ASTRID AND THE GIRL IN THE TANGERINE DRESS

An Astrid Price Mystery

ALAN RODERICK

ILLUSTRATIONS ELLA J WILDING

WANT MORE OF ASTRID? TRY THESE...

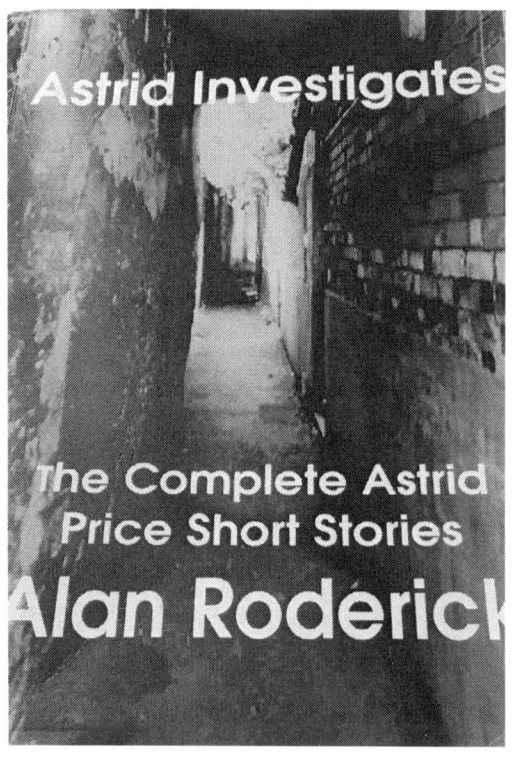

Marc Harshman, Poet Laureate, West Virginia: *What fun! I love... Astrid, her vibrancy, and the subtle cleverness with which she goes after the truth, as well as the humour.*

CATH DRWG PUBLISHING: £9-99

Jonathan Edwards, Costa Prize Poetry Winner, 2015: *This is a truly wonderful book. Anyone who... loves detective fiction, will have a ball reading this novel. We swing through these pages, enjoying Astrid's adventures and the playful set pieces, but what's most impressive about this novel is the author's distinctive style and voice. The prose is entertaining, witty and well-crafted, and it's a pleasure to be in this author's company. A joyous and memorable read.*

CATH DRWG PUBLISHING: £9-99

CATH DRWG PUBLISHING

LUČKA, THE ORIGINAL CATH DRWG,
PHOTOGRAPH ALAN RODERICK

First Published in 2021 by Cath Drwg Publishing.
Copyright © Alan Roderick. This edition, June, 2021.

The moral right of Alan Roderick to be identified as the author of this work has been asserted in accordance with the Copyright, Designs and Patents Act, 1988.

This book is a work of fiction. Names, characters, businesses. organisations, places and events are either the product of the author's imagination or are used fictitiously. Any resemblance to actual persons, living or dead, events or localities is entirely coincidental.

All rights reserved. No part of this publication may be reproduced or transmitted in any form, or by any means, electronic or mechanical, including photocopy, recording or any information storage and retrieval system, without permission in writing from the author and publisher.

Cover Design Copyright © Ella J Wilding 2021

Illustrations Copyright © Ella J Wilding 2021

Typeset in Calibri and Helvetica Neue by Alan Roderick

Contact: alanroderick11@outlook.com

FOR BOŽENA ALWAYS *UND FÜR IMMER UND EWIG*

By the Same Author

NON-FICTION

The Music of Fair Tongues
The Folklore of Gwent
Unknown Gwent
The Folklore of Glamorgan
The Ghosts of Gwent
Johnny! The Story of the Happy Warrior
A Gwent Anthology (Edited)
Travels in Gwent (Edited)
The Newport Kaleidoscope
Newport Rugby Greats
The Pubs of Newport
Haunted Gwent
The Gwent Christmas Book (Edited)
The Dragon Entertains

FICTION

Astrid Investigates (The Complete Astrid Price Short Stories)
Astrid and the Golden Lovespoons (An Astrid Price Mystery)

POETRY

After You'd Gone: Poems 2016 to 2020
Selected Poems: 1978 to 2015
Twelve Days In Intensive Care: October 21st to November 1st, 2010, A Poetic Record
Božena's Book (Edited)

AUTHOR'S NOTE

I started writing this book on August 12th, 2010. Then again on March 13th, 2012. And again on October 29th, 2012. Yet again on May 12th, 2013.

For various reasons, however, it remained, like Schubert's famous symphony, unfinished.

And now, my latest effort begun on November 26th, 2020 and finished in the early months of 2021. So, if at first. . .

PS: I compiled the text mainly on Pages on my iPad and inserted the illustrations using the Pages app on my iPad and on my MacBook Air. The fonts used were Calibri and Helvetica Neue.

Alan Roderick, Newport, June/July, 2021

ACKNOWLEDGEMENTS

MY HEARTFELT THANKS GO TO ELLA J WILDING FOR HER WONDERFUL ILLUSTRATIONS AND COVER DESIGN. THEY ARE A TRIUMPH.

I OWE MANY GRATEFUL THANKS ALSO TO ROB SMITH FOR HIS INVALUABLE EXPERTISE AND TECHNICAL HELP WITH THE ILLUSTRATIONS AND COVER DESIGN.

LIST OF ILLUSTRATIONS

1. "You want me to find a girl in a tangerine dress . . ." Page 4
2. Yes, dearie, what is it? What do you want? Page 23
3. I plied my paddle with smooth, efficient strokes towards the opposite shore. Page 55
4. "There's someone waiting for you upstairs," said Stakis, his hands, as usual, deep inside a big pile of potatoes. Page 91
5. She was strumming the ukulele à la George Formby. Page 117
6. They fell upon each other. Page 156
7. I was there, looking at what used to be Culloden Jimmie and at Stakis, holding the knife. Page 203
8. Sometimes, too, I would pick a secluded spot and go through my Tai chi exercises. Page 217
9. She wore some kind of overall. Page 220

10. In the rear passenger seat behind Iolo was a big red teddy bear. Page 241
11. Stakis was sitting there on the bed, looking lost and forlorn. Page 260
12. That left only the Parrot Man, Daniel Owen. I dialled his number. Page 274
13. I was looking at a one-storey Tudor farmhouse. Page 280
14. As I landed on top of them, I pressed first the Welsh Dragon ring on my left hand, aiming at Crad. Page 299
15. Slowly, and very carefully, I removed the golden yellow daffodil motif brooch from my Titian coloured hair. Page 322
16. I caught the flash of the great big handled knife as it plunged towards me. Page 351
17. "Don't let it drop, for Cymru's sake!" Page 372
18. A full moon was shining, high up in a clear sky. Page 380

ASTRID AND THE GIRL IN THE TANGERINE DRESS

CHAPTER 1

What would you do if someone came to you in their hour of need, desperate for your help, but the whole thing screamed wild goose chase at you, the mother of all wild goose chases? Would you think to yourself, I'm not touching this with a Second World War German Tiger Tank? Would you, once you had stopped laughing, send them away with a couple of fleas in their ear, or would you fob them off with some well-meaning, but ultimately, empty platitudes?

Well, if you're a private detective like me, you listen carefully to what they have to say, and then, if business is bad and you're short of the readies, you state your financial terms, take their money and do the best you can. That's what I did when Edward Henry Davies walked into my life.

It must have been about ten in the morning, I'd already washed and breakfasted, fired up the computer, seated myself at my desk, and begun checking in tray and out tray, sharpening my pencils, flicking through correspondence, you know the sort of thing – getting ready for business. I was about to check the laptop computer and review the state of my cases when a faint, diffident sounding knock came at my office door.

"Come on in," I said, 'it's open."

The man who came in must have been around six

feet I estimated. He was wearing a blue t-shirt with the words, 'I left my heart in Upper Bangor,' emblazoned on the front, black shorts and sockless trainers.

"Mrs Price," he said, "Mrs Astrid Price, the private detective?"

"That's what it says on the door, my friend," I said, what can I do for you?"

"Well, Mrs Price," he said, taking the chair opposite to me, "my name is Edward Henry Davies but my friends call me 'Aitch' for short."

"Pleased to meet you, Mr Davies," I said. "Any relation to William Henry Davies?"

"No, I've never heard of that gentleman," he said, "Who is he? A friend of yours?"

"Oh, just someone I know," I said, "now about this case of yours, why exactly have you come to see me and what can I do for you?"

As my prospective client started to speak, I looked at him more closely. His brown hair was tied back in a ponytail, he sported a brown, goatee beard and, after he had spoken to me for a while, I knew that he was the possessor of a pronounced 'Gog,' that is North Wales stroke Gwynedd, accent. After I'd heard him out, I brushed my fingers back through my hair and gave him what I hoped was a sympathetic look.

"Let me get this straight," I said, tapping my rounders bat with the fingers of my right hand. "You want me to find a woman for you, a woman you've only seen once, and that for just a few minutes, but all you've got to go on is that she had some sort of small dog with her, when you saw her that time in the cemetery?"

"Well, not quite, Mrs Price," said my prospective new client, "she was wearing a tangerine dress when I saw her . . ."

Bloody Blackpool supporters, I thought, ever since they'd got to the promised land of the English Premiership, they were everywhere, but I said, "this dog, what did it look like? Did it have a name? What did she call it?"

"Well, Mrs Price," said the client, giving me a helpless look, "the trouble is all these small dogs look the same to me, and I wasn't taking too much notice of him, I was concentrating on her after all, but I think she called him Victor, or Hector, or Nestor, or something like that, perhaps?"

"Okay," I said, giving him a more positive look of my own, "Not much to go on is it, really, when you come to think about it. May I ask why you're so anxious to trace this woman?"

The client looked embarrassed. He avoided looking at me, his throat sounding as if he had a whole regiment of frogs in there, fighting for supremacy. Eventually, he managed to gain control of himself, quell the frogs and clear his blocked throat. "Do you believe in love at first sight, Mrs Price," he said, "you know, what the French call *le coup de foudre*, the stroke of lightning.

You want me to find a girl in a tangerine dress . . .

Before I saw her, I didn't, but now I do."

Again his eyes roamed the room, my office, looking at everything except me. My client was young, probably in his mid to late twenties. I figured he would have found it hard to talk about love, especially to a complete stranger, never mind all this stuff about *coups de foudre*.

A part of me felt like saying to him, "Let me get this straight, you want me to find a girl for you, a girl in a tangerine dress – what do you think I am, some sort of dating agency? I'm a private detective, for Cymru's sake," but being the soft touch that I am, I didn't, instead I decided to give him a break, besides I had nothing else on at the moment, pounding a few doors for a couple of days wouldn't hurt me, and whilst I was on this wild dog chase, searching for Hector, Nestor, or whatever his name was, and his tangerine dressed mistress, I could console myself with the thought that something better might be coming along soon, something I might have more chance of solving.

"All right," I said, "I'll do it but only for a week and at the end of that time, if I haven't located her – well, all bets are off. In the meantime, it'll cost you fifty Glyndwrs per day plus expenses. By the way, I need fifty in advance, let's just call it a deposit, non-returnable, of course."

"Yes, yes," said Edward Henry Davies, reaching into his coat pocket, bringing out five crisp ten Glyndwr notes (he'd obviously been to the bank or hole in the wall before coming to see me) and passing them over the desk towards me.

"Thanks," I said, picking them up and giving them a fond squeeze, it was always nice to make the acquaintance of unsullied, brand new notes, straight from the Welsh Republican Mint at Llantrisant; even if I had the feeling they wouldn't be part of my gang for very long.

"Hold on," I said, as Edward Henry Davies rose to go, "which cemetery are we talking about? Pantglas or Nant yr Eos?"

"Nant yr Eos. (The Brook of the Nightingale, although it was a long time since any nightingales had sung there, I can tell you.) In the twin city of Maendy," he said. "Here, I've brought you some photos I took of the exact place where she put the dog over the wall and then climbed over herself." And he passed an envelope over the desk towards me.

"When were these taken?" I said, "on the actual day you saw her?'

"No, no," he said, "On that special day I made the mistake of leaving my mobile at home so when I saw her I couldn't take any pictures. Besides, it's not exactly the done thing, is it, going up to complete strangers in a public place and taking photos of them with your mobile phone. What would she have said to me? These were taken a few days later when I was trying to find her again."

"Did you notice anything unusual?" I said, "Any sign of a struggle, anything she might have dropped, the ground disturbed, anything like that?"

"No," he said, "I looked as carefully as I could, but I couldn't see anything. Maybe you with your trained eye . . ."

"I'll check," I said, "but I don't hold out too much hope. When did you say all this happened?"

"Monday, August 1st," he said. Two weeks ago, I thought, people have been walking all over that ground since then, how am I supposed to find anything after two weeks, but I said, "don't worry, there might still be something there, some clue you may have overlooked. By the way, did you speak to her at all? It might be useful if we knew she had some sort of accent or a particular tone of voice."

"No," he said, "I was just building up to it, but then she jumped over the wall and I didn't want to alarm her by following straight after. You know, all this talk of stalkers there's been in the press lately . . . Then by the time I finally plucked up the courage to follow her, there was no sign of her or the dog anywhere. I've tried putting discreet personal ads in the local paper, Mrs Price, but no joy, and I was too embarrassed to go round sticking those notices on lampposts you see people doing when they've lost their dog or cat. They would think I was crazy. I did think about knocking on that row of houses just opposite the cemetery to see if someone had noticed anything, but then I felt like a fool, so . . ."

"You came to me," I said.

"Yes," he said. "I'd heard people speaking highly of you and then there was the rugby connection, you having played outside half for Wales and all . . . I obviously couldn't go to the Welsh Republican Police; they'd have laughed me out of the station with the little I had to go on. I did try, though; I like to think I wasn't completely useless. For two weeks solid, I kept going back to the same spot at the same time, but she never showed. I can still see her now pushing that dog of hers over the cemetery wall into Coed Melyn Park. I ask myself a thousand times a day, why, oh why didn't I have my mobile phone with me that day. Just one picture of her might have made all the difference . . ."

My client's voice trembled and he looked as if he was going to go at any time. I'm a compassionate girl, none more so, and, besides, I didn't want anybody's salt tears falling on my office floor, you never know, it might be bad for business, so I discreetly pushed the box of tissues lying on my desk towards him. He snuffled a bit, blew his nose and dabbed his eyes with another tissue.

"Can you help me, Mrs Price; I can't stop thinking about this girl. Is there something wrong with me?"

"You've just got it bad, that's all," I said, "it might be passing infatuation, who knows, but right now, it's all that matters to you. Look, I can't make any promises, but I'll do what I can. Give me a week to ten days and I'll make some enquiries. In the meantime, leave your details with me. You know, address, telephone number, email, all that sort of thing." I passed my notepad and pencil over the desk towards Edward Henry Davies. He took them and scribbled down his particulars in a shaky hand.

"Right," I said, standing up to let him know his time was up, "I'll be in touch as soon as I find anything." Edward Henry Davies nodded and left without saying a further word. The audience over, I put my feet on one of the few vacant spaces my cluttered desk had to offer and began to think. Was this guy genuine? Did he really expect me to find someone using the rubbish description he had given me and with no photograph? And if not, what was the point of it all? Still, he had been prepared to part with the fifty Glyndwrs up front and seemed prepared to pay more.

Was he really in love with Miss Tangerine Dress, or was there some other reason he was so anxious to find her? At the back of my mind, some faint, distant memory stirred, something about a *Songs of Praise* programme years ago, when some guy watching TV at home on his sofa had seen a girl, singing in a church choir somewhere, miles away from the town he was living in, who had given him a massive dose of that *coup de foudre* Edward Henry Davies had been talking about.

Most people would have left it at that, and gone on to find someone nearer, not quite so far away, someone living in the same town perhaps, but this guy took the time and trouble to track her down, and eventually they married in the very same church, where he had first seen her singing on that TV programme. So, maybe there was hope for Edward Henry Davies after all, although I can't say I was really convinced. Still, I would do what he wanted, make enquiries, bang a few doors, visit Nant yr Eos cemetery, interview people and give him a fully written up report, summarising all my findings. It was the least I could do after he'd paid me and, that way, my conscience would be clear when I placed his hard earned money into my rather depleted bank account.

    I spent the next hour or so on my Apple laptop checking out back copies of our national newspaper *Y Byd* (The World) since August 1st, but nowhere could I find any mention of a woman having gone missing, with, or without, a dog. For all I knew, she could have just been visiting the place, staying with relatives maybe, and was long gone back to where she belonged. Or she could have gone on holiday, perhaps or had fallen ill and was now in hospital. Any number of things could have happened. Maybe Edward Henry Davies had imagined it all — stranger things had happened. Maybe Edward Henry Davies was some kind of nut who liked giving his money away to private detectives. Maybe, maybe, so many maybes. I sighed and got up from my desk. There was no way round it; I was going to have to go to Nant yr Eos myself.

First, I packed my rounders bat, the special one a man in Aberbargoed had made for me: you could make it small enough to fit into a coat pocket, but press a little button on the side and, hey Prestatyn, it would expand back to full size. I also took a recorder/blow pipe the same man had designed and built. It looked just like a mini recorder and you could even play a tune on it, but it was capable of firing small darts, which could put people to sleep for a while from a distance of about fifty feet. I wasn't expecting trouble, you understand, but as my old mam always used to say, one could never be too careful. I put the answer phone on, just in case anyone was desperate enough to want to contact me, locked the door to my office and went downstairs.

Stakis Theodorakis, my landlord, confidant and occasional helper was inside *The Lying Cod* fish bar, potato peeler poised at the ready, staring at his daily fix of *Y Byd* (The World).

"Hi, Stakis," I said, "I'm just going out for a moment, there are a few things I need to check. If any clients come calling, can you take their details for me, or ask them to leave a message?"

"Sure, Astrid," he said. "Sure thing. Got a new case on? That guy who left earlier, perhaps? He seemed to be in an almighty hurry . . ."

I nodded, anxious to be on my way.

"Need any help?" he said, waving his potato peeler in the air, "you know, I'm always there for you."

"I know, Stakis," I said, "and thanks for your kind offer, but I'm all right. I've got a feeling this won't take very long, I can't really see any way of getting to the bottom of it, but if I do need any help, yours will be the first name on my list, Stakis, you know that," and I patted his hand gently.

"Okay," he said, "you know, I'll be ready, willing and able. Stakis is always willing and able where you're concerned, Astrid. In the meantime, would you like me to keep something back for you?" and he gestured toward the pile of unpeeled potatoes waiting patiently there in front of him.

"D'you know what?" I said, "I fancy a bit of a change when I get back, something Greek, perhaps. You know, just like your old mam used to make. Surprise me. Anything with vegetables in it, I've become a bit of a semi-veggie lately. I've got to go, but leave your mobile on in case I need to call you."

"Just one thing before you go," he said, pointing at his copy of *Y Byd* (The World). "It says here . . ."

Those dreaded words, I thought, 'it says here . . .' I love Stakis to bits, I really do, but as soon as he says those words, I know I am not going to get away in a hurry.

"What does it say?" I said, hoping my impatience

wasn't showing too much.

"It says two more of those new Super Dragons have been taken from different parts of Casnewydd. That's about the fifth or sixth one to go since they started appearing on our streets."

The Super Dragons were one of Casnewydd City Council's better moves. Since their launch, two or three weeks ago, they had brightened up the cityscape with their colourful and cheerful appearance. I liked them, as did most people I knew. Made of fibreglass in a Bangor factory, they stood five feet tall and had been painted and decorated by a variety of local artists. In a few months' time they were due to be auctioned, all the benefits going to needy charities, but at the rate they were disappearing, there weren't going to be all that many left to go under the hammer.

"That's terrible," Stakis, I said, "who could be doing such a thing and why, I don't know what Casnewydd's coming to, but I have to go, there's a client anxious for news, see you . . ." And with that I was gone, heading for my pride and joy, my all yellow *Pwca*, which was parked at the back of Stakis's fish shop.

I got in and closed the door behind me. Above me, the sky was as blue as a Cardiff City football supporter's shirt, and not just any old shirt, one which had been dipped in a dye of an ultra shade of blue, with not a cloud of any description to trouble it.

It looked like it was going to be another hot one.

For days now the heat had been hovering around the 30-degree mark or just below. Some people were finding it difficult to sleep and more than a few tempers were beginning to fray, although I had to say I liked it, the hotter the better for me, within reason, of course. It was the talk of the twin cities. No one had seen anything like it in the Welsh Republic since 1976, whenever that was.

Twenty-five degrees and rising — said the announcer on the *Pwca's* radio — that's what I wanted to hear, a summer that was a proper summer, not like those watery washouts we usually got. So far, August had been more than kind to the Welsh Republic, temperatures were up and the sun looked as if it was never going to take its hat off as it came out to play, day after succeeding day.

I started the *Pwca* and headed east over the river towards our twin city of Maendy and the Nant yr Eos Cemetery. Talk about money for old rope, this was going to be easy; I could feel it in my Brecon Carreg bottled mineral water.

CHAPTER 2

As I crossed the river and drove along Kathryn Jenkins Avenue, and down Mary Thomas Terrace, past the boarded up fronts, charity shops, estate agents, assorted takeaways and local convenience stores, I took a look out of my rear view mirror. Nothing unusual, just a shiny, gleaming new *Hebog* (or Hawk, otherwise known as the latest Welsh motorbike sensation) chugging steadily behind me, the driver's face obscured by a futuristic looking dark helmet. The *Hebog* was still with me when I turned into Alex Jones Drive and when I entered Gethin Jones Close it was still there, following patiently on behind. Normally, I would have been suspicious of somebody apparently following me, but today I was not anticipating any trouble and, sure enough, as I reached the gates of Nant yr Eos Cemetery and pulled in to stop, the *Hebog* went sailing by, heading north towards the Celtic Banner Golf Course.

    I got out of the car and cast a glance at the row of three terraced houses right opposite the cemetery gates. Later, I needed to knock on those doors, to find out if anyone had seen anything on the night that Edward Henry Davies had met the love of his life, but for now, I needed to check out the exact spot where Tangerine Girl had climbed over the wall with Nestor or Hector or whatever his name was. Maybe I would find a clue after all, a clue that would crack this case wide open, but I wasn't about to rush down to Ladbrooke's Cymru and put my Breton striped t-shirt on it. I walked briskly past the small Jewish cemetery, and then onto the main part of Nant yr Eos, glancing at the other gravestones as I went. A lot of them looked as if they hadn't been attended to since the time of the Chartist Uprising, some in particular were in a bad state of repair and jutting out at all kinds of precarious looking angles. I stopped and took out the photographs that Edward Henry Davies had given me.

Yes, there it was, X marks the spot. So this was where Tangerine Girl had climbed over the wall some two weeks ago. I followed in her footsteps. It wasn't hard; the wall wasn't particularly high in this part of the cemetery. Then I stopped again and took a careful look all around me. I don't know what I was expecting to find, a piece of fabric from a tangerine coloured dress, perhaps, an envelope addressed to Astrid Price, Master Detective, maybe, telling me everything that had taken place on that fateful day, or a piece of paper giving me an address I could follow up in my search for clues.

Surprise, surprise, there was nothing, nothing of that kind anyway. I stooped to my knees, pulled out my folding magnifying glass (yes, I did have one) and looked again, very intently. Still nothing. Then I got up and looked around me. I was now in Coed Melyn Park, with the cemetery to my left, but the trees weren't letting me in on their secrets. What had happened that evening? For the first time I began to wonder if Tangerine Girl and Hector the wonder dog hadn't been abducted. I made a circle in my mind's eye and looked at it as thoroughly as I could, but the grass was about as forthcoming as the trees. I made another circle, then another and another until I had covered quite a bit of ground, but one private detective working alone is liable to miss something, however detailed and thorough her search. Which way had woman and dog gone? That was another thing I didn't know.

Damn Edward Henry Davies and his vagueness, I was just going to have to do the best I could, even if I had to take a couple of hours doing it, still, someone else was paying, I told myself and paused to look under yet another tree when, suddenly, I thought I heard something, something like a slight whoosh and the next thing I knew, that something was thudding into the tree just above my head, something with what looked like a piece of paper attached to it.

Instinctively, I ripped the paper from the bolt or whatever it was that had embedded itself in the tree, stuffed it in my pocket and turned quickly. For all I knew, there might be another of these things coming my way pretty soon, and whoever was firing them didn't appear to have me on their Christmas card list. Then I saw him? Her? I couldn't be sure, whoever it was had a futuristic looking dark helmet on their head. They were about fifty yards away, right where I and Tangerine Girl had gone over the wall.

I just had a brief glimpse of what looked like some kind of gun or pistol they were holding in their hand. They saw me at the same time as I saw them and took off back towards the cemetery gates at a rapid pace with me after them, but by the time I reached the wall, there was no sign of them. Still, I kept going, pushing myself to the limits and got back to the gates, just in time to see The Helmet riding off on the back of a shiny, gleaming new *Hebog*. He/she seemed to be in an awful hurry, as if they had suddenly remembered their waterbed had been leaking since early that morning.

Well, I thought, you can run, but you're not going to outpace me, not with me driving the *Pwca*. I climbed in, slammed the car into first gear and set off up the road after The Helmet. It was only a matter of time, I thought, before I would be having a serious conversation with this person, telling them I didn't take kindly to being shot at.

Or so I thought, but fate was to intervene in the shape of the Welsh Republican Police. I could see the *Hebog* in the distance and felt myself getting ever closer when, suddenly, I saw the two policemen standing in the middle of the road between two big black police vans. Their hands were in the air and they were flagging me down. Bloody, bastard, sod it, I thought and I swear, for one brief, roadblock busting moment, I was tempted to drive straight through them and scatter the representatives of law and order, but then common sense kicked in and I thought better of it. After all, I had a private investigator's licence to protect. Inwardly cursing I pulled up and wound down my window, as the two men walked towards me, looking resplendent in their red, white and green uniforms, their hands on their holstered guns, poised for trouble.

"Sorry to bother you, madam," said the taller of the two, "just a routine check, nothing to worry about."

"Yes," said his companion, eyeing me up and down, "this won't take very long, not very long at all," and he began inspecting the *Pwca*.

"What's all this about, officers?" I said, "I'm in a bit of a hurry, you see, I'm late for my little nephew's birthday party."

The shorter of the two policemen looked at me more closely, "hey, don't I know you," he said, "aren't you that rugby player? What's your name again? Hey, Jude, look who we've stopped, it's Astrid Price."

Jude looked up from his inspection of the *Pwca's* rear wheel tyres and came towards me. "So it is," he said, "I thought her face looked familiar."

Strangely enough, their accents were not the local Casnewydd ones I was used to and, if I had to put a bet on it, I would have said they were more Gwynedd way, maybe Anglesey, somewhere around North Wales anyhow. Still, in the new Republic, people moved around a lot more, took their job opportunities where they could find them . . .

"Why the roadblock, boys?" I said. "Come on, you can tell me, we being more or less on the same side and all . . . who is it you're looking for? Our friends The Edwards?"

"Sorry, Astrid, no can do, you know we can't give out classified information to members of the public," said Jude, tapping the side of his nose conspiratorially, "well, everything seems to be in order, we won't detain you any longer, wouldn't want you to be late for that birthday party now, would we . . ."

I smiled and waved as I drove on but inwardly I was seething. No chance now of catching The Helmet, he or she would be long gone. And I couldn't just turn around and go back the way I had come, not after all that palaver about nephews and birthday parties.

About a mile or so further up the road I managed to make a detour and double back on myself, eventually arriving in front of the cemetery gates without any signs of any more roadblocks. I stopped the car about fifty yards away from the row of three terraced houses and pulled on a pair of sensible looking glasses. Then I piled my shoulder length Titian red hair up into a bun with the help of a few hairpins and covered it with a bowler hat. I also took a clipboard and pen from the glove compartment and was just about to get out of the car, when I remembered the piece of paper wrapped round the bolt The Helmet had shot at me. I took it out of my pocket and uncrumpled it. It was printed, not handwritten, in Welsh, and it said:

"Keep your nose out of what doesn't concern you, Price. Signed: A Well Wisher."

Charming, I thought, it was always nice to be loved. I put the paper back in my pocket and headed for the first of the terraced houses, clipboard and pen at the ready. The house looked as if it hadn't been lived in for months, the grass was overgrown and the front doors and windows were boarded up. There was an air of neglect about the whole place. I thought about knocking just in case, but then shook my head and moved onto the next one. This place, although never likely to feature on the front cover of *Welsh Homes and Gardens* was a decided improvement. The area in front of the house was paved and someone had taken the time and trouble to put out a few potted plants and hanging baskets. I knocked and waited. I didn't have long to wait.

The door was opened by a six-foot, shaven headed, bare-chested, unshaven man looking about fifty years old. His naked belly was hanging over his trousers. In his left hand he was clutching a bottle of Casnewydd's Finest Ale. He looked as if he was partial to putting away more food and drink than any number of visitors to the Abergavenny Food Festival. He looked at me bleary-eyed. It was not an aesthetically pleasing sight. "Yeah," he almost bellowed in my ear, "what do you want? I told the last one, I'm not buying any Welsh encyclopaedias."

There was just a hint of a foreign accent there, I thought, but I couldn't quite call to mind what it was. *Pnawn Da*/Good afternoon, sir," I said, "if you could just spare a minute of your valuable time. . ." but before I could get any further, he had slammed the door shut on me, leaving me stranded in mid-sentence.

Great, I thought, things were not going too well, maybe third time lucky . . .? The last house looked the best of the lot. There was a small box tree in the garden and the front window was crowded with owls of all shapes and sizes, there were barn owls, tawny owls, little owls, snowy owls, all sorts of different owls, not real ones of course, these owls were made of wood, plastic, stone and any other material you could think of. They looked colourful, bright and cheerful which was more than I was feeling at this precise moment.

I knocked three times using the metal owl shaped knocker. Then I waited. Nothing. No sound from within the house, no sound from the road outside, this was definitely not turning out to be one of my better days, but I was determined to get something out of it, so I knocked again, this time louder. Eventually, I heard the sound of footsteps approaching, then bolts being drawn as the door opened a fraction, pulling on its chain. I could just make out a grey permed head over thick-

Yes, dearie, what is it? What do you want?

rimmed glasses, staring inquisitively at me.

"Yes, dearie," said a high pitched, unnatural sounding voice belonging to the Perm, "what is it? What do you want?"

I put on my best Mona Lisa smile and waved a card I had run up on the computer a few nights ago. It probably wouldn't have stood up to any intense scrutiny, but on occasions like this could just about pass muster.

"*Pnawn Da*/Good afternoon, madam," I said, "my name is Doctor Kate Roberts, from the Department of Psychology at the University of Casnewydd, and I'm conducting a survey on behalf of the Welsh Republican Government..."

"What's that you say, dearie, you'll have to speak up a bit, I'm a bit hard of hearing, you know."

If she'd had a stick, she would have no doubt waved it, but she didn't, so I repeated my spiel, laying particular emphasis on the Welsh Republican Government bit.

"Welsh Republican Government, my eye," said the Perm, sounding more querulous than ever, "what have they ever done for us, we should go back in with England, that's what I say, we were better off with them. Why, when I..."

"It'll only take a few minutes of your time, madam," I said "and everyone who takes part gets the chance to win a prize."

"What sort of prize?" said the Perm, looking at

me more keenly now and sounding a little more interested.

"Oh, there's a whole list of them," I said, "What happens is this. Once the survey is finished, I send the details to the government and then they send you a list of prizes to choose from, with a stamped addressed envelope for you to reply, of course."

"I see," she said, "well, what is it you want to know? Fire away, young woman, I haven't got all day, you know."

"Right," I said. "The Welsh Republican Government, in conjunction with the University of Casnewydd, is trying to measure the memory and observation powers of its citizens. So, on August 1st, just gone, they sent a young female student into the cemetery, just over the road from here, and into the park nearby. She was wearing a tangerine dress and had a small dog with her. What I want to know is this: did you see this girl and her dog and, if so, what can you tell me about the two of them? What did they look like, all that sort of thing?"

"What kind of a damn fool test is that?" said the Perm, "August 1st, August 1st, that's almost two weeks ago, I can hardly remember what happened five minutes ago, let alone the last fortnight."

"Do try and think," I said, "those prizes are really very good, well worth having, I can tell you. Now, I'm only allowed to tell you she was wearing a tangerine dress and had a small dog with her. The rest of the information has to come from you. Does that ring any bells? Any bells at all?"

"Let me see," said the Perm, "tangerine dress, a tangerine dress . . ? What was she, a Blackpool supporter? What's a Blackpool supporter doing in Casnewydd? And why come all the way out here to this Godforsaken place?"

This was getting me nowhere. "Maybe if I could come in," I said, "sit down and have a cup of tea, perhaps, maybe that would help you to remember more clearly."

"Sorry, dearie," said the Perm, "I can't allow that I'm afraid, there've been too many burglaries in Casnewydd lately, I keep reading about them in *Y Byd* (The World), you look all right, but . . ." And she started to pull the door shut.

"Wait," I said, "stop, are you sure you didn't see the dog . . . what about your prize, you must remember something, surely . . ." but I was talking to myself, the retreating footsteps inside the house were not listening to me. This was one subterfuge that wasn't turning out too well. "I'm leaving my card behind, just in case," I said, pushing it through the letterbox, "if you do think of anything, please get in touch with me," although I didn't hold out too much hope on that score. As I drove away, I thought I saw a curtain twitch at the beer-swilling gent's house, but I couldn't be sure.

CHAPTER 3

"So, you're going back there again," said Stakis, ladling the steaming hot vegetable Moussaka onto my waiting plate, "in the middle of the night . . . what are you, crazy? Why can't you wait until the next morning and go back, and do whatever you have to do, in broad daylight?"

"Hey, Stakis," I said, in between mouthfuls, "this is not half bad. You're improving. You'll have to get your old mam to give me the recipe."

"Never mind all that," he said, "what about curfew? How are you going to get round that?"

"Ah yes," I said, "now that might just be a problem . . ." The controversial curfew had been recently introduced by President Hopkin, Mary to her adoring fans, who had been elected five years ago, on a 'Those Were The Days Ticket,' and had lost no time in throwing her weight around. I had my views on that, my theory was, that as Ireland had had so many presidents called Mary, we Welsh figured we had to have one too, Celtic solidarity and all that.

Anyway, the curfew operated from midnight to seven a.m. and was the latest in a long line of measures, designed to combat the growing threat of The Hammers of Edward, or Edwards for short, a terrorist group who objected violently to the severance of the link with

England and the coming of Welsh independence. So far no one had been killed, the Edwards confining their activities to minor irritants, such as blowing up post boxes, painting out Welsh language signs, robbing corner shops run by little old ladies etc., although there were growing signs that they were about to escalate their activities.

Train lines had been disrupted and attacks made on isolated, rural Welsh Republican Police stations. Word on the street was that they were threatening something big soon — 'a happening' – as they liked to call it. I'd had a run in with The Edwards myself once, not so long ago, whilst trying to discover the truth behind the story of the Golden Lovespoons, and it wasn't an experience I particularly wanted to repeat. I could understand the authorities getting twitchy about what would happen next . . .

As for the curfew, people were divided as to its effectiveness, the licensing trade in particular, and the taxi firms, had not been at all pleased, and the burgling fraternity was less than impressed, but President Hopkin had evoked the Emergency Powers Act and pushed the legislation through the *Senedd* or Welsh Republican Parliament.

"But why do you have to do this in the dark?" Stakis was saying, "what's wrong with the day time, for Cymru's sake?"

"Because I need to remove that foot long bolt

from the tree in Coed Melyn Park," I said, "and I don't fancy doing it with an audience of one pensioner and his dog watching me. I need to search that wood free from prying eyes and idle tittle-tattle. Besides, you never know, I might find something else; I didn't have a proper chance to look things over the last time, what with The Helmet person firing at me and all."

"Yeah, yeah, that's all well and good, but what about the curfew?"

"I've thought about that," I said, "it's easy really. I go there before the midnight hour, make myself comfortable somewhere I can't be seen, wait a few hours and then . . ."

"Oh, yeah," said Stakis, "you drive up there in your *Pwca,* which no one is going to notice on account of it being a brighter shade of yellow, and everything. Don't you think those people from this afternoon will recognise it?"

"A good point," I said, "you can drive me up there in your car . . ."

"Me," he said, "I'll be here minding the shop, serving hungry customers."

"Oh, Big Zorba can do that till you get back," I said, "you trust him, don't you?"

"Of course," said Stakis, "isn't he my first cousin?"

"Well, there you are then," I said, "that's settled. Now I'm off to my flat for a while, give me a call at ten."

The flat was in exactly the same condition as when I had left it all those hours ago. No one had broken or entered, but there were several messages on the answer phone. I switched it on and listened:

1. *"Hi, Astrid, it's Daniel, Daniel Owen, give me a call, Gelert is pining for you."*
2. *"I know it's early, Mrs Price, but is there any news? Edward Henry Davies."*
3. *"Astrid Price? The Great Detective? You don't know me, but I know you. I'm watching you – be warned."*

This last voice sounded muffled as if whoever had delivered the threatening message had done so with a handkerchief over their mouth. It was also hard to tell whether it was a man or a woman doing the talking.

Inside the flat it was hot, twenty-eight degrees at least. I changed into something cooler and more comfortable, made myself an Astrid special, lay back on the bed and gazed at the ceiling. What had I learnt so far? Well, not that much really. I was still not sure whether Tangerine Girl existed, outside of Edward Henry Davies's no doubt vivid imagination. I had found no evidence as to her existence; on the other hand I had found no evidence of her not existing either. So the jury was still out on that one.

Then there was the little matter of someone taking a shot at me. Why? What for? I had no clue, and couldn't think of any reason why anyone would want me off the case. Damn that bloody roadblock, I'd have caught The Helmet, no problem at all, if the Republicans hadn't been around to stop me. Hang on . . . Wait just a little beer-drinking minute . . . Now that I came to think of it, that Republican roadblock had proved very convenient for The Helmet, a bit too convenient, perhaps. Were those two Republicans real Republicans, after all?

Then there was the anonymous phone call made by someone obviously trying to disguise their voice. Again, the question was why? Why try and warn me off? Didn't they know that was like the proverbial red rag to a Pamplona bull and more likely to heighten my ardour rather than cool it? Maybe someone was just playing about; maybe someone from my past, who held a grudge against me, was trying to wind me up, like the Victorians did the Tredegar Town Clock. But who? That could apply to a lot of people. I took a sip of my drink and wondered. As usual, I was caught in a thick fog of questions and very few answers.

I thought about my plan for tonight. What if Stakis were right and I was making a big mistake . . . Sure, it was risky, I knew that, but I needed to get a closer look at that bolt The Helmet had fired at me, once I got that I could get in touch with my man in Aberbargoed and ask him what he thought. That sort of technical wizardry thing was going to be right up his street . . . then again, what if it wasn't there, what if someone had purloined it in my absence? And, more importantly, after Stakis had dropped me off at the Nant yr Eos Cemetery, how was I going to get back to my flat above *The Lying Cod*?

Sure, I had been bullish with Stakis, but at present, all I had in mind was a vague idea of waiting out the time inside the cemetery until curfew was over and then walking back into Casnewydd as bold as the Bedwas, Trethomas and Machen Brass Band. But the more I thought about it, the less this plan appealed to me, think Astrid, think, you're supposed to be The Great Detective? (Even the voice on the telephone said so, although I don't think they really believed it somehow, even masked by a muffled handkerchief, the heavy sarcasm still came through.) Is this really the best you can come up with?

I could take my chances of course, hit the back streets and minor roads and get back into the City that way, it was well known the Welsh Republican Police were fond of hogging the main thoroughfares on curfew Night, but against that there were those persistent rumours of AWR (Army of the Welsh Republic) Special Forces (especially The Llywelyn the Last Brigade) being drafted in to help out every so often, and they would have no qualms in operating in the back alleys and quiet, dark corners of the City. Oh, this was getting me nowhere . . . I needed a break from all this thinking;

sometimes a woman could do too much thinking . . .

I needed something to eat. No point in going out on a job nursing an empty stomach. I busied myself in the kitchen for a while, then, job done, I sat down in front of the television, with my bowl of steaming hot *cawl* (Welsh broth), just like *Nain* (north Welsh for grandmother) used to make, and switched it on ready for my daily dose of bad news from the Welsh Republic and the rest of the world, and was just in time to hear a familiar sounding voice solemnly intoning the words, *"God Bless the Welsh Republic."* There was a pause, then the announcer broke in:

"That was an extract from a speech by President Mary Hopkin, speaking at today's security debate in parliament. We now bring you the rest of the news. Two more Super Dragons have been taken from their positions in different parts of the City of Casnewydd. The police are investigating and appealing for witnesses to come forward."

Then there were a couple of fairly uninteresting items to begin with about reservoirs drying up and the latest hosepipe ban and then the nation's favourite reporter, blonde bombshell Brigantia Lightfoot filled the screen.

She was standing on the steps of what looked like a Town Hall, somewhere in the North, telling us that

The Welsh Republican Police were still looking for the original recording of *Mae Hen Wlad Fy Nhadau*, the Welsh National Anthem, which had been taken from its museum case in Caernarfon.

She went on to say that it had been recorded in London by the Gramophone Company on Saturday, March 11th, 1899 by a singer called Madge Breese. It was important, because it was thought to have been the first Welsh language recording ever made.

There were already fears that it had been smuggled out of the country and sold to some unscrupulous rich collector. According to Brigantia, the Welsh Republican Police were at a loss to know who had taken the iconic recording, but involvement by organised criminal gangs, or even the proscribed terrorist organisation, The Hammers of Edward could not be ruled out.

In the meantime, the body of a man who had been found hidden in dense undergrowth not far from Bangor City Centre, at around the same time the Madge Breese recording had been stolen, had been identified as John Henry Sienkiewicz, or Polish John, a small time crook, well known in North Wales criminal circles. He had been stabbed in the back with what the local police somewhat inelegantly described as 'a great big handled knife.' But, emphasised Brigantia, the police were, as yet, not making any connection between the two seemingly disparate events.

Then Brigantia pulled her rabbit out of the hat: she played the complete one minute and seventeen seconds of the original Madge Breese recording, the one that all the fuss was about.

Backed by a piano accompaniment, Madge was giving it her all, but her voice sounded shaky and quivering, a relic of a bygone age and a reminder of a time totally different to our own.

I continued to half listen to Brigantia and her appeals for any fresh information and proceeded to attack my bowl of *cawl*. Hmm, I mused, the North seemed to be having a bit of a bad press lately. First, there had been that business with The Ruthin Strangler, then all the hoo-hah over The Mould Mangler and quite recently the press had gone to town on The Denbigh Jangler, so called because he rattled his keys in the faces of his victims, before relieving them of all their belongings.

And now this. It seemed to me there might be quite a few fanatical Welsh Americans who would pay good money to get their hands on that recording. A pity it was all happening up north, I could have maybe got a slice of that action for myself, but what was I talking about, I had my hands full down here; there was plenty to worry about in the south, never mind the north. Just as I was finishing my bowl of *cawl*, I half heard the words

"Along the English border . . ."

"Oh, oh," I thought, the fragile peace with England seemed to be in danger of breaking down again. And the Super Dragons seemed to be continuing their disappearing act. At this rate, there were going to be none of them left before very long. Gloom and Doom, it was all Doom and Gloom. If Doom didn't get you, Gloom surely would.

There was only so much bad news I could bear in one day. I switched off the television and meditated/dozed for about half an hour or so.

About nine o'clock I started to get ready. I had decided to wear sensible shoes with a good grip, in case I needed to run quickly, the rest of my outfit was as black as a New Zealand rugby shirt; black trousers, black jumper, and black gloves. I also dug out a particularly fetching black balaclava of mine. I didn't want to glow in the dark, I wanted to blend into the darkness, not stand out from it. Then I packed Excalibur, my trusty rounders bat, and a little watertight packet I hoped might come in handy later, night vision goggles and a tool kit to work on the tree. It all fitted neatly into a medium sized, lightweight black rucksack. Stakis was right about one thing: I was going to have to be careful, if the Republicans found me with all this gear, I would have to come up with a pretty good explanation, or else I could be looking at a long stretch in Portmeirion.

With that in mind, I didn't want to present a vision of black to anyone seeing me riding in Stakis's car.

I pulled on a white trench coat, and then I piled my shoulder length Titian red hair up into a bun, with the help of a few hairpins, and placed a brown Fedora hat à la Humphrey Bogart in *The Big Sleep* on my head. Then I took a good, long look at the person in the mirror looking back at me. Perfect, *bendigedig*, even if I did say so myself.

As for the white trench coat, once we got to Nant yr Eos Cemetery, I would be able to reverse it, to reveal a black trench coat on the other side. I was feeling better already, what could possibly go wrong? This was going to be a piece of Welsh cake; a proper bakestone, I could feel it in my Brecon Carreg bottled water. The only thing I really had to worry about was not fear itself, but the police helicopter, if they decided to fly that tonight, I might be in trouble. Now, where did I put that cheap pay as you go phone, the one I'd been keeping for an emergency . . .?

CHAPTER 4

"I don't like this, Astrid," said Stakis as we crossed over the river in his car. "I don't like this at all. It's far too dangerous. What if . . ."

" . . . Gavin Henson gets back with Charlotte Church and starts playing rugby again," I said, "what if . . . what if . . . give it a rest, Stakis, and keep your eyes on the road, the last thing we want is an accident at this time of night. And remember what I told you, take a roundabout route; I don't want us going straight there. I don't think anybody's following us, but you can't be too careful, as my old mam used to say." I took a good look in Stakis's rear view mirror, it was true, it didn't look as if anyone was following us, but . . .

"Yeah, well," he said, "you're always so confident, aren't you, but how exactly are you going to get back home after you get this bolt out of the tree, if it's still there, that is. You know I can't come back to fetch you, the penalties for curfew breakers are really strict and I have a business to think of . . ."

"I've been thinking about that," I said, as Stakis pulled up alongside the Nant yr Eos cemetery wall, "and the truth is I'm still not sure. Any ideas?"

"Yes," he said, "I can turn this car back right now, and we can all sleep soundly in our beds, instead of putting our careers, our livelihoods and our freedoms on the line. Besides you don't know what's out there waiting for you, not everyone's as frightened to death of curfew as I am, you know."

"Aw, Stakis," I said, patting his arm affectionately, "it's nice to know someone cares, but this is one of those times where a girl's got to do what a girl's got to do . . . besides, I've got Excalibur with me, one tap on the knee with her and the curfew breakers are going to regret ever deciding to come out tonight."

"Yeah, yeah," he said, "so you say, but what if they have guns, what then? It's no good, I'm still not convinced and I can't even call you on your mobile as you're worried about the noise giving you away . . ."

"Nothing's going to happen," I said, "I get in, I get the bolt and I get out again, then I get back to *The Lying Cod*, it's as simple as that, a two-year-old child could do it."

"That's what I'm worried about the most," said Stakis, "you — acting like a two-year-old child. I don't know, Astrid, this doesn't feel right, what would Morgan have said?"

"Well, he's not here to tell us, is he?" I said, "look, Stakis, I have to do what I think is right." I gave him a quick, fleeting peck on the cheek. "Now go, go, no sense in both of us getting into trouble and don't beep the horn as you're driving off."

"I'm not that stupid," he said.

"I know," I said, "but listen, if you should get

stopped on the way back, you know nothing about me, right, you were just out for an evening drive, you're worried about the business and you just wanted to take your mind off things . . . And Stakis, if I'm not back by ten tomorrow morning, get in touch with Inspector Sergeant, he'll know what to do, no, wait, don't, if I'm unlucky, he might be questioning me anyway, wait a whole twenty-four hours and then contact him."

"All right, but tell me this, how are you going to get back over the river?" said Stakis.

"Don't worry," I said, "what I said earlier on about not having a clue wasn't strictly correct, I have got a plan, a trick up my sleeve, a clever ruse I can call on, crossing that river will be like taking Pell's mint humbugs from a sleeping four-year-old child, I just can't wait."

"What are you going to do? Walk over it? Wouldn't that just be like you?" he said.

"You'll see," I said, "or rather you won't, as you won't be there, but I'll tell you all about it later."

I took a quick look around me, there didn't seem to be anyone coming or any late stragglers mooching about, or taking their dog for a last chance to relieve itself before curfew. I took off the Fedora, rolled it up and put it in my trench coat pocket. Then I folded the trench coat, stowed it away in my rucksack and put on the balaclava, "how do I look?" I said.

"Wonderful," he said, "Zeta Jones herself couldn't have looked better . . ."

Before he could say anymore, I gave Stakis another quick peck on the cheek and then I was out of the car, over the low cemetery wall and down over the other side. I heard Stakis doing a quick three-point turn and heading back in the direction of Casnewydd and then I was on my own, the night fast closing in around me.

For a few minutes, I stayed where I was, listening, watching, but I heard nothing, no cars whizzing past, no drunken pedestrians on their way home from the pub. My heart was beginning to pound, the adrenalin starting to pump, maybe this wasn't such a good idea after all, maybe Stakis was right, and maybe there was something wrong with me.

Bloody Stakis, what did he want to go on about Morgan for? As George Harrison might have said, it was all too much. I felt like I wanted to cry, great heaving big sobs, and lose myself in my sorrow, but I had to keep a check on my emotions, I had to stay strong. What use was a weepy private investigator? About as much use as a Welsh archer at the battle of Agincourt with paper arrows, probably. I had to get a grip on myself.

Weeping and sobbing wasn't going to bring Morgan back any time soon. Cymru knows there wasn't a day went by when I didn't think about my dear, departed husband shot down in the course of an investigation, when we were both young private eyes starting out together, but now I needed all my wits about me, Morgan would always be with me, but now wasn't the time for me to get emotional. I took my first tentative steps in the direction of where I knew the tree with the bolt would be, stopping every so often to listen and look around me, hoping I was the only human being abroad in the cemetery at this time of night.

These night vision goggles were good; I had to give full marks to the manufacturers. I could see as clearly as if it were a bright, sunshiny day. I moved steadily towards the place where The Helmet had shot at me. So far, so good, I was right; this was going to be a proper piece of Welsh cake, a real doddle, and an absolute cinch.

I walked on cautiously, but at a steady pace. Discarded cigarette butts, empty drink cans and old plastic bottles which had once contained industrial strength cider littered the ground around a few of the cemetery's many benches. Somebody had been having a good time, well, what they thought of as a good time.

Then, I heard it. An owl was hooting in the cemetery, that eerie noise it made sounding triple magnified to me in my present state of mind. There it was again, no it sounded more like two of them, there was a call and response element about it, but was it real or was it human voices I was hearing. I shook my head, stop it Astrid, you're getting paranoid, concentrate, you came here to do a job, not get scared out of your wits.

As I moved (soundlessly, I hoped) between the

gravestones, pausing every so often to look and listen, I became aware of the moon coming out of the shadow of a dark cloud and beginning to perambulate across the night sky. "Here I am," the full moon seemed to say, "look at me, aren't I beautiful?"

Yes, you sure are, honey, was the answer to that one, I thought, but I wish you'd stay out of sight a bit more. Then it was away again, vanishing into a long line of asymmetrical dark clouds. Now, I was right next to the place where Tangerine Girl had vaulted the wall. Still no sounds around me, no footsteps coming near, no warning shouts, no accusing cries. Well, in for a penny, in for a Welsh pound, I always say and I cleared the wall. Now I was almost at my journey's end, the tree was there in front of me, standing out in all its stark beauty, I started reaching for the tool kit in the back of my rucksack, but where was the . . .?

Bloody, sodding bastard it, the bolt had gone from the tree, there was no sign of it anywhere. Now what? I sank to my knees in rage and frustration, it was all I could do to stop myself from howling out my anger, and alerting anybody who might possibly be near, and meant me harm. Morgan, where are you when I need you? All this way for nothing, I had put myself at risk for nothing, absolutely nothing and now I still had to cross the river, get back to Casnewydd and run the gauntlet of any patrols wandering about, upholding the curfew. I could have kicked myself for being such an idiot. Why did I never listen to Stakis . . .? Why did I always think I had the answer to everything? What was the matter with me?

How long all this went on, Cymru alone knows, but eventually I began to calm down a bit. Maybe the bolt had loosened of its own accord and fallen down out of the tree and, holding on to this forlorn hope like a gambler to his last precious chip at the Rhyl Casino, I paced the ground around, looking intently, wishing the bolt to be there somewhere, anywhere, but of course it wasn't. I tried again and again, going further each time, but it was hopeless. I had about as much chance of finding an orange tree growing on top of the municipal rubbish dump in Merthyr Tydfil.

There was nothing for it now, I had to lick my self-inflicted wounds and get back to the City as best as I could, the idea of spending the rest of the night here, surrounded by gravestones and being hooted at by the occasional owl or owls, not to mention who knew what horrors of the night, preparing to engulf me at any moment, was a non-starter as far as I was concerned. I began to retrace my footsteps and make my way back to the main road. I don't know whether it was by design or whether my feet had somehow instinctively taken me there without me knowing, but I suddenly found myself right next to the row of terraced houses where I had earlier made my unsuccessful enquiries about the girl in the tangerine dress.

I moved slowly and cautiously, almost crouching down in my anxiety not to be noticed. What was that the Perm had said to me about a lot of burglaries going on around here? I didn't want her alerting the forces of law and order to my presence, right now, the last thing I wanted was a question and answer session with them. I crept carefully nearer the wall. Now, I could see the houses clearly, but I was fairly sure, whoever was in them, they couldn't see me. They looked dark and empty, as if they had fallen into a deep, deep sleep. Then I heard the long, mournful sound of the sirens coming from the direction of Maendy town centre — curfew had started, from now on I was fair game for anyone and everyone who wanted to perform a citizen's arrest on me, shop me to the Republicans or generally make my life a misery. It was not a good time to be out and about and walking the streets.

I was about to slip over the wall and take my chances with the plan I had formulated, but not revealed to Stakis, better he didn't know about such things, if he was stopped and questioned, when I saw lights being switched on and heard sounds coming from within the two houses I had visited. Just like any number of cats, my curiosity got the better of me. I decided to stick around for a while to see just what I might see.

CHAPTER 5

Reader, what I saw was this: both the bare-chested man and the woman with the perm from earlier on, came outside and stood on the pavement in front of their houses, only now the bare-chested man was fully clothed. They seemed to be waiting for something, but what? They should have been inside, the pair of them, didn't they know there was a curfew on, even just standing outside of your own house could get you into trouble, if a Welsh Republican Police vehicle happened to come by at this moment . . .

And, wouldn't you just know it, two black police vans came hurtling round the corner and skidded to a halt, but instead of running back indoors, Bare Chest and Perm didn't flinch an inch. The doors of the vans opened, and the two policemen who had stopped me from catching up with The Helmet, stepped down. All four exchanged greetings and began to talk; I could hear them quite clearly in the still pleasantly warm night air.

"Is that delivery Mrs Big ordered ready for us?" said the policeman I knew as Jude.

"Yes," said Bare Chest. "We've got them all waiting for you. Any idea what she wants them for?"

"Not a clue," said Jude, "best not to ask, you know what she's like. Where are they?"

"The usual place," said Bare Chest and he and

Perm moved towards the first of the terraced houses, the one with the overgrown grass and the boarded up doors and windows. Bare Chest pointed some kind of remote control thing at the front door of the house and, to my surprise, it swung silently open.

"Hurry," said Jude, "I'm not expecting any patrols along here, but you never know, they could decide to run a check on this stretch of road at any time."

"Right you are," said Bare Chest and he and Perm disappeared inside the house whilst the two policemen stood guard outside. Before long they reappeared, pushing and pulling a gaily coloured, multi-designed, and five-foot tall, fibreglass Super Dragon out on to the road.

Interesting, I thought, very interesting, so this is where Casnewydd's Super Dragons have been ending up. The four of them then manhandled the fibreglass creature into the back of Jude's van and then the same process was repeated with a second, equally bright and beautiful Super Dragon, only this time, they placed it in the back of the other policeman's van.

I was tempted, sorely tempted, to mount a one-woman rescue mission and give these thieving desperadoes a taste of what Excalibur could do, but there were four of them after all and who knows how many guns they had between them. Instead, I had an idea. I took out the cheap pay as you go phone I had brought with me, switched it on, muffling the sound as best I could between my gloves. I needn't have worried;

the four of them had their hands full with the dragons and were heaving and panting, not to mention talking almost at the tops of their voices. I knew we were out of the way here, but really, their self-confidence was ridiculous. Anyway, I got the phone up and running and sent a text message to my favourite Welsh Republican Police Officer.

"Dear Inspector Sergeant," I wrote, "a terrorist outrage is about to be committed at . . ." and I gave the exact location of the three cottages, "if you hurry, you can catch The Hammers of Edward red-handed. Signed From One Who Knows."

My hope was that the Republicans would arrive in time, but even if they were too late, it would give me a chance to slip away unnoticed, and there would be at least one less patrol car to worry about on my way home.

Meanwhile, the four across the road had finished their work and begun talking again, they seemed to be in no hurry, and maybe Inspector Sergeant would catch them after all.

For the first time, I became aware of Perm's voice. She looked old, but somehow she didn't sound so old anymore, and the way she had helped pull the Super Dragons around, well, that hadn't been too old either. And now I came to think of it, her voice had lost its earlier high-pitched, querulous quality, it was no longer the voice of an old woman, but that of a young girl in her mid-twenties, perhaps.

"Hey, Joe," she said to one of the Republican Police men, "it seems all four of us have something in common —an encounter with the famous Mrs Astrid Price . . ."

"Yes," said Joe, "you should have seen her face when we flagged her down, it was a picture, wasn't it, Jude?"

"Yes," said Jude, "it was all I could do to stop myself from laughing out loud, and you say she came here afterwards?"

"She was here all right," said Bare Chest, "poking her nose into things that don't concern her, but we saw her off all right, she didn't get anything from us, calls herself The Great Detective, the woman hasn't got a clue," and he spat vigorously at the gutter.

Why, you bastards, I thought, you bloody, sodding bastards, just let me get at you, I'll show you who hasn't got a clue, and it was all I could do to stop myself running out there and confronting them, but luckily for me, perhaps, Jude and Joe were already saying their goodbyes and getting back into their vans. Then they both drove off in different directions, whilst Bare Chest and Perm moved back towards their houses. The odds were evening up now and, not for the first time that evening, I was tempted to have a go, but just as the two entered their houses, there came the screeching sound of a police siren approaching fast from the direction of Maendy town centre. It looked like someone had taken notice of my text message after all.

Good, exactly what I wanted. I started to move away in the direction of Casnewydd as silently as I could. When I got to a particularly dark spot I went over the cemetery wall. I could hear nothing, not even my friendly neighbourhood owl, or was that owls. I stooped, rummaged in my rucksack and pulled out a pair of roller blades, attaching them to the soles of my shoes. These were no ordinary roller blades; these were not even Marks & Spencer Cymru roller blades. These were super charged, go anywhere, take me home Daddy, almost silent roller blades. This was more like it.

Now I was up and away and flying, the back roads and alleyways were deserted and I made good progress, even the backs of the houses I passed seemed dark and empty, people were going to bed early, cowed by the curfew. Once or twice I thought I heard a sound, but it turned out to be only cats going about their nocturnal business, untroubled by any curfew imposed by mere men and women, this was going better than I thought, not long now and I would be home in my own bed, sleeping the sleep of the righteous, and well deserved it would be, too, but when I rounded the corner of a particularly disreputable looking lane lined with wheelie bins, I found myself staring at the sight of a gun-toting soldier, about twenty feet away from me, barring my way to the centre of the city and freedom, this must be one of the crack Llywelyn the Last Brigade Special Forces, the rumour mill had been working overtime on, during the last few weeks.

He must have seen me at about the same time I saw him and raised his gun towards me, before I really knew what was happening and then, in that particularly (peculiarly?) authoritative tone all soldiers and policemen and figures with guns in their hands seem to imbibe with their mother's milk, he said, or rather shouted, "Halt, in the name of the Welsh Republic, or I fire."

CHAPTER 6

Great, I thought, *bendigedig*, that's all I need, what am I going to do now – surrender meekly and go quietly, like a Welsh lamb to the slaughter, and have nothing to look forward to but some awkward questioning? Turn tail and hope he won't shoot me? What would Charlie Chan have done? Or Rip Kirby or Dick Barton or any of a hundred other fictional detectives? As usual, these guys weren't around to argue the pros and cons with. There was only one thing to do really, and I was going to do it, even though I am as loath as the next woman to cause physical pain to the splendid men (and women) of our armed forces. Before you could say Tonypandy or even Tonyrefail, I was charging straight at the soldier, as fast as I could, shouting 'Boudicca,' at the top of my voice, in a possibly vain attempt to disorientate and distract him.

I was lucky, maybe he was reluctant to shoot, maybe he was just tired and the long night was getting to him, or maybe my shouting "Boudicca" had actually spooked him on my behalf, but he let me get within a few feet of him, without pulling the trigger, and then I was launching myself into the air, feet first, going straight for him, and before he could fire, I was hurtling into his shoulder, dislodging the gun from his grip and dropping him to the floor. It was all I could do to maintain control as I landed, but I managed it somehow, thank Cymru, and then I was gliding on, the adrenalin pulling me through and away and round the next corner.

By then he must have got to his feet, because I heard the sound of the shot or shots behind me thudding harmlessly into the brick wall of the alley. Then I heard him running and there were more shots but I was leading a charmed life, nothing hit me, I was invincible, gliding on and on, until I knew I had left the soldier far behind.

The question was: where were his colleagues, were they even now rushing to his aid, eager to catch the furtive curfew breaker, or had he radioed on ahead and very soon I would be caught in an ambush? I didn't know and couldn't worry about it. I kept going, what else could I do, but I was more careful now, my air of over confidence from earlier on, dampened somewhat, but as five, maybe ten, minutes went by and there was still no sign of anyone in hot pursuit or trying to block my path, I began to think, maybe I was going to make it after all.

Then I rounded a corner and there it was, stretched out in front of me, the Brown River, separating the twin cities of Maendy and Casnewydd, the last hurdle, once over that and I was more or less home and dry, or so I hoped. As I neared the water's edge, I stopped for a moment to check if I was being followed. Good, I could hear no one, but I forced myself to count slowly up to one minute. Still, no sound of anyone on my trail, not even your average neighbourhood hell hound. I was alone with my thoughts and feelings and the night, just the way I wanted it. I waited an extra minute for good luck, and then I took out the lightweight packet I had stowed away in my rucksack before setting out on this night's adventure. I pressed the button in its side and, almost silently, with a gentle whoosh it expanded in front of my eyes to become a watertight mini coracle strong enough to bear my weight and with its own single paddle to guide the craft. Thank Cymru for my man in Aberbargoed, I thought, what would I do without his technical wizardry.

I hoisted my passport to freedom and a good night's sleep over my head and made my way down to the riverbank. No sign of Republican or Army patrols, thank Cymru, they must be further downstream, manning the bridges, or on a tea break somewhere. I looked but could not see any cigarettes glowing dimly in the dark, no torches illuminating the night; it was just me, my coracle and the water to cross.

I placed the coracle in the water and stepped gingerly in. Bye, bye, Maendy, I thought. Now, how did it go again? Yes, it was all coming back to me, I knew that female bonding course I went on with the Welsh Women's Rugby Team, learning to coracle, on the Teifi and Tywi rivers, would come in handy someday. As I plied my paddle with smooth, efficient strokes towards the opposite shore, I began to relax for the first time

I plied my paddle with smooth, efficient strokes towards the opposite shore

that night, not too much, of course, it didn't do to be too confident in my line of work, but just enough for me to feel increasingly more comfortable and at ease with myself.

True, the night had ended in failure, as far as achieving my main goal was concerned, but I was still in one piece, I had learnt something, not much, but something about what was happening to the Super Dragons of Casnewydd, and pretty soon I would be safe and warm in the security of my own trusted bed.

As I reached the halfway point of the river, I stopped paddling and listened again as intently as I could. Luckily for me, there was still no sign of the Welsh Republican Police helicopter, my biggest fear of the night, and I didn't think the police launches would penetrate this far upstream. I looked all around me with the high-powered night vision goggles, but could see no one about. Then I took the cheap mobile phone, I had used earlier at Nant yr Eos to phone Inspector Sergeant, out of my pocket and slipped it silently into the water. If I were to be caught, I didn't want that to possibly incriminate me. Then I resumed paddling my coracle with slow rhythmic strokes pulling me ever onwards towards my goal.

In what seemed to be no time at all, I had reached the opposite bank and was pulling the coracle ashore. Again, I checked and waited, straining all the listening nerves in my body, striving to hear the slightest sound. Nothing, I heard nothing, my luck was in. I pressed the button embedded in the coracle three times and, with the same gentle whoosh, it subsided back into the same rectangular shape it had been before I took to the water.

    I folded it carefully and tucked it away inside my rucksack. Then I clambered up the sides of the riverbank and, once on top, accelerated away on my roller blades through the back streets of Casnewydd, heading towards *The Lying Cod* and Price Towers, I was almost there.

    Now, I was within two streets of *The Lying Cod*. *Make Elin Fflur Minister of Music – Now!* said the graffiti on one high, red brick wall I passed. On a nearby lamppost someone had plastered a poster with the words *Vote Ivor Hale and The Generous Party —Money in Your Pocket* written on it. Somewhere up above in an upstairs apartment, I could faintly hear the sound of some mournful Welsh *Fado* singing on the radio — just like the Portuguese *Fado*, if you really want to know, only not quite as cheerful. Not far to go now and I would be where I wanted to be . . . home and dry . . . and in my bed, sleeping the sleep of the just.

    Careful, Astrid, what if someone is there, lying in wait for you, gun in hand, ready to put the handcuffs on? I tried to put such negative thoughts to the back of my mind, I was so near, so very near, nothing was going to stop me now.

And I was right. I made it to the door of my flat without further incident. Never had a flat above a chip shop seemed so warm and welcoming and so inviting. I undressed and had a warming, invigorating, refreshing shower. Then, feeling much better, I unpacked the rucksack and placed the clothes I had worn for the night in the laundry basket, taking good care to mix them well up with the rest of the washing. I wasn't really expecting a visit any time soon, but you never knew. Then I took to the strength and security of my bed. For a while, I lay there, trying to make sense of the night's events.

Who was this mysterious Mrs Big and what did she want with the Casnewydd Super Dragons? Were Jude and his partner real, if somewhat corrupt policemen, or were they impostors just pretending to be officers of the law. What part did Perm and Bare Chest have to play in all the goings-on? And what did Tangerine Girl have to do with any of this, if anything? None of it made much sense to me and it wasn't long before sleep had penetrated my outer defences, scaled the walls of my castle and stormed my inner citadel, leaving me deep within the land of dreams.

How long I slept for, I don't know, but I was suddenly awoken by the sound of a loud and persistent banging on my office door. I turned over and buried my head in the pillow, hoping it would go away. It didn't. Reluctantly, no, make that very reluctantly, I rose and made my way towards the door, grabbing Excalibur as I went. For all I knew, it could be anybody out there. Now, I could hear the voices, one in particular was shouting, "Open up in the name of the Welsh Republic, open . . ."

"All right, all right," I said, "I'm coming, what are you trying to do? Wake all of Cymru up? Don't you know there's a curfew on?"

I was pretty sure it was the Republicans knocking so loudly at this ungodly hour, but I gripped Excalibur tightly, just in case, and pulled back the chain on the door.

"What's all this about?" I said, "Can't a law-abiding citizen get any sleep anymore? Show some identity, please."

"We don't need any identity where you're concerned, Price," said a voice I thought I recognised, "open up, there's a good girl."

Rubbing my, still heavy with sleep, eyes, I did as I was told. Two men were standing in front of me, one in uniform, the other in plain clothes, the moustache of one of them looking even longer and more mournful than the last time I had seen it. The moustache was in plain clothes, the other man in uniform.

"Inspector Sergeant," I said, "PC Pritchard, to what do I owe this unexpected honour, how long has it been now, since last we met . . . come in, come in, both of you and have a seat. Sorry my office is in such a mess. I don't know, these cleaners, nowadays . . ."

Pritchard looked disdainfully around him before

sitting down. I could see he was itching to whip out his handkerchief and wipe the seat but he somehow resisted the urge to do so. Inspector Sergeant stood for a few seconds before he too joined his subordinate in sitting opposite me.

For a few moments there was silence between us, then Pritchard said, "We have been alerted by the Maendy Police Department as to a serious violation of the current curfew laws. What were you doing at Nant yr Eos Cemetery tonight, Price, not leaving flowers there by any chance, were you, or drinking after hours with some of your underage mates? Breaking the curfew is a serious breach of the laws of the Republic."

"Me, Officer Pritchard," I said, "you must be joking, I value my Private Investigator's Licence too much to indulge in any illegal activities. Besides, I've been in bed ever since the siren went off."

"Can you prove that?" said the inspector, "was there anybody with you at the time?"

"In bed, you mean?" I said, "let's see now, who was there with me, let me think, no, nobody, unfortunately, I haven't been doing too well on the bed front lately."

"Sorry to hear that," said Pritchard, although he didn't sound very sorry to me, "but let's tell the truth for once, shall we, we didn't come here to talk about your private life. After you left Nant yr Eos, you were seen, we have a witness, an extremely reliable witness."

"Oh, really," I said, "he or she must be very unreliable then, because I was never at Nant yr Eos in the first place. Why would I want to go there anyway? Cemeteries at night, not my thing, I can tell you, too spooky by far, ooh, dead creepy," and I gave an involuntary shudder and quite convincing it looked too, if I do say so myself.

"Anyway, at the risk of repeating myself, why in the name of Cymru, would I want to go to Nant yr Eos, Inspector? That's in Maendy, for Cymru's sake, you know I never go over there, what would I want to go over there for, there's nothing there for me, I'm a good Casnewydd girl, you know that. I never know the names of the streets in Maendy for starters, I have to ask for directions all the time — it's like a foreign country to me over there. Besides, how would I get over the river, what with all those lights and patrol boats and armed sentries, with orders to shoot to kill at curfew time?"

"This witness," said the Inspector, stolidly ignoring my impassioned speech, "is a member of our glorious armed forces and, therefore, a trained observer. He claims he was attacked by some person unknown whilst in the act of discharging his duty. He further claims that this person looked like a woman. A tall, slim, athletic looking woman dressed all in black. Whilst attacking him, this woman. . . Miss X, shall we call her, for the sake of argument, shouted something . . ."

"Yes," said Pritchard, "he's not terribly sure, but

he thinks it was something like 'Boudicca'. . ."

"Really," I said, "well, there you are then, it's probably someone with a grasp of our ancient Celtic past. I wonder who it could be. . . I know, it must be some member of the Boudiccan Appreciation Society out and about after a night on the tiles. You know — those people who meet in The Iceni Club every first Thursday of the month, I've often been tempted to go myself, but never got round to it."

"It must be one of them; I hear they get a lot of women going to their meetings. There's your villain, Inspector, that's who you're looking for, not law-abiding citizens sitting at home, minding their own business, waiting for curfew to be over . . ."

"Such as yourself, I suppose," said Inspector Sergeant, "tucked up in bed with a nice cup of Fair Trade cocoa were you?"

"Of course, Inspector," I said, "but how did you know? Since when have you been psychic?"

"Oh, just a hunch," said the inspector, "sometimes I strike lucky."

"The soldier said it sounded like a woman's voice to him," Pritchard said, "the attacker, I mean, with just a soupçon of North Walian to it. Now we know, and you know, that you spent your formative years in the north of the Republic . . ."

Just a soupçon, I thought, somewhat inconsequentially; what was wrong with a hint, a touch, a flavour . . . but I said, "and very happy ones they were too, but that description could apply to anyone, well, maybe not my ex-Welsh team-mate, Big Bertha Rees. As for the North Walian bit, I'm not the only one living in Casnewydd with a northern background. There's my sister Delyth, why don't you ask her?"

"We did," said Inspector Sergeant, "but as you very well know, Astrid, she is still Welsh Republican Ambassador to the Court of King Sean Connery I in Scotland and currently living in Edinburgh. What would she be doing, curfew breaking in the middle of the night at Nant yr Eos Cemetery? Seeking out some old acquaintances?"

"Well, she was always very highly strung," I said, "couldn't stand the same routine all the time . . . I wouldn't be surprised if she fancied a change from all those kilts."

"That's ridiculous, Price, and you know it," said PC Pritchard, "you'll be telling us next your old friend, Big Bertha Rees, has been flying through the air knocking over one of our soldiers."

"Well, since, you mention it," I said, "I have heard . . ."

"Oh, shut up, Price," said Inspector Sergeant, "you make me sick with your constant lies, evasions and equivocations, we have it on good authority, a woman resembling you was seen haranguing and harassing law abiding citizens, living opposite Nant yr Eos Cemetery, not long before the curfew breaking incident, and then someone contacted us to say we should get to Nant yr Eos as soon as possible, as a terrorist act was about to be committed . . ."

"Surely, Inspector, you don't suspect me," I said, "why, I'm cut to the quick . . ."

"You can be cut all you like," said Pritchard, putting in his ten Gwynfors' worth, "we're on to you, Price, and one of these days we're going to get you, you just wait and see."

Doesn't this bloke ever play a different record, I thought, but I said, "this is beginning to sound more and more like police harassment to me, PC Pritchard, what would President Hopkin say if she knew this sort of thing was going on?"

"Knowing you, I expect you voted for her at the last election," said Inspector Sergeant, fingering his moustache once more . . .

"Now, now, Inspector," I said, "you're forgetting the privacy of the ballot box and all that, we're not living in a dictatorship yet."

"Yeah, but for how long," said Pritchard. He looked as if he wanted to say something else as well, but stopped when he caught the Inspector looking at him.

Abruptly, Sergeant looked at the both of us and clasped his hands. He seemed to be coming to some sort of decision. "Well," he finally said, "we must be going, things to do and all that. I'm sure Astrid has a lot ahead of her on what looks as if it's going to be another hot day, but Pritchard is right, don't leave Casnewydd, Mrs Price, without informing us first and watch your step, you're not invincible, you know."

"Thank you so much for those heartfelt words of advice, Inspector," I said, as I ushered them both out, "You can rely on me. If I can help the Welsh Republican Police in any way, I'm honoured to do so . . ."

"Yeah, yeah," said Pritchard, anxious to get his final parting shot in before the door closed on him, "you have your fun now, Price, but remember what I said . . ." and then the two of them were gone, their police regulation footwear clumping down the stairs, leaving me alone with my thoughts.

No sense in going back to bed now, I thought —I was wide awake and the mournful sound of the siren was beginning to be heard all over the City, curfew had been lifted and we were free to go about our business for the next seventeen hours at least.

I made myself a cup of tea and two slices of whole-wheat toast, thinly spread with raspberry jam, and sat down at the kitchen table. Suddenly the room echoed to the sound of my mobile playing our national anthem, the Tich Gwilym accented *Mae Hen Wlad Fy Nhadau* or The Old Land of My Fathers. Someone was trying to get in touch with me, I half expected it to be Edward Henry Davies, anxious for more information on Tangerine Dress Girl, the love of his life, but it was Stakis, anxious for news of my adventures. Damn, I should have texted him as soon as I got in after my encounter with the gun-toting soldier, but it had clean slipped my mind, and then Sergeant and Pritchard with their suspicions — wasn't there anybody else they could interrogate in Casnewydd, why pick on me all the time —had pushed the thought even further to the back of my list of priorities.

"RU OK?" read his message —short and sharp and to the point.

"Yes, It's getting better all the time, I have just finished reading The Black Book of Carmarthen – I really enjoyed it," I texted back — our code words for everything in the allotment was hunky dory.

My duty done, I finished breakfast, washed and got myself ready and contemplated my next move. Things weren't right was the only idea that sprang to mind, I was getting nowhere, not only was I no nearer to finding Tangerine Dress Girl, I had stumbled into some kind of sub plot involving Casnewydd Super Dragons and what might, or might not, be bogus policemen. What did it all mean, what was it all about, Alfie?

I got up and, without really noticing it, began to slip into The Form — my Tai Chi moves; they calmed me down and helped me think more clearly. In fact most of my better ideas came to me, as I was gliding in and out of the almost hypnotic, rhythmic movements. A lot of the time the truth, or the best way forward, was staring me in the face anyway, just waiting for me to reach out and grab it, but what the hell, I wasn't hurting anybody and I liked sliding slowly, gracefully from move to move. So it was that when this morning's episode of The Form was over, I knew just what to do. It was time to renew acquaintances with Perm and Bare Chest again, and maybe this time Excalibur would have something to say to the pair of them . . .

CHAPTER 7

It was election time in the Welsh Republic. Those five years certainly came round fast. The parties were jostling for position and the strongest party would elect the President from amongst their number. Everywhere you went there were posters. Cajoling, exhorting, urging, begging you to give this or that particular party your all-important vote. Vote for me, me, me! One of them in the window of the Rebecca Riots café implored me to do something right and vote for the Benevolent Despot Party.

"Save money," it said, *"abolish Parliament, let just one person, with your best interests at heart, make all the right decisions."* Another, distinctly tatty looking, poster read, *"Vote for Ivor Hale, of The Generous Party. He'll see you right."*

Maybe he would, and maybe he wouldn't, but right at this moment, I had other things on my mind . . . I drove the *Pwca* fast, but not so fast as to cause annoyance to the guardians of law and order, I had had enough of them for a while, and it wasn't long before I was pulling up in front of the same three terraced houses I was beginning to know so well.

Once out of the car, I marched straight up to Perm's house, anxious for some answers and was about to knock, when I noticed three things I hadn't noticed before. Don't they always say everything goes in threes? The first was a brown cardboard notice in the front window on which someone had written in an exquisite copperplate hand: "*Hi, Astrid. I knew you'd be back.*" Someone's taking the *pissoir* here, I thought, cheeky bastard.

The second thing I noticed was that the name of the house above the door was *Salem* and the third thing I noticed was that the door was ever so slightly ajar. I knocked anyway, I'm polite that way, three times if you must know, and then I pushed the door wide open. "Hello," I shouted in my best Casnewydd accent, "anyone at home, it's only the milk woman; I've got that Goji Berry yoghurt you asked for."

Still no answer, the house was as quiet as a pub full of English rugby fans, who have just watched Cymru cross for their last try at Twickenham, to make the final score line 32 nil with just seconds to go. I shouted again "and I've brought that Welsh goat's cheese you wanted — all the way from Mynydd Gelli Wastad . . ."

No reply. If there was anybody there, they obviously didn't feel very much like talking. Well, in for a penny, in for a Welsh pound. Who lives in a house like this? I was about to find out as I shouldered Excalibur and walked in, closing the door behind me.

I walked down the ground floor passage past the stairs leading to the upper storey, moving as slowly and as carefully, as that Frenchman who had crossed between the two sets of 'knitting needles,' holding the Casnewydd Michael Sheen Pedestrian Footbridge up, not so long ago. Mind you, he had done it on a tightrope suspended some 79 metres up in the air, and with a six foot balancing pole in his hands, so he had very good reason to be careful. On my left was a room with the door closed, I kicked it open and charged in, ready for anything that came my way. Nothing did, the room was completely empty, but stank of stale cigarette smoke. The small room before the kitchen was also as empty as a vandal's head after a few drinks on a Friday night, but the kitchen offered a table and two chairs, plus a stove with a few pots and pans, and an antique looking washbasin. Like all the other rooms on the ground floor, this one too reeked of cigarettes, as if Chain Smokers Incorporated had been holding their annual conference here. The toilet cum bathroom was just as bad but the kitchen did at least have something to offer my trained eye.

    There was an envelope lying on the kitchen table with a name written on it —my name —in an elegant, Victorian copperplate style, just like the one on the cardboard notice in the front windows. I got a long spoon from one of the kitchen drawers and knocked it away as far as I could. Nothing happened. Good, I thought, it didn't seem to be booby trapped, but just to make sure, I dropped a heavy saucepan from the kitchen oven on top of it, leaping back as I did so. Again, nothing happened, it appeared to be all right, but still I waited a full five minutes before I picked it up and looked at it, just to make sure. Inside, on a piece of expensive looking notepaper, probably Swiss or German, it said, still written in the same elegant hand,

"What took you so long, O Great Detective? Sorry, but you're too late, young Astrid. Better luck next time? Yours, ever, Mrs Big."

Ha, ha, very funny, what a comedian, a right little joker. I couldn't stop laughing; it was all I could do to stop myself from rolling in the aisles. I hadn't laughed so much since the tears rolled down my face at . . . well, you get the picture.

I stuffed the envelope and note into my pocket, resolved to look at them again later, and went upstairs. I was still as vigilant as ever, but by now, I had the distinct impression I was alone in this house, and whoever had been here before wasn't likely to be coming back in a hurry. There were four rooms on the top floor — three bedrooms and a shower cum toilet. That was full of the usual left over smoke but two of the bedrooms were free of it. I looked around as carefully as I could, but whoever had been here had not left me very much in the way of clues. Time to get systematic, Astrid, order and method may bring results. If I'd had a fine tooth comb I'd have used it. As it was, I got down on all fours and swept each room with my eyes. Nothing. The 'comedian' who had left me the note was playing one last joke on me. I got to the third and final bedroom and repeated my modus operandi. There didn't seem to be anything here either.

I was just about to give all this up as a bad job and go and explore the garden when I saw it . . . tucked into the corner of the room was a tiny square piece of tangerine coloured fabric . . . if I hadn't been looking so intently, I would surely have missed it. Well, well, it wasn't one hundred per cent, gilt edged proof, but it looked as if Edward Henry Davies might not have been living in a dream world after all. I stuffed the square of fabric in my other pocket and gave the garden the once over. Nothing to report there, the stinging nettles had it pretty much all to themselves.

Before leaving the place I stood in front of Perm's house and stared. Something was missing. What was it? Something I'd seen before wasn't there anymore. Then it struck me —all the owls had gone. The front window, which had once been full of owls of all shapes, sizes and descriptions, was now as empty as my bank account halfway through the month. Perm had obviously taken them all with her. Were they just living as squatters? Sleeping on the floor in sleeping bags? Just using the house until such time, as they no longer had any use for them? Who knew? I didn't and such speculation wasn't getting me any further forward.

So I tried Bare Chest's house although I didn't expect him to be at home. It was pretty much the same story, enough stale smoke hanging in the air to keep an addict going for weeks, didn't these guys ever open any windows, a kitchen that might have been fashionable in the 1930s but now looked like a museum piece and that was about it — no note for me this time.

Next, I looked at the first house, the one with the neglected garden, from which the pair had conjured up the Super Dragons, on the night I had broken curfew, but if I was expecting any clues which would solve this mystery, once and for all, I was again sadly disappointed. There was nothing, no hint of any solution to my problems. I was no further forward than before.

Leaving the houses behind me, I sat in the *Pwca*; my hands on the steering wheel, thinking. I had a lot to think about. Where had Perm and Bare Chest gone? Could Perm have been Tangerine Girl in disguise or had the pair kidnapped her? And if so, why? That latter scenario, by the way, might explain the tangerine square I had found. And where was the dog? There had been no sign of him. And there had been no barking, when I first knocked on the doors, and came face to face with Perm and Bare Chest. I needed answers and I needed them fast —it was time to pay someone a visit . . . someone who might just know what was going on, and even more importantly, perhaps, who was behind it all.

CHAPTER 8

From outside, the public house known as *The Clinging Man* looked the same as ever, its weather-beaten sign hanging in the air, depicting a tear-stained man, clinging desperately on to the left leg of a fast retreating woman, its colours bleached with age. On the wall of the pub someone had scrawled in a somewhat shaky hand using an aerosol can, the words, *"Tell Laura I Love Her."* Tell her yourself, I thought, can't you see I'm really rather busy right now.

Inside, the pub hadn't changed a bit either, the same old threadbare carpets on the floor, the same old dartboard, the toilets which, it was rumoured, had had a preservation order slapped on them by *Cadw*, the Welsh Republic's heritage body, the ripped faux leather chairs and benches, the same old jukebox, playing the same old tunes, standing guard in the same old corner. Once upon a time, the walls and the ceilings would have been stained a deep, dark shade of brown, but since the Welsh Republic had brought in a hotly debated smoking ban, *The Clinging Man* was at least clean in this respect.

In the back bar, sitting on an ancient settle, I found Big Bertha Rees, who had played prop to my outside half, when we both starred for the Welsh Women's Rugby Team. Bertha looked as if she had been poured into her seat with as much tender loving care, as a top notch barmaid, or barman, would have poured a bottle of Casnewydd's Finest Ale into a waiting glass.

If Big Bertha had been big during her playing days, her dimensions were now verging on the huge. There were those who said that she never got out of her seat, that the landlord let her sleep there at night, that he had tried bringing in a crane to lift her, but had had to give it up as a bad job, but I didn't believe them, I had a suspicion that she could still put on a useful turn of speed, if the need arose.

Normally, Big Bertha would have had a coterie of male admirers surrounding her — despite her size she seemed to exercise some kind of fascination over the opposite sex — and yes, like a lot of, shall we say, slightly overweight women, she had quite a pretty face, but today she was on her own, nursing a pint in her two big hands. As I walked towards her, she looked up from her drink.

"Well, well," she said, "look what the Siamese has brought in. If it isn't the ball dropper herself, Astrid, pass it to me, and I'll let it slip, bloody Price."

God, the woman had a memory like three herds of elephants. One time and one time only, I had dropped the ball with the All Black line at my mercy . . . that winning try would have been the difference between success and failure in the World Cup Final and Bertha had never let me forget it. Little did she care that it had been raining canines and felines, at the time, and the ball was like a bar of soap which had been dipped in oil and then rubbed thoroughly in a tub of grease. Props expected the fancy Dan dilettantes in the backs to deliver, when they had the chance. In Bertha's eyes, I was a failure and always would be, which didn't stop her taking my money, whenever she got the chance.

"Oh, don't start that again, Bertha," I said, "that was years ago, can't you just get over it like everybody else?"

"Yeah, well," she said. "You'd like that, wouldn't you and maybe you're right, but every time I see you, it all comes back to me. What do you want anyway? Information on the cheap again, I suppose?"

"Of course," I said, "what can you tell me?"

"Rumours are rife on the streets," she said, tapping the side of her nose in an attempt to appear mysterious.

"What sorts of rumours?" I said.

"You know," she said, "somebody is supposed to be hiring imported muscle, bringing in heavies from abroad. . . They don't need to fly them in through Caerdydd or Bangor or bring them in via the main ports anymore, they just land them on some secluded beach at dead of night and away to go . . ."

"Do these people have names?" I said.

"Do they ever," she said, "the list reads like an International Hoods Who's Who. The talk is of guys like Georg Alptraum, the Hamburg hit man, a nasty piece of work by all accounts. Then there's the Columbian, Rodrigo Rodriguez, Herb the Serb, Cocky Marciano from New York, Marseille's Monsieur Dieu, those are the sort of people we're talking about — they're just a few of the names that have been going the rounds. The home grown article, like Red Iolo, for instance, nobody seems to be interested in them anymore."

Red Iolo, I thought, there was a blast from the past and one I hadn't heard of for a while. He was a villain, of course, but there was something of the old school 'lovable rogue' about him, some hint of a saving grace and he sported a neat line in Panama hats, but I said, "Monsieur Dieu, Mister God, why do they call him that?"

"Because he has the power of life and death over people, that's why," she said. "He tells them to pray, and then, after they've finished praying, he either lets them have it, or lets them go."

Charming, I thought, what a nice man, but I said, "a bit like the old Roman emperors, then?"

"Yes," she said, "just like them. There's also talk of the northern mafia moving in — you know, the Wrexham-Bangor-Llandudno-Rhyl connection. Something big's going down, but I don't know what it is. These are interesting times we live in, Astrid, English troops massing at the border; threats from London, the vultures are circling . . ."

You're telling me, I thought, and a bit too noisily

for my liking, but I said, "and the Republicans, what do they make of all this imported muscle, you're talking about, coming onto their turf?"

"Look, Astrid," she said, "the Republicans are undermanned, underwomanned and underpaid, and you know it, and everybody else knows it. It's all they can do to keep the lid on the local low life without outsiders coming in to stir the pot."

"What about a Mrs Big," I said, "does that name mean anything to you?"

"Can't say that it does," she said, and her eyes seemed to bear out the truth of what she was saying, "Why, should it?"

I ignored her question and followed up with another one of my own. "What about these missing Casnewydd Super Dragons, Bertha?" I said, "anything you can tell me about them?"

"Only that those not vandalised, by the Casnewydd literati, seem to have been stolen. Why would anyone want to do that?"

You tell me, I thought, you're the one who's supposed to have her ear to the ground, but I said, "I'm afraid you're not being much help here, Bertha, what about a missing girl wearing a tangerine dress? She had some sort of dog with her the last time she was seen."

"Tangerine dress?" said Bertha, "what is she, some sort of Blackpool supporter? Why would I know anything about her? What did she do? Rob a bank? And as for the dog, well, dogs go missing every day; you know that as well as I do. I tell you what, I'll ask around, see what I can find out, but it'll cost you . . ."

"How much?" I said wearily. "How much do you want this time?"

"Well, seeing as it's you, Astrid," she said, "let's just say I like seeing Owain Glyndwr's face – in fact I like seeing it so much, I'd like to see it five times in all, if you see what I mean?"

"Of course," I said, "who wouldn't," pulling out five ten Glyndwr notes from my pocket, counting them and pushing them over the table towards Bertha.

"Great," she said, "*bendigedig*, I love renewing acquaintance with our national hero; it gives me a thrill every single time I see his picture on a banknote."

"I'm sure it does," I said, "but just you make sure you come up with something useful. You know my number, don't you?"

"Of course," she said, "who could forget the number of the great Astrid Price, Wales's answer to Sherlock Holmes himself? And don't worry, ball dropper, if I can't come up with anything useful, I'll give you your money back, less my fifty per cent commission, of course."

"You're so good to me, Bertha," I said, "they should rename you Bertha the Generous."

"Bertha the Generous," she said, "I like that, maybe I'll start signing all my autographs that way, it's got a certain ring to it."

"Hasn't it just," I said, "if only it were true . . . well, I was going to buy you a pint, but now you've got most of my money, I don't think I'll bother, see ya . . ."

And with that I got up from my chair and left *The Clinging Man* behind me. I was now the proud possessor of information, concerning international gangsterdom, but as far as the girl in the tangerine dress was concerned, I was not really any further forward than before.

So, what now, my love? It felt as if I were riding a juggernaut which would career along, regardless for a while, gathering momentum with each passing minute, and then, all of a sudden, would come to an abrupt, jarring full stop, before picking up pace again — if the old Celtic gods of Luck were smiling on me, that is.

If this were a Raymond Chandler novel, now would be about the time for a man (or, in our more enlightened days, a woman or a young girl) with a smoking gun to appear and move the action on a bit. Not that I'm a particular fan of people with smoking guns, you understand – in my experience, they tend to be a little bit too trigger-happy for my liking. I waited, but nothing happened. Wherever the men or women with guns were, they certainly weren't in the car park of *The Clinging Man* at this time of the morning.

I started the engine and eased the *Pwca* out into the City's teeming traffic. Somewhere out there, perhaps, were Tangerine Girl and that dog of hers, just waiting for me to do my Knightess in shining armour bit, and come along and rescue them, but whether they were dead or alive, I had no way of knowing, I needed to find out. I was about as much further forward as one of those writers stuck on the same page for weeks and suffering badly from a chronic and incurable case of the dreaded 'writers' block. Now, more than ever, I desperately needed a breakthrough, any kind of breakthrough, but I had no idea where it was going to come from, still less when . . .

CHAPTER 9

Stuck in a traffic jam on Dafydd ap Gwilym Road, it was hot and just a little sticky. I was feeling the need for refreshment; I should have had a drink in *The Clinging Man* after all. I could have just parked the *Pwca*, I suppose, and taken the city's well-organised and efficient underground system and got there quicker, but I love my *Pwca*, love it more than Richard Burton ever loved Elizabeth Taylor, loved it so much that even time spent alone with it, in the mother of all traffic jams, would have seemed bearable.

I called my answer phone. Only one new call: Edward Henry Davies asking me to get in touch again. I dialled his number on my mobile.

"Look," I said, "if you can drag yourself away from whatever you're doing, I haven't got time to talk right now, but there's been a new development. Can you meet me at *Die Sachertorte* in about fifteen minutes from now?"

I was about to hang up, when Davies's voice cut in. He sounded breathless as if he had been running. Maybe he had been writing after all and had had to run downstairs to answer the phone. Maybe . . .

"Yes," he said, "I think I can manage that, but can't you tell me . . .?"

"Sorry," I said, "got to go, the traffic's started

moving again. Don't be late; I can't abide men who are late." I put the phone down and concentrated on the traffic again, it looked as if it was beginning to move at last . . . food and drink, here I come.

Die Sachertorte was the latest sensation to hit the streets of Casnewydd. It was a Viennese style coffee house full of fattening, cream filled delights, cheesecakes, gateaux of all kinds, those little pancakes — *Palatschinken*, they called them, filled with all sorts of sweet, enticing things, *Kaiserschmarrn* made from eggs, milk, sugar and flour, and of course the ultimate Viennese chocolate concoction, the eponymous *Sachertorte*.

The coffee house was decorated in the style of the fin de siècle Austro-Hungarian monarchy, with pictures of the Emperor Franz Josef I, the Hofburg and old Vienna adorning the dark, wood panelled walls, reflected back on each other by the carefully designed and strategically placed antique mirrors. Personally, I could have done with some Gustav Klimt reproductions lining the walls myself, but then you can't have everything, I suppose. Discreet background music was provided by the various members of the Strauss family, plus the occasional tune by other composers, such as compositions like the *Radetzkymarsch*. As soon as you opened the front door, the fragrant smell of freshly ground coffee delicately assailed your nostrils and, once inside, there were inviting nooks and crannies, little hideaways, where you could have that oh, so private conversation, without fear of being eavesdropped or spied upon. It was run by a husband and wife team who had learnt their trade in Austria's capital and knew how to provide an experience, which would appeal to all five senses. Everybody who was anybody in Casnewydd society just had to be there, darling. I loved it, loved it to bits and I wasn't the only one, some lunch times people were fighting one other to get in there.

So, when I finally finished battling my way through the traffic and got to *Die Sachertorte*, I was feeling good, in anticipation of the pleasures to come. I might have been ten minutes late, but never mind, it would do Edward Henry Davies good to wait, that's what I always told my male acquaintances anyway. Closing the door behind me, I scanned the room to see who was who. There was a babble of noise, everybody talking at once and trying to get their point across. The place was heaving, as I knew it would be. Looking closer, I saw a middle-aged couple sitting together, but reading separate newspapers. At the table next to them were two middle-aged men, clutching their pints of cool light-coloured Austrian lager, huddled over their phones, consulting the Internet, emailing friends and ignoring each other completely. These people were just the tip of the Titanic; as usual the place was packed with the good burghers of Casnewydd, all demanding their sugar rush and insisting that their coffee and cake addiction be satisfied as quickly as possible.

But where was Edward Henry Davies? I couldn't see him anywhere. I hoped he wasn't going to stand me up on our first date. (Well, second, if you counted the interview in my office.) Then I saw him. Good, he was right at the back of the coffee house waving a copy of *Y Byd* (The World) at me from one of those little booths, just made for confidentiality, and a private tête à tête.

I excused me my way through the throng and took a seat opposite him and within seconds, or so it seemed, a waitress was at my shoulder, in her smartly pressed black and white uniform, an Austrian hussar's shako on her head, wanting to know my order.

"Coffee, please," I said, "with a small carton of cream on the side and just a little piece of your delicious *Sachertorte*. No, make that a medium piece," I said, as she started to move away, "I'm feeling a little Gregory Peckerish."

Before you could say Rhosllanerchrugog or Betws Gwerful Goch or even Llyn y Fan Fach the waitress had brought my order, and mighty delicious it looked, too. Hmm, this is good, I thought, this is really good, I could eat more of this, but I won't, got to watch those calories, you know.

As soon as she had gone, I turned my attention to Edward Henry Davies.

"So, what exactly is it that you do?" I said.

"Well, Mrs Price," he said, "I'm a playwright or at

least I'm trying to be."

"Oh, really," I said, "what kind of plays do you do?"

"I specialise in alternative histories," he said, but he must have noticed my quizzical look, because he hesitated and then, after a few seconds' thought, took the plunge. "You know the sort of thing," he said, "William the Conqueror, getting a Saxon axe buried in his head in 1066, and Harold winning the battle of Hastings. Or the Welsh, sorry I mean the Cymry, I was forgetting about the presidential decree . . ."

I nodded. This latest move by Mary Hopkin, our new president, was proving to be a bone of contention with many people. Basically, it meant that all 'slave' names, as she insisted on calling them: Wales, Newport, Swansea, Welsh etc. were effectively outlawed and banned from official usage, only their Welsh language equivalents being allowed, but she hadn't got around to banning them from being used in ordinary conversations between members of the public yet. Maybe that was coming . . .

"Go on," I said, 'what about the Cymry?"

"Well," he said, "what if the boot had been on the other foot? What if the Normans had been confined to what is now the territory of the Welsh Republic, and our ancestors, the Cymry had invaded from northern Europe and subjugated them? Would we have been as nasty to the Normans as they were to us? Or what about

Bonnie Prince Charlie?"

"What about him?" I said.

"Well, if he had carried on to London, instead of stopping at Derby and turning round and going back to Scotland, who knows what might have happened."

"Who, indeed?" I nodded noncommittally. Hmm, I thought, I couldn't really see these plays packing many bums on seats, but I said, "so what were you doing in the cemetery that day? Why weren't you at home writing or researching in the library or on the Internet?"

"Two words, Mrs Price," he said, "the author's worst enemy: writer's block. Sometimes I get stuck and can't think of anything else to write. So I go for a walk. I find it clears the air and you'd be surprised how often ideas and thoughts come to me when I'm just strolling about, minding my own business."

"So the cemetery is one of these usual walks, is it?" I said.

"Yes," he said, "although I do try to vary my routine a bit, so as not to get stale. Anyway, as you can probably tell, I'm not from around these parts originally. I moved south just to be near the big Welsh theatres, but house prices these days in Caerdydd . . ." he shrugged his shoulders, "so Casnewydd seemed like the next best option."

I nodded. It was time to get back to the business in hand, the reason why we two were sitting together in *die Sachertorte* in the first place.

"Mr Davies," I said, "this girl you want me to find. Can you still remember what her dress looked like, even after all this time has gone by?"

"I think so," he said, looking at me almost pleadingly. "Why? Have you . . .?"

"Don't get your hopes up," I said, "it may be something and nothing," and I produced the scrap of tangerine fabric I had found in the Perm's house.

He looked at it and then back at me, "where . . . where did you get this?" he said. "It looks like part of her dress all right, but as you say, after all this time, I can't be sure, it could belong to anyone . . . where did you find it, Mrs Price?"

"That doesn't matter," I said, "let's just say it might be a step in the right direction, that's all, although there's still a long way to go and I make no guarantees. Right now, I'm still pursuing my inquiries, which reminds me I really must be going. Thanks for the coffee and cake, I'll keep in touch. As I say, don't get your hopes up too high; she may be miles away from here for all we know. I'll keep in touch." And with that I was gone, leaving a bemused Edward Henry Davies sitting there, clutching his coffee cup.

He looked like he was going to cry. For a moment, I almost felt sorry for him, then I told myself someone had to keep their wits about them if that girl of his was ever going to be found. I still had plenty to do and miles to go before I slept. These investigations didn't solve themselves. I was supposed to be the private detective, it was up to me to find this elusive girl in the tangerine dress, if she was still walking the planet, that is, and report back to Edward Henry Davies. And if I couldn't find her? Well, then, that would be a blow to my professional pride, but I would just have to 'woman up' and tell the love struck dreamer my best efforts had failed and, in my professional opinion, he would be better off forgetting all about this particular girl and finding somebody else to love, somebody who didn't make a habit of disappearing off the very face of the Welsh Republic.

    I shut the door of *Die Sachertorte* behind me and climbed into the *Pwca*. I didn't want to but somehow I felt I needed to reacquaint myself with my office, call it women's intuition, call it what you will . . .

CHAPTER 10

"There's someone waiting for you upstairs," said Stakis, his hands, as usual, deep inside a big pile of potatoes, "I had to let her in, she was most insistent. I told her I didn't know when you'd be back, but she wouldn't take no for an answer and it didn't help that you weren't answering your phone again . . ."

"Ah," I said, which was all the apology he was going to get. "What did she say her name was?"

"She didn't," said Stakis, "but she looked pretty determined to me. I'd watch my step if I were you."

I climbed the steps to my office cum flat, Stakis's warning ringing in my ears, the smell of his cooking assailing my nostrils. What now, I thought, didn't I have enough on my plate already with chasing after girls in tangerine dresses, who seemed to have vanished as successfully as my money, at the end of a Friday night out. Now, now, Astrid, this wasn't the attitude to adopt. Think fresh clients, new sources of money, more interesting cases maybe. I opened the door and there she sat, staring fixedly at my desk, as if doing so would bring the answer to all her problems. I coughed politely. I would soon get to the bottom of all this, I was a detective, that's what I did, and Reader; this is what I found out.

Culloden Jimmie was missing and nobody

"There's someone waiting for you upstairs," said Stakis, his hands, as usual, deep inside a big pile of potatoes

knew why. Not the police. Not his closest associates. (Or, if they did know, they weren't telling anybody.) Not even his wife knew the reason for his disappearance, least of all his wife. How did I know all this? I knew all this, not because I was there, when it happened, or because I'd read it in the pages of *Y Byd* (The World) over breakfast that morning, but because the woman he'd shared most of his adult life with, was sitting across the table from me, telling me everything, describing in graphic detail the circumstances in which Culloden Jimmie, or James, as she insisted on calling him, had disappeared from off the face of our beloved Welsh Republic.

Mrs Culloden Jimmie was not what I had expected. If asked to take a lie detector case, I would have guessed that she would have been a mousy, dowdy kind of woman, nothing to send a note home with the carrier pigeon about. Instead, she was well groomed, elegantly dressed and handsome for her age, she must have been in her early sixties, yet the carefully coiffured and bobbed blonde hair cut, the expensive, but not too expensive, spectacles, the trendy black Kipling handbag and the lively demeanour all belied her age. This was a woman who had no intention of letting herself go.

Now Culloden Jimmie may have been a lot of things, but he was no great shakes in the sartorial department and he always gave the impression, to me at least, of not being too concerned about his personal appearance. So to say I was surprised when I found her in my office and she announced who she was, well, you could have knocked me down with a Casnewydd City Council Buildings Department wrecking ball. I looked at her expectantly.

"All right, he was a villain," she said in an accent, with which you could have cut a haggis with a claymore, even though she must have been living in what was now the Welsh Republic for God knows how long. It was as thick as Scotch broth or Cock-a-Leekie soup. Cymru knows what part of Scotland she came from, at school my strongpoint had never been geography, particularly, Scottish geography. I know, it's a shocking admission to make from someone, whose sister is the Welsh Republican Ambassador to the court of King Sean Connery I, and I don't want to make a big song and dance about my ignorance, but all I knew is that she came from up there somewhere.

"But he never did anything nasty," she said, "well, not really nasty, he was a . . ."

"Lovable rogue?" I said, "gentleman villain?" churning out all the old clichés. She'd be telling me next any number of flies would have been safe in Culloden's company. The man was a saint, an absolute saint; there were no two ways about it . . . Still, a wife is entitled to look at her recently vanished husband through a rose coloured prism, I suppose.

"He had been on his way home from the pub, you say?"

"Yes, Mrs Price," she said, *The Welsh Bankrupt,* down by Tommy Farr Close, his favourite, his local, he was in there most nights."

I nodded. I'd been in there a few times myself, strictly business, of course. "But why come to me," I said, "why not let the Welsh Republican Police get on with their job."

"Them," she said, "the WRP, don't make me laugh, Mrs Price, they were about as much use as one of those Japanese paper umbrellas in a thunderstorm." She paused, as if something had just occurred to her.

"I can't afford to pay you very much, Mrs Price," she said.

Here it comes, I thought, the usual sob story. Jimmie must have had something stashed away surely — he wasn't a complete idiot, after all, or maybe he was, and had frittered away all his ill-gotten gains, what did I know about the state of his personal finances, but I said, more fool me:

"Don't worry about that; pay me what you can when you can. Now, about Jimmie and his disappearance – I'll try my best to find him, but I make no promises. Has he ever gone missing before?"

"No, Mrs Price, this is the first time. I tell you I'm sick with worry, what can have happened to him? It's been seven days now, and there's been no word, no phone call, no emails, no texts —nothing, nothing at all."

Seven days. I looked at my desk calendar, that

would mean Jimmie had left all he loved in this world behind him on August 12th. "Have you got a photograph?" I said, "a good likeness? I'll need one to show the punters when I ask around."

"Yes, of course," she said, "I've brought one with me," and she handed me what appeared to be a recently taken photograph of Culloden on holiday somewhere, soaking up the sun.

"That'll do nicely," I said, "and I need a contact number from you, somewhere I can get in touch with you easily."

She wrote a number down on a piece of paper and handed that to me as well.

"Telephone number, Casnewydd 230 946, address, 84, Dick Richardson Street," I said, "I know the place."

"Yes," she said, "you can reach me there most hours of the day and night. God knows I spend enough time there in front of the telephone, waiting for it to ring, waiting for him to call."

"Don't give up," I said in what I hoped was an encouraging, and not a patronising, tone. "I know it's hard, but try to look on the bright side of things. People go missing every day of the week, they hide out, hole up somewhere, get whatever it is on their mind out of their system. Then they come back after a few days and pick up the strings of their old lives again. Maybe that's what your husband's doing?"

"That's what the Republicans said, The Welsh Republican Police, your friends and helpers, as they like to call themselves. Don't make me laugh. 'He'll be back,' they said, 'he's probably out casing some joint somewhere, he'll turn up, don't you worry, Mrs MacLean, just like the proverbial bad penny, we know all about his sort round here, don't we, boys?' Fat lot of good they were, Mrs Price, it was all just a big joke to them, they weren't taking James's disappearance seriously enough for my liking, sure they pretended to be interested, said they'd put a man on the case and all that, but I could tell their hearts weren't in it, not really. After all, what is he to them — just a small time thief and fixer, a troublemaker, that's all. That's why I came to you, Mrs Price, James and his friends had a lot of respect for you, they said, after your husband got killed the way he did, you put a lot of time and effort into making that detective agency of yours work."

In spite of myself, I was touched and just a little bit flattered, but this wasn't about me, this was about finding another human being who, for all I knew, didn't want to be found, had his own very personal reasons for not wanting to be found, but whom I was going to have to find, if only to satisfy my own incipient curiosity.

"Now, forgive me," I said, "it's none of my business, I know, but I have to ask you this, Was Culloden, I mean James, seeing someone else. Was everything all right between the two of you? It might help me in tracking him down."

She took it on the chin, all right, I have to give her that, she didn't slam me with her handbag or burst into tears, or walk off in a huff or anything like that.

"Well, Mrs Price," she said, "you're right, I suppose, if it'll help you with your enquiries . . . I can't deny there haven't been stormy waters from time to time and James has been known to have an eye for the ladies, but lately, we've been getting on so well, it's almost been like the first days we met, so, no, I don't think he was seeing anybody, but I'm beginning to think I don't know anything anymore. Maybe I didn't know him as well as I thought I did."

Time to move on swiftly, I thought, but I said, "Was he planning anything, do you know? Had he something in mind? Was he working on a job of some kind? Something that might interest the Welsh Republican Police?"

"I don't know," she said, "I didn't want to know, to tell you the truth. Besides, he never talked to me about his work, 'what you don't know, won't hurt you,' he always used to say."

Words of wisdom, indeed, I thought, but I said: "did he leave any note, any message, anything to say where he was going and what he was doing?"

"No, nothing," she said. "The first I knew he was gone was the next day. I woke up to find myself alone, well, nothing unusual in that, he'd often stay out all night. Once he'd started drinking, met some cronies of his, it was the devil of a job to get him to stop."

"Again, I have to ask you this," I said, "did he have any enemies, anyone who would want to see him depart this life before his allotted three score years and ten?"

"Well, in his line of work . . ." she shrugged her shoulders, "that's an occupational hazard, I suppose, but no, there's no one outstanding that I can think of, no one who held a real, cast iron grudge against him."

"What about the Missing Persons Bureau Cymru?" I said, "Have they been any help?"

"They try," she said, "God, do they try and they're well meaning, but they're overwhelmed, Mrs Price. So many people go missing, I never realised how many till James . . ."

She broke off and reached for a tissue from her handbag. I let her regain her composure and then I said: "so how do you think I can help, Mrs MacLean, one individual working alone. You've already said the Welsh Republican Police and the Missing Persons Bureau can't cope, so how do you think I can find James?"

"Well, you've got contacts," she said, "you must have, you know Casnewydd and you must have done this sort of work before, I mean, I thought every private eye tracked down and hunted people who'd gone missing for whatever reason . . . isn't that part of your bread and butter? Besides, I trust you, I know you won't let me down."

"He could be over the border in England by now," I said, "and, if he is, you're going to need a London private dick and money, big money. Then again, he might be up North, Bangor, Wrexham, somewhere like that. He could even be in Europe or America, for all we know. Or he could . . ."

"I know," she said, "I try not to think about that. It's the only thing that keeps me going. The thought that somehow, somewhere, he's still alive."

I nodded. "Is his passport gone?" I said, "has he withdrawn any money from his bank account? Did he take his car with him when he left?"

"No," she said, "nothing's been touched, everything is just as he left it."

"Any distinguishing marks?" I said, "anything that would make him stand out from the crowd?"

"He always had, sorry, has a deeply pessimistic streak in him," she said. "Apart from that, no, he has no distinguishing marks."

"What about his friends?" I said. "Red Iolo and the others —The Plank, Rassau Tony and Two Fingered Geraint? Do they know anything?"

"They say they know nothing," she said, "that his disappearing is as much a surprise to them as to everybody else."

"And you believe them?" I said, "You think they're telling the truth?"

"I don't know," she said, "I really don't know

anything anymore, they could be lying, they could all be in this together, I just don't know, Mrs Price, I was hoping you would be able to find out for me."

There it was again: this reliance on me, this hope, this trust, I hoped I would be up to it.

"He could have changed his appearance," I said, "could be changing it now, as we speak. Are you sure he hasn't got any distinguishing marks, anything that wouldn't be so easy to change?"

"Yes," she said, "how could I have forgotten? It must be all this stress I've been under, I don't know whether I'm coming or going. He has two tattoos, one on each arm. The left one says: *I fought the law* and the right one says: *and the law won.*"

"There was no ransom note?" I said, "no demands for money?"

"No," she said, with just the barest hint of irritation in her voice, "I told you, I've received no communication of any kind, either from James, or from anyone else, purporting to know of his whereabouts."

I could feel this interview was drawing to a close, there wasn't much more I was going to learn from this session, but I still had another question to ask, one I felt hadn't been completely answered earlier in our conversation.

"Are you sure James hasn't run off with another woman?" I said. "I mean that might be one logical explanation . . ." My words hung in the air like stalactites in the deepest depths of the Pant yr Ogof Caves.

"Let's just say that James had learned from past experience it wasn't wise to dally with other women, and not to push me too far. Let's just leave it at that, shall we?" said Culloden Jimmie's wife. "And now, if you'll excuse me, I really must be going, a home doesn't look after itself you know. I'll show myself out, Mrs Price, and don't worry about the money; I'll let you have some as soon as I'm able." And she rose, pushed back her chair and left me alone with my thoughts.

CHAPTER 11

There was something cold about Mrs Culloden Jimmie, I couldn't quite put my digit on it, but it was there in the background, like a lone piper playing a mournful lament on a hill somewhere in the distance. Well, maybe I'd get to the bottom of it and maybe I wouldn't, I'm not Superwoman, even if I think I am sometimes. Maybe I was just seeing things that weren't there like my psychic *nain* (grandmother) years ago back home in North Wales. Maybe it was time to stop worrying about intangibles and start to get to grips with this case. That was what I was getting paid for after all, although Cymru knew how much money I would get, if any, at the end of it all.

After she had gone, I took a closer look at the photograph Mrs Culloden Jimmie had given me. A clean-shaven face, short, greying curly hair looked up at me. By now, of course, he could have started to grow a beard; he could have shaved his head, that was still the fashion with a lot of men now.

As I stared at the face in the photograph, staring back at me, I began to wonder what I had let myself in for. Wasn't it enough that I had one missing person to chase after without having to get involved in a search for another one? What was I: some kind of one-woman missing persons bureau? Why hadn't I politely but regretfully declined the case: pressure of work etc., impossibility of one woman having all the resources to investigate properly, if the Welsh Republicans couldn't find Jimmie, what hope would I have etc., etc. But I hadn't declined the case, had I, I'd accepted it and now I was stuck with it, for the foreseeable future at least. Well, I'd just have to give it a go and see what came of things, who knows, I might be able to make some progress.

A thought struck my mind. Might the two cases be related? Daft as it might sound, might Culloden Jimmie have done a runner with the girl in the tangerine dress? Stranger things had happened . . . no, it was too ridiculous to contemplate, there was more chance of my becoming the next President of the United States, than of those two having known each other. I would have to think again, but first I needed something to eat, it had been a long day.

I decided to eat out. Somehow, I didn't fancy any of Stakis's chips today nor even one of his vegetable moussakas. I didn't even fancy sending out to Montalbano's pizza joint for a takeaway. Hang on a minute . . . there was a new restaurant specialising in Scots/Irish Gaelic fusion cuisine called *Bia Blasta* (Delicious Food) that had opened recently in the Calon Lan area of the city. I decided to give it a try. I would check it out; maybe get a takeaway, if I didn't fancy eating in the place itself. Who knows, a night in at home with my feet up watching the TV, good food, good drink, good company, my own company —it might be just what I wanted. Or maybe not. Maybe, I needed someone else's company as well. Maybe I needed to hear a familiar voice.

What I really needed was a good cwtsh. I picked up my mobile phone and dialled a well-known number.

"Hey, Bird Man," I said, "Long time, no see. Fancy a bite to eat tonight? I hear that new Gaelic fusion restaurant is very good. How about I meet you there at nine p.m. sharp?"

"Hi, Astrid," said Daniel Owen, "where have you been all this time? Gelert's been pining for you."

Gelert was an African Grey Parrot in Daniel Owen's care, who had been a great help to me in one of my earlier cases, when I had become involved in a series of murders and a search for two missing golden lovespoons.

"I know, I know," I said, "I've been neglecting him, but I promise to get over to see him as soon as I can. Trouble is, I'm a bit bogged down with some cases at the moment and progress is slow, very slow."

"Perhaps Gelert could help you there," said Daniel Owen, "you know that's one clever parrot . . ."

"You might be right at that," I said, "look, I've got to go, are we on for tonight? We can talk more about Gelert then."

"Sure," said Owen, "sounds good to me, you've

got a deal, see you later . . ."

"I'm looking forward to it," I said and ended the call.

As I drove towards the *Bia Blasta,* I passed a patrol of Welsh Republican Policemen, guns at the ready, intent on flushing out enemies of the state, which got me to thinking: What were those two cops' names again? The ones who stopped me at the roadblock? For the life of me, I couldn't remember what they were called; indeed, I had somehow forgotten their names entirely. I stretched my brains out on the rack and tightened the lever. Think, woman, think, what were they called? Jules and Jim? John and James? Jack and Jake? Could be, but it didn't sound quite right, somehow. Jude, that was it, Jude and Joe.

Then I saw him. A man was walking towards me, holding a drinks can in his left hand. There was something familiar about him, where had I seen him before? Suddenly, without bothering to look, he ditched the drinks can in the middle of the pavement and carried right on walking. My civic pride affronted, it was all I could do to stop myself from getting out of the car, and remonstrating with him, for so carelessly littering the thoroughfares of our fair city. Then it came to me. This uncouth litter lout was none other than my old 'friend', Jude, whose improvised roadblock had stopped me from pursuing The Helmet and finding out who he or she really was. I was surprised he hadn't noticed me or, if not me, my bright yellow *Pwca*. That took some not noticing, I would have thought.

A rage came over me. I had this overwhelming desire to charge out of the car, tackle him literally and metaphorically, rugby tackle him to his knees, and then to bash the truth out of him with the help of Excalibur. That was one way of doing things. The other, and perhaps more profitable way was to shadow him from behind without his noticing and to see where we would eventually end up. There was, of course, a third alternative: I could just simply phone my old friends in the Welsh Republican Police and let them sort things out, but what would I say to them, I had no real evidence against this guy, other than wounded pride, and it was my word against his, as far as taking the Casnewydd Super Dragons was concerned. I couldn't see them rushing to my assistance somehow.

No, I would just have to follow him and see what came up. I piled up my hair, reached into the glove compartment, and fished out my blonde wig, adjusting it on my head using the driver's mirror. I added a pair of dark glasses to complete my disguise, got out of the car and started walking behind him at what I hoped was a reasonable distance, one which would not arouse suspicion on his part.

I needn't have worried, by now my quarry was deep in conversation with somebody on his mobile phone, and probably wouldn't have noticed if Catherine

Zeta Jones had sashayed past him, singing *She'll be coming round the mountain when she comes* and wearing nothing but a few strategically placed red, white and green fig leaves. Good, he was oblivious to me and all my desires and ambitions, but I wasn't near enough to hear what he was saying, apart from the odd, meaningless word.

He continued walking at a swift pace up Sir William ap Thomas Drive, not looking to the left or right of him, still intent on speaking into his phone. By now the houses were beginning to get bigger and be set further back from the street. We were entering that part of town where the *crachach*, that wealthy, bordering on filthy rich, wheeler dealer, intellectual, media savvy, powerhouse section of Casnewydd society liked to lay its head at night. It beat living over a fish and chip shop hands down, I had to admit. One day, Astrid, one day, I found myself musing, all this will be yours . . . I shook myself involuntarily, get a grip, woman, concentrate on the matter in hand, you're supposed to be following someone, don't blow it now . . . I gave the houses another cursory glance, none of them looked like the sort of place Jude would be likely to own, not on his Republican salary, if he really was a Republican, that is. So, where was he heading and why?

I didn't have long to wait before I got the answer to that question. At the far end of Sir William ap Thomas Drive, he halted in front of a Georgian style house cum small mansion, which looked as if it had just stepped out of the pages of a Jane Austen novel. So much so, in fact, that I found myself half expecting the lady writer herself to drive up in her carriage and four at any moment and be escorted down by the waiting footman. But to my disappointment, she failed to show. Oh, well. You can't have everything, although I sometimes think it would be nice to have something every now and again. Then I saw Jude pause at the big wrought iron gates and ring a bell set into one of the two flanking stone pillars.

"Yes," came a metallic sounding voice, presumably coming from the house itself. Jude put his phone in his pocket, leaned into the speaker and said something I couldn't quite catch. It sounded suspiciously like *Hen Ffordd Gymreig O Fyw*, or the Old Welsh Way of Life, to me, but I couldn't be sure at that distance.

Then the gates opened wide enough to admit him. I thought about rushing the gates before they closed, so that I could get in too, but that would really be giving the game away. Instead, I sauntered past, as if I was Mrs I Haven't A Care In The World, watching Jude's back heading towards the house, and making a mental note of the house name: *Yspryd y Nos* or Spirit of the Night. I walked on for a further five minutes, just in case somebody might be watching from the house, trying to give the impression I was only out for a stroll enjoying the sunshine, then I crossed to the other side of the street and doubled back on myself.

The house was still exactly the same as the first time I had seen it, but showed little, if no, sign of life. I could see the speaker set into the pillar supporting the gates and was tempted to say something, anything just so that I could gain admittance. But, of course, there might have been a special password, which I had no way of knowing, and I didn't want to arouse suspicions — not just yet anyway. Somehow I didn't think they would have fixed on 'Open Sesame' as their password for the day. The password could have been the *Hen Ffordd Gymreig O Fyw*, or the Old Welsh Way of Life, I thought I had heard earlier, but I didn't want to risk anything at this stage of the game by calling attention to myself, especially if I had misheard the password.

So I carried on walking, back to the *Pwca* and, not for the first time, I had a lot to think about. I needed to get into that house and have a look around, but how? It was probably wired up with all the latest technological marvels to deter and expose would-be intruders and, even if I did succeed in getting in, Cymru knew how many people were inside there. Were there dogs running free in the grounds? I didn't know. There was so much I didn't know, but this wasn't the time or the place to indulge in philosophical agonising over the state of my knowledge, or rather lack of it.

I took off my blonde wig, and stashed my dark glasses away, then I leaned back in my seat and rested my hands on the steering wheel. Who did I have for back up? There wasn't a great deal of choice. Cagney and Lacey weren't available; more's the pity. The Parrot Man, Daniel Owen? From what I knew of him, he was brave, but inexperienced, and didn't exactly inspire confidence, when faced with a backs to the wall crisis type situation. Edward Henry Davies? Well, he was paying good money to me to work for him, not to be roped in as my assistant when the going got tough. Stakis was a fryer, not a fighter. No, I was on my own. Notice how I'd automatically ruled out calling in the Republicans — I wasn't exactly the flavour of any month with them right now.

Thinking about Stakis gave me an idea, I phoned *The Lying Cod*. "Hey, Stakis," I said. "Can you . . ."

"Hey, Astrid," he said, "how's my favourite private eye, what would you like to eat, I've had some very fresh sea bass delivered, just now as a matter of fact. Do you think we could . . .?"

"Sorry, Stakis," I said, "but I've got other fish to fry, I mean other plans for the evening. Look, don't get alarmed, it's probably nothing, but if I don't ring you again in an hour's time, can you give me one of our *special* phone calls?"

"Astrid Price," said Stakis, "what are you involved in now? You get back over here immediately and let the Welsh Republican Police deal with it, that's what they're paid for . . ."

"Sorry, Stakis," I said, "I have to go, don't forget

to make that call will you, in an hour's time . . ." and I hung up.

Still deep in thought, I drove the few miles to the *Bia Blasta* restaurant, mulling over the day's events. I was so engrossed in my own problems, and their possible or probable solutions, that I hardly noticed the black sedan car coming slowly to a halt behind me. Indeed, I was so wrapped up in my ponderings, and wondering what I would choose as my main course at the Gaelic restaurant, that I scarcely noticed the three men tapping at my car window, two of whom had guns and shaven heads and one of whom I recognised.

"Sorry, Astrid," said Red Iolo, doffing his trademark Panama hat and spotlighting his balding head, "these two are down from the North and haven't a clue where anything is. So I have to drive them around, like, take them everywhere, until they get to know their way about."

"Can't they afford a Sat Nav?" I said, "I hear there are some good ones, going cheap in Tescos Cymru."

"Well," said Iolo, "like I said, I was hired to show these guys around and be their driver, just until they find their feet and get to know the city. Well, you've got to get work where you can now; I didn't know they were coming after you. Nothing personal, you understand . . . I don't want any trouble."

"That's all right, Iolo," I said, "don't worry about

it, I'm sure they're paying you well for your services. I'd just watch your back, if I were you. By the way, who did you say hired you? Come on, you can tell me. And what about your old friend, Culloden Jimmie? Where is he? Do you know?"

"Cut the crap, Iolo and don't talk to the prisoner, we'll do the talking," said one of the hoods, a tall, blond, blue-eyed guy, with a pronounced Teutonic accent and shaven head, who seemed to take a particular pleasure in showing me just how long his gun was, "and you too, Price, we're taking you in."

"Oh, how romantic," I said, "you really do know how to speak to a girl, don't you. What next? Flowers, chocolates, champagne? And where exactly are you taking me? Paris? Rome? Las Vegas? New York, Abertridwr maybe? Pray, do tell."

"That's for us to know and you to find out, Price," said the other hood, smaller than the first and with a pair of fashionably trendy dark glasses, but with the obligatory shaven head. I didn't need to be a great detective to tell that, unlike his colleague, he was probably French. "Now, get going, not everyone's as patient as Georg here."

"Yeah," said the German giant, "do as he says, or it will be the worst for you."

"All right, big boy," I said, "keep your hair on. Oh, I forgot, you haven't got any, have you? Still, never mind, don't look so peeved, I'm coming, I'm coming. After all, what choice do I have?"

"No choice, whatsoever," said Dark Glasses. Get your motor running, Iolo, we have places to go and people to meet."

Red Iolo avoided looking at me but did as he was told and started the car. I found myself sitting in the back with the German giant whilst Dark Glasses took his seat in the front next to Iolo. I took a quick backward glance through the rear window. I recognised my erstwhile dinner date, Daniel Owen, coming swiftly towards the car, and hoped that he would have the presence of mind to take down the make and number and notify the Welsh Republican Police of my fate. He was almost up to the car when the engine sprang into life and we were away.

"Allow me to introduce myself," said the German as the car accelerated onwards, "my name is Alptraum, Georg Alptraum, and this is my friend and colleague, Monsieur Dieu. Red Iolo, you already know . . ."

"Hey, Alptraum," said Monsieur Dieu, "Don't tell that psycho ginger bitch anything, the less she knows, the better."

"What good will it do her?" said Alptraum. "She knows she's just bought a one-way ticket to oblivion. I'm her worst nightmare come true and she'd better believe it."

"Yeah, yeah," I said, "I bet you say that to all the private detectives you meet, I've heard all that stuff

113

before, tell me something new, something I don't know. Like where are the girl in the tangerine dress and Culloden Jimmie and what's going on with the Casnewydd Super Dragons?"

Iolo kept his eyes on the road. The two hoods exchanged glances, but nobody said anything. I took a closer look at the blond, blue-eyed Germanic hunk. Yes, yes, I know it's clichéd and all that, but that's really what he looked like. Anyway, in spite of myself, I felt feelings stirring within me and not the sort of feelings where I wanted to take his face outside and introduce it to the pavement. No, these were feelings bordering on the amorous, what was the matter with me, the man was a cold-blooded killer and no doubt pictured on wanted posters all over Europe. Get a grip on yourself, Astrid; you should be trying to send this guy away for a long trip to a Welsh Republican prison, not measuring him up for a pas de deux under the duvet.

"How come you speak such good English anyway, Alptraum," I said, "I thought you were from that place the Beatles started out. Oh, what was it called now . . . ?"

"Liverpool?" said Alptraum, "and no, I'm not from there. Do I sound as if I come from there? I thought everyone knew where I came from, even you, Price."

"No," I said, "the place in North Germany. You know the one, come on, you must know it. What's it called again? Bremen? Lübeck? Cuxhaven?"

"I think you mean Hamburg, and as far as my

English is concerned, well, I had a German father and an English mother, Price, that answer your question?" he said, shooting me a look that was supposed to freeze me to the marrow, but ended up having quite the opposite effect.

For a while there was silence. Alptraum continued to point his gun at me and look *macho* whilst the other two said nothing. Alptraum and Monsieur Dieu seemed pretty sure of themselves, confident in the knowledge that they had me just where they wanted me. What would Inspector Clouseau have done? Cymru knows. But he wasn't there to ask. Do not go gently, Astrid, I thought, do not go gently, but how? They had the firepower and, if it came to the push, Red Iolo would surely side with them, hoods' honour and all that. I would have to bide my time, wait for an opportunity . . . then I became aware of where we were going. The Jane Austen house, where I had seen Jude go in through the gates, loomed up before us.

This time, Red Iolo rang the bell and mumbled something. The gates swung open and we swept through. Iolo parked the car in front of the house and he and Monsieur Dieu got out, then Alptraum motioned me to do the same. "Go park the car and make yourself scarce," he said to Iolo, "we'll take care of this from now on."

Iolo mouthed a silent apology in my direction, as if he knew what was in store for me, but averted his eyes as Dieu and Alptraum pushed me up the steps and through the front door. I found myself in a large hall with pictures of nineteenth-century English country houses on the walls. From one of the adjoining rooms I heard what sounded like music being played. Alptraum knocked on the door of the room and who should open it, but my old friend from Nant yr Eos Cemetery — Bare Chest.

His belly, although by this time fully clothed, was still hanging over his trousers, and looking even bigger than the first time I had seen it, what's more, it was inviting, no, positively demanding a swift punch to the gut. At that moment, I wanted, more than anything, to do it. I longed to ram my fist into the gargantuan folds of flesh. There was only the lingering fear that, once the fist was in, I would never be able to get it back out again. Patience, Astrid, patience, hang on in there, choose the time, the right time and the moment.

He looked at me and laughed. Over the sound of the music, he said, "They're here, Mrs Big, and they've brought her with them."

"Then show the lady in, Herb, why don't you," said a female voice I didn't recognise, "where are your manners already?"

The woman they called Mrs Big, all five feet three of her, it seemed to my trained private detective eye, must have been around her mid to late forties. Wearing what looked like an expensive top and dark slacks with a

She was strumming the ukulele à la George Formby

white Basque beret, perched on top of her close cropped, expensively styled blonde hair, she wasn't ugly exactly, but neither did she possess the kind of good looks that would turn your head in a crowd. Cymru knows why, she was strumming the ukulele à la George Formby. It sounded as if she were singing, "with my little stick of Denbigh rock . . ." in a high, querulous, strangely hypnotic voice. Or was it Tenby? Denbigh rock? Tenby rock? Who cared? I certainly didn't. I had other things to worry about. Like how had I got myself into this mess and, more importantly, how was I going to get out of it?

"What's with the music?" I said, "and why am I getting a private performance?"

"Quiet, don't interrupt her, she's practising, this is her practice hour," said Herb giving me one of those if looks could kill looks, I would have been dead and buried and somewhere at the bottom of the deepest mine shaft in the Rhondda valley by now.

Suddenly Mrs Big stopped playing and put down her ukulele. "Hand me a ciggy, please," she said to no one in particular, but the assorted minions got the message and rushed to do her bidding. "I need to think. I need some of that old tobacco inside me."

She pulled out what appeared to be a solid gold lighter from the handbag on the table next to her. I couldn't be sure, but I thought I detected the word *'Biggie'* inscribed on its side.

"There, that's better. The first draw is always the

best I find, suck the nicotine right down into the old lungs . . . Now, just what are we going to do with you, Mrs Price?"

"You could always let me go," I said, "I promise not to tell anyone about you and your nefarious activities, Girl Guide's honour. I even promise not to talk about this gang of international hoodlums you've assembled. What were their names again now? You see, I've forgotten them already. Well, I'll be going then, now that's settled. Nice meeting you, Mrs Big. I'll find my own way back to my car and that takeaway meal I was all set to have, before your goons stepped in . . ."

And I started off calmly and slowly, heading for the door, for all the world as if I was just going to put the cat out for the night. For one gloriously silly moment, I thought I was going to make it, but Mrs Big had other ideas.

"Not so fast, Mrs Price," she said, "Georg, Monsieur Dieu, the lady still has unfinished business with us. If she takes a step further, shoot her in the leg, that ought to slow her down a bit."

"All right, all right," I said, "only kidding, you've made your point, you've convinced me, I'll stick around for just a little while longer, but then I really must be going."

"Somehow I have the feeling, Mrs Price, you're not going to be with us for very much longer," said Mrs Big. "What do you think boys?"

"No, Mrs Big, she sure isn't," said the assorted sycophantic hoods, nodding their shaven heads in unison and already looking forward enormously to helping me on my way out of this life and into the next one.

"See what I mean, Mrs Price," said the woman they called Mrs Big, "such obliging young men, they'd do anything for me, anything I asked them to . . ."

Yeah, I thought, cheat, lie, steal and murder amongst other things, but I said, "how lucky you are to have such willing accomplices, they must be a constant joy to you and a comfort in your old age."

Mrs Big looked at me closely but I could see it wasn't the look of love that was in her eyes. She thought for a while and then said, "I think Astrid needs a little haircut, don't you, Herb the Serb?"

"Yeah, that style is so passé nowadays," said Herb, "all it needs is a little clippety-clip and she'll look ten thousand times better. Now where did I put those garden shears? I know I've seen them somewhere."

"Wait," I said, "before you do that —you seem to be two missing —what happened to Cocky? And Rodrigo Rodriguez, I was looking forward to meeting him."

"Cocky Marciano, you mean, such a nice boy, a perfect gentleman, I always think," said Mrs Big. "Oh, he couldn't make it, urgent family business meeting in New York, or was it New Jersey? Who knows, one of the two, anyway. As for Rodrigo Rodriguez, Mrs Price, don't worry about him, he'll be here soon enough."

"A pity," I said, "I was looking forward to meeting those two. Still, three out of five ain't bad, as I always say. Anyway, Mrs Big, while I'm here, and just out of interest of course, what exactly have you done with Culloden Jimmie and that girl with the tangerine dress I've been looking for? And, before I forget, do tell where you've put all those Super Dragons; Casnewydd is missing them so much."

Mrs Big gave me another long look. Somehow I got the impression it wasn't exactly full of the milk of human kindness. Oh, well, you can't please everybody, I suppose. Her three assorted hoods glanced at each other.

"I don't have to tell you anything, snooper," she said. "Go get those shears, Herb, and then I think it will be time to send Mrs Price on a long journey, one she won't be coming back from in a hurry."

Bare Chest's face lit up, he took a step towards the door, I had the feeling he was going to enjoy what would happen next more than I would. Time to do something, Astrid, what would Miss Marple have done? I didn't know, but there was only one thing I intended doing. So I did it. "Stop," I said, "wait, isn't the condemned woman entitled to a hearty breakfast or a last wish or something like that . . ."

"Go on," said Mrs Big, sounding interested in spite of herself, I must have appealed to what was left of her better nature, "What do you propose?"

"Well, forget about the breakfast," I said, "it's too late for that now and I don't really feel hungry anymore anyway. How about I play you a little tune on my recorder? I'm sure you'll like it, Mrs Big, you're a musical woman after all. It's one of my own compositions, *Women of Harlech.*"

"Sure," said Mrs Big, "why not, but only on one condition . . ."

"Of course," I said, thinking one had to humour these criminal masterminds, "and what would that be?"

"That you answer a question I have for you, Mrs Price," she said, "just the one question . . ."

"Go ahead," I said, "what is it?" not having a clue what was coming.

"Right," she said, "what 1960s Liverpool group had a hit with *Some Other Guy,* Mrs Price? Was it (a) The Big Five (b) The Big Yin or (c) The Big Three? No helping her now, Georg."

What! I thought, is this woman serious? How in Cymru's name am I supposed to know that, but I said, "what happens if I get it wrong?"

"Well, in that case, Mrs Price, the boys here shoot you dead on the spot, don't you, boys?"

"Yes, Mrs Big," said Alptraum and Dieu in unison, "we shoot her dead on the spot."

"Well, if that's how you feel," I said, "I'd better give you an answer . . ." eeny-meeny, miney-mo, catch a yeti by his toe, think, Astrid, think, what is it, (a), (b) or (c)? Oh, what the heck, pick any letter and go down fighting anyway. "C," I said, "C, The Big Three, it's The Big Three."

"Congratulations, Mrs Price," said Mrs Big, clapping her hands in glee, "you've passed the test with flying colours. It was indeed The Big Three."

Thank Cymru for that, I thought, but I said, "Does that mean I get to go then? Well, it's been nice meeting you all; I can't tell you how nice."

"Not so fast, Mrs Price," said Mrs Big, "first you perform your party piece for us and after that, Herb and the boys can take care of you. It's called deferred gratification, Mrs Price, or delayed gratification or something like that. On their part, of course, not on yours. Where's this recorder of yours then? I'm getting quite anxious to hear it."

"Oh, it's just in my pocket," I said, "I'll get it out now," and I went to put my hand into my jacket but at the sight of my hand moving, Alptraum and Dieu raised their guns and shouted in unison, "hands up, Price, don't move."

"Sorry," I said, "I was forgetting I was amongst friends. Would one of you like to search me, then?"

"What," said Mrs Big, "haven't you searched her yet? You fools, what do I pay you people for?"

"Sorry, Mrs Big," said Alptraum, "we were going to, but she kept talking and talking and somehow we forgot."

"Well, do it now, you big German lummox," said Mrs Big, "and do it quickly, it'll soon be time for my nightcap."

Monsieur Dieu kept a watchful eye on proceedings whilst Alptraum's practised hands patted me down; he had obviously done this sort of thing before.

"Ooh, Georg," I said, "did that give you a thrill, well, did it, you German muscle man? I didn't think you cared, maybe you'll take me to the *Bia Blasta* later on for some Gaelic fusion, I feel my appetite returning."

"Shut up, Price, what's the matter with you, don't you ever stop talking, yakity-yak-yakity-yak, all the time, don't you ever get fed up with the sound of your own voice?" said the Hamburg hit man.

"Ooh, Georg," I said, "anymore of this and you'll be carving me a love spoon next."

"And what do you keep looking at me like that for?" said the big German. "Can't you look somewhere else?"

"Well," I said, "you know how, when you walk into an art gallery, and you see this beautiful painting that really knocks you out like Gustav Klimt's painting of *The Kiss* in that museum in Vienna? And, no matter how hard you try, you just can't stop looking at it? Well, that's the way I feel about you, honey bunch, you great big burning hunk of German manhood, you."

Alptraum, looking anything but flattered at these remarks, just glared at me and with a shout of triumph pulled out my mobile phone and my recorder. Right on time the room resounded to the strains of Titch Gwilym's version of our beloved Welsh National Anthem.

"That'll be for me," I said, "mind if I answer?"

"Answer the phone, Georg," said Mrs Big, "and step away from Price, you'll be blocking Monsieur Dieu's line of fire."

Alptraum did what he was told on both counts. "Hello," he said. "Hello, what? No, no, you must have the wrong number. No, I told you, what are you talking about, no one here ordered hake and haddock fish cakes with a small chips and a dash of tartar sauce with mushy peas on the side. No, we don't want any bread and butter to go with it or cans of coca cola, reduced sugar, or no reduced sugar. No, there's nobody here by the name of Zephaniah Williams, what kind of a name is that, anyway? I told you, you've got the wrong number." He switched off the phone and handed it to Mrs Big.

"Who was that?" she said.

"God knows," said Georg, "some idiot delivery guy on a bike who couldn't find his delivery address, I could hardly understand what he was saying, sounded like deepest Glaswegian to me."

"Never mind," said Mrs Big, "not to worry, we'll check her phone later on when she's no longer any use for it. In the meantime, Mrs Price, your big moment has arrived. I believe you have a musical offering for us . . . being a musician myself, I'm really looking forward to your impromptu performance."

Not as much as I am, I thought, not half as much as I am, but I said, "Why, of course, I'm sure you'll like it, Mrs B, I may call you that, I hope, everyone else I've played it to and there's been quite a few of them, I can tell you, has been really knocked out by it," and, slowly and very deliberately, I raised the recorder to my lips.

CHAPTER 12

I took a deep breath and looked around, making sure I knew exactly where everyone was. Stakis's phone call meant the cavalry would be on their way eventually, but in the meantime I had to help myself.

"Well, get on with it then," came Mrs Big's voice, seemingly from afar, "I want to hear this great composition."

And get on with it I did. Soundlessly the first dart from Aberbargoed Man's recorder pipe slammed into Georg Alptraum's body. I don't know who was more surprised, Alptraum or Monsieur Dieu as the German's body slid slowly to the floor. Then it was the Frenchman's turn, I ducked and swerved to avoid any shots from him as I aimed my second dart and there he was, flat out cold on the floor. Even the massed ranks of the French rugby union faithful, gathered together to sing the *Marseillaise,* couldn't have woken him up.

I was dimly aware of Mrs Big grabbing her ukulele and running for the door, but I was more concerned with the figure of Herb the Serb advancing towards me, screaming and shouting. "You bloody woman," he said, "you got those two, but you won't get me. Let's see you get out of a Belgrade Bear Hug."

Brave words, Herb, I thought, but I said nothing as I fired my third dart, bringing the Balkan bruiser to an abrupt halt, just feet away from me, his arms flailing, his eyes spitting defiance as they glazed over. As they did, I heard the sound of a car starting up outside, and then moving away at a rapid rate of knots. That would be Mrs Big and Red Iolo leaving us, I presumed.

With no way of pursuing them, I surveyed the scene around me. The three hoods were sleeping like babes in the wood but they wouldn't stay that way forever. I had to work fast. First, I relieved the two goons of their guns, then I searched Herb the Serb — no weapons, an identity card in Cyrillic script, plenty of money – Euros, Glyndwrs, English pounds but no clue that would help me in my search for my two missing persons.

Not much luck either with Dieu or Alptraum, again they weren't short of money, but the stamps on their passports seemed to indicate that they hadn't been in the Welsh Republic for very long. There was little else of any use to me in the three men's wallets — no open sesame that would crack the case, no hand drawn maps with X marks the spot, no detailed Plans A, B and C for me to follow. Ah, well, no one ever said this was going to be easy.

My phone rang again to the strains of Titch Gwilym's version of *Hen Wlad Fy Nhadau*. "Hello," said a well-known voice in my ear, "hake and haddock fish cakes for Zephaniah Williams, hake and haddock fish cakes . . ."

"It's all right, Stakis," I said, "you can cut the pretence, everything's under control at this end. How long have I got before the Republicans get here?"

"About five to ten minutes, I suppose," said Stakis. "After I got in touch with your friend Inspector Sergeant and told him I was worried, they traced your phone signal and sent a few squad cars out to find you. Are you sure you're all right?"

"I'm fine, Stakis," I said, "everything under control here. I'll tell you all about it when I get back. In the meantime I've got some babysitting to attend to . . ." And yes, my three friends were starting to come round, Alptraum was opening his eyes and the other two were showing signs of life. "Quick, Georg," I said, "before the Republicans get here, why did Mrs Big hire you and what do you know about the missing Super Dragons?"

"Don't tell her anything, Alptraum," said Monsieur Dieu.

"Yeah, that's right," said Herb the Serb, "tell that woman nothing. Let her find out for herself. If she *can*. She's supposed to be the Master Detective."

"Boys, boys," I said, pointing their own guns at them, "why so churlish, you're going to have to tell the Republicans anyway, they're going to be here soon, so why not me as well? Come on; tell Astrid, you know it makes sense."

Silence from the Three Amigos. A silence that was broken by the wailing sound of one, maybe two

Welsh Republican Police squad cars on their way to the scene of the crime.

"Your last chance, gentlemen," I said, "tell momma, why don't you, hey, how about I shoot one of you in the leg? We could say you were trying to escape. Would that loosen your tongues a bit? Come on, who'd like to volunteer? Herb? Mrs Big ran out on you; don't forget, without so much as a backward glance . . . I might let you go if you play ball," but I was wasting my time and my breath, the three stooges obviously had their very own version of the Sicilian Mafia *Omerta* going on between them. What would Inspector Montalbano have done? Who knew or even had a clue? I didn't know and, as usual, he wasn't there to tell me himself.

What I did have was our very own Inspector Sergeant and his assistant, PC Pritchard, who now stood before me, together with a whole posse of uniformed Republicans, both male and female.

"That's a nice pair of guns you've got there, Price," said PC Pritchard, "I thought you didn't believe in firearms."

"I don't," I said, "not usually, anyway, but they come in handy, sometimes, especially when you're dealing with a bunch of hardened desperadoes. Oh, I must be forgetting my manners. Inspector, PC Pritchard, let me introduce to you the one and only Georg Alptraum, Monsieur Dieu and Herb the Serb."

"Well, well," said Inspector Sergeant, "and what

might those three be doing here? More to the point, what are *you* doing here, Price, playing nursemaid to them?"

"I could ask the same question of you, Inspector," I said. "How come you've ridden to my rescue so quickly, like Arthur on a foaming white charger, I didn't think anybody knew I was here."

"Oh, we had two calls. The girl on the desk said one was from some Glaswegian calling himself Zephaniah Williams," said PC Pritchard, "said he'd seen some damsel in distress being dragged into this house kicking and screaming by two armed hoodlums. Said he didn't know what the world was coming to, said the woman looked really attractive and it was a real shame what those guys were doing to her . . ."

"The second call, well, you're not going to believe this, Price — she said the second call said a woman had been abducted by three suspicious looking characters not far from the *Bia Blasta* restaurant, gave an excellent description of the make and car number, apparently, but get this, she said the caller sounded just like a parrot was calling, but how she figured that one out, I don't know."

"Well, PC Pritchard," I said, "you don't need me to tell you there are some real jokers around in this city — they'd do anything for a laugh."

"Normally," said Inspector Sergeant, fingering his mournful looking moustache and giving his subordinate an exasperated look, "we wouldn't have bothered to come ourselves, or just sent the local neighbourhood bobby round, but with these new guidelines from above, well, we . . ."

"And I'm really glad you did, Inspector," I said, "you too, PC Pritchard, and, if I ever meet them, I really must shake the hands of those public spirited members of the public who alerted you to my plight. I'm sure you'll find suitable accommodation for our continental brethren here, but be careful with Herb, he bites. By the way, do you think one of your colleagues could give me a lift back up to the *Bia Blasta*? I had to leave my car up there when these jokers abducted me . . ."

"Yeah, sure, why not," said Inspector Sergeant, "would you like us to pander to your pan Celtic obsessions too and pay for your meal as well, while we're at it and throw in a bottle of wine on top, I'm sure they do a decent Highlands and Islands vintage . . ."

"Well, now you mention it," I said, "That would be quite nice."

"You must be joking, Price," said the inspector, "you're not going anywhere for a while, you've got some explaining to do along with your foreign friends. Take her guns, Pritchard, and put her in the next room whilst we question these guys."

"With pleasure, Inspector," said PC Pritchard, "after you, Price, you heard what the inspector said."

Well, there's no pleasing some people is there?

You present them with some of the most wanted criminals in all Europe, dished up on a plate for them, without them having to so much as lift a finger and then they go all sarcastic and officious on you. Then they leave you hanging around for hours on end while they question the said criminals before condescending to give you the third degree when your turn comes round. They threaten you with all sorts of unmentionables and won't even let you in on what the thugs said to them, even though they can see you're dying to know. Eventually, they let you go with the usual warnings not to leave town, keep your nose clean, stay out of trouble, don't do anything the Pope in Rome, the Archbishop of Cymru and the Chief Rabbi wouldn't do, etc, etc.

In the end I had to call Stakis to get me out of there and back to the *Pwca*. Going to the *Bia Blasta* was of course by now out of the question, they'd long since shut, so I had to make do with some of Stakis's leftovers when we got back. Then I had to listen to Stakis telling me how foolish I had been and would I never learn etc, so far I'd been lucky but these villains I kept going up against were going to be the death of me, if I wasn't careful, and so on and so on. God he was just like my mother — nag, nag, nag and then some more. I knew he meant well and had my best interests at heart and had got me out of many a jam before now, but I needed time to think, not to be lectured at, however well disposed towards me the lecturer. Hadn't I had enough lecturing tonight to last me from the Welsh Republican Police?

So, when I finally found myself in bed, alone, in case you're wondering, I asked myself what had I learnt this evening that I hadn't known before. Well . . . not that much really. I now knew that the Welsh Republican Police were in no hurry to let me in on what they'd managed to squeeze out of Georg Alptraum and his pals. I also knew that Mrs Big was still at large, but where exactly . . . She could still be in Casnewydd in a safe house somewhere, holed up with Red Iolo and maybe a few others, plotting revenge on me, or she could have crossed the border into England. She could have decided to return to the north and the Wrexham-Bangor-Llandudno triangle, for all I knew.

So, not much there really. I was also no further forward in the search for my two missing persons. I had the feeling Edward Henry Davies, and Mrs Culloden Jimmie, were not going to be very pleased with me. They were expecting a return for their money and I couldn't blame them. So far all I'd done was go down a lot of blind alleys with no pot of information at the end of them. Nor did I know why Mrs Big and her friends were so interested in the Casnewydd Super Dragons. There must be some reason; these people didn't do anything for nothing.

I was like a juggler —but not a very good one — instead of keeping balls up in the air, I was dropping them all over the place, nothing stuck. Big Bertha would have had a field day, watching me. Think, Astrid, think, you're supposed to be The Great Detective. No, it wouldn't come.

Oh, well, as Fleetwood Mac's Peter Green might have said, all this thinking was getting me nowhere. Tomorrow was going to be another day, *ein neuer Tag* as Georg Alptraum might have said, maybe something would occur to me then, maybe I would uncover the clue of all clues, the answer I was searching for to all these riddles, maybe . . . or maybe not. The duvet felt comfortable and inviting, I turned out the light, turned over and began my journey into the land of dreams.

CHAPTER 13

Sunday dawned bright and early, as every Sunday ought to, and I went downstairs to find Stakis reading that morning's edition of *Sulyn*, our national Sunday newspaper.

"What have the great and the good got to say for themselves today, Stakis," I said, "any news that might interest me? Any unsolved crimes, murders, misdemeanours I might get my teeth into? Any more Casnewydd Super Dragons been abducted?"

"Can't say that there is, really," he said, "but there's an article here which might interest you. It's all about Caratacus ap Cadwaladr."

"Who?" I said. "Spartacus who?"

"No, not Spartacus," said Stakis. "Caratacus, Caratacus ap Cadwaladr. Haven't you heard of him? He's a street poet, well versed in the strict Welsh metres of *cynghanedd*, a good writer of the Welsh verse forms *englynion* and *cywyddau* and he's coming to Casnewydd tonight to read his poetry in the upstairs bar of *The Red Herring*.

"Do you fancy going? We could make an evening of it, with a few drinks and something to eat afterwards. He's a proper poet and a good one too and he's a whizz with all those Welsh language verse forms, you know, the ones you always wanted to master, but found too complicated to bother with, like *cynghanedd, englynion* and *cywyddau*. Did you know that there are eight types of *englynion* alone?"

"Can't say that I did," I said, feeling my eyes beginning to glaze over at an alarming rate, although I like and relate to a lot of poetry, the strict metres aren't exactly my cup of Glengettie tea.

"Well, what do you think?" said Stakis, not letting me off the hook that easily.

"About what?" I said, "about the chances of the Casnewydd Gwent Dragons in the new season's Magner's League. Oh, you mean about *cynghanedd* and all that stuff?"

"Of course," said Stakis, "don't you try and dodge the issue, Astrid Price, you know exactly what I mean. Will you come with me to see one of Cymru's premier poets, Caratacus ap Cadwaladr? Big Zorba can look after the shop for that night. Don't tell me you don't want to come. He has a growing reputation as a brilliant performance poet. People rave about him wherever he goes."

Do they, I thought, the things you find when flicking through the Sunday newspaper, but I said, "I don't know yet, Stakis, I might be busy that night, I'll tell you nearer the time."

"Well," he said, looking intently at his newspaper, "it says here that Caratacus ap Cadwaladr has written some verses, especially in honour of the Casnewydd

Super Dragons, it should be worth going to see him, just to hear those. . ."

I must have still looked doubtful, because he continued, "it also says here that they'll be serving free faggots and peas after the event, when there'll be a chance to ask Caratacus ap Cadwaladr questions about his work. And not just any old faggots and peas – these are going to be provided by Michel Noir, head chef at *La Galloise et Le Chat Andalou,* Casnewydd's newest French eatery. He will be demonstrating his latest take on nouvelle Welsh cuisine. And there's wine from the Tintern vineyards to sample too. How could anyone possibly refuse?"

Good old Stakis, any mention of food and he was right there. Still what would be the harm in making his day and going with him? If things got too heavy on the literary front, I could always feign a headache, or plead a migraine attack, and hi-tail it out of there and back home to bed. Of course, it wouldn't be right to leave my old friend in the lurch, but my absence would mean more faggots and peas for him to consume.

"Right, Stakis," I said, "you're on, we'll both go together, but if it's what I think it might be: full of four letter words and obscene expressions, I might have to leave before the reading's over."

"It's a deal," said Stakis, "and just like Edith Piaf, I know you won't regret it, *Sulyn* is never wrong. We'll take my car and I'll knock on your door when it's time to go, oh, I just can't wait . . ."

"All right, Stakis," I said, "try not to get too excited; it's only a poetry reading for Cymru's sake. In the meantime, I'm going for a run down by the canal and maybe a bite to eat, see ya, don't forget to take my calls . . ."

As I headed towards the canal and my rather infrequent morning jogs the newspaper placards yelled at me: *Missing Madge recording — police baffled — psychics called in,* but I had other things to think about. For a start, I was still no further forward with my enquiries and, for all I knew, both Culloden Jimmie and the girl in the tangerine dress could be halfway to Mexico by now, maybe together, maybe alone. On the other hand, they could both be dead and buried, again either alone or separately, in a place known only to their killers.

And what about Mrs Big? Where was she holed up? Was she still in the country? Or had she fled for pastures new? I had taken some of her hired hands out of the game with the help of my musical blowpipe but, for all I knew, she might have quite a few killers on her books, any one of whom might very well be out to get me. This depressing thought caused me to cast more than a few worried glances over my shoulder so that, at times, I more than once bumped into my fellow morning joggers. Fellow joggers . . Wait a minute; wait just a daffodil picking minute, any one of them could be Mrs

Big's hired assassins or assassin, just itching to put a bullet in my back or in my front for that matter. Now, now, Astrid, relax, calm down, don't be so paranoid, they wouldn't try anything in broad daylight, with all these people around, would they . . .?

Luckily, before I could talk myself any further into a panic of my own making, *The Oval Ball* hove into view and I decided to stop for a caffeine injection of the tea variety and maybe just a little cake on the side, it might do me some good.

The Oval Ball was a canal side café run by Goronwy, who in his younger days had been a more than passable hooker (not that kind of hooker) on the rugby field, hence the name of his establishment. It was unlikely ever to win any Michelin stars, but it was beloved of lorry drivers, canal barge owners, members of the general public, ex-rugby players and connoisseurs of a good Welsh breakfast alike.

I sat myself down in my favourite place next to a window overlooking the canal and cradled the industrial sized mug of steaming, hot tea in both hands.

"Hey, Goronwy," I said, looking around the room which was, as usual, beginning to fill up with people coming in for their fried egg sandwiches and full Welsh breakfasts, "where's that *Bara Brith* and those bakestones I ordered. Jogging on this towpath is hungry work, I'll have you know."

"Coming up, Astrid," said Goronwy from behind

his counter. "I've only got one pair of hands, I'll have *you* know."

In reality, of course, he had about four or five people working behind the counter, cooking and clearing up, all of whom were completely devoted to him. He was just one of those people who enjoyed the occasional moan, that was all.

"Here you are," said Goronwy, placing my order in front of me before thumping me playfully in the shoulder and sitting down opposite me. Don't get me wrong, I liked Goronwy, and, as greasy spoons went, his was right up there with the best, but sometimes he was a little too larger than life. Still well built and strong, even if his best days were behind him, he was one of those men who didn't know his own strength.

"Oi, Astrid," he bellowed into my left ear in a deafening shout, his voice resonating through the room, "you know what, sometimes I feel just like that little Dutch boy, I'm so rushed off my feet."

"What Dutch boy?" I said.

"You know what Dutch boy," said Goronwy, "the one that put his finger in Offa's Dyke, you know, to keep the water out."

"Oh, that Dutch boy," I said, and then before he could continue with his line of attack, I switched direction, "seen any suspicious looking characters around here lately, Goronwy?" I said.

"Apart from yourself, you mean," he said, "I can't

say that I have. What sort of suspicious characters?"

"Well, not the sort of people you'd normally see going up and down your towpath," I said, "hard looking men with curious looking bulges in their pockets, men from the continent who wouldn't think twice about jumping the queue in front of little old ladies — those sort of people."

"Hired hoods from abroad you mean, packing pistols in their pockets and up to no good," he said. "No, I can't say I've noticed anybody like that in *The Oval Ball* recently. Those sort of people tend to gravitate more towards the city, more money to be had there."

"What about the grapevine?" I said, "Have you heard anything through it? More specifically, what's the word on the canal footpath about Culloden Jimmie?"

"All I know about Culloden is that someone told me he's gone missing," said Goronwy, "I have an idea he was in here about a month ago, though, as I recall he had a bowl of *cawl* (Welsh broth) and a hunk of bread to go with it. Was it him? You know I'm not too sure now. Didn't say much, mind, seemed to be in a bit of a hurry to me . . ."

"Was he alone?" I said, "or did he have company? He didn't have a girl in a tangerine dress with him, did he, a girl who just happened to have a dog with her?"

"Now, now, Astrid, you know it's more than my job's worth, what would the Welsh Republican

Government's Department of Health and Safety have to say to me, let alone my customers, no the dog would have been tied up outside."

"So he did have a girl with him," I said. "And she did have a dog with her? Was she wearing a tangerine dress?" almost falling over myself in my eagerness to get at the information.

"Let me think," said Goronwy, taking off his chef's hat, and scratching the few hairs left on his head, "did he have a girl with him, was there a dog? Oh, you're getting me all confused, now, the place was busy, there were people everywhere, taking their dogs for a walk and stopping by for a bite and a cuppa. Was Culloden Jimmie ever there at all? My memory's going, Astrid, I thought I knew the answer to your question, but now I'm not so sure."

"Sorry, Astrid, that I couldn't have been more help, by the way, are you going to that poetry reading tonight, I've heard it's going to be very good . . ."

"Oh, don't you start," I said, "I've heard enough about that from Stakis to last me for the next few days."

"Well, I'll leave you to it then, Astrid," said Goronwy, "those Welsh breakfasts don't cook themselves, you know," and he clapped me on the shoulder, turned and walked back to serve some more customers.

Great. Just great, I thought, *bendigedig*, as I jogged back along the towpath towards *The Lying Cod*.

Goronwy had been no use, no use at all and I was still no further forward in my quest for my two missing persons, the Casnewydd Super Dragons, the whereabouts of Mrs Big, the answer to a woman's prayers, the meaning of life, you name it — I couldn't find it. More than that I had no idea, absolutely no idea, of how to proceed further, call myself a detective, my dead husband Morgan would be spinning in his grave. I would have to reach for my *How to Be a Private Detective* manual as soon as I got home. There was no doubt about it, I had reached a low ebb, my tide was a long way out, right out, further out than the one on the beach at Weston-Super-Mare, I felt depressed, and about as useless as Goronwy's so-called information, and all I had to look forward to was Stakis's poetry evening. That had better be good or the fish fryer would never hear the last of it . . .

CHAPTER 14

Well, when we got there, with Stakis looking like the cat that had just won a year's supply of free cream, the upstairs room of *The Red Herring* was looking fuller than the inside of my old mam's fridge after she'd just come back from shopping. We were lucky enough to grab a table for two right at the back of the room. The bar staff were being kept busy, slaking the customers' insatiable thirsts, but I managed to catch the eye of Aneurin, the friendly barman, and brought back two foaming pints of Casnewydd's Finest Ale.

"*Iechyd da*, Stakis," I said, "your very good health," and scanned the room around me. I didn't see anyone I actively recognised, but as I didn't exactly spend much of my time going to poetry readings, perhaps this wasn't so surprising. The usual regulars of *The Red Herring* had given this occasion a wide berth and were all in the downstairs bar doing what they did most nights — drinking and putting the world and its intractable problems to rights.

Upstairs, where the poetry reading was about to take place, there were a few couples talking animatedly and some couples, not so animated, looking bored, hardly talking at all. There were individuals standing round the sides of the room, clutching their pint as if it were the only thing left between them and a life of misery and then there were the real poetry buffs, their heads craned over slim volumes of, presumably, Caratacus ap Cadwaladr's poetry. And there were the usual groups of men sitting together, but not communicating with each other in any way. They were fondling their mobile phones, gazing raptly at them and intent on who knows what exactly? Emailing their friends, looking up some obscure facts on the Internet or just playing with their darling, their 'magic lantern' for the sake of it, because they had to. They were oblivious to anything else, to the world, any world, other than their own cyber, virtual reality one. They could hardly even remember to take the occasional sip of the beer, so lovingly brought to them by Aneurin and his bar staff. Take a picture of them and you could call it *The Death of Conversation Come to Pass.*

This Caratacus ap Cadwaladr would have to be something special if he was going to drag their attention away from the light of their lives, their dearest love. Losers, the lot of them, when did you last see a bunch of women, sitting around, checking their mobiles, ignoring everything and everyone around them. Well, maybe they did, maybe they were just as bad as the men and maybe I didn't move in the right circles anymore, maybe I just didn't get the whole mobile phone thing. For me, it was a means to an end, namely: getting in touch with someone, speaking to someone when they weren't there in the same place as you. Maybe I was too old fashioned for my own good. I was beginning to get all introspective again when, somewhere in the background, a harp began softly to play, the lights started to dim and a ripple of applause thrilled through the crowd. Here we go, I thought, this is it. It's either going to be a complete disaster and I'll have to play my migraine/headache get-out-of-jail card after about five minutes, or I'll love every last *cynghanedd* pouting, *englyn* spouting, *cwydd* shouting minute of it. I was about to find out. Caratacus ap Cadwaladr — do your worst, this girl is ready.

The tremor of excitement rose to a crescendo — what was this guy – some kind of pop star —drowning out the harp music and then Caratacus ap Cadwaladr was making his way through the crowd, stepping up to the microphone, waving a nonchalant hand in greeting. He was clutching a sheaf of papers in his left hand and a pair of reading glasses in his right. He had dark, wavy hair and a brownish black goatee beard. I estimated he was about twenty-five or twenty-six years old, twenty-eight maybe, at a pinch. He looked straight at the audience and said, or rather shouted, "Good evening, Casnewydd, how's it hanging," and then, in a slightly lower tone, "I've always wanted to say that."

I bet you say that to every town you go to, I thought, but now the poet, after a brief few words on the joys of *cynghanedd* in general and *englynion* and *cywyddau* in particular, was launching into his first poem and I had the uncomfortable feeling that, out of all the audience, he was eyeballing me in particular, reading his poem to no one else, other than me. It might have been my imagination, but that's the way it seemed to me, that was the distinct impression I was getting.

"Stakis," I said, turning to my escort for the night, "this guy's looking right at me, just watch him."

"It's not what you think," said Stakis, "he's not interested in you as such. That's what they all do. *Sulyn* had an article on it: fix a member of the audience in your sights, and your work comes across much better. Caratacus ap Cadwaladr is well known for it."

"I see," I said, but I wasn't entirely convinced, I know when someone's trying to give me the once over, and this guy's interest wasn't purely poetic, I could tell, whatever Stakis and *Sulyn* might say.

Still, I had to admit, although it irritated me to say it, some of his poetry wasn't half bad and quite amusing at times. He had a strong, clear reading voice, with just the faintest trace of a North Wales accent in his speech, and once I got used to his direct, unerring gaze fixed right on me, I grew to enjoy the tirades against the Roman occupation of Cymru in one particular epic, the sniping at our present Welsh way of life in some snappy *englynion* and the short, but unadorned and touching, but not mawkish love poems. His *cwydd* entitled *Inside a North Wales Betting Shop* was frankly hilarious and he did a stunning rendition of what, so Stakis assured me —

he'd read it in *Sulyn*, was his magnum opus: *Mab Darogan*, The Son of Prophecy.

As I said, he read clearly, fluently and forcefully, tracing the lines with his fingers, and then pausing, to stab the air with those self-same fingers, as if to emphasise a point, and all the time, he was looking up from his papers, scanning the faces of the back row of the audience, before inevitably, or so it seemed to me, coming back to fix his gaze on yours truly.

After about twenty, maybe thirty minutes and before I knew it, the performance was drawing to a close and Caratacus was intoning: "thank you, thank you, you've been such a lovely audience I'd like to take you home with me, but I couldn't leave here tonight without sharing with you my thoughts on the phenomenon that is the Casnewydd Super Dragons. Since arriving in your fair city I've had opportunities to survey a few of them and I must say, I'm really impressed. Very colourful, very imaginative, very artistic they are, all of them. So thanks to the city fathers for finally getting something right and here it is, my final poem for the night: *Ode to a Super Dragon*."

This is it, I thought, pay attention, Astrid, maybe this guy knows something about the missing dragons, that you don't know, perhaps he'll put in a few clues in his poem for you. I listened intently and carefully, as carefully as someone who has just been told by a gun-toting thug, that he is going to say something and say it only once, and he'd like to have it repeated back to him word for word, if you don't mind. So, I listened, but I can't say it made all that much sense to me, it certainly didn't bring me any further forward in my eyes, as far as the missing dragons were concerned, unless, of course, he was using code that only certain members of the audience would understand . . .

"What was that last one all about?" I said to Stakis, grabbing his arm in a proprietorial kind of way, as the clapping showed no signs of dying down.

"I've no idea," he said, "I'll have to see what *Sulyn* says next week, but wasn't it great? Those guys with the mobile phones were even shouting out 'encore' —you don't hear that very often at a poetry reading."

No, I'm sure you don't, I thought, not from my limited experience of such events. Oh well, if I understood it or not, that last poem had gone down a storm with everybody else. Even Aneurin and his bar staff were stomping their feet and cheering. In spite of myself, I found myself clapping with the rest of them whilst Stakis was a-hooting and a-hollering in his own unique way. He too had enjoyed the night so far. In fact he was all for staying behind after the reading to buy one of the books, Caratacus ap Cadwaladr was selling, and have it signed by the author.

Naturally, I feigned indifference, when, secretly, one part of me was quite anxious to make the poet's acquaintance. So I pretended to protest, after all, I was supposed to be Stakis's date for the night. So, I pleaded things to do, cases to solve, beds to sleep in, etc. but Stakis insisted and, as I made a great show of telling him, I really hadn't the heart to spoil his fun; it was his evening after all. So we joined the queue of about ten to twelve people waiting to speak to the great man and have their newly purchased books autographed, and, eventually, there we were — standing right in front of him. He looked even more good looking from close up, than he did before, standing in front of the microphone, reading poems to me alone, in my back row seat.

Caratacus ap Cadwaladr's slim volume of poetry was entitled *I Was a Fugitive from the Celtic Twilight*. I picked up one of the books and said, "this one's on me Stakis," and when my old friend demurred, I insisted, saying, "no, please, Stakis, it's my treat and my pleasure, if you don't let me do this for you, I'll never speak to you again."

Caratacus ap Cadwaladr was watching our little pantomime with a half-smile playing around his lips. "You're obviously a woman of taste and discernment, Miss . . ." he said and lifted his pen ready to sign, but before he could do so, I jumped right in. "Make it out to Stakis Theodorakis, please," I said.

Caratacus ap Cadwaladr smiled again, this time a full smile, which filled his entire face. "I'm afraid, you'll have to spell that for me, Miss, my Greek is a little rusty, I'm afraid."

I obliged, saying, "Can you add the date and the place as well, please. I want this to be a great souvenir of a wonderful night out."

Ap Cadwaladr signed with a flamboyant flourish and then I said, "So tell me, Mr ap Cadwaladr, what exactly were the thought processes behind that last poem tonight, the one about the Super Dragons, and what did it all mean exactly?"

"Oh, please," he said, "I like everyone to call me Caratacus, especially exceedingly pretty women such as yourself, Miss . . .? Maybe we could have a drink when I'm finished here and I could explain the poem to you in greater detail? Who knows, perhaps you could be my muse?"

A fast mover and a flatterer, too, I thought, Stakis could learn some things from him, and corny, very corny as well, but even so, a tiny little part of me was secretly pleased all the same, so I said, "Astrid, Astrid Price, Caratacus, and it's Mrs, not Miss."

"I'm sorry," said Caratacus ap Cadwaladr, "you didn't seem to be wearing a ring of any kind. I just assumed . . . well, you know . . . is this Mr Price?" and he nodded his head towards Stakis who was standing next to me.

"No, it's not," said Stakis, "not that it's any business of yours. And what gave you the idea we wanted to drink with you anyway?"

Caratacus ap Cadwaladr raised both his hands in

a peace-making gesture, "hey, man, no worries," he said, "I'm here to sign books and read my poetry, not start a war with anyone, peace and love and all that sort of commotion . . ."

"Yeah, Stakis," I said, "Calm down, Mr ap Cadwaladr was only trying to be friendly."

"A bit too friendly, if you ask me," said Stakis, "we've come here to get a book signed, not to go out drinking with people we've never met before."

Just then, before things could escalate any further, a woman pushed in front of us without so much as a gentleman's excuse me. Like a lot of people I see, she looked vaguely familiar to me, but I couldn't quite recall where and when I'd seen her before. Her hair was dyed a strange mixture of a kind of garish frijid pink and shocking blue colour. She was wearing an owl pendant over her owl motif tee-shirt, long, dangling owl earrings and not much else. Or so it seemed, the eye being instantly drawn to the owl motifs, and not whatever it was she happened to be wearing. I looked at her again.

She didn't look old, she didn't look old at all, in fact, she looked to be more in her mid-twenties, nor did that garish hair betray any sign of a perm. No, it couldn't be . . . but that owl fixation . . . Coincidence? Could be, of course, but on the other hand, how often did you see someone wearing distinctive owl based jewellery in this fair city of ours. I decided to investigate. That's what I'm supposed to do after all. I tried the subtle approach. I'm good at that.

"Hey, you," I said, "that's right, you, queue jumper, you with all the owls. The one who's just pushed in. Are you really a closet Sheffield Wednesday supporter, or do you just like birds that only come out at night?" (All right, I know some owls fly by day, but what the heck, I was thinking on the hoof.)

"What?" she said, giving me one of those if looks could kill, I would be lying abandoned and no longer breathing, battered and severely bruised at the bottom of a disused slate quarry, somewhere in the wilds of North Wales by now looks, "what in Cymru's name are you talking about? I don't think I know you. Do I know you?"

Then, without waiting for an answer from me, as if I no longer existed, she turned to Caratacus ap Cadwaladr. "Caratacus," she said, "Crad, it's been so long. Too long. Have you missed me?"

"Sharona, my Sharona," said the poet, "Sharona Haf, you don't know how much I've missed you. Where have you been these last few months? My darling little thespian, how is the acting profession going? Well, I hope?"

"Not so good, Crad," she said, "I had to get a job as part of a knife throwing act in the circus for a while to tide me over."

"And did you flinch?" He said, teasingly, "what with all those knives thudding in next to you?"

"You know me, Caratacus ap Cadwaladr," she said, "I never flinch. *I was the one* throwing the knives. The others were doing the flinching." And she laughed but it wasn't a particularly pleasant sound.

Then the two of them fell upon each other like the Greeks upon the Trojans and were embracing and doing that hands all over each other stuff, that makes anyone else standing not a million miles away, want to reach for the sick bucket.

Stakis and I were quite forgotten in the love-in, and somehow I didn't think I was going to get that drink and moment alone with ap Cadwaladr now. It was then I noticed the faint, but unmistakable, lingering smell of stale cigarette smoke coming from the direction of Sharona Haf. It didn't need a Jim Rockford to tell me she could chain smoke for Cymru. She was obviously a smoker and a heavy one at that. The circumstantial evidence was beginning to pile up, but I still had no real, positive, categorical, undeniable proof.

This time I decided to employ the direct approach. "Hey," I said, "queue jumper, Sharona, or whatever your name is, how's Mrs Big these days? It must have been quite a shock for you when your old sparring partner, Herb the Serb, was taken in by the Republicans? How is he by the way? Have you been to see him? And what about those two fake police pals of yours? What were their names again, Jude and Dude? Joe and Mo? Seen them lately? Or any more Super

They fell upon each other

Dragons?"

Reluctantly, Sharona Haf disentangled herself from her poet friend's clutches. "What," she said, giving me one of those if looks could kill, I would have been halfway to the bottom of the Welsh Sea or the Cardiff Channel by now. "What is this — Twenty Questions? What is the matter with you, woman? Caratacus, what in Cymru's name is she talking about. Is she demented or something. Who is this woman? Who is she anyway?"

"I don't know," said Caratacus ap Cadwaladr. "She calls herself Price, Mrs Astrid Price, she just turned up for the performance and wanted me to autograph one of my books for her."

"Price, Price, Astrid Price . . . wait just a leek-throwing minute," said Sharona, "isn't she some kind of washed-up Welsh Baseball star? You know, I never could understand the attraction of that game, I mean it's only played in Liverpool and Newport and Cardiff."

"Hey," said Stakis, "less of the slave names, if you please, the President says we're to call them Casnewydd and Caerdydd from now on, she said so in her latest broadcast."

"The President, the President," said Sharona, "ooh, the President said this, the President said that. Ooh, you're getting me all scared now. Let's all bow down to the President in case something dreadful happens. I'll bet you're frightened to death of breaking the curfew laws, aren't you?"

"No, I'm not," said Stakis, "I laugh in the face of the curfew laws, ask anybody who knows me."

"Huh," said Sharona Haf. "So you say. Who are you anyway, butting in to things, which don't concern you? Who is this guy, Caratacus?"

"He seems to be some sort of friend of Mrs Price's," said ap Cadwaladr, "a bit argumentative, if you ask me. He's tried to pick a fight with me already."

"Hey," said Stakis, "who are you calling argumentative, and just for the record, Miss-whatever-your-name is, Astrid wasn't a baseball player, but one of the finest female outside halves ever to pull on a number 10 shirt for Wales."

"Come on, Stakis," I said, "let's go, don't make a fuss, you can buy me that drink you've been threatening to get me for ages, I'm sure Miss Haf and Mr ap Cadwaladr have got better things to do than bandy words with the likes of us."

"But you started it," said Stakis as I propelled him towards the door, "You accused that owl girl of something. What exactly did you accuse her of?"

"Not now, Stakis," I whispered in his ear, "later, this is not the time or place. Let's get back in the car. Smile at the people as we go out now, there's a good boy."

"Right, Stakis," I said as soon as we were safely ensconced in his car, "the minute those two come out, I want you to do me a favour."

"What sort of favour? he said, "nothing illegal, I hope."

"No, no," I said, "nothing like that, if they split up, I just want you to follow Caratacus ap Cadwaladr and tell me where he goes, I'll take the girl. If they leave together on foot, I'll follow them myself, if they drive or take a taxi, we'll both follow them in your car. Got it?"

"What?" said Stakis, "how am I supposed to follow anybody? I'm a fish fryer, not a private detective. That's your job."

"It's easy," I said. "Just look in a few shop windows every now and then and pretend to be minding your own business, if he stops, you stop. If he rumbles you and says anything, just bluff it out, I'm sure you'll think of something, tell him you're on the lookout for another fish and chip shop premises. Business is booming, just lie, Stakis, for Cymru's sake. I want to know where he goes and whom he talks to, if he talks to anybody, that is. Try and be discreet, if possible."

"But what about curfew?" said Stakis, "we have to be back indoors before curfew strikes, the penalties are really severe. I might lose my licence."

"Screw your courage to the sticking place and stop worrying so much, Stakis," I said. "We've got a couple of hours left before curfew starts and, anyway, you may not have to follow him, they may leave together. If you're that worried about curfew, stop following him at the point you think you need to get back home in time."

"Okay, you know best, I suppose," said Stakis and, then, before I could stop him, he had turned on the radio; well it was his car after all.

"After the recent clashes featuring the Welsh Republican Navy in the waters of the Cardiff Channel and the Welsh Sea," said the announcer, *"The Foreign Minister, Margaret Hanmer, spent the day in frank but friendly discussions with her counterparts in London and Dublin. She described the mood as. . ."*

But I never did get to discover what she described the mood as, because just then Caratacus ap Cadwaladr and Sharona Haf emerged from the entrance of *The Red Herring* beaming at each other and holding hands. The next thing I knew they were billing and cooing at each other like two collared doves sitting on a branch of a tree in someone's garden. It was enough to make even the most hardened operative want to reach for the sick bag. As for Stakis . . . well, he didn't know where to look.

"Quick," I said to him, "now's our chance, which way is the ginger tom going to jump?"

"How should I know . . ." said Stakis, but my question was answered as the two said goodbye and ap Cadwaladr turned left down Ivor Novello Street and, after a few brief seconds of hesitation, Sharona went in the opposite direction up Shirley Bassey Street,

"Right," I said, "we're on, be brave Stakis and remember what I told you." The last I saw of him he was trailing somewhat reluctantly in Caratacus ap Cadwaladr's wake, and trying desperately not to look conspicuous, but at least he was following instructions.

Now it was my turn. I wondered where Sharona Haf would lead me, perhaps to Mrs Big's hideout, perhaps to the missing Super Dragons. I might even hit the jackpot and chance upon Culloden Jimmie and the girl in the tangerine dress.

So far, so good, she didn't appear to be aware of me following her and kept up a steady pace. No need to stop and pretend to look in shop windows here, she appeared to be so wrapped up in her own thoughts.

As she continued down Dorothy Squires Terrace we passed a crowd of women standing in front of a shop window, gazing at a rather opulent looking wedding dress, but she showed no reaction, head up, carrying straight on, not looking to the right or the left.

As she turned into Malcolm Vaughan Street, I moved to follow her when, suddenly, I became dimly aware of a nondescript looking car pulling up behind me. Strange, I hadn't heard anything. It must be one of those new, silent cars the Welsh Republican Government was investing so much money in to try and combat the soaring fuel costs we were all suffering from. Instinctively, I turned my head, but before I could do anything, two men about the same height, dressed in black berets, dark glasses and camouflage gear, had gripped my arms and pressed what looked very much like guns into my face.

"Get in the car," said the one gripping my left arm.

Not again, I thought, but I said, "Look, can't you see I'm in the middle of an . . ."

"As if I give a flying ruck . . . The car, now. If you know what's good for you," said the one gripping my right arm.

I got in the car. I learnt a long time ago it was best not to argue with gun-toting *hombres*, especially two such mean-looking ones as these. "What nice shooters," I said, "have you had them long?" No answer. "Whereto then, boys?" I said, "somewhere by the sea, I hope, I fancy the Gower Peninsula myself at this time of year. No, well, I have heard it said that Strata Florida is very nice in August."

Still no answer. I gave up. The car did a U-turn and sped away with four silent men and one very thoughtful woman inside it.

CHAPTER 15

As we drove along, thoughts spun in my brain like a souped-up Victorian child's spinning top. Whose clutches was I in now? Had Mrs Big surfaced yet again to wreak a terrible revenge on me? The four guys in the car didn't look like, or act like, any of her henchmen, but who could be sure. Maybe the Edwards had returned to punish me for past misdeeds, or some other third party, as yet unknown, was out to get me. The truth was, I had no idea. All I really knew was that I was in a car with four men with guns, when I didn't have one. The odds didn't look right, nor did they look good.

As I continued to beat up my brain, looking for answers, I weighed up my chances of escaping. They, too, did not look good. I was wedged between two of the men in the back seat, their guns pushed against my sides. The driver and his companion sat stony-faced, their eyes on the road, not that I could see their eyes because of the dark glasses all four wore. It was hard to see a way of getting out of the position in which I now found myself. This time there would be no saving, last minute phone call from Stakis. Poor Stakis, in all the 'excitement' I'd forgotten all about him. I dreaded to think what had happened to him. Where was he now, lying alone and abandoned at the bottom of some dark alley after Caratacus ap Cadwaladr had spotted he was being followed, and decided to beat him up just for the hell of it. Maybe Mrs Big's thugs were interrogating him at this very minute. Poor Stakis wouldn't like that; I had really dropped him in it this time.

That had been one of my less brilliant ideas. What was I thinking, sending my old friend and landlord out on a potentially dangerous mission, when he palpably wasn't prepared for it? But I had myself to worry about. Maybe this was the end of the line for me, never mind Stakis, maybe the final whistle was about to blow time on my career and I was about to become a missing person statistic myself, there would be no more cases for me to stumble through haltingly, searching desperately for clues, any clue, this car would return from wherever we were bound, but with only four men inside it, the sole woman passenger would have met her end (mourned by whom? by anybody?) on some isolated hill top, miles from anywhere, which no one ever visited, even in the summertime . . . maybe I would meet Morgan again, maybe not, who knew, nobody knew, this time I was going down with nobody to help me . . .

Don't go down that road, Astrid, snap out of it; pull yourself together, while there's life there's . . . and all that baloney-maloney. At least I could try to take one or two of them with me, when the time came, give them something to remember me by, make them work to earn Mrs Big's money. And yes, give them one for Stakis while

I was at it.

I was so deep in my own musings that I almost forgot to look where we were going. For some reason they hadn't blindfolded me, but I had been too busy wondering about what was in store for me to take much notice of my surroundings.

"But this is . . ." I said.

"Yes, Mrs Price," said the man next to the driver, "this is the way to the Welsh Republican Police Headquarters, Casnewydd, pull up here, Sergeant."

As the car came to a halt, the two guys next to me motioned me out of the vehicle and up the steps leading into the building. As one of them pushed open the doors, I could see I was expected.

"Mrs Price, how nice to see you again, how kind of you to call by," said PC Pritchard, "follow me if you would . . ."

"Have I got any choice?" I said.

"None whatsoever," said Pritchard, "we just want you to help us with our enquiries, that's all. Thank you gentlemen for bringing Mrs Price in."

My erstwhile companions nodded curtly, pushed me forward and took their leave.

"What's all this about, Constable Pritchard, who were those men and why have they brought me here?"

"Technically speaking, Mrs Price, that's none of your business, but as I'm feeling in a particularly good mood tonight, I'm going to tell you, those men are members of the Llywelyn the Last Brigade, part of the Army of the Welsh Republic's Special Forces and they brought you here tonight to take part in an identity parade."

"But what have I got do with an identity parade?" I said, "and why can't you send any of your own men to fetch me? Since when has the army been doing your dirty work for you?"

"Short-staffed, I'm afraid, Price," said Pritchard, "besides we work very closely together with the armed forces, especially now, under the current emergency laws."

"Talking about short-staffed," I said, "Are you sure you can manage by yourself? And where's Inspector Sergeant tonight, then? Playing ludo with his cronies in the back bar of *The Welsh Bankrupt* again, I suppose?"

"If you must know, Mrs Astrid Price," said Pritchard, "Inspector Sergeant has gone to the theatre tonight with his wife . . ."

"I thought the pantomime didn't start until Christmas," I said.

"Ha, ha, very funny, Price, it must be the way you tell them, he's gone to that experimental fringe theatre on the banks of the Brown River, what's it called. . . that's it, he's gone to the Square House. They're showing a play by some unknown author, what's his name again, Jedward something, or was it Tedward, could have been Nedward . . ."

"Edward H Davies," I said.

"Yes, that's it," said Pritchard, "Edward H Davies, but how did you know?"

"You're forgetting I'm what they call a master detective," I said, "and I keep up with the arts pages of *Y Byd* (The World). What's the play called?"

"Oh, it's on the tip of my tongue," said Pritchard, "what's it called now . . . I know, that's it . . . some sort of long winded title, something like *What If William Had Got The Arrow In The Eye?*"

That sounded like the Edward H Davies I knew and loved, I thought, but I said, "is it any good?"

"How should I know," said Pritchard, giving his best imitation of a Frenchman shrugging his shoulders, "I haven't seen it, it all sounds a bit avant-garde to me, if you want my opinion. If you're that interested, you'll have to ask the inspector when you see him next. Anyway, that's enough of the pleasantries, follow me, Price, we have work to do."

Well, look on the bright side, Astrid; at least it's not Mrs Big and her minions you've got to worry about. Just humour the little bastard Pritchard and we'd soon be out of here.

We went down two flights of steps to a door marked Interview Room Rhys Gethin Suite, where another guy was waiting for us, but instead of a police uniform, this one, a tall, well built, dark haired guy, was wearing a black beret, dark glasses and camouflage gear, just like the gang of four who had abducted me on the street and brought me here.

"Allow me to introduce Lieutenant Pryderi," said Pritchard, "not his real name of course," as dark glasses guy bowed stiffly. He seemed vaguely familiar to me, but I couldn't quite place him, he hadn't been with the others in the car just now, but there was something about him I thought I'd seen before . . .

"Of course," I said, "but where are all the other potential suspects? And why is Lieutenant Pryderi in here with us, anyway? Shouldn't he be in the other room behind that special glass you guys have? What sort of identity parade is this?"

"A one-woman identity parade of course," said Pritchard, "and before you start, it may be technically illegal, but under the current powers granted to us by the President to combat the present state of emergency, we can do practically what we like. The police and the armed forces are working together, Price, to keep the Welsh Republic safe so that people like you can sleep soundly in their beds at night. Now put on this balaclava, jump through the air and shout 'Boudicca' at the top of your voice."

"What!" I said, "are you serious? I wouldn't be seen dead wearing this balaclava, it's not fashionable, it's not trendy, it's cheap and nasty, Cymru knows who wore it last or where it's been. I demand a phone call and my lawyer. You've heard of him no doubt – John

Frost, the Iceman we call him, he'll soon get me out of here."

"Demand all you like," said Pritchard, "it'll do you no good. And you can forget John Frost. He's not going to help you. Didn't you hear what I just said? Under the powers granted to me by the President . . ."

"Yeah, yeah," I said, "don't tell me, I'm not allowed my legal rights and it's all the fault of the President. Well, she's not getting my vote, that's for sure. What are we living in — some kind of police state? I've a good mind to kick this unclean balaclava of yours straight into touch, walk straight out of here and dare you to do your worst. What are you going to do? Force me to listen to recordings of male voice choirs from the valleys for hours on end?"

"Don't tempt me, Price," said PC Pritchard. "Don't give me any ideas you might regret . . ."

"Here, take mine," said Lieutenant Pryderi, in what seemed to be an accent-free voice, as far as I could tell, handing me what seemed to be a sparkling, brand new, fashionable looking balaclava. "Freshly washed this morning and never been worn, your old mam would be proud to wear it."

"Why thank you, Lieutenant Pryderi," I said, "thank you, kind sir, you see, PC Pritchard, why can't you have manners like that?"

"Oh, just get on with it Price," said PC Pritchard, "we haven't got time for your nonsense, you're not the only case in the file book, you know."

"All right," I said, "but I warn you to expect a visit from Lawyer Frost."

"Oh, stop it, please," said Pritchard, "you've got me trembling like a naked man with no fig leaf in a force ten gale. I'm shivering in my size eleven boots. Now watch carefully, Lieutenant Pryderi, and tell me if she's the one."

Well, I don't mind telling you I felt a right *twp* (idiot) standing there in front of these two strangers, well, Pritchard wasn't a stranger, but he wasn't exactly a bosom pal either, but Lieutenant Pryderi certainly was, even if I had met him briefly that one night when he had attempted to shoot at me. I found myself beginning to take a closer interest in this soldier, perhaps behind all those dark glasses, black beret and camouflage gear, there was a real person trying to get out. I looked him up and down a bit. Now that I could get a closer look at him, I could see that he was about my height. How old was he, twenty-eight, twenty-nine? Of course, the last time I saw him I had been too busy trying to make my escape to notice any of these minor details. Well, in other circumstances, he might have been worth a punt . . .

"Price," said PC Pritchard, "are you going to put on that balaclava and jump, or do I have to put you in a cell for the night, maybe a few nights if our new special powers run to it."

"Well, PC Pritchard," I said, "how high would you like me to jump exactly? What would get your motor running?"

"You're the rugby player," said Pritchard, "just imagine you're back in training. Why not jump as high as you did on the night you broke the curfew. You know, when you attacked Lieutenant Pryderi here."

What a bastard, eh. I don't know why, but I had a hunch he didn't like me very much. And after all those Christmas cards I'd sent him. Oh well, in for a penny, in for a Welsh pound, I suppose, I didn't much fancy going through with this ridiculous charade, but I fancied a night or two in the cells even less. I put on Lieutenant Pryderi's balaclava, I motioned the two men to stand back, I took a few steps, I jumped, letting loose a blood curdling cry of 'Boudicca,' and making no attempt to hold anything back, I figured that Pritchard would know if I was trying to con him, I also figured that, if the worst came to the worst, Lawyer Frost would be able to get me out of there, sooner or later. Surely, he would be able to find a way round these ridiculous new police powers the President had so unthinkingly granted.

Pritchard looked expectantly at Lieutenant Pryderi. "Well?" he said.

"Well, what?" said Pryderi.

"What do you mean 'well, what?'" said Pritchard, "is she or is she not the person who jumped into you and knocked you down on the night you were on sentry duty?"

"Sorry to disappoint you, but one wild banshee woman screaming 'Boudicca' at the top of her voice sounds very much the same as another to my untrained ear," said Lieutenant Pryderi, "besides it was dark, very dark and it all happened so fast . . ."

"But did this person jump as high as Price?" said Pritchard, reluctant to let his quarry go, now that his moment of triumph was so near.

"I told you," said Pryderi, "it was dark, it happened so quickly, I was trying to get a shot off, then the next thing I knew I was eating dirt. Besides, she's right, why didn't you hold a proper identity parade like any cop worth his *Halen Môn* (salt from Anglesey) would have done. Just what sort of a cop are you, PC Pritchard? And before you start on me with your emergency powers spiel, just remember I'm a member of the Llywelyn the Last Brigade and that still counts for something in this Republic of ours. I don't know why I let you talk me into taking part in this farce in the first place. Let this woman go, or I swear I'll find this Lawyer Frost of hers myself and bring him round here."

Well said, Lieutenant Pryderi, or whatever your real name is, that's telling him I thought, but I said, "You heard the soldier, Officer, either charge me or release me and let me go."

Pritchard glared at the two of us for what seemed to be a long minute, he was obviously having trouble trying to formulate his words. He took a few deep breaths. "All right, Price," he finally managed to say, "you win for now, but you haven't heard the last of this . . ."

"I'm sure I haven't, Officer," I said, "I know you'll think of some other way to get to see me again. Just like you, I do *so* enjoy our meetings. Do give my regards to Inspector Sergeant. I have missed seeing him this evening. In the meantime, can I have the taxi fare back to *The Lying Cod*? And shall I send Lawyer Frost round to see you in the morning for a cosy little chat . . . ?"

"Get your own taxi, Price," said PC Pritchard, "and you can stick your Lawyer Frost where the sun don't shine and I don't mean Llanelli. Now get out of my sight the pair of you, I've got work to do."

"Charming," I said to Lieutenant Pryderi as we headed for the exit.

"Wasn't he just?" said Pryderi, "fairly oozed it . . . look, I'm sorry about all that back there. It wasn't my idea, believe me, I just got kind of carried away with the whole thing. He was very persuasive, he and that senior officer of his, what's his name again – Sergeant, that's it, Inspector Sergeant."

"Don't worry about it," I said, "it'll be some time before I can bring myself to look at another balaclava again, I can tell you. Still there's no harm done, Pritchard's an idiot, that's all. Don't take any notice of him, I don't."

By now we had reached the car park. I was just about to say my goodbyes and make my own way back home when Pryderi made me an offer I could have refused, but somehow didn't think I would.

"All the same," said Pryderi, "I feel I owe you something, a drink at least, maybe a nightcap."

Lieutenant Pryderi, I thought, what took you so long, but I said, "I thought you elite Special Forces guys were confined to barracks and wrapped up warm in bed with a cup of Fair Trade cocoa every night at ten o'clock. I thought you had no time to spend buying drinks for strange women. Besides, I never go out with strange men whose names I don't know."

"But you do know . . ." he said.

"Yeah, yeah," I said, "and if your name's Pryderi, I'm the wife of the governor of the Bank of Cymru. Come on, what's your real name, you can tell me, everybody tells me everything."

"I'd like to, Mrs Price, I really would," he said, "but you know, state secrets and all that, let's just leave it at Pryderi for the time being, shall we. Besides, you've got some secrets of your own, if I'm not very much mistaken."

"I don't know what you're talking about, I'm sure," I said, "you must be confusing me with some other woman, Lieutenant Pryderi. You haven't met my sister, Delyth, have you? Now she's the one for secrets, why I could tell you stories about her that would . . ."

"It *was* you, wasn't it" he said, "I know it was you."

"Was me what?" I said, "what are you on about now, you don't half jump around in your conversations, Pryderi, I'll give you that."

"It *was* you that jumped at me that night of the curfew," he said, "it *was* you that shouted 'Boudicca' and you I nearly shot at, would have shot at, if you hadn't been too quick for me. I knew it was you all the time, even before all that palaver with the balaclava, but I didn't want to give Pritchard the satisfaction of sending you down for breaking the curfew."

"You've lost me again, Pryderi," I said, "you've spent too many nights alone out by yourself watching for curfew breakers, soldier. Whoever attacked you that night it wasn't me, I've always had the utmost respect for our armed forces. Ask my sister Delyth, ask anyone who knows me."

"But I don't want to ask anyone else," he said, "I want to ask you. Now, are you coming for that drink or not? Let's finish this conversation somewhere more atmospheric than the Welsh Republican Police car park."

As usual, I was in three minds what to do. Sometimes I think my middle name is *Indecision* and not the one my old mam and dad gave me. Would Lieutenant Pryderi be the yeast to my dough? I didn't know. Cymru alone knew. The time to hesitate was through. I jumped in with both feet, but refrained from shouting 'Boudicca' as I did so. "All right," I said, "you've persuaded me, a late night coffee at my favourite Austrian coffee house, and maybe just an ever so tiny slice of *Strudel* to go with it, sounds just the thing to me. Come on, it's only round the corner."

As we walked through the doors of *Die Sachertorte,* the first thing we heard was not the usual Strauss waltzes, I was used to in the daytime, but an Anton Karas look-a-like playing the Harry Lime theme from the film *The Third Man* on his zither. Obviously, the proprietors adopted a different musical policy for the evening clientele.

"Where shall we sit?" said Pryderi.

"Aw, anywhere will do," I said, "just find us a place where we can be nice and quiet and have a conversation without being disturbed. There are a few things I want to ask you."

"And there are a few things I want to ask you too," said Pryderi. "I'd like to know just exactly what you were doing on the night we first met."

"Now, don't start that again," I said, "anyway, I get to ask the questions first because I'm the private detective, remember?"

But I never got to ask any questions of Lieutenant Pryderi (not at that time anyway), nor did I get to sit down and enjoy a dose of Viennese coffee house coffee, because just then the dulcet tones of Tich Gwilym and his interpretation of our national anthem rang out on my mobile phone.

Oh, no, Stakis. I was ashamed to say I'd clean forgotten about him.

"Hello, Astrid," he said, "Why haven't you called? I've been worried sick. Look, I'm in that new pub, *The Leek and Daffodil*, you know, that one on Shaking Stevens Square."

"That place with the new tapas bar?" I said, "That's only just opened? What are you doing in there, you don't even like Spanish food."

"Yes," he said, "and Astrid . . . I need help, lots of it . . . they're coming, they've . . . oh, no, help me, please."

The phone went dead as if Stakis or, more worryingly, someone else, had switched it off.

CHAPTER 16

"Trouble?" said Pryderi; his face showing more than the usual concern a stranger would have felt.

"I'm afraid so," I said, "I'm sorry, I have to go, a dear friend is in difficulties and it's all my fault, I'll never forgive myself if something happens to him."

"Shall I come with you?" said Pryderi, "we can take my car, you know, two heads and all that."

"Yes, no, oh, I don't know," I said, "look, I don't want to get you into trouble as well. Besides it could be dangerous."

"It's no trouble," he said, "didn't I take an oath to protect and defend the population of the Welsh Republic? Especially the good-looking members of it. Lead on, Mrs Price, and I'll follow."

"All right," I said, "but remember I did warn you. I can't be responsible for your safety. Come on, let's go, we have to hurry, I just hope I'm not too late."

As we left *Die Sachertorte* the Anton Karas look-a-like was blasting out *Goodnight, Vienna* ever so discreetly on his zither. I didn't know about Vienna, I just hoped and prayed it wasn't Goodnight, Stakis and that I wouldn't have my faithful friend on my conscience for the rest of my time on this earth.

The Leek and Daffodil stood on the corner of Quiet Woman's Row and Tryweryn Avenue and was one of those new builds, all chrome and glass and designer interiors straight from the factory. Despite its name it specialised in steaks, *paninis* and *ciabattas* for the lunchtime commuter crowd, besides selling a wide variety of Spanish and South American beers, with waiters wearing *sombreros* and other outlandish gear, somebody at head office thought fitted the Latin American theme. It also boasted its own resident *flamenco* troupe five nights a week, Monday till Friday. It wasn't my glass of *vino tinto* nor could I imagine Stakis wanting to visit it of his own accord, but it was just the sort of place that poseur, Caratacus ap Cadwaladr, would frequent, if indeed Stakis had followed him there and the two of them were inside. For all I knew, Sharona Haf might be in there with them too. She could easily have made it in the time that I'd been distracted by PC Pritchard and his nonsense.

That was the 64,000 Glyndwr question. Who exactly was inside? Was Stakis there? Or had he been spirited away into the night just like Tangerine Dress Girl and Culloden Jimmie? There was only one way to find out.

"Are we going in?" said Pryderi.

"No, wait a minute," I said, "first, I'm going to have a look around. Stay here and wait till I come back, if anyone asks what you're doing, say you're waiting for a friend which is true. Don't do anything I wouldn't do, I'll be back before you can say Llanfihangel Tor y Mynydd."

The Leek and Daffodil was a long, low, one-storey building. Annoyingly, it had the type of windows which you could see out from but not look into. Besides the front door, it had a rear entrance, but nothing much seemed to be happening. No cries for help, no screams of blue murder that I could decipher anyway. I sauntered slowly round the building, taking my time, and trying to give the impression that I did this every day of the week.

When I got back to Pryderi, I had little, if anything to report.

"Are we going in now then?" he said.

"I am, but you're not," I said. "For all we know, this could be a trap. If it is, there's no need for the both of us to be caught. You wait here and keep watch. If you hear me shout 'Boudicca,' come-a-running and be prepared for action. If I haven't returned within fifteen minutes – well, as much as it pains me to say it, call PC Pritchard and let him know what's happened. I'm going in, wish me luck."

"Sure," said Pryderi, "but shouldn't I come with you . . ."

"Don't worry," I said, "I'm used to this sort of thing and I've got Excalibur with me."

"Who, or what, is Excalibur," he said, sounding slightly bemused.

"Excalibur is a very dear friend," I said "and he's going to help me find someone else I love very dearly. It is a far, far better thing that I do now than I have ever done . . ."

"Wait," said Pryderi, "before you go, my real name's Powell, Richard Powell. I thought you might like to know before . . ."

"I know," I said, "thanks, I appreciate your telling me, does this mean I can call you Dick?" and with that I was away and heading for the door of *The Leek and Daffodil*, Pryderi's despairing cry of "well, I wouldn't go quite that far," echoing in my ears as I tried to look a lot more nonchalant than I felt. Over the front door stood a poster telling anyone who was interested that Scotch Bonnet and the Vindaloos (they must be really hot) were performing at this venue on Saturday night, all the way from Gwaun-Cae-Gurwen, and not to be missed. Somehow, I didn't think I would be going. I pushed open the door (well, someone had to) and walked right in.

Easy now, Astrid, subtly does it, whatever you do, don't draw attention to yourself, I thought, so I slammed the door behind me and shouted, "Pizza delivery for Zephaniah Williams, pizza delivery for Zephaniah Williams!"

That ought to get their attention. They were a disparate looking bunch if ever I saw one: not surprisingly, they were men for the most part, sitting there, sipping their sherry or downing pints of Iberian lager or drinking glasses of Malaga red. Men out with their wives and girlfriends, men out with other men's wives and girlfriends, men enjoying other men's company, and the odd group of women laughing and joking together. Most of them were so busy oléing to each other and making mini-Mexican waves, they scarcely had time to give me a second glance. I gave the room a more than careful scan, but nowhere could I see any sign of Stakis or anyone else I knew. Time to get pally with the barman.

The barman wore his jet-black hair, combed down in a fringe, over his forehead. The hair looked dyed and he looked old before his time. He had on an open-necked, long-sleeved shirt, completely covered with meadow flower motifs. He looked me up and down a bit, with what passed for disdain in these parts.

"There's no one here by that name," he said, "anyway, why would anyone want to bother with pizza when we have some of the finest tapas ever recorded on offer here – eat your heart out, Seville, San Sebastian, Bilbao and all those other places," and he waved a languid hand in the direction of the said tapas — a truly vast array of various culinary delicacies.

I had to admit they looked good and I would have been sorely tempted if I had not been in the middle of an important mission, namely, to find Stakis. That was my main priority; right . . . still, they did look very good . . . maybe later, when I had tracked down my missing friend.

"Strange," I said, "I could have sworn the restaurant said the call came from here. What did you say your name was again?"

"I didn't," he said, "but you can call me Al."

"Okay, Al," I said, "Have you had any . . ."

"Stop," he said, "stop, I was only joking, pulling your leg, see, my real name is Dafydd, but most people call me Daf for short."

"Okay, Daf," I said, trying not to laugh too hard at his winsome way with witticisms, "have you had any new faces in tonight, people unaware of the delights of your tapas bar? They might have ordered a pizza before they cast their eyes on your truly dazzling display of delicacies . . ."

Daf the barman preened himself ever so slightly. "Well, now you mention it," he said, "there was that odd looking couple and the guy who came in after them . . . I've never seen any of them before."

"What did they look like?" I said.

"Well, to tell you the truth, I didn't take that much notice of the two men," he said, "the girl, now – her hair — couldn't seem to make up its mind whether it was pink or blue and she seemed to have some sort of owl fixation, owls everywhere you looked, really weird, I asked her whether she was a Sheffield Wednesday supporter, but she gave me a mouthful, said she couldn't stand football. The guy with her had dark, wavy hair and some sort of goatee beard. The second guy took more notice of the tapas than the odd couple. Now, I come to think of it, he seemed a bit nervous, kept looking over his shoulder, all the time, toying with his drink. We don't like that sort of thing in here — customers should drink up and order another one, none of this shall I, shan't I business..."

"Where are they now?" I said.

"Oh, they left in a hurry," he said, "not long before you came in. Three or four other guys came in and they all left together. Although the odd looking couple didn't seem to have anything to do with the guy who came in after them.... yet, they all left together with those four other guys..."

"These four other guys, did they have bulges in their pockets?"

"What, wallets you mean?" said Daf, "can't say as I noticed, seeing as how none of them came up to the bar to order a drink, bloody teetotallers, no doubt..."

"Did they say where they were going?" I said.

"Can't say that they did," he said, "and I didn't ask them. Besides, I was too busy washing glasses to take much notice of what they were saying."

Somehow, I doubted the veracity of that last remark. "There's twenty Glyndwrs for you and a free pizza, if you can remember anything else," I said.

"Well, now," he said, fingering the twenty Glyndwr note I had just passed him, "you say the pizza will be on its way to me before I can say Llanfairpwllgwyngyll etc, etc, and I get to keep the money as well..."

I nodded, "all yours," I said.

"Well, in that case," he said, "I seem to remember one of them saying something about a little place they had stashed away in Cwm Hyfryd. What was the word he used? 'Hideaway', I think he said. Or something like that. Hey, you ask a lot of questions for a pizza delivery woman. And why is a stunner like you a pizza delivery woman in the first place? What's all this about anyway?"

"Can't tell you I'm afraid," I said, "they made me swear a Hippocratic Oath, before I was allowed to deliver my first pizza."

"Your Hippopotamus what?" he said.

"Look it up," I said, "enjoy your pizza. *Tara, rwan.*" (Bye for now.)

As I left *The Leek and Daffodil* and its bemused barman behind me, the flamenco troupe were just warming up. As I shut the door behind me I noticed something that I hadn't noticed before. Not far from the door, there was a scrunched up beer mat just lying there, as if someone had dropped it by accident — bloody litter louts, I thought, there should be a law against them, but then something made me stop and retrace my footsteps. I bent down, picked up the crumpled beer mat and unwrapped it carefully. Inside there were just two words, scrawled and obviously written in a hurry. The words backed up what Daf the barman had told me, they were Cwm Hyfryd and were written in Stakis Theodorakis's fair hand, or I was going back in time to put an arrow in William the Conqueror's eye personally. Stakis must somehow have managed to drop it, without his captors noticing, in the hope that I would find it later.

"Cwm Hyfryd," I said to Lieutenant Pryderi, "whoever's got him, and it looks like Caratacus ap Cadwaladr and Sharona Haf are involved, have taken him to Cwm Hyfryd."

Pryderi didn't exactly blanch, after all, he was a member of an elite force, but he didn't look that ecstatic either. I wasn't feeling too pleased myself.

"It could be a bluff," I said, "they could have dropped loud hints about Cwm Hyfryd just to fool the barman, Stakis and anyone else who came looking for him, i.e, me. For all I know, they could be anywhere in Casnewydd right now or even Maendy or somewhere else altogether..."

"Well," he said, "there's not much we can do about it tonight, I've got to get back to barracks and I'm sure you don't want to run the risk of being caught curfew breaking..."

His lips were about to form the word 'again,' but I stopped him. "Yeah," I said, "you're probably right, let's go."

"I am right," he said me, "believe me, things will look better in the morning."

I heard his words, but they didn't strike me as

being said with very much conviction and, driving back in the car towards *The Lying Cod,* the atmosphere just about rivalled Napoléon's retreat from Moscow for cheerfulness. I was deep in my own thoughts, weighed down by a burden of guilt: if only I hadn't been so irresponsible and cavalier with my treatment of Stakis. What was I thinking, sending him off all alone on a shadowing mission when I should have known that he wouldn't be up to it. As the car pulled up next to my front door, I didn't have the heart to invite Pryderi up for a nightcap. One part of me was tempted, the part which always enjoyed male company, but it would have seemed disrespectful to Stakis. Anyway, it wasn't Pryderi's fight or his problem. He had already done enough for me by getting me out of that tight jam with PC Pritchard. I couldn't expect him to put his army career in jeopardy for someone he hardly knew and another person he didn't know at all. Besides I suddenly felt so tired, I felt as if I were physically and mentally exhausted. I needed a shower. I needed a warm bath. I needed an even warmer bed. Then I needed to think, to form a plan of action, one which was going to be better than the previous ones I had come up with.

   Pryderi was saying something, it sounded like "are you going to be good?"

   "What?" I said, "what do you mean, am I going to be good?"

   "Look," he said, "I've got to get back for duty, I

can't tell you where, but it isn't Cwm Hyfryd, just don't do anything silly, all right?"

    I watched him as his car drove off and headed towards the military district at Pantycelyn. Then I climbed the stairs to my flat. Pryderi needn't have worried. I had no intention of going back out again, and wandering the streets, in a vain reflex action attempt to find Stakis. He deserved better than that. I had some thinking to do and some sleep to catch up on; I needed to be at my best for what the morning would bring. Maybe Pryderi was right, maybe things would look better in a few hours' time, but for now there were a few phone calls I needed to make before my head hit that pillow. Then to sleep, perchance to etc, but more importantly, sleep. I needed desperately to recharge my batteries; I had a big day ahead of me tomorrow.

CHAPTER 17

Litter strewn streets. Dog mess covering the pavements. Abandoned drinks cans lying everywhere. Refuse containers overflowing with rubbish. Recycling bins of all shapes and colours lining the thoroughfare in front of the two-up, two-down houses, that hadn't seen a lick of paint, since the last time Queen Victoria had visited. The place had long since seen better days. Loud music blasted from open upper floor windows. Dogs howling behind closed doors. Drunks sitting on dilapidated benches, swigging from long bottles of cheap cider and shouting and bawling at each other. One forlorn trainer lying there, alone on the pavement, shorn of its mate.

What few election posters there were around here, hung tattered and forlorn from lampposts or telegraph poles or lay in the gutter, mangled and torn, along with all the other flotsam and jetsam of urban life. There were scarcely any in the windows of private houses. I spotted just one for the Generous Party and their leader, Ivor Hale. Oh, well, this was what passed for another Pleasant Valley Sunday I supposed.

Welcome to Cwm Hyfryd, Astrid. What was it that Sherlock Holmes had once said about the least salubrious parts of London – 'East of Aldgate always carry a firearm.' Well, the great detective would have loved Cwm Hyfryd. It was the kind of place where angels feared to tread, Welsh Republican Policemen went round in pairs, using an armoured car as their vehicle of choice and even the scavenging seagulls and pigeons didn't linger very long. It was the kind of place where politicians refrained from taking visiting foreign dignitaries on walkabouts, if they could possibly help it, it was the kind of place where people would come up to you in the street, asking you to give them a Glyndwr or two, please, if you would, so that they could get home on the bus, to catch their dying sister's last breaths, when you knew, and they knew, and everyone else knew that catching a bus was the last thing on their minds. It was the kind of place where . . . well, you get the picture.

Just ahead of me, I saw two hooded youths, engaged in what I assumed was one of those witty, drawing room type conversations, so typical of these parts. As I came up to them, they did not give me as much as a backward glance let alone a forward one. They were wearing identical clothing, same footwear, same baseball caps, same matching outfits. "Where you been hiding, man?" said the one.

"Nowhere, man, just keeping out of trouble," said the other and pulled out a packet of cheap looking cigarettes, with what seemed to be Cyrillic writing on the packet, offering one to his companion. I toyed with the idea of asking them whether they had seen Mrs Big and her cohorts lately, but then thought better of it. I would probably have had to explain what cohorts meant, they would then probably have professed their ignorance or, more likely, given me a mouthful of choice verbal abuse and I would then have felt obliged to give them a lesson in manners, thus wasting valuable time and drawing attention to myself, something I really did not want to do. I ignored them and walked on at a fast pace. The less time I spent in this place the better.

I turned the corner and a cat ran right across my path. I looked to see if it was black — just my luck, a ginger tom had crossed my path. Never mind, on and on I went, past streets with names like Freddy Welsh Boulevard, Joe Erskine Drive, Jimmy Wilde Walk, Johnny Owen Crescent, Howard Winstone Avenue, Johnny Basham Circle. In fact, I began to think I was going round in circles myself. Talk about the mother and father of all wild goose chases. But then I saw it. When it came, it came as a surprise to me and probably everyone else who saw it. It looked as out of place as an Indian elephant playing the piano on top of an Antarctic ice floe and nothing like the rest of Cwm Hyfryd. It was a late Victorian looking house, embellished with a riot of ornate gables, sash windows and chimneys. One wall was completely covered with ivy, totally obscuring the top floor windows.

At a pinch, it might have been worth climbing up there and getting inside that way, but not now in the daylight, when everyone could see what I was doing. On the roof I could see what looked like seven starlings on top of the chimney pots. What were they waiting for, I fleetingly wondered, before I heard a woman singing from somewhere inside the house — a sweet, honey-dripping, mellifluous sound that made you want to hear more. It sounded like something I knew, but I couldn't be sure. For a few moments, I thought it was *Dafydd y Garreg Wen* or David of the White Rock, but as I got nearer, I realised what the tune was — it was *Ar Lan y Môr* or Along the Seashore.

As I got even nearer I noticed that on either side of the door to the house, there were nine-foot tall sunflowers in the front garden. Over the door I could just make out the name of the house in fading green letters – *Hyddgen*. I noticed something else as well . . .

A man was standing at the bottom of the steps, leading up to the front door of the house, early on this balmy August evening; his jacket draped over his shoulders French style. In one hand he held a cigarette, in the other a mobile phone clamped to his ear.

Nothing unusual about that, of course, it was a scene repeated up and down the country, thousands of times a day. What was unusual was the suspicious looking bulge in his trouser pocket. Of course he could have been just pleased to see me, I suppose, but then he hadn't seen me yet, he was so busy with his telephone conversation. Now that I got nearer again, I could begin to hear what he was saying. It wasn't Welsh and it wasn't English, it sounded more like some kind of Spanish, but not the Castilian variety, there didn't appear to be any of the thuh thuh sounds in it as in *civilizacion*, *Zaragoza* etc, if you see what I mean.

"Rodrigo Rodriguez?" I said. "Señor Rodrigo Rodriguez?"

"*Si*," he said, "I am he, but how. . ."

"Oh, just a hunch," I said, "a lucky guess, a shot in the dark, women's intuition, you name it, I've got it. You look tired, Rodrigo, let me play you a little lullaby I wrote all by myself, with no one helping me, you'll like it, believe me," and I pulled out the recorder I had had specially made in Aberbargoed.

"Hey," said Rodrigo, "what are you . . ."

But it was too late; before he could pull out his gun I had planted two of my darts into his left shoulder. I wanted this guy to be out for a while. As he began to fall, I helped him ease gently to the ground — well, I'm good like that, helpful is my middle name — then I dragged him out of sight into the conveniently placed bushes. Oh, yes, and I frisked him too while I was at it — he had a well-thumbed copy of Gabriel Garcia Marquez's book, *One Hundred Years of Solitude* on his person and a betting slip for a horse called *Mab Darogan* (The Son of Prophecy) running in the 2.30 at Chepstow. Worth a punt maybe, if I got out of all this in time? Two different passports, a mobile phone, a wad of money — Welsh, English and some Euros, a packet of cigarettes and a cheap lighter. I let him keep all that – I wasn't greedy – but I took the shooter he'd been trying to pull on me, before I incapacitated him. I had a feeling that might come in handy later.

So far, so very, very good. "The duck is plucked," I said into the tiny microphone, which was hidden under my left jacket lapel, courtesy of my technical wizard from Aberbargoed. I didn't have long to wait. Within seconds a white van was pulling almost noiselessly up to the kerb and out climbed Lieutenant Pryderi and Daniel Owen.

"Take this baby to the Casnewydd city limits," I said, pointing to Rodriguez's prone form, "and give him his copy of Gabriel Garcia Marquez's *One Hundred Years of Solitude*. It'll give him something to read while he's trying to find his way back."

"Right," said Pryderi (I still couldn't get used to calling him Richard Powell) "and what are you going to do?"

"I'm going in to see what I can find," I said, "where's Big Zorba?"

"Round the corner, waiting for your signal," said Daniel Owen, "good luck," and he and Pryderi hauled a comatose Rodriguez to his feet between them. "Come on, big boy," said Pryderi, "we've got places to go."

Once the two of them had gone, taking their prisoner with them, I held a hurried, whispered conversation with Big Zorba. He was all for going into the house with me, but I prevailed on him to give me fifteen minutes and, then, if I hadn't returned, send for the cavalry. Then I set my mobile phone to record, just in case I happened to have any interesting conversations, once I was in the house. I'd found no keys on Rodrigo Rodriguez and, as I suspected, the front door to the house was open. I pushed it gently, holding Excalibur, my rounders bat, straight out in front of me.

I was in a long hall with three doors on its left hand side, all closed, and a staircase leading to an upper floor. Straight in front of me, there was another closed door. I stood stock still, listening, but could hear nothing apart from the sound of the woman still singing and that, I realised now, was coming from upstairs. Slowly, I moved forward, trying to make as little noise as possible. When I got to the first door on my left, I stopped. What to do? Kick it open? Open it quietly and with as little noise as possible? Leave it and go on to the next one? Go back outside and ask Big Zorba for his opinion? What would Adrian Monk have done? Who knows? I didn't know, I had no clue, knowing him, he'd probably have gone into some sort of panic attack, but I couldn't afford to go down that road, I didn't have the luxury of a capable assistant and a compliant police force to fall back on. There was nothing else for it; I would just have to give it the full Ponty. So I did. I gave it the full Ponty, everything I had, no holds barred, holding nothing back, I threw everything into it, like the cook anxious to use up all the items in his, or her, store cupboard in a fragrant, aromatic, sweet-smelling, delicious stew.

I opened the door as quietly as the quietest chapel mouse, nerves jangling as to what I might find on the other side. I needn't have worried, the room was small, but furnished in good taste, and seemed to be some kind of lounge, but apart from me, there was no one in it. The next two doors I tried were empty too, now for the door straight in front of me.

Once again I stopped to listen, my fingers caressing Excalibur. Now, the only sound I could hear was my own breathing, the woman upstairs seemed to have stopped singing, I hoped that didn't mean she would be coming downstairs to join me at any minute. Was she the only person in the house? Was Stakis here at all or had they spirited him away somewhere else? Only one way to find out. I opened the door in front of me with more confidence than I was actually feeling.

I found myself in a room with a television, a fridge, a table and two chairs. On one of the chairs a man was sitting, drinking coffee from a tall white mug, whilst reading today's copy of *Y Byd* (The World). Next to him on the table was an object, that looked suspiciously like a gun to me, but was it within his reach? I moved closer towards the table and he looked up in surprise, the face he showed me, seeming somehow familiar. It took me a second to realise it, but I knew I was looking at my old 'friend,' Jude, the not so genuine policeman. Or was he? I still wasn't quite sure.

"Hey, Jude," I said, "fancy meeting you here, just come to read your gas meter, it won't take long. Everything okay, I hope, you look as if you've just seen The Ghost Cat and all her kittens."

"Price," he said, and it was almost all he could do to get the words out, "what are you . . . how did you . . . ?"

"Get in?" I said, "Simple, I just opened the door and walked in. Isn't that what you did, Jude? That is your real name, isn't it, by the way? Jude, I mean? Are you really a member of the Welsh Republican Police, Jude, or do you just go about impersonating them and hindering ordinary citizens in the pursuit of their civic duties?"

"Go climb a monkey tree, Price, I don't know what you're talking about," said Jude.

"Oh, I think you do," I said, "I think you know very well what I'm talking about, and I also think I know very well what you're thinking, hunk. You're thinking, can I reach the gun on this table, before she thumps me with her rounders bat, in a sensitive part of my anatomy. It all depends how plucky you feel, I suppose. Do you feel plucky, hunk, well do you? Go ahead, hunk, reach for the gun, make your play."

I could see Jude looking at me and I could almost hear him thinking. Shall I? Shan't I? Is she faster than me? Why didn't I put the gun where I could reach it more easily? But I'd had enough of mind games, before he could make his move, I flicked out Excalibur, sending the gun crashing to the other side of the room, then I kicked over the table and, with a look of desperation on his face he was coming for me, but, oh dear, I seemed to have, somehow, made contact with a most sensitive part of Jude's anatomy after all.

Down he went, like a bag of the finest Maris Pipers, gasping for breath. While he continued to pretend to writhe in agony — he must have spent too much of his spare time watching the English Premiership on *Sgorio*, the Welsh Language football programme —I searched him quickly and thoroughly. Ah, just what I was looking for, a pair of handcuffs — maybe Jude was a proper policeman after all. Then, while he was still feeling sorry for himself, I yanked both his hands behind him and handcuffed him to the chair he had so recently been sitting on. I put the table back up and left the keys on it, in front of him so that he would have something to look at while I was gone. There, that ought to keep him happy for a while.

Then I threw a quick glance at the copy of *Y Byd* (The World) Jude had been reading. Well, well, very interesting, it seemed that my old friends, Georg Alptraum, Monsieur Dieu and Herb the Serb, were going to be spending some time in Portmeirion before being summarily deported from the Welsh Republic, that should leave Mrs Big with a few holes to fill in her own private army, for the time being at least. Now for the upstairs in this rambling old house. And what might I find there? But I needed some answers to a few questions that had been troubling me. Maybe my old friend Jude would be in a cooperative mood, but somehow I had my doubts. Some men can be so unforgiving.

"Right," I said, jumping on the table and dangling my legs from it, "who's upstairs? Mrs Big? Red Iolo? Joe, your partner in crime? I've really missed him, you know. Stakis? What have you done with Stakis, Jude? Come on, tell Astrid – think of me as, well not a father figure, obviously, but someone you can confide in, confess your misdeeds to . . ."

"Go boil an egg, Price," said Jude between gasps, "I'm telling you nothing."

"Really," I said, "nothing at all? What would PC Pritchard say if he knew you were on Mrs Big's payroll? More to the point, what would Inspector Sergeant say? Where is Mrs Big by the way? And who's that upstairs singing? Nice voice. Anyone I know? Go on, Jude, you can talk to me . . ."

"Oh, go chew on a rock, Price, or better still slide down a cliff in Rhossili Bay, why don't you?" said Jude, "Mrs Big is where you'll never find her."

"Is that so?" I said, "Is Tangerine Girl with her or Culloden Jimmie? What's that you say? Don't feel like talking anymore? Well, I'm sorry to hear that. I'd better be going then, things to do and all that. I'll let PC Pritchard know you're here. Maybe he'll send Joe along to set you free. Oh, is that your big toe I've stepped on, dear me, I can be so clumsy at times. I'm so sorry . . . *Tara rwan* (bye for now). Be sure to give my love to your friend Joe, won't you?"

I shut the door behind me, leaving Jude to stew in his own juice for a while. What now, my love, as Shirley Bassey might have said. Well, it didn't need an Hercule Poirot and his little grey cells to tell me that upstairs was the obvious answer, but before climbing I waited and listened again, but the only sound I heard was Jude moaning and groaning.

Slowly, I began to mount the steps, testing each one carefully before putting my full weight down. There didn't seem to be any creaking, but as my old mam always used to tell me, you couldn't be too careful. At least this time, if I did meet anybody, I was armed to the teeth, what with Jude and Rodriguez's guns and my very own Excalibur.

I got to the top without incident and found myself on a spacious landing with four doors leading off, all of them closed. I stopped to listen again. There were no sounds coming from behind any of the closed doors. For all I knew, there could be villains waiting behind each one, just itching to do me in or dent my ego at the very least. On the other hand, all four rooms could be completely empty. Or . . . I could just stand here puzzling over the various combinations that might or might not await me, or I could do something.

Right, time to do something, but what — bull in a china shop or something more subtle? Any minute now, Jude was going to get over his bruised ego and start yelling. Perhaps I should have given him one of my tranquilliser darts as a parting present. Oh, well, too late now, in for a penny, in for a Welsh pound. I tapped on the first door ever so gently with Excalibur and watched it swing open — nothing. One down, three to go. I did the same with the next door and the next door. Still nothing, nobody in any of the rooms, I was alone with my thoughts.

Now, there was only one door left. I listened intently but couldn't hear anything. I thought about kicking this door in and entering with my two guns blazing, just like Billy the Kid or John Wayne on a bad day with a splitting headache, shooting first and asking questions afterwards. Why not? Nobody seemed to want to answer my questions anyway. Now, now, Astrid, calm down, keep that head up, relax, control yourself, imagine yourself opening the door gently, ever so gently, just like all the others . . . that's it, slowly does it . . . now imagine you are stepping inside, in your mind's eye see yourself not shooting, unless it was absolutely necessary, of course . . .

Enough imagining, what was that about four tries for a Welshwoman, maybe this time I would find something. Slowly, very slowly I opened the fourth door to see what I would find . . .

CHAPTER 18

I had found something all right and that something was Culloden Jimmie. There was no need to look any further for the missing Scotsman. Even, from where I was standing, I could see the tattoos on his bare arms, what was that his wife had said to me – "He has two tattoos, one on each arm. The left one says: *I fought the law* and the right one says: *and the law won.*" They were plainly visible. One of my searches at least was over.

Poor old Culloden. He would never see his native Isle of Barra or speak Scots Gaelic to anybody ever again; nor would he ever do anything else for that matter — his body lay stretched out on the floor of the room and I had seen enough dead bodies to know that this one was never going to do a Lazarus on me. In the great scheme of things, it had obviously not been one of Culloden's better days.

I sighed inwardly, a deep and mournful sigh, whichever way you looked at it; it was hard to put a positive spin on what had happened to him. It was harder still to realise that, kneeling next to the body, his hands grasping a great big handled knife, was my friend and confidant, Stakis Theodorakis . . .

You know how it is when everything seems to be in slow motion, nothing seems to move very quickly and everything has a dream like quality about it? Well, that's

I was there, looking at what used to be Culloden Jimmie
and at Stakis, holding the knife

how it seemed to me now. I was there looking at what used to be Culloden Jimmie and at Stakis, holding the knife, and time stood still. By a great effort of will, I forced myself to break the spell. "Stakis, what are you doing?" I said, "put the knife down, your finger prints must be all over it," but Stakis just gave me a stunned, uncomprehending look, he was obviously in deep shock. I took a step towards him, saying, "Stakis, it's me, Astrid, put the knife down, do it for me, please."

"Yeah, Stakis, put the knife down," said a voice from behind me, a voice I knew all too well. I turned and found myself looking at Inspector Sergeant and PC Richard Pritchard; they must have crept up on me during that brief interlude when I first discovered Stakis, the body and the knife.

Suddenly, before any of us could react, Stakis dropped the knife with a clatter and rushed towards me. "Astrid," he said, throwing both his arms around my neck, "thank Cymru, you've come, it's been hell, sheer hell. I couldn't have stood it for much longer. That crazy woman with the beret, playing the ukulele at all hours of the day and night and, when she wasn't doing that, asking me questions about obscure sixties groups I'd never heard of . . . I mean just who are The Undertakers and who cares who Rory Storm and the Hurricanes' drummer was?"

"But the worst one was that Sharona Haf; she's a devil woman, Astrid, no, that's not right, the devil himself would hide from her. And yet she has the loveliest singing voice — it just doesn't make sense. She was in here just now, blowing smoke in my face and threatening to carve me up with that big German knife of hers. All the way from Solingen, she kept telling me, none of your cheap supermarket rubbish. She abseiled out of the window just now, just before you got to me."

"And the food . . . you wouldn't believe the food they gave me — all I had was bread and water whilst they gorged themselves on fish and chips from, do you know where – *The Lying Cod*, that's where, oh the cheek of it and then they ate Monmouth Pudding for afters, oh, I'm so glad you're here, Astrid. Wait a minute, what's he doing here? And who's he?"

I pulled Stakis's arms from my neck long enough to see Daniel Owen and Pryderi had just entered the room.

"Oh," I said, "well, Daniel, you know, of course, and this . . . this is Lieutenant Pryderi."

Stakis gave Pryderi a long hard look. "Don't tell me," he said, "let me guess, he's a friend of yours, another . . . new friend of yours I don't know about. Where did you meet him, at The Silurian Club, I suppose?"

"Now, now, Stakis," I said, "Daniel and Lieutenant Pryderi are here to help you, you should be grateful to them instead of doing your Nicholas Anelka impression and acting like The Incredible Sulk. What's more,

Lieutenant Pryderi has given up his day off work to be here."

"I'll bet he has," said Stakis. "What's happened to you, Astrid, you used to be able to solve all these cases on your own with no help from anybody . . . now you seem to require all this assistance . . ." and he waved a derisory finger in the direction of my two little helpers.

"Oh, stop moaning, Stakis," I said, "and be grateful you've been rescued. Anyway, we've got to get out of here, who knows when the bad guys might come back . . . can you walk Stakis, are you fit enough?"

"Of course," he said, "what do you take me for? No, don't answer that . . . just take me back home, I need some food. Food, food . . ."

"It's prison food you'll be eating for the next few days at least, Stakis," said Inspector Sergeant, "read him his rights, Pritchard and slap the cuffs on him. Then get onto the station, we need reinforcements here quickly."

"You can't be serious," I said, "Stakis wouldn't harm a tarantula and you know it. It's Sharona Haf you should be after, she's just abseiled out the window, you heard what Stakis said. And that rogue cop downstairs, what's his name again — Jude. Arrest him and start looking for Mrs Big while you're at it, she must be behind all this or I'm the King of Siam."

"What rogue policeman, Price?" said Inspector Sergeant, "there's no one downstairs and you know it. There's no one in the house apart from me, Pritchard and you and your friends . . . by the way, what are you all doing here anyway? A social call, is it? Not that your company appears to have done Culloden Jimmie much good. I think you'd all better accompany Stakis to the station — every one of you has got a lot of explaining to do. Pritchard, where are those reinforcements?"

"Sir," said Pritchard, "Sir, there's something you should know."

"What?" said Inspector Pritchard, "what is it? Well, speak up, man."

"I think you should know, sir, that this man here is Lieutenant Pryderi . . ."

"What!" said the inspector, "who in Cymru's name is Lieutenant Pryderi?"

"You know, sir, the one I was telling you about, the member of The Llywelyn the Last Brigade, the one who refused to pick Price out at my identity parade . . . "

"Just a minute," said Pryderi, "this woman and her friends are acting under my direct orders. They were helping me follow up an important lead in the Madge Breese case."

"What!" said PC Pritchard, "what are you talking about? We've got you all bang to rights, breaking and entering into a private house, Stakis standing over a dead body with the murder weapon in his hand; we'll see what you've all got to say down at the station."

"Fine," said Pryderi, "if that's what you want, but perhaps you won't mind me phoning my superiors before we go? You realise of course that The Llywelyn the Last Brigade does not come under the jurisdiction of the Welsh Republican Police?"

"Well," said Pritchard, "that might apply to you, Lieutenant, but Price and the other two certainly do come under our jurisdiction, as you put it. Let's go, we've wasted enough time already."

"Wait a minute, Pritchard," said Inspector Sergeant, "let's not be too hasty here, Lieutenant Pryderi may have a point. He can go for now, but we need to talk to Price and Daniel Owen and Stakis is coming with us, he has, after all, been found in possession of what appears to be the murder weapon. I take it you have no objection to that, Lieutenant?"

"None at all," said Pryderi, shooting me a glance which seemed to say, "I can't help you any further, I'm afraid."

Well, to cut the proverbial long story short, after much grilling, gratuitous insults and attempted third degree, Sergeant and Pritchard were obliged to let me loose on bail, thanks to the good offices of my lawyer, the Iceman, John Frost. Lawyer Frost was a tall, thin man with a shock of white hair and a deep voice, who, in his spare time, was a big noise with the local Chartist Re-Enactment Society. On this particular evening he also managed to square it for Daniel Owen and myself, despite all the Emergency Laws Sergeant and Pritchard were trying to throw at us, although even he couldn't swing it for Stakis — he was going to have to spend a few more nights in custody at the Welsh President's pleasure, unless I could find some way of getting to the bottom of all this.

Police stations are not my favourite places in all the world, I must say, and I'd seen enough of the inside of the Welsh Republican Police Headquarters, Casnewydd, over the last few days, to last me for a while, I can tell you. Then, as I left the station, I was surprised to see Lieutenant Pryderi waiting outside. He looked as if he had been waiting there for some time. For me? Maybe he had been just standing there, at a bit of a loose end, wondering what to do with the rest of his evening, or life, perhaps. I started to thank him for all that he had done for us, but he cut me short . . .

"No need to thank me," he said. "I've heard all about you, Price. Some of the men at the barracks remember you when you were still playing for Casnewydd Ladies, before you'd made it into the Welsh side. Like a female David Watkins, they said you were, only taller, of course, no one could catch you, apparently, or so the men said."

"Oh, Lieutenant Pryderi," I said, "Stop it, you're making me blush." But inwardly I glowed —it's always nice to be recognised and to know that, somehow, deep down inside, you've still got it.

"That's twice now you've put your neck on the line for me, Lieutenant Pryderi," I said. "How can I possibly repay you?"

"I think you know how, Astrid Price," he said.

"Why, Lieutenant Pryderi," I said, "I do declare you're making me positively blush."

"I'd like to do more than that," he began, but I cut him off.

"Sorry, Pryderi," I said, "you're a good looking guy in a smart uniform and I've got a lot of time for you, but right now all I can think of is springing Stakis from the clutches of the Welsh Republican Police. Besides, I wouldn't want you to get in trouble with your employers. I wouldn't put it past that weasel Pritchard to be on the phone to them right now."

If Pryderi was disappointed to hear this, he didn't show it. All that army training, I suppose. I laid a consolatory hand on his shoulder. And, in spite of myself, I began to feel the slightest flickering of something I maybe didn't quite understand myself. And, for one, oh so, fleeting moment, I wanted to do more than just place my hand on this man's shoulder, a man I hardly knew, a man I had barely just met.

Oh, Astrid, Astrid, I thought to myself, has it come to this? Have you forgotten Morgan, dearest Morgan already? Is he so easy to betray? And, of course, I had been neglecting his grave terribly of late, not to mention that of my poor old mam, God rest her soul.

Sure, never a day went by without me thinking of them both, but lately, I was becoming more and more pre-occupied with other matters, like how, exactly, in the name of Cymru, was I ever going to get to the bottom of all these mysteries, riddles and conundrums which kept crowding in on me and making my life a complete misery.

In my defence, all I could think of was that I wouldn't say I wanted to jump into this soldier's trousers exactly, but there *was* something about him, there was no denying he *had* something.

"How will I get in touch with you, Pryderi, I mean Richard," I said.

"You won't," he said, "Everything our end is classified, you know, extremely hush hush, all that sort of thing . . . Give me your number and I'll call you, whenever I'm able to, that is."

"Oh, and Price . . ."

"Yes," I said.

"Just now . . ."

"What about just now?"

"Just now, I was talking about a candle lit dinner for two at a top Casnewydd hostelry, no expenses spared. Not what you appeared to think . . ."

Oh, I thought to myself, feeling not very tall at all. Jump in with both feet, Astrid, why don't you, and don't forget to shoot yourself in both of them at the same time, while you're at it. Idiot, moron, complete and utter fool . . .

His voice trailed off. He kissed me lightly on the

cheek and then he was gone, like one of those fanciful will-o'-the-wisps in the night, you read about in ghost stories, leaving me feeling more than just a little alone and wondering quite what was going on here.

Of course, the police had interviewed each one of us separately, so I had no idea what Stakis and the other two had said to them. As I made my way back to *The Lying Cod*, I had some questions of my own I wanted answered: like who had killed Culloden Jimmie and why? Was he mixed up in some business I didn't know about? All the signs seemed to point towards Sharona Haf. What was that Stakis had said about that big German knife of hers? But there was no guarantee she had anything to do with Culloden's death.

Presumably it was she who had freed bent cop Jude, and alerted Sergeant and Pritchard, after abseiling down through the window. That was one little lady I needed to ask some questions, if I ever caught up with her again, that is. Who knew where she was now? Safely holed up in some hideaway with Mrs Big and what was left of her minions, perhaps? I needed to find those people and quickly if I was going to be of any use to poor old Stakis. Which reminded me, I needed to ask Stakis what exactly had happened to him since his ill-fated attempt to shadow Caratacus ap Cadwaladr had gone so badly wrong. And last, but certainly not least, what the hell was I playing at with Richard Powell, aka Lieutenant Pryderi, of The Llywelyn the Last Brigade?

It was with a very heavy heart that I made my way back to *The Lying Cod*. The place just wasn't the same without Stakis standing there, waving his fish fryer at all and sundry, laughing and joking, or peeling potatoes. Big Zorba would have to step in now and run things until such time as Stakis got out, if he ever did get out . . .

I was there, I saw what happened and even I had to admit the evidence did not look good. Maybe Stakis was prison bound and there was nothing I could do to save him. For just one fleeting moment, the ignoble thought crossed my mind that maybe Stakis had actually done the deed. After all, we had all seen him there in that room, in that house in Cwm Hyfryd, with the knife in his hand, the lifeless body of Culloden Jimmie lying next to him . . . but I shook that thought off with a shudder. No, never in a million years would Stakis ever have done something like that. It simply wasn't in his nature.

When I got back to my flat I just didn't feel like eating anything, my normally healthy appetite had gone and I found myself searching for something to do, anything to take my mind off things, I switched on the radio just in time to hear there was still no progress in the hunt for the missing Madge Breese recording and then the announcer's honeyed tones were intoning:

And now we take you over to a party political broadcast brought to you by Orson Workshy and The

United Grafters' Party.

Thanks, but no thanks, I thought to myself, no disrespect to Orson Workshy and his merry men etc, etc, but I wasn't that desperate, so I switched off the radio, showered, cleaned my teeth and climbed into bed. I'd like to say I spent all night tossing and turning, thinking of ways to spring Stakis from his incarceration, but I didn't, I was so exhausted I just turned over and dived headlong into the land of deep, deep sleep. The last thing I remember thinking before all the lights went out was that old cliché tomorrow is another day . . .

CHAPTER 19

Rome, they say, is built on seven hills, but the city I lived in, the City of Casnewydd, seemed to have far more than that, although I had long since ceased trying to count them. Hills with names like Bryn Derwen and Bryn Terfel, Brynhyfryd and Bryn Meredith, to name but four, long winding hills with twists in the tail that took you by surprise, short sharp hills that sorted out the unwary after the first few, gut-wrenching yards, leaving them gasping for air, hills verging on the perpendicular; steep, almost vertical climbs where it became a struggle to put one foot in front of the other, vertiginous inclines that seemed to go up and up and never end, hills to cause enough huffing and puffing to blow anyone's house down, hills that looked as if they had been designed by Pythagoras, but a Pythagoras with a grudge against walkers and pedestrians. At any minute you expected to see mountain goats cavorting on the pavements, Sherpa Tensing talking to Sir Edmund Hilary or hear the sound of distant yodelling.

Sure, there were flat areas in the City, low-lying tracts of land where any passing Dutchman would have felt at home, but they lacked . . . What was the word — oomph, charisma, pizzazz, *chutzpah*, excitement? Whatever you liked to call it, these pancake nether lands just did not cut it, try as they might, they could not hack it. Through no fault of their own, they weren't, well, they just weren't hills. The hills were alive with the sound of the City, they shook to its rhythm and pounded to its beat, they were its pulsating heart.

On warm summer nights, when it got too hot to sleep, and sometimes even in winter, but mostly when I needed to think, to find a way forward, the hills would call to me. At such times, I would get into my car and drive, up into the highest hills overlooking the City and let my eyes roam over the tidal Brown River far below, thinking of what needed to be done.

Sometimes, too, I would pick a secluded spot and go through my Tai Chi exercises. So it was no surprise that I found myself here again on a late summer night, not long after we had found Stakis holding a murderous knife in his hand, pondering and wondering just what I was going to do to solve this, there was no other word for it, intractable, case and get Stakis out of that Welsh Republican Police cell and make him a free man once again.

I sat behind the steering wheel of the *Pwca* and stared at the scenery. The scenery stared right back but it didn't offer me any clues or startling revelations. It didn't say to me, why not try this line of enquiry, or interview these people, it just stood there and looked pretty, so after a while of just sitting there and not coming up with anything very much, I decided to get out

Sometimes, too, I would pick a secluded spot and go through my Tai Chi exercises

of the car and stretch my legs a bit.

There was nobody about so, without even thinking very much about it, I started to move effortlessly into the form, passing from Fishes in Eight, through Single Whip and onto Stork Spreads Wings. When I reached Strum the Lute I was pretty much in tune with myself, God, the universe and all other points philosophical. By Embrace Tiger Return to Mountain, a sense of well-being had enveloped me, had I really been so worried about the fate of Culloden Jimmie, and when I reached Step Back and Repulse Monkey I had almost forgotten about girls in tangerine dresses, Super Dragons, Mrs Big and her minions and all the other loose ends that had been exercising my mental facilities to date.

Almost, but not quite. As I moved into Golden Cock Stands on One Leg, the vague outlines of a plan were beginning to form in my mind, it wasn't perfect but it might just work. Anyway, what did I have to lose, I said to myself finishing the Long Form with Step Up, Parry and Punch, I certainly wasn't getting anywhere with my usual methods.

CHAPTER 20

So the following morning saw me paying a visit to Super Dragon Central (aka an empty shop which Casnewydd City Council had temporarily taken over). It was fairly early but various local artists were hard at work putting the finishing touches to some ten or twelve fibreglass dragon bodies, drinking coffee or standing back and admiring their handiwork. The dragons must have been about five feet high from head to hoof.

I wandered around the room, taking a good look around me. There were pots of paint, palette knives and brushes everywhere, old newspapers were strewn over parts of the floor and here and there battered old armchairs and sofas offered a welcome rest to visitor and artist alike.

The artists believed in variety all right. No two dragons were exactly the same, some were painted in bright, bold attractive colours, others featured a *smorgasbord* of differing motifs, local and international, whilst still others were covered in surreal flights of fancy, where the artist had really let their imagination take flight and soar to the heavens. I had to admit they all looked really good and it would have been hard choosing a winner from amongst them.

I moved around the room for a while checking out both dragons and artists. Eventually I settled on one

She wore some kind of overall

woman who looked like she might be amenable. Her hair was tucked under a sort of bluish red turban and she wore some kind of overall, which had once upon a time been white but was now covered with paint, old and new.

"Good morning," I said, "sorry to interrupt you, my name is Augusta Hall. I'm a journalist working in Bangor and I'm down here visiting my sister Delyth for a few days. I heard about your scheme and thought my readers up in the north might be interested. It's a really great idea."

"Pleased to meet you," she said, extending her hand. "Branwen Guest at your service. Hey, you look awfully familiar. Don't I know you, aren't you the one who wrote *How Mean Was My Valley*?"

"Not guilty," I said, "you must be mistaking me for someone else, don't worry, it happens all the time."

"Yes, you must be right," she said, looking at me closely as if she still didn't quite believe me, "I must be thinking of some other Augusta Hall. Or maybe I'm thinking about someone else altogether?"

"Yeah, maybe," I said, "it's probably because I'm a journalist, I suppose. It's the pencils, you see. People automatically confuse me with writers they've heard of . . ."

"Yes . . ." she said, nodding her head in agreement, but it was clear that she still wasn't entirely convinced. I had the feeling I was going to have my work cut out with this one.

"Do you mind if I ask you a few questions?" I said.

"No, not at all," she said, "Fire away . . . I'll do my best to answer, but wait a dragon painting minute . . . I know who you are . . . you're that cricketer, the one who played for Wales, the one that kept getting out all the time, she had Titian red hair just like yours."

"Wrong again," I said, "I'm afraid, sport and me are like Jose Mourinho and Barcelona or Tottenham and Arsenal, the two just don't mix. Now, if I could just get onto those questions . . ."

Easy now, Astrid, don't rush things, build up gradually . . . "Right," I said, "have you had any Scotsmen come to see you with tattoos on their arms or girls in tangerine dresses pulling their pet dogs behind them?"

"I must say, Augusta, you do ask some very strange questions," said Branwen Guest, "not at all like the other journalists we're used to . . ."

"Ah," I said, "that's because *my* readers like a lot of local colour, something to spice things up a bit. They simply love hearing about big, brawny Scotsman with tattoos on both arms. Maybe the left one might say: *I fought the law* and the right one might say: *and the law won.* You know, that kind of thing. Or the girl in the tangerine dress might have a dog with her and that dog might be called Victor, or Hector, or Nestor, or Vector or something like that — any of this ring any bells?"

"No, not really, Augusta," she said, "I'm sure I would have noticed if anybody like that had come to watch us at work."

"All right," I said, "Where do the dragons come from? Are they made in Wales?"

"Oh yes," said Branwen Guest, "they're from the north, they're made in Bangor."

"I see," I said, "and do you get many people coming to see you while you work, people from the north of the Republic, perhaps?"

"Well, it's funny you should say that," said Branwen Guest, stooping to apply a finishing touch to one of her dragons, "we have had quite a few people down from the North lately and, now that I come to think of it, some of them were quite peculiar . . ."

"Oh, in what way?" I said, "did any of them have tattoos or dogs with them?"

"No, no, it wasn't that," she said, "Really, Augusta, you do seem to have an unhealthy fascination for tattoos and dogs, I must say. No, I'm thinking more of the woman with the ukulele, the one with the white beret."

"Ukulele?" I said, "she had a ukulele with her?"

"Yes," said Branwen, "and she insisted on giving us a tune as well. I forget what she played now, but I remember it was quite good. There was something else about her . . . now, what was it . . . yes, that's it, she offered to buy one of our dragons. Well, I told her she couldn't. They weren't ours to sell; they belonged to the City of Casnewydd. Well, she went all round the room, touching our dragons and tapping them, almost as if she were looking for something. She seemed to be particularly interested in the new ones that had come in quite recently. And then she did another strange thing."

"And what was that?" I said.

"Well," said Branwen, "she said if I could answer a question she was going to put to me, she would give me five hundred Glyndwrs for an unpainted dragon of her choice. Plus two tickets for the Haydn Beethoven concert at the Central Hall. They say he's very good, you know, for someone born and bred in Llanfairfechan, but I still had to refuse, even though she went as high as eight hundred Glyndwrs. Well, I was tempted of course, but I had to tell her. Look, I said, I've already told you, they're not mine to sell, they belong to the City of Casnewydd, but she went ahead and asked her silly question anyway . . ."

"And what was the question?" I said, "Can you remember it? Anything to do with Madge Breese?"

"Funnily enough, I can," said Branwen Guest, "it was so bizarre, it stuck in my memory, but it was nothing to do with Madge Breese. Oh, isn't that whole thing dreadful . . . She said 'can you tell me who sang lead vocals with Freddie and the Dreamers? Was it (a) Freddie Garrity (b) Freddie Mercury or (c) Freddie Cannon?' "Well, how should I know? I didn't have a clue;

I'm not that old, I told her. She just laughed, said it was just a bit of fun, that's all and that she had to be going."

"Did she have anybody with her?" I said.

"Yes," said Branwen, "two foreign looking gentlemen. Well, they didn't look very Welsh anyway. As far as I remember, they were pretty big and quite well built. They seemed to be very interested in our dragons as well. Oh, and they kept looking around all the time, their eyes were everywhere as if they were expecting something to happen."

"And did it?" I said.

"Did what?" she said.

"Something happen?"

"No, the three of them left and we just carried on working and closed up and went home as usual. To tell you the truth, I was glad when they left; it was all getting a bit creepy."

"Tell me," I said, and I wasn't quite sure myself, why I was asking this question, "was this before the Madge Breese recording was stolen or after? Can you remember?"

"Let me see now," she said, "that's a tough one, I may need to consult my diary for the answer to that one," and she pulled out a battered looking little black book and started to leaf through it. "Ah, yes," she said. "Here it is . . . strange, there's nothing here, I thought I'd written everything down on that particular day. Most peculiar, I must have forgotten to do it for some reason.

Probably had to do a lot of shopping that day. You know how it is, if you don't write something down, it's gone before you can say 'Show me the way to Penrhyndeudraeth.'"

"Oh, well," I said, "I won't take up any more of your valuable time, thanks for all your help, I'll give you a good write-up as soon as I get back to Bangor."

"Of course, Bangor," said Branwen Guest, hitting herself on the forehead, "silly me, why didn't I think of it before. That woman . . . the one with the ukulele, she said she and her friends had just come from Bangor. And another thing . . . she gave me something, I'd forgotten all about that as well. Now where did I put it?" and she began rummaging round in various pockets.

Eventually, she succeeded in pulling out a piece of battered, tattered looking white card. "Ah, there you are," she said triumphantly, "I knew I'd put you somewhere. You know, Augusta, just before she left, the woman said to me, 'if you change your mind about selling one of the dragons, give me a ring on this number.'"

"May I see," I said, extending my left hand, "I might, you know . . . want to get in touch with her myself, background information for my article and all that . . ."

"Yes, yes, of course," said Branwen and she handed me the card. I turned it over. In bold black type, it said: **AMBER BERNSTEIN: BUYER AND**

COLLECTOR OF MEMORABLE ANTIQUES and underneath there was what looked like a mobile number: **071400 21409**.

Touchdown. We have lift-off. Cue fireworks, explosions, cheerleaders, ticker-tape parades, sirens blowing and all sorts of razzamatazz. Until now, the case had been about as clear and transparent as the mud on the banks of the Brown River. If anything, it had been even muddier. Now, at last, I might be getting somewhere. The number could be a dead end of course; it might be one of those pay as you go deals using a cheap throwaway phone. Nevertheless, it was some light in the tunnel — time would tell whether it turned out to be a mere will o' the wisp.

"Thank you once again," I said, resisting the temptation to physically embrace Branwen Guest. "You've been more than helpful, good luck with the Super Dragons. Now I really must be going – editor's deadlines, you know, don't worry; I'll see myself out. *Tara rwan* . . ." (Bye for now.)

Once outside on the pavement, I paused to take stock. There appeared to be no one around, nobody seemed to be interested in my movements, it didn't look like I was being followed. I turned and walked through a deserted underpass.

Normally, the subways and underpasses of the city were full of buskers plying their trade, churning out the latest chart topper from years ago and recycling old

Bob Dylan hits that even he had forgotten about. It was open to question whether they paid royalties to the Performing Arts Society of Cymru. Somehow I doubted it.

Anyway, at this time of night, the buskers must have all gone home to count their money and work on their repertoire for the following day, as no one seemed to be around here either. Even the city's pigeons, those indefatigable hoovers-up of human waste and food droppings, were nowhere to be seen.

I glanced idly to my right. On the wall of the underpass someone with nothing better to do had scrawled The English Settlers' Party electoral slogan, *'The Republic has failed - reunion with England now.'* Underneath, someone else had painted the words *'vote Benevolent Despot – you know it makes sense'*. Who said political debate in the Welsh Republic was dead?

I took out my mobile and dialled the number Branwen Guest had given me. It took a little while and then the dialling tone cut in. Seconds later I heard a man's voice at the other end of the line. It was a clear strong voice with just the faintest trace of a North Wales accent about it and, for some reason, it sounded vaguely familiar. "Yeah?" the voice said, "who is it? What do you want?"

Charming, I thought, but I put on my best 'posh bird' voice. "Hello," I said, "I'd like to speak to Amber Bernstein, is she available?"

"Who wants to know?" said the voice.

"My name's Augusta Hall," I said. I'm a journalist working in Bangor and I'm down here visiting my sister Delyth for a few days. She's working down here you know, just for the summer. She told me about the Casnewydd Super Dragons and I thought my readers up in the north might be interested. Anyway, a woman I met named Branwen Guest, who was painting one of the Super Dragons, was kind enough to give me Amber Bernstein's number . . . She also gave me some intriguing new information . . ."

"Did she now," said the voice, "Augusta Hall, yeah, I've heard of you. Say, aren't you the one who wrote *How Mean Was My Valley*?"

"Well . . ." I began, but the voice was interrupting me, "hang on a minute," it said, "let me clear this first . . ." There was the sound of a conversation going on in the background and somebody saying something I couldn't quite catch and then the voice came back on. Where had I heard it before? "Yeah," it was saying, "I'm sure Amber would like to see you. She's really interested in all that Super Dragon stuff. Do you know *The Lord Raglan*?"

"I think so," I said, "my sister, Delyth, may have mentioned it to me, isn't it some sort of pub, one of those gastro places . . ."

"Yeah," said the voice, "it's easy enough to find, it's one of those new places just opened up on John

Uzzell Street, you know in the heart of the city's business quarter . . . Be there at 7 p.m. tonight sharp won't you and I mean sharp, Amber's very particular about punctuality, very particular. Be sure to bring a rolled up copy of *Y Byd* with you, oh and stand underneath the clock so that we'll be able to recognise you. And Augusta . . ."

"Yes?" I said.

"One more thing. Don't forget to come alone. Leave your sister behind tonight. Amber doesn't like to have too many visitors all crowding her at the same time. She's eccentric that way."

CHAPTER 21

So there I was at twenty to seven that night, standing in John Uzzell Street, on the opposite side of the road to *The Lord Raglan*, idly twirling my rolled up copy of *Y Byd*. Things seemed quiet enough, most of the office workers appeared to have gone home, the street itself was deserted and nobody appeared to be going in or out of the building and there were no sounds of any drunken brawls or loud behaviour emanating from the place. Quiet was good, very good and there was also no sign of the usual group of nicotine addicts, congregating outside the entrance to the pub, chewing the fat and, whether they intended to or not, ever so slightly intimidating any potential customers.

Ideally, I should have let someone know where I was going – Daniel Owen or Désirée Protheroe perhaps. Wasn't that what all the experts on internet dating said you should do. Still, what could possibly go wrong? I would be in a public place, meeting with one, perhaps two or three, strangers discussing the sudden and somewhat inexplicable surge in interest in Casnewydd's Super Dragons. It was going to be the mother of all doddles . . . I could feel it in my designer Brecon Carreg bottled water.

Nevertheless, something, call it female intuition, call it a private eye's hunch, call it a sixth sense, call it what you will, made me pull out my mobile phone and dial. As my old mam used to say, you could never be too careful. An answer phone machine cut in. Normally, answer phones were one of my pet hates but on this occasion I was prepared to make an exception.

"Dan," I said, "it's Astrid, hope you and Gelert are both well. Look, I need your help. I'm following up a lead I've got in this case I'm pursuing. I need someone to cover my back just in case the worst comes to the worst. Can you stand by your telephone? If you don't hear from me within twenty-four hours, call the Republicans. If I phone you, or you phone me, and you hear me use the word Olwen in a phrase or sentence, call the Republicans – something will have gone badly wrong. If on the other hand, I use the code word Blodeuwedd, everything in Sophia Gardens will be lovely. If you get a text from me, one of those code words is going to be in it. Have you got that? Write it down, memorise it, don't forget it, it could be the difference between you and Gelert seeing me in one piece again or not. And Dan . . . if anyone other than me answers my phone, call the Republicans, remember, I'm counting on you."

I put the phone away and looked around me. As far as I could see, there still appeared to be no one around. John Uzzell Street seemed to have shut up shop for the night. To go in or not to go in? As somebody once said, that was the question. Somewhere in the far distance, I could hear the sound of dies being cast and armies crossing their own personal Rubicons.

Well, in for a penny, in for a Welsh pound. I crossed the road, whistling *Happy Days are here again* silently to myself. Inside the pub, I seemed to have the place more or less to myself. There was just one old bloke at the back of the pub, drinking cans out of a plastic bag and trying not to let the barman see him.

There was no one else about that I could see, apart from the barman himself, a doleful looking bloke with a drooping moustache who shot me a less than welcoming glance before retreating once more behind the pages of his *Welsh Bugle*. I walked towards him, casting an appreciative eye over the gleaming array of hand pumps with their enticing names, but I wasn't here to sample *The Lord Raglan's* beer.

"Has Michael Finn been in?" I said, by way of an icebreaker.

"What? Who?" he said, in a pronounced Maendy accent and reluctantly lowering the pages of his paper.

"Never mind," I said, "where's the clock?"

"Clock," he said, "clock, look around you, which one do you want?"

He was right. They were everywhere, big ones, small ones, some as big as your arm. Some detective I was, not to have noticed them straightaway. Memo to self, wake up Astrid, people are depending on you. That Amber Bernstein, that was some sense of humour she had.

"Pour me a pint of Old Gwentian," I said, "that always goes down well." The barman did as he was told and I took up a seat where, unlike Wild Bill Hickok, *my* back was against the wall and I had a clear view of anyone entering or leaving the pub. I pretended to take an interest in *Y Byd's* cryptic crossword whilst keeping my eyes and ears open. I'd like to say the beer was up there with the finest I'd ever tasted but it was passable at best. The workers in the business quarter obviously weren't the greatest connoisseurs of beer in the world.

When seven o'clock came, what seemed to be all the timepieces in the pub started chiming and booming out the hour. After that, time passed, as it was wont to do. The barman and I both perused our respective papers. I waited. Nothing happened. No sign of the mysterious Amber Bernstein. No sign of anyone in fact.

Then at 7.15 p.m. precisely, all the clocks went off again. Amidst all the cacophony I could faintly make out the sign of a telephone ringing, but it wasn't my mobile. It was the pub's telephone behind the bar. It rang and kept ringing. "Aren't you going to answer that?" I said.

Reluctantly, Speedy Gonzales picked up the still ringing phone. "Yes, this is *The Lord Raglan.* Who? What? Hang on a minute . . . I'll ask. It's for you," he said, proffering me the phone.

"Me?" I said, "but nobody . . ."

"You're the only one I can see carrying a rolled

up copy of *Y Byd*," he said, "speaking personally, I prefer *The Welsh Bugle*, there's a better class of article in the *Bugle*, I always find."

"Yeah, right," I thought, but I said nothing and took the phone.

"Yeah," I said, "who is this?"

"Augusta Hall?" said a voice I was beginning to know, a clear strong voice with just the faintest trace of a North Wales accent about it.

"Yes," I said, "who's this?" knowing full well who it was.

"There's been a change of plan, Augusta," said the voice, ignoring my question. "Amber can't make it tonight, sorry about that, she wants you to come out to Cwrt-y-bela instead. Know where that is? make sure you're there at 3.30 p.m. sharp tomorrow. She'll be expecting you. Make sure you're there on time, Amber likes people to be punctual."

"What, all the way up there," I nearly blurted out, before I stopped myself in the nick of time, having just realised I was supposed to be from Bangor, and wouldn't be expected to know where such a remote, out of the way place as Cwrt-y-bela was.

"Never heard of it," I said, "how do I get there?" but the voice seemed happy enough to give me directions and I made a show of repeating them two or three times. "Good," the voice said, "that's settled then. We'll look forward to seeing you tomorrow."

A thought suddenly occurred to me. One of those hunches I get from time to time . . . "Hey," I said, before the voice could ring off, "Your Amber Bernstein, she wouldn't by any chance be a George Formby fan, would she?"

"Why, Augusta," said the voice, "whatever gave you that idea?"

"Just a shot in the dark," I said, "I get them sometimes. Cwrt-y-bela it is, then."

There was no reply, only the sound of a mobile phone being switched off.

"Anybody interesting?" said the barman who did not appear in the least bit interested. "Only Kathryn Jenkins after my autograph," I said, "she will keep pestering me. Well, I'll be on my way, then, you know, things to do . . . "

"Yeah, sure," said the barman, "come again, do" and buried his head in the pages of his paper again.

I left the delights of *The Lord Raglan* behind me and stood on the pavement of John Uzzell Street mulling things over as to my next move, when my ears suddenly became aware of a discordant caterwauling coming my way. Two figures were coming towards me singing, if that was the right word, *We'll keep the Welsh flag flying high* – revellers, maybe? At first, I didn't take that much notice, but as they came nearer, I could see that they were dressed as David Lloyd George impersonators. Strange, I thought, the annual David Lloyd George convention had long since left town. Then they were upon me.

"Got a light, love?" said the first one in a voice that sounded vaguely familiar to me. It was a strong, clear voice with just the faintest trace of a North Wales accent about it. Where had I heard it before?

"Sorry, *Cariad*, the last time I smoked was behind the school bike sheds," I said.

Then the second impersonator chimed in. Whoever it was behind the Lloyd George mask there was the faint, but unmistakable, lingering smell of stale cigarette smoke coming from their direction. "You've dropped your keys, *Cariad*," she said, a woman's voice then, and, as she did so, there was the sound of something jangling to the ground behind me.

Instinctively, and without thinking, I turned to look in the direction of the sound. Big mistake. I felt, rather than heard, the blunt instrument crashing into the side of my head.

The last thing I remembered thinking was what a sucker I'd been to drop my guard like that. Then I was falling, falling from the top of Snowdon without a safety net to catch me, down into some deep, dark abyss of my own making.

CHAPTER 22

I was having the strangest dream. I was lying in a wood full of bluebells. Swallows were darting low over a nearby river, swishing and hurrying here and there, searching for food. What did it all mean? I had no idea and I couldn't ask Sigmund Freud or Carl Jung for an explanation —these people were never around when you wanted them.

Anyway, all of a sudden, the birds were gone and my favourite Columbian, Rodrigo Rodriguez, was pointing his gun at me and saying, "Everyone has a shelf life and yours; Señora, has just about reached its limit." It was only now I realised that he spoke with a pronounced lisp. Poseur, I thought, haven't you got anything better to do than threaten private detectives going about the course of their lawful business, but I said nothing. What was there to say? He was probably right. Meanwhile outside the open door, Sharona Haf was half humming, half singing *Ar Hyd y Nos,* or All Through the Night, to herself whilst sharpening one of her many knives from Solingen.

Then she stopped and looked at me. "You know too much about the Super Dragons and Madge Breese, Price, we can't possibly let you go. You'll have to die, won't she, Rodrigo?" The Colombian nodded and gave me a pitying look. Carefully, I considered my position. I wouldn't say things were bad exactly, but my prospects looked nowhere near as good as a wet weekend spent in Barry Island with no money and no prospects of any arriving soon.

Then Sharona and Rodriguez and their threats all disappeared from view and I was dozing desultorily for a while, drifting in and out of consciousness, until even I had to admit defeat and wake up. But I wasn't in my nice warm bed, safe above *The Lying Cod*, oh, no, I was somewhere I really didn't want to be, somewhere I would have preferred to avoid. And as for my head . . .

CHAPTER 23

It was beginning to get dark, how long I'd been out for, I didn't know. Slowly, and painfully, I became more aware of my surroundings. I was sitting in the passenger seat of a car and someone – who? Sharona? Rodriguez? The David Lloyd George impersonators? — had very thoughtfully done up my safety belt for me.

Gradually I began to realise that I wasn't the only person in the car. Oh, no. Sitting, or rather slumped, in the driving seat next to me, a great big handled knife protruding from his body, was a man whom I guessed to be in his mid to late fifties, a man whom I recognised . . . He was wearing a Panama hat over what I knew was a balding head. First Culloden Jimmie and now Red Iolo. Some person, or persons unknown, seemed to be systematically working their way through the leading lights of our local criminal underworld.

Then I became aware of another presence in the car beside Red Iolo and myself, it must have been my psychic side coming out, I suppose. I turned my head and looked around me. In the rear passenger seat behind Iolo was a big red teddy bear whom I didn't recognise. Just like Iolo, he didn't appear to be moving very much and, as I looked closer I could see some sort of note pinned to the teddy bear's body, a great big handled knife holding it in place, and on the note was

In the rear passenger seat behind lolo was a big red teddy bear

written in big black letters: 'unlike his friend, this one talked too much'. Well, well, well, I thought, somebody seems to have spending a lot of money on big handled knives lately.

I don't mind telling you, at this precise moment, I felt like putting my head in my hands and crying, either that or running from the scene as fast as I could, but somehow I resisted both these urges and forced myself to calm down. Think, Astrid, think. Keep that head up. *Nil Disperandum* etc. This was so obviously a set up — ten to one my fingerprints were all over the knife. For all I knew, they could have been all over the car as well. I pulled out a handkerchief and carefully and thoroughly wiped every available surface I could find.

It probably wouldn't be enough to prevent me getting another visit from Cymru's Finest —The Welsh Republican Police —but I had to try. Maybe it would be enough to distract their attention away from me, maybe they would have enough on their plate, with other fish to fry, to bother about me, but I wasn't going to count on it. Then I turned my attention to the knife and Red Iolo's body.

Sorry, Iolo, you weren't such a bad guy, I thought inwardly, as I tried to remove whatever prints of mine had been put on it by whoever had brought me here, but then, Iolo was probably past all caring now anyway. As I worked I became aware that the car looked vaguely familiar to me. Yes, that was it, this was the car which

Red Iolo had driven to Mrs Big's with me and Georg Alptraum and Monsieur Dieu as his passengers.

When I was satisfied and sure I was finished, I sat there for a while in silence, surveying my handwork and thinking. Someone, I thought, whilst trying to ignore the pain in my head, obviously had it in for me and mine, they had framed Stakis for the murder of Culloden Jimmie and now they were trying to frame me for the murder of Red Iolo. Yes, someone was out to get me, all right, but who and why? Who hadn't I sent any Christmas cards to lately?

For one brief moment I thought about setting the car on fire to really try and destroy any possible evidence against me, but then, not having smoked for years, I had nothing — no matches, no lighter, not even the proverbial two sticks to rub together and besides I didn't really fancy setting dead bodies alight —I didn't have the heart to do it.

Then, somewhere in the distance, I heard the faint sound of a police siren approaching and breaking in on my musings. Why did police cars always have to have their sirens on full blast to let the bad guys know they were coming, I thought, if anything it was counterproductive and rather giving the game away. Then I realised, they were coming for me. There was no time to lose, the way the Welsh Republican Police drove, they would be on me within minutes, if not seconds. I said a silent farewell to Red Iolo and the big red teddy bear and eased myself out of the car.

The sound of the sirens was getting nearer. I looked around me. To the left of the car I could see what looked like motorbike tracks leading away into the distance. Otherwise I was on a country road in what appeared to be the middle of nowhere. There were no houses, no farms, nothing I could see, no cover apart from a few straggly looking hedges. It seemed to me I was in the Cwrt-y-bela area of the Casnewydd City Limits, a wild and remote place, where few, if any, city dwellers went, if they could help it, but I couldn't be sure, I was still feeling none too good from the effects of the blow to my head and the shock of finding Red Iolo, a dead Red Iolo, sitting there beside me. Things were looking bleak.

What would Harry Houdini have done? As usual, the great man showed no signs of coming round the corner and enlightening me. Nothing for it, but to make up my own mind then. I didn't really have a great deal of choice. I could have ducked behind the nearest hedge I suppose, but didn't really fancy my chances, the Republicans would soon have flushed me out, and so I took the only course open to me. I started to run as fast as I could away from the sound of the oncoming sirens, hoping the discovery of the body would keep the Republicans off my track for a while at least.

Four or five minutes passed and I had slowed to a steady lope. Think of it as a training run, Astrid, I told myself, just another one of those daily keep fit sessions. I still didn't recognise where I was and there were no distinguishing landmarks to help me out, but at least I was putting some distance between myself and Red Iolo. Maybe I should have stuck around, spun the Republicans some yarn as to why I happened to be sitting in a car with a dead man and a teddy bear in the back seat. Maybe they would have believed me, maybe not. Too late now.

Why were there no signposts around here? I knew the Welsh Republic was suffering a severe financial squeeze and cuts were everywhere, but this was ridiculous. So far I seemed to be the only person on the road, no sound of any cars or buses or motorbikes, no cycles, nothing, not even a pair of roller skates. Good, that was the way I liked it. Good too, to know that all those years spent running the Casnewydd City Marathon had come in handy. The sound of the sirens seemed to have stopped; presumably the Republicans had found Iolo's dead body and were carrying out an investigation which, I hoped, would not be thorough enough to implicate me in any way.

I began to slow to a walk, the immediate danger seemed to be past at least for the time being. I would have to keep going until I came to a signpost, bus stop, or some other symbol of civilisation, something which would give me some kind of indication as to where exactly I was.

So I continued on my way for a while at least until, to my surprise, I came across a tree with an election poster taped to it – who would have put up an election poster in this Godforsaken place I wondered and stopped to take a closer look. The poster was exhorting me and anyone else who passed this way – not that would be very many I supposed – to put their cross on the ballot paper for Orson Workshy and The United Grafters' Party. It also gave brief details of the party's manifesto — if you could call it that. In spite of myself I became so engrossed in reading this nonsense that I forgot all about the Republicans and my attempts to get away from them and back to civilisation. Then I suddenly became aware of something — I sensed, rather than heard it, coming up behind me.

I turned, half expecting trouble, or at least the Republicans with a warrant for my arrest for murder, but instead I found myself looking at a shiny, gleaming new *Hebog* and a voice I thought I recognised telling me to "Jump on, Mrs Price, jump on."

CHAPTER 24

Well, to say I was surprised was an understatement; you could have knocked me down with a cromlech. I was looking straight at a motorbike rider wearing a futuristic looking dark helmet and around six feet in height by my best estimate. Very faintly, somewhere at the back of my brain, alarm bells began to ring. Where had I seen a *Hebog* recently? And in what circumstances? I had a vague memory . . . never mind, it would have to come to me later.

More pressingly, what if this guy was one of Mrs Big's minions sent with a gun and a silencer to give me a passport into the next world. I braced myself for whatever was coming next, do not go gently, Astrid . . . but when he pushed up his visor, I could see he was Edward Henry Davies who had started me out on this hunt for tangerine dress girl, a hunt which, so far at least, was proving pretty fruitless. What's more, and I still couldn't quite believe it, he was sitting astride the aforementioned brand new *Hebog* or Hawk.

No wonder I hadn't heard it coming up behind me, he must have switched on its built-in silencer. Perfected by Welsh scientists working out of the new hush hush research centre in Carmarthenshire, it was the latest technological marvel in what was proving to be a golden age for Welsh science and technology.

Motor biking circles were thrilled with it, but so far only a few had been made and it cost an absolute fortune to buy. If its rider wanted to, he, or she, could make the *Hebog* as silent as it was possible to get, you genuinely couldn't hear it approaching which is why the military were said to be very interested in developing its potential.

"What are you doing here?" I said, once I had recovered from my initial surprise.

"I could ask you the same question, Mrs Price," he said, "You're a long way from your usual city beat out here."

"I thought you were a penniless playwright," I said, "What are you doing on a bike like this?"

"Ah," he said, after what seemed to be a slight moment of hesitation, or maybe I was just seeing things that weren't there, "a rich aunt died and left me some money . . . I've always fancied one of these and, when the opportunity arose, well, I took it. I got it from Offa's Bikes. Do you like it?"

Fair enough, I thought, but I said, "yes, but what *are* you doing here and, more to the point, where is *here* anyway? I'm not sure I recognise this place at all."

"We're in Cwrt-y-bela, Mrs Price," he said, "one of the most wild and remote areas in the Casnewydd City limits. I would have thought an-on-the ball private eye like yourself would have known that."

Yeah, I thought, an-on-the-ball private eye like

myself should have known a lot of things, but I said, "yeah, of course, Cwrt-y-bela, I was acting on a tip off regarding your case, you know, Miss Tangerine Dress. The guy wouldn't tell me where we were going, blindfolded me and brought me here. Then he took off the blindfold, told me to wait here and said the contact I needed would be along in ten minutes. Well, an hour's gone by and no sign of anybody, until you showed up of course. I'm beginning to think the tip off has been having a little joke at my expense . . ."

"Anyway, if it's so wild and remote, why are you here then instead of pen pushing? Isn't there a drama about Aneurin Bevan, becoming Prime Minister of the United Kingdom, exercising your imagination and just itching to work its way out of your system?"

"You know, Mrs Price," he said, "you might be on to something there; I shall have to give the matter some serious thought. Anyway, jump on, unless you want to walk back to Casnewydd that is, there are no buses around here, you know, not even a Welsh Fargo one."

"Wait," I said, "did you pass anyone along the way? Or see anything unusual?"

"The Republicans, Mrs Price?" he said, "I heard their sirens, but saw no one. Why, are they after you?"

"No, no, of course not," I said, "let's get going then, shall we? I'm sure you've got things to be doing in Casnewydd."

"Yes," he said, "but before we go, is there any . . .

I mean, have you made any progress regarding my case, you know the girl in the tangerine dress?"

I was tempted to say none whatsoever, I've been too busy stumbling over dead bodies to pay much attention to girls, who may or may not still be in the Casnewydd area, and who may or may not still be wearing the same old tangerine dress they were last seen in weeks ago, but I didn't. Something told me that Tangerine Dress Girl had some part to play in all this — the dead Casnewydd gangsters, Stakis's wrongful arrest for murder, the attempt to frame me, the missing Super Dragons — the list seemed endless. So I came up with some anodyne, diplomatic explanation as to why I hadn't exactly been rooting up any trees lately in my pursuit of the mysterious Miss Tangerine Dress and it seemed to satisfy him, for the moment at least.

"You can drop me off at the Chartist Mural," I said, "I can walk the rest of the way, it's not far and I need to think."

The journey back to Casnewydd took no time at all on the *Hebog* and I was soon waving goodbye to Edward Henry Davies, promising faithfully to get in touch as soon as I had any news of Tangerine Dress Girl. I walked the remaining streets back to *The Lying Cod*, not really caring whether anybody was following me or not. As I opened the door to the fish shop and prepared to mount the stairs to my flat, Big Zorba, Stakis's cousin, gave me a cheery wave from behind the counter but it wasn't the same without Stakis himself being there . . .

I pushed open the door to my flat to find a whole stack of bills and election literature waiting for me there on the mat. I threw it a cursory glance — it was the usual stuff, *Get President Hopkin Elected Again, Vote Those Were The Days, You Know It Makes Sense* plus a whole pile of leaflets from all the other competing parties. Too tired to pick them up, I left them where they were, littering the floor. Then I lay down on the bed, close to tears. The way I felt now I couldn't face another visit from the Welsh Republican Police and the dynamic duo Sergeant and Pritchard. I had had enough of those two for a while. By now their forensics team must surely have gone through that car and Red Iolo's body with the finest of fine tooth combs and although I had tried very hard to remove any trace of my presence in that car, I had been in a rush and must almost certainly have missed something.

Again, I felt like crying, everything was piling up, I was getting nowhere with the case, I was a useless private dick, I had failed Stakis . . . failed everybody. Stakis. My feeling sorry for myself wasn't going to do him any good, was it. In a bid to cheer myself up, I ran a bath, lit some aromatherapy candles, got out the fine smelling soaps and let the warm, luxuriating water flow over me, easing all the stresses and tensions of the day out of my body. If I'd still been smoking (I hadn't for years) I would have lit a cigarette as well, though I stopped short of adding a rubber ducky to the proceedings. I thought about turning the radio on, maybe there would be some soothing Welsh *Fado* music playing on one of the stations to ease my troubled mind, but decided against it, I needed to concentrate. What had I learned today? That somebody was out to get me and would stop at nothing to incriminate me and mine in their nefarious web —but why? As usual I had no clue.

And how was I going to prove Stakis's innocence. I knew he was about as capable of committing murder as I was of painting one of Kyffin Williams's Snowdon mountain scenes on the back of a cardboard box, but that wouldn't cut much ice with the judges. I had to come up with something soon, time was running short.

Then there was the possibility that Edward Henry Davies, my alternative playwright, might not be all that he seemed. What exactly had he been doing up there in the wilds of Cwrt-y-bela and why? Soaking luxuriously, I pondered this question and a few others that had been troubling me for a while.

For some reason, it all seemed somehow interconnected — the missing Super Dragons, Madge Breese and her recording of the National Anthem, the murders and the related attempts to frame me and Stakis for them, Mrs Big and her criminal henchmen, Tangerine Dress Girl and Sharona Haf — it was all threatening to get too much for me if I didn't bring it under control. I ran some more hot water into the bath and tried to relax.

Just who was Tangerine Girl and what was her role in all of this? Were she and Sharona Haf one and the same person? What was Caratacus ap Cadwaladr's role in all this? Was he just an innocent performance poet with a penchant for dodgy girlfriends? Or something more sinister? A lot more sinister? I took my feet out of the water, placed them on the edge of the bath, leant back and pondered some more. The answers still weren't coming.

CHAPTER 25

I was sleeping the sleep of the just . . . I was having this delicious dream in which, for once, I got to be the one holding all the shooters and lording it over the bad guys who hurried to answer my every whim. I was on the point of telling them what to do next, waving my guns in the air, as I did so, when I suddenly became dimly aware of a loud and insistent knocking, not in my dream, you understand, but somewhere not very far away from me, a banging which seemed to be getting louder and louder.

Reluctantly, I switched on the bedside lamp and looked at my alarm clock. 4 a.m. 4 o'clock in the morning. Who could possibly be banging on my door at this time? As if I didn't know and then, as if to confirm my worst fears, PC Pritchard's voice coming through loud and clear. "Open up, Price, this is the Welsh Republican Police. We know you're in there," it seemed to be saying to me in my rather confused state.

Was this why they made these visits in the middle of the night when you were disorientated and still half asleep—so that they could catch you out with awkward questions when your brain wasn't functioning properly? I decided to stall.

"Hang on, can't you," I said, "it's the middle of the night. I need to brush my hair, wash my face, put some clothes on. Give a lady some space, won't you?"

Then came Sergeant's voice. "You've got five minutes, Price," it said, "then we're breaking down the door, ready or not." And it sounded as if he meant it.

Hurriedly, I splashed some water on my face, dragged a brush through my hair and pulled on a dressing gown. It wasn't great but, under the circumstances, it would have to do. Then, and only then, did I open the door to my unwelcome visitors.

Instead of the two I was expecting, there were three of them. Yes, Sergeant and Pritchard were there but they had a woman with them — a WPC, a woman so tall and thin, she looked as if she were walking on stilts. For some reason I couldn't quite figure out, she looked strangely familiar to me. Anyway, the three of them barged their way past me into the room without so much as a "Good morning, Mrs Price," or "hello, Astrid, sorry to disturb your beauty sleep."

"Inspector Sergeant, PC Pritchard, how nice to see you again," I said, "but what would Lawyer Frost have to say about such a visit at this time of the morning and who's your little friend, if I may ask." Then I looked at the woman more closely, the rugby ball dropped and I knew where I had seen her before. "'Stilts'," I said, "Tall Girl, what are you doing here? I haven't seen you since the last time you played second row for us in the Welsh Women's Rugby Team."

'Stilts' or Tall Girl looked at me coolly but then, it was all coming back to me now, you could never really call us the best of friends, she was a forward, I was one of the 'fancy dan' backs and an outside half at that and never the twain . . . "It's WPC Sempringham now, Astrid, or perhaps I should call you Mrs Price, now I'm on official business," she said, "WPC Gwenllian Sempringham and proud to wear the uniform of the Welsh Republican Police."

Of course, Gwenllian Sempringham. Her name was a bit of a mouthful even back then and the obvious move would have been to call her Gwen, but we, being rugby players, had to go one better and give her a nickname and, because of her physical stature, Tall Girl or 'Stilts' was the one that had stuck.

"Yeah, yeah," said Pritchard, rudely interrupting my reverie, "let's skip the Old Welsh Rugby Girls reunion act and let's get down to business, shall we? Why did you kill Red Iolo, Price, what had he ever done to you?"

I stared at Pritchard in disbelief. "What are you talking about?" I said, "I haven't seen Red Iolo since he drove me to Mrs Big's house along with that German gangster guy and the French assassin."

"Then why were your finger prints all over the car in which we found his dead body? And what exactly were you doing out there, far from home, in Cwrt-y-bela?" said Inspector Sergeant.

Now I knew they were on unsure ground —I had done a pretty fair job of removing any traces of my prints from that car, at the most, I must have missed only a few of my prints when I was cleaning up.

"What would I be doing all the way out there?" I said, "in that Godforsaken place? You'll be saying I'm a regular visitor to out of the way places like Caer Llwynog next. No, I'm a Casnewydd girl. I rarely stray outside the Casnewydd City Limits. Well, apart from the occasional, reluctant foray to the Twin City of Maendy, of course. You can ask Stakis. He'll tell you . . ." And then I remembered. "If he were here, of course."

The inspector laughed, a short, sharp laugh, but there was no mirth behind the sound. "But he isn't, is he, as you very well know, he's enjoying the hospitality of the Welsh Republic at the moment. And even if he were here, that argument wouldn't hold water, Price," he said, "as if Stakis wouldn't crawl through an Hieronymus Bosch inspired vision of hell on his hands and knees just to get to you. Everyone knows that. No, try again, Price, you'll have to do better than that . . . we're looking for more reliable witnesses than Mr Stakis Theodorakis."

"Does that mean I can't see Stakis tomorrow, then, Inspector?" I said.

"I don't see why not, not that it'll do you much good, I should have thought. We've got him bang to rights, his prints are all over that knife we found him with," Sergeant said, "but I'm a fair man, if you really want to see him, be at the station, nine o'clock sharp, we'll have an officer waiting for you . . ."

Well, after that, they kept on trying to grill me, and get me to confess to the killing of Red Iolo, and a host of other unsolved crimes they were trying to solve, but I batted away all their deliveries, insisting that even if my fingerprints were in Red Iolo's car, this was only because he had once driven me to Mrs Big's mansion, and what in Cymru's name would I be doing in Cwrt-y-bela anyway, and, eventually, after what seemed like hours, but was probably only around forty-five minutes, they gave up and left me in peace with a stern warning not to leave those Casnewydd City Limits I professed to be so fond of and a parting shot of "We'll get you, Price, you see if we don't," from my dearest friend PC Richard Pritchard.

By the time they left it was hardly worth going back to bed, so I didn't. Instead, I went through my usual morning routine, showering, eating; teeth cleaning etc, although I had to practically force the food down me, my appetite was still inside the Welsh Republican Police Headquarters, Casnewydd along with Stakis . . . Poor Stakis, I hadn't been very good to him, had I, but I was about to make it up to him, even if only in a very small way . . .

CHAPTER 26

I left *The Lying Cod* bright and early and in time for my appointment at the Welsh Republican Police Station. To my surprise, 'Stilts' was at the reception desk waiting for me, together with another male officer I didn't know.

"'Stilts'," I said, "I mean, Tall Girl, I mean WPC Sempringham, I didn't expect to see you here so early, especially after your late night visit yesterday."

She smiled, a bleak, wan smile. "You know how it is," she said, "duty calls."

Doesn't it just, I thought, but I said, "I've come to see Stakis, I mean the prisoner, Stakis Theodorakis."

"I know, Astrid, I mean, Mrs Price," she said, "I've been told to take you down there and wait with you whilst you speak to him. Come with me, please." She came out from behind the desk and we descended together into the bowels, I mean down three or four flights, of the Welsh Republican Police station till we came to the block of cells. Once there she whipped out a bunch of keys and opened the third door on the left.

Stakis was sitting there on the bed, looking lost and forlorn. He looked up and saw me and an expression of pure joy crossed his careworn face.

"Astrid," he said, "I'm so glad to see you. The food here in this Welsh Republican Police Station is terrible, worse even than that stuff they gave me **Stakis**

Stakis was sitting there on the bed, looking lost and forlorn

that house in Cwm Hyfryd."

"That's what I came to talk to you about, Stakis," I said. "That house in Cwm Hyfryd. The people who held you prisoner there, what sort of things did they talk about? You know Mrs Big and Sharona Haf — when they weren't singing and playing the ukulele. Was that poet —Caratacus ap Cadwaladr —was he ever there?"

"But I thought you came to get me out of here," he said, "that's what you came for, isn't it? What about my application for bail? What's Lawyer Frost doing?"

"Lawyer Frost is doing his best," I said, "the thing is, Stakis," I said, "with all these new emergency laws the government has brought in, nobody's getting any bail at the moment. You'll just have to hang on in there for a while longer, Stakis."

For a moment, I thought he was going to cry, but he seemed to pull himself together, and I ploughed on. "That's why I've come to see you," I said, "I want to get you out, of course I do, Big Zorba does his best, but *The Lying Cod's* not the same without you, old friend. I need to ask you about your time in Cwm Hyfryd to see if you can tell me anything that might help me with my investigations."

"Well, they did say something about not being able to find The Welsh National Anthem," he said, "they kept saying they were looking for it, but couldn't find it anywhere or something like that. It sounded like a load of old rubbish to me. To tell you the truth, after a while, I just switched off and stopped listening to what they were saying, I just wanted to get out of there."

"But did they mention any names at all, Stakis," I said. "Think, man, think. This just might be important. Did they say anything at all about Madge Breese whilst you were there?"

"Who? Madge who? Didn't you hear me, Astrid? After a while I just gave up on what they were talking about and retreated into my own thoughts. I told you that already. Wait a minute though, I seem to remember there was one name they mentioned quite a lot," he said. "What was it again? Dostoevsky? Tchaikovsky? Lermontov? It's no good, it's gone. I don't know, it sounded Russian to me, maybe Polish, perhaps, something Slav, anyway. Or was it Bulgarian, I don't know. You know me, Astrid, all these foreign names sound the same to me."

"Time's up," said 'Stilts', "you'll have to go now, Astrid, I'm afraid."

"Just one more minute," said Stakis, "please," and then to me, "what about that new guy then, Astrid?"

"What new guy?" I said.

"You know the one I mean," he said, "that bloody soldier who was with you in the house in Cwm Hyfryd. Strideri or Ryderi, or whatever his name is, does he mean anything to you?"

"Oh, you mean, Lieutenant Pryderi," I said, "why,

he's just a friend like Daniel Rowlands, you know, The Bird Man."

"I've seen you look at him, Astrid, remember," he said "and it's not the way you look at The Parrot Man."

"Aw, Stakis," I said, "you know I love you . . ."

"That's what you say," he said, "but it's not the way you look at me either, Astrid, it's different." And then, desperately, a fierce whispering into my ear, "Get me out of here, Astrid, please. You can take her, I know you can, I can put her uniform on and we can walk out of here together. Then I can help you solve the case . . ."

"Sorry, old friend," I said, "I can't do that, you know, I can't."

"Hey, you two," said 'Stilts', "no whispering. You know the rules, Theodorakis. Come on Astrid, time's up."

"I have to go," I said to Stakis, "keep your spirits up. Hold that head high. We, I, we're going to get you out of here. Remember that. You've been a great help. I'll be in touch."

"What was that all about then?" said 'Stilts' as we climbed the stairs back to the top of the building.

"What was what all about?" I said.

"You know, all that whispering going on between you two at the end there."

"Oh that," I said, "I'm very much afraid Stakis is feeling a bit alone and confused at the moment. He wanted me to go and lay some flowers on his mother's grave, bit of a tall order, I'm afraid as she's buried in

Greece somewhere . . . now where was that exactly?"

"Strange," said 'Stilts', "and there was I thinking he was asking you to 'take me out' and help him make his great escape out of here."

"Take you out, Gwenllian," I said, "why I wouldn't know where to start."

"Oh, I think you would, Astrid," she said, "I think you would, all right . . . " and with that she left me standing there to ponder my thoughts, such as they were.

CHAPTER 27

Outside, the sun was blistering down out of a hot, hot sky on to man (and woman and child of course) and beast below. It was going to be another fine day, a day for visiting the beach, talking to friends, sitting outside with a relaxing drink, leisurely walking in the countryside or just pottering around in the back garden, doing what you wanted to, in short, all the civilised joys of modern life but none of that applied to me today, I could not afford to spend the time daydreaming, lazing on a sunny afternoon, oh, no, I had other things to do, had another errand to perform, another task I had to carry out that I wasn't remotely looking forward to in the slightest.

I put the *Pwca* into first and rapidly ramped up the gears as I accelerated away to my next destination. What if Stakis was right, I thought, what if I were falling for Pryderi? I hardly knew the man, knew next to nothing about him in fact and didn't I have enough on my Wedgwood dinner plate as it was without complicating matters further with a possible romantic interest? Anyway, who knew what his feelings were towards me?

Stakis's state of health was beginning to bother me too, he had looked really down, just now, in that police cell. He must have been desperate to try to get me to take out 'Stilts' and help him escape. I was no expert but was he perhaps suffering from post traumatic stress disorder after his experiences in Cwm Hyfryd? I would have to get Lawyer Frost to see if he could take in a medical expert to inspect him when he next visited.

Whilst driving and thinking, I kept casting the occasional glance in my rear view window, just in case anyone was following me, force of habit, I suppose, but either all was clear or I was losing my grip. I took a few wrong turnings and detours and speeded up and slowed down just to be sure, but again nothing seemed to be untoward.

Now came that part of the day I wasn't looking forward to one little bit. It was one of the hardest things I had ever had to do, but it had to be done. I had phoned ahead to say I was coming and the front door was open, no need to knock.

After the formalities were over, the how are yous etc, the polite offers of tea and biscuits just as politely declined, I got straight down to business. "I'm sorry for your loss," I said. "Really sorry, believe me, but is there anything you can tell me that might help me find the people who took Jimmie from you and from this world? Did he ever say anything about The Welsh National Anthem for example. Or Madge Breese? Or anyone with a Slav sounding surname? Try to think. It sounds random but the answers to these questions might turn out to be quite important."

Mrs Culloden Jimmie folded her hands and

looked at me. "I can't really recall anything, Mrs Price," she said, "as I told you before, he never really talked to me about his 'work'. Didn't want to get me involved, he always said. I'm sorry I can't be more helpful . . . "

"That's all right," I said, "if you do think of anything, anything at all, even if it seems unimportant, do get in touch, it could be of use—you know where to find me now?"

"Yes," she said, "I've got your card in a safe place. Wait a minute, what did you say about Slav sounding surnames? One night, a few weeks back, I just happened to overhear Jimmie talking to one of his cronies on the phone and there was one name that cropped up a couple of times in the conversation. What was it now? Oh, I've got a memory like a sieve nowadays—something like Cybulski or Lewandowski, maybe? Or was it Andrzej Wajda? Could it have been Zbigniew Lewandowski or Robert Cybulski? Or maybe the other way around? I might not even be pronouncing it right. My Slav languages are a bit rusty, you know."

Her pronunciation sounded all right to me, but what did I know? I struggled at times with Welsh and English, for starters, let alone anything beyond the borders of the Welsh Republic. Whoever this mysterious Slav guy was and he was fast acquiring a multitude of different names on my travels, somehow I didn't think I was going to glean anything more from this interview. I rose to go. "Don't worry," I said, "that'll give me something to work on, another piece in the jigsaw. I'll be on my way, then, if you need anything, anything at all, don't hesitate to contact me. And the Republicans are on the case now, as well. I'm sure they'll . . ."

"The Republicans . . ." she almost spat out the word. "You and I both know, Mrs Price, that the Republicans have little or no intention of wasting their time looking for the person who . . . Find whoever killed Culloden, Mrs Price, find them and bring them to justice, that's all I ask," she said. "He was a bastard, but he was *my* bastard."

I nodded. "I'll do my best," I said, even though I knew it was a tall order. Well, what would you have done? Mrs Culloden Jimmie looked rough, really rough, rougher than the roughest diamond you could imagine, but I saw through her restless, unprepossessing exterior. Underneath beat a proverbial heart of gold, just made for Neil Young to sing about. I made my excuses and left before I saw her start to cry. Her last words before I left were, "He wasn't likely to get a pension in his line of work, was he now?" No, I thought, as I closed the front door behind me, leaving the freshly minted widow to her overwhelming grief and her memories, he surely wasn't.

CHAPTER 28

I drove back to *The Lying Cod* and busied myself with preparations for the trip to Cwrt-y-bela Farm — hoping to banish all negative thoughts from my mind – they weren't doing me or Stakis any good. Before leaving, just to be on the safe side, you understand, I placed a golden yellow daffodil motif brooch (courtesy of my friend from Aberbargoed) in my hair because I wanted to look good and because I *was* worth it and most of all, because it might come in handy later on, you never knew, although I really, really didn't want to use it, if I could at all help it. Anyway, I also put on two rings, also especially made by my man in Aberbargoed, one on each hand, one featuring a red dragon rampant and the other a map of our beloved Cymru, just in case—you never knew when those two babies might come in handy.

When I thought I was good and ready, I said a final Good Luck prayer to myself and closed the door behind me. As I went down the stairs, I passed on the chip butty Big Zorba offered me, by way of lunch on the move, as he prepared to start life standing in for Stakis, until he was released, if he ever was, if I could fill in the missing holes in the jigsaw puzzle to get him out of Welsh Republican police custody. If, if, if . . . I climbed into the *Pwca* and got my motor running. Just like Canned Heat I was on the road again. I was on the road again.

The tide was up on the Brown River and two mallard drakes were chugging gallantly along, the second one some distance behind the other, but catching up gradually. They hugged the shoreline, whilst in the middle of the river an abandoned tyre floated serenely upstream without a care in the world. All of a sudden I felt just like that second duck, always destined to be playing catch-up, always fated to be one step behind. Somewhere high above, a small aeroplane was heading towards its destination, wherever that was. Over the Cardiff Channel to England perhaps?

The news coming over the radio did nothing to improve my mood. Reports were coming in that the rivers were at a very low level, if not almost dry, some of them, and I wasn't in the least bit surprised. Even the trees were beginning to wilt and beg for mercy. I felt hot, hot, hot, hot and sticky. I wanted to stand in a cold shower, I wanted to pour cool, refreshing water all over me, I wanted to take a drink to ease my thirst, but I had to keep going, I had work to do, places to go and people to find, that was what I was being paid for. Boy, but it was hot, hot, hot. It was so hot that if I'd wanted to I could have done the old fried egg on the pavement trick. If I'd wanted to . . . but I had other things on my mind, like where was my next clue coming from . . . did I say it was hot? I should have been on the nearest beach wearing my best bikini, polishing my tan. I should have been out in a boat on the Caerdydd/Cardiff Channel, as we were now having to call what used to be called the Bristol Channel, but I wasn't, I was here sweltering in the hot sun, driving my *Pwca* towards Cwrt-y-bela Farm, hoping to stumble across some clues, any clues that would help me forward in this most intransigent of cases. No doubt about it, I had those summertime blues.

It could have been worse, I suppose, at least I wasn't breaking any rocks in the hot sun, but driving along Gareth Bale Boulevard trying not to think of the Caerdydd Channel and the Welsh Sea and all these other new names for everything we were having to get used to.

I picked up the phone and dialled an old estate agent friend of mine, Désirée Protheroe, whom I had known since we were girls together in Craig yr Haul High School, and who had helped me out in a previous case when I had become embroiled in searching for a pair of Golden Lovespoons.

"Hey, Désirée," I said, "it's Astrid, I need some help. Can I pick your brains?"

Désirée's North Wales accented tones came trickling down the line like melting honey. It made me feel quite homesick.

"All right, Astrid?" she said, "What do you want now, you only ever ring me when you want something."

"Désirée," I said, "how can you say such a thing, but now you mention it, there is just one little question I wanted to ask you. What can you tell me about Cwrt-y-bela Farm?"

"Have you never heard of client confidentiality, Astrid," she said, "we're not supposed to give out information over the phone to anyone, especially prying private eyes like yourself."

"Aw, come on, Désirée," I said, "what's the harm in a little gossip between friends. Besides, you know me; I only have my fellow citizens' best interests at heart. And anyway, this could help me crack a most difficult case."

"Oh, all right, then," she said, "as it's you. Cwrt-y-bela, Cwrt-y-bela, give me a minute" and there was the sound of papers rustling, Then Désirée came back on the line. "Sixteenth century farmhouse" she said, "with a lot of traditional features, been on the market for a while, but let quite recently. Somebody from the North, I believe, the Bangor area. From what the locals say, whoever's taken the property likes to keep themselves to themselves, although there's been a lot of coming and going apparently. At all hours of the day and night apparently — even during curfew. Why so interested? The country wouldn't suit you, Astrid. You're a city girl."

"Thanks, Désirée," I said, "you've been a great help as always. We really must have that drink together sometime."

"Yeah, right," said Désirée, "just as long as it's not propping up the bar in *The Clinging Man*," and hung up.

CHAPTER 29

Cwrt-y-bela —the Court of the pine marten – never mind, the pine marten, I was going to have to be pretty agile myself on this one. For a start, I needed to tell someone where I was going, so that, if things did go wrong, they could alert the Republicans. In the past I had always used Stakis, but it was no good calling him, he was locked up somewhere deep in the dungeons of the Welsh Republican Police Headquarters, Casnewydd.

I needed to arrange a code word again with someone, so they would know everything was all right or vice versa. I wanted to try Pryderi, but I hadn't heard from him for days and he would be Cymru knows where now, probably somewhere on manoeuvres along the border with England or, for all I knew, camping out by the Irish, sorry, the Welsh, Sea and besides it was definitely more than his job was worth to be involved any further with me. And anyway, I didn't have his number, did I? I didn't know Edward Henry Davies well enough to trust him; It was no good asking the Republicans; they would just laugh me out of court and tell me where to go.

That left only the Parrot Man, Daniel Owen. I dialled his number.

"Look, Dan," I said, after the opening formalities, enquiring after each other's health and asking after

That left only the Parrot Man, Daniel Owen. I dialled his number

Gelert's health were over, "I'm going to Cwrt-y-bela Farm, I'm following up a lead I've got in this case I'm pursuing. I'll be taking the *Pwca*. I need someone to cover my back just in case the worst comes to the worst.

"Can you stand by your telephone? If you don't hear from me within twenty-four hours, call the Republicans. I know I've told you all this before, but If I phone you, or you phone me, and you hear me use the codeword, I think we're going to need a new one, just in case—let's just say if I use Flat Holm in a phrase or sentence, call the Republicans – something will have gone badly wrong. If on the other I use the code word Steep Holm, everything in Sophia Gardens will be lovely. If you get a text from me, one of those code words is going to be in it. Have you got that? Write it down, memorise it, don't forget it, it could be the difference between you and Gelert seeing me in one piece again or not. And Dan . . . if anyone other than me answers my phone, call the Republicans, remember, I'm counting on you."

"Yeah, I've got all that" he said, "all written down and remembered. But shouldn't I come with you, two heads are better and all that sort of stuff . . ."

"Thanks, Dan," I said, "I appreciate that, but it's no good the two of us walking into a potential trap, at the moment you're more use to me where you are. I plan to reconnoitre the place later this afternoon, see how the land lies. Then I'll make a decision whether or not to keep the appointment tomorrow. And Dan, ring me every hour, on the hour within reason. Now go and look after those parrots of yours. Love to Gelert."

Somewhere between the Crindau roundabout and the Eglwysnewydd turnoff my phone rang. Strictly speaking, this was an illegal manoeuvre while driving, but, what the hell, there was nobody about and everyone else was doing it all the time anyway. "Hello," said a voice I didn't recognise but which, somehow, still sounded vaguely familiar, it sounded like a man's voice, but it also sounded muffled as if whoever was calling, was speaking through a handkerchief. "Is that Astrid Price, the private detective?"

"Yes," I said, "who is it? What do you want? Look, if it's about that outstanding tax bill, my cheque's in the post . . ."

"Mrs Price," said the voice, sounding more muffled than ever, "whatever you do, don't go down to Cwrt-y-bela Farm. They're . . ."

"Why not?" I said, "and who are they?" but the unknown caller had hung up, or maybe somebody else had hung up for them. As I continued on my way to the isolated, remote farmhouse the road signs became fewer and fewer and my mood became more and more melancholy. Up here they were a different breed I found myself musing. Up here, the City might not even exist; such was the all-pervading sense of isolation.

What were those instructions the voice on the

telephone had given me again? Turn left at T*he Coal Miners' Arms,* go right at *The Melted Cheese Inn* and then carry on, straight ahead, for the next two or three miles until I came to a fork in the road. It was all pretty flat up here, I said to myself, not much cover for any self respecting private dick, aiming to creep up on his or her quarry unawares.

Then suddenly the *Pwca* rounded a corner and I could see a building —what was that Désirée had said, something about a sixteenth century farmhouse — stretched out in front of me about two or three miles away. This must be it. There was nothing else for miles. I brought the *Pwca* to a halt, time for some serious thinking. What to do now? Well, there were a number of possibilities that occurred to me. I could either carry on driving and head straight for the farmhouse, test out their defences, as it were, ring their bell and come up with some sob story, like could I please have a glass of water, the heat was really getting to me, or put on my best Belfast accent, tell them I was lost and could they please, please help me out, but then, that ran the risk of whoever was inside the farmhouse, if there was anybody inside the farmhouse, recognising me and maybe detaining me against my will with perhaps some malice aforethought and I didn't want that.

Or I could forget about the farmhouse for today at least, turn the car round, head back to the bright lights of Casnewydd as fast as I could and consider my best course of action over an Astrid special or two. In the end and, after giving all the various possibilities very careful consideration, I decided I had come all this way, so I might as well drive a mile or so extra further down the road and take a closer look at Cwrt-y-bela Farm.

Then, I stopped the car again, got out and trained my high powered binoculars on the object of my interest. It was then that I became aware of the all embracing silence, a silence which was strangely overwhelming, almost oppressive, there were no birds to be heard, no blackbirds singing, no thrushes calling, no sparrows chirping, not even a crow caw-cawing, nothing.

It looked like the birds were giving this place a wide berth. Maybe it was a signal for me to do the same . . .

CHAPTER 30

And why would there be birds singing? There were no hedges, no trees, no nothing, no cover for miles around. And why would anyone build a farmhouse way out here? It was not a place I would want to spend much of my time. In spite of myself, I shuddered involuntarily. Get a grip on yourself, Astrid, I said to myself, focus on the job in hand . . .

Unless, of course, it was because of its proximity to the sea . . . The sea, The Welsh Sea, as we now had to call the stretch of water between Holyhead and Dublin, Fishguard and Rosslare, after the latest presidential decree. Ideal for smuggling goods and people in from the North of the Republic, especially if you did not want to attract the attention of the authorities. It made sense now I came to think of it —was that what Mrs Big and her cohorts were up to at Cwrt-y-bela farmhouse? If indeed Mrs Big and her cohorts were still in the South. For all I knew they might have left for Bangor and the North days ago.

I was looking at a long, low, black and white framed, one-storey Tudor farmhouse with a few outbuildings alongside. There appeared to be no one about, no sign of life, although there was one car parked outside what seemed to be the main entrance. For all I knew, there may have been others parked inside those

I was looking at a one-storey Tudor farmhouse

outbuildings or, more worryingly, other vehicles coming back to the house just as I was here, alone and isolated in this desolate country, looking to see what I could see. Maybe, they were just around the corner, heading for me as I continued to scan the building.

There was also a nagging doubt in the back of my mind, growing bigger by the minute, here was I scrutinising the farmhouse through my binoculars —who was to say there wasn't someone inside the place doing the same to me? I switched the binoculars to long distance camera mode and took a few shots of Cwrt-y-bela farmhouse, something to refresh my memory for later on. Then I got back in the *Pwca* and returned the way I had come, glad to get out of there and just a little, a tiny little bit wiser.

On the way home, the M Pedwar (M4) Motorway was solid, bumper to bumper. I had plenty to think about, as I waited for the traffic to move, like how in Cymru's name was I going to get anywhere near that farmhouse without being spotted? It was possibly, make that probably, bristling with Mrs Big's minions always anxious to help me on my way to the next world, if she gave the word. It needed a military mastermind, it needed a Pryderi that would come up with a workable plan. Pryderi. Ah, Pryderi . . . Cymru alone knew where he was. For a brief moment I thought of sending the Parrot Man up there to try the glass of water/I'm lost in the wilderness trick and see what he could see but I almost immediately dismissed the motion. I'd already lost Stakis and it wouldn't do to send another amateur to do my dirty work for me.

As I left the motorway and drove further along The Brown River, back towards *The Lying* Cod and home, I saw a blue balloon floating down stream plus a few jackdaws foraging at the water's edge where the mud gave way to a sparse collection of stony outcrops and small, half-filled pools. Were they trying to tell me something? Perhaps they were. Keep going, never give up, the answer is there somewhere, if you are just patient enough to carry on digging for it. But enough of such musings. I was beginning to depress myself, not an unusual occurrence, I must say, but now wasn't the time for fits of melancholy. Keep a clear head, Astrid, get a grip, Concentrate on the weather, yes, that was it; take my mind off more pressing matters. I threw a brief glance out of the *Pwca's* window. It was the sort of day you would spend time in the frozen foods or milk and yoghurt section of the supermarket, just to keep cool.

Which reminded me, I was running low on supplies. Well, even a detective has to eat. And cook, and clean, and wash up, and pay the bills. I was beginning to depress myself again, so I pulled the *Pwca* into one of those pile 'em high and flog 'em cheap discount joints — Waldi — its sign with its sausage dog motif was hanging limply in the heat, put my one Glyndwr coin in the trolley and wheeled my way round the brightly lit parallel aisles full of products the supermarket hoped would attract my attention.

But I had a list of items inside my head. Bread, check, potatoes, check, milk, check, fruit and veg ditto, something to drink and one or two special treats maybe, this was turning into one quest I was getting the hang of. Anyway, I cruised the aisles on autopilot, putting stuff in, taking it out again, looking at labels, vaguely thinking about what I was going to eat that night and how long it was going to take me to prepare and not really concentrating on anything really when I suddenly became half aware of the couple in front of me.

She was wearing a rock, the size of Gibraltar, or maybe even bigger, on her left hand and her hair was dyed a strange mixture of garish frijid pink and shocking blue, while he had dark, wavy hair and a brownish black goatee beard and looked about twenty-five or twenty-six years old, twenty-eight maybe, at a pinch.

It didn't need a Captain Hastings or a Dr Watson to tell me I was looking straight at that lovely couple otherwise known as Sharona Haf and Caratacus ap Cadwaladr. Now, I could have performed a citizen's arrest upon the two of them, I suppose, but I wasn't exactly anxious that they should see me. The trouble was your average supermarket is not exactly chock full of places to hide, especially your pile 'em high, flog 'em cheap variety.

Just like those tired of life people running from

the bulls in Pamplona, I might very soon be on the horns of a dilemma. Any minute now, either Sharona Haf or Caratacus ap Cadwaladr, or both together, were going to turn round and see me. And then what would we do — engage in civilised conversation about the weather? Discuss the latest edition of *Poetry Cymru*? Maybe rubbish all those poor poems the editor of this month's *New Cymru Review* had chosen to feature? Somehow, I doubted it. Where were those dark glasses and blond wig when I needed them. In desperation, I plucked a box of cereal from the nearest shelf and placed it in front of my face, pretending to study the list of ingredients intently.

But I needn't have worried. The gruesome twosome were so wrapped up in each other, pawing one another incessantly and gazing fondly into each other's eyes that I could have probably driven past in a 4x4, playing *Women of Harlech* at full blast and they wouldn't have noticed. Think, Astrid, think. Sooner or later, lover boy and girl were going to snap out of it and take an interest in their surroundings, namely me.

What to do? Confront them? Call the Welsh Republican Police on my mobile? Tackle them (both literally and metaphorically)? What would Inspector Morse and Lewis have done? Cymru alone knew. I would have to shift for myself. I did the only thing possible. Or rather, the only thing that occurred to me at the time. Still holding the cereal packet in front of me, I advanced towards 'Bonnie and Clyde.' "Excuse me, please," I said in my best 'posh bird', voice, ready for their inevitable reaction but they just stood aside to let me pass without so much as a glance in my direction.

So far, so very, very good. Now to get out of there and, once the pair got into their car, discreetly follow them to wherever they were headed. I got through the checkout without any undue alarums – nobody recognised me, nobody called my name, nobody said "reach for the sky, Price" and I made my way to the *Pwca* and proceeded to load the groceries into the boot of the Pwca. That done, I turned and started to walk towards the driver's seat, but I never made it . . .

CHAPTER 31

"Not that car, Price, this car, get in, won't you," said a voice with a distinct North Walian twang I thought I recognised.

I looked up. Wouldn't you just know it, the voice belonged to my old 'friend', the poet, Caratacus ap Cadwaladr and standing next to him was none other than Sharona Haf, the Solingen knife girl, grinning from ear to ear . . . and not in a pleasant way either.

"Thought we hadn't seen you, didn't you?" she said. "A fine detective, you are, hiding behind a cereal packet and thinking we wouldn't notice . . . Now do as Crad says and get in the car, you can sit in the back with me."

"And if I refuse," I said.

"Refuse all you like," she said, "Crad will then just have to blow your head off with that shiny big new gun he got for Christmas. Would be a shame to ruin Waldi's nice new forecourt but needs must. And don't think of shouting for help, Price, then we really would have to shoot you. Besides, no one here is going to help you, they're all too busy sorting their shopping out and trying to get home as fast as they can. Pity about *your* shopping though . . . After all that thought and effort you put into it. Still you won't need it where you're going now, will you . . . Now get in the car, just look upon it as us taking you for a little ride in the country . . ."

Oh, no, not again, I thought to myself, I was really getting fed up with people taking me for a ride to places I didn't want to go, but what choice did I have. I got into their car, Sharona Haf's gun pressed into my side and Caratacus pulled away from Waldi, leaving me to figure how I was going to get out of this one with the odds very much stacked against me.

CHAPTER 32

We were standing in the kitchen of Cwrt-y-bela farmhouse, a state of the art kitchen with all mod cons, obviously designed by some twenty-first century designer, aiming to recreate some late sixteenth-century Tudor chic, which put my so-called kitchen above *The Lying Cod* to the deepest blushing shame. I could see a number of doors leading off to various rooms in the house, I assumed, but what really caught my eye was the exquisite looking knife rack holding some distinctly wicked looking knives, looking for all the world as if they had been especially flown in all the way from Solingen by special request of Sharona Haf. I hoped she wasn't going to practise her knife act on me later.

From the moment I had got into their car I had had half an inkling that we were on our way to Cwrt-y-bela Farm and so it had proved. No need, therefore, for a military style operation to get into the place, the villains had obligingly brought me to it themselves. Normally on such a drive as this I would have been talking ten to the dozen, trying to unsettle those who were taking me where I didn't want to go, but for some unknown reason, I had decided on this occasion to keep my powder dry. Now I was here though, I let it all go.

"What a really nice place you have here," I said, smiling my sweetest, Welsh unsalted butter wouldn't melt in my mouth smile, "thank you so much for inviting me. And where's Mrs Big? Shouldn't she be here? She is the leader of your gang, isn't she? Did she kill Culloden Jimmie and Red Iolo, or did she get one of you to do her dirty work for her? And why does she want the Super Dragons so much?"

"My, my, such a lot of questions," said Caratacus ap Cadwaladr, "shall we tell her, Shar, shall we?"

"No, don't tell her anything," said Sharona Haf, "let her go to her grave not knowing. I say finish her off now and let's get out of here, who knows when the Republicans might decide to put in an appearance."

What a cutie, eh? I knew that Sharona Haf was a nasty piece of work, the first time I saw her which seemed a long time ago now. And that big hair of hers, nothing but a lot of cheap and nasty extensions which were going to give her scalp a lot of trouble in years to come.

Outside, out of a cloudless sky, the life giving sun was beating down, twenty-five degrees in the shade which was just how I liked it. If I was going to go, then this was as good a day as any I suppose, but just like the reluctant child that has been sent to bed, I didn't want to go, that was the point. I didn't want to join the ancestors just yet, there were so many things I hadn't done, so much I needed to do. Out there in the Welsh Republic, people were making love, going about their daily business, laughing and crying, enjoying their favourite meal, walking the dog, sunbathing in the back garden, savouring a quiet drink, trying and failing to read *Ulysses*, watching TV, or even, Cymru save us, knocking on doors and canvassing for votes in the upcoming presidential election, a whole host of things which were shortly going to be denied me forever.

Faintly in the background there was some mournful Welsh *Fado* singing on the radio — a haunting, plaintive sound —ordinarily, it would have held me transfixed with its beauty, but now I had other things to think about, like how I was going to get out of this latest fine mess I'd got myself into.

Not for the first time, I found myself staring down the barrels of two enormous guns. Not for the first time, I regretted not having specified a gun on that special Christmas list I had sent to Santa — an enormous one, for my own personal protection, you understand. Too late now. I didn't even have my trusty rounders bat Excalibur with me to confront the villains. Don't you just hate it when you're in a room full of people, all of whom have shooters, and you haven't got one and they're all pointing the said shooters at you.

Well, it was just like that now with Sharona and Caratacus both taking great delight in pointing their guns in my direction. And so here I was, standing in the kitchen of Cwrt-y-bela farmhouse, wondering what in Cymru's name to do next, staring down the barrels of two enormous guns pointing straight at me, the people holding them bearing me no good will whatsoever. What would Wyatt Earp have done? Blasted 'em all into the next world with his Colt 45, probably, not really an option under my present circumstances. Somewhere deep within me I sighed, a long drawn out sigh, a sigh of resignation, perhaps. Was this the way the Welsh cake, or bakestone, as we always called it at home, was finally going to crumble?

"I must say you have been a busy bee, Augusta, running around in all those circles, blundering up and down all those blind alleys," Sharona Haf said, rousing me from my reverie. "Or should I call you Astrid, that is your name isn't it? The so called ace rugby player? Has-been, more like. Astrid Price, the bumbling detective? Why I've seen better Private Eyes in the pages of one of those cheap, second hand, Oxfam Cymru crime novels."

She was standing right in front of me and I'm sorry to have to say this but she stank of smoke and cigarettes and lighting up in dark corners and illicit drags on cancer bringing fags. I wouldn't exactly say she was a psychopath, but she was certainly beginning to scare the hell out of me. It would be a pleasure, a real pleasure to sort her out once and for all, and I was going to enjoy setting about her, if only I could manage to find a way of relieving her of the great big gun she was pointing right at my pretty face.

Besides, I needed to keep a cool head, to set personal feelings aside, for the time being at least. Just then, my mobile phone rang out to the Tich Gwilym accented strains of our beloved National Anthem.

"Now who could that be?" I said. "Maybe it's Inspector Sergeant and PC Pritchard come to rescue me. Now wouldn't that be nice, we could make a fivesome at Poker."

"Shut up, Price," Sharona said roughly. "Just slide the phone gently on to the table and none of your private dick tricks, mind, these guns are loaded."

I did as I was told and slid the phone gently on to the table, I made it a rule never to argue with people with guns, especially with anyone as unpredictable as Sharona.

"Yes," she said, "who is this and what do you want . . . no, no, there's nobody by that name here, you must have got a wrong number, no, I don't know anything about a Pryderi and his pigs" and she hung up.

Pryderi, I thought, all those days spent waiting and now he calls and what a time for him to call. Was I pining for Pryderi? Did I want to see him again? For the life of me, I couldn't say. I didn't know. I didn't know what I wanted, but for a few brief seconds, the mere mention of his name caused hope to burn brightly within my breast, but even if he could put two and two together and come up with a big fat four, by the time he got here, I might well be sinking deeper than a stone in the waves of the Welsh Sea so conveniently positioned not far from Cwrt-y-bela farmhouse.

"Who was that?" said Caratacus.

"Some madman called Dick Powell, kept going on about some bloke called Pryderi and his pigs. You do have some funny friends, Price, I must say."

"Never heard of him," I said, "he's no friend of mine and I don't know anything about pigs, must have been a wrong number, as you said."

Just then my phone rang again —who could it be this time, I wondered, me having such an extensive list of friends and all.

"My, my," said Sharona, as she picked it up, "you really do have a lot of friends, don't you, or maybe it's the pig man again, still hasn't found the right number."

"Yes, who is it and what do you want?" (Any other time, I would have been lost in admiration at Sharona's beguiling telephone manner but, right now, all I could think of was how to relieve her and Caratacus of those two guns they kept pointing in my direction.) "What, no, I don't want to spend a fortnight on Steep Holm, thank you very much, however cheap it is. Goodbye and don't call again."

"Who was that?" said Caratacus, lovingly fingering his gun but making sure to keep it trained unwaveringly on me.

"Oh, some other idiot," said Sharona, " trying to sell me a cheap holiday on Steep Holm or Flat Holm or somewhere. I had a job to understand him. There was all this noise in the background —sounded like a load of parrots going ten to the dozen . . . You wouldn't know anything about that now, would you, Price?"

"Who me?" I said, "I keep getting these kind of crank calls all the time, Cymru knows who these people are and where they get my phone number from. It's an occupational hazard, I suppose."

Sharona gave me a withering look, one of those if looks could kill, I would have dropped stone dead on to the floor by now and, unlike Lazarus, never risen again, looks, but she didn't seem entirely convinced. Never mind, I thought, the Parrot Man, Daniel Owen, had managed to contact me. Two of my allies had got through. The question was would either of them be able to get here in time? Possibly, very possibly, but I wasn't about to bet Stakis Theodorakis's *Lying Cod* fish shop on it.

"It's a pity about you, Price," Caratacus ap Cadwaladr said, interrupting my thoughts and with beads of sweat beginning to glisten on his forehead — the hot weather, or something else? "A real shame. I could have written poems about you, you could have been my muse, my inspiration, the woman that got my creative juices going – but now . . . well, you see my dilemma, I'm sure, I'm afraid I'm going to have to kill you. The best I might be able to do for you would be a funereal ode . . ."

Faced with this enticing prospect, I thought to myself —what would Steve Temple have done? I didn't know and, as usual, there was no sign of her rushing around the corner with husband Paul in tow and a whole battalion of the Metropolitan Police to help me out, so I did the only thing possible – I stalled.

"Now, let's not be too hasty," I said, "tell me more about this muse business, I'm sure we can work something out. If anyone's going to write a poem about me, it's got to be you surely? Let's sit down and talk about it. You know, tell me some more about all those *englynion* and *cywyddau*. Forget about Sharona, why not come back to my place and give me a private poetry reading, if you see what I mean. You'll find me most appreciative, I'm sure . . ."

"Don't listen to her," said Sharona, "can't you see what she's doing, she's playing for time, she's not interested in you or your poetry, shoot her and get it over with."

Did I detect just the faintest hint of jealousy there? It would have been just like Sharona to be less than magnanimous. I inched nearer. There were two of them to one of me, and, as usual, all the guns were with them, not great odds but it could have been worse. Now, to go out with a bang or with a whimper? That was the question. Or, in the immortal words of Elvis, 'it was now or never'.

"No, we can't kill her yet," Caratacus ap Cadwaladr said, "We have to wait until the others get here, see what Mrs Big says . . ."

"Oh, can't you ever make a decision by yourself, Crad," Sharona said, "I say shoot her now, get it over with, shoot her in the back then we can always say she was trying to escape."

This was all getting a bit serious now for my liking, I didn't want to be shot anywhere, if I could help it, least of all in the back, so in desperation I tried a shot of my own, this one a shot in the dark— what did I have to lose after all . . . "Where's the dog, Sharona?" I said.

"What dog?" she said. "What are you talking about now, you crazy woman?"

"You know the one I mean," I said. "Hector, Nestor, Victor, whatever his name was. Did you practise on him, eh? Did you? Stick a knife in him too? You must be running out of them by now, surely. Solingen must be hard put to keep up with the demand. Did you stick Nestor just for the practice like or are you just a raving psychopath . . . who can't control herself?"

"Why, you, you . . . ginger-haired, South Walian bitch," said Sharona, taking a threatening step towards me, "Call yourself a private detective? I'll give you knives. I'll stick one in you, I'll teach you to talk to me like that."

I stood my ground. "And what about that tangerine dress of yours," I said, "is that still hanging in your cupboard somewhere? Do you pull it on at night and look at yourself in the mirror and think how glamorous you are? Oh and by the way, Shar, just between ourselves, get it right, would you, my hair's Titian, for Cymru's sake, Titian, not ginger, would you like me to spell it for you," smiling my sweetest, honey flavoured smile.

Well, this must have tipped her right over the edge, as the next thing I knew, she was charging straight at me, forgetting all about the gun she was waving in her hand. Luckily for me, she wasn't holding one of her special knives from Solingen at the time. Luckily for me, too, Caratacus just managed to insert himself between us, shouting "Stop it, Shar, can't you see she's trying to wind *you* up now."

It was a half chance, scarcely even that, but maybe it was all I needed. What would Inspector Rebus have done? As usual, I had no clue and there was little chance of him coming to save me, now or ever. I would have to do it the Eric Carmen way, all by myself. And it really was now or never, as Mr Presley would have said or rather sung. I had to go for it, no other choice, really, and so I did . . .

CHAPTER 33

I drew myself up to my full height and launched myself into the air, aiming a drop kick at the precious pair, at the same time yelling "Boudicca", that ancient Celtic war cry at the top of my voice, almost frightening myself, as I did so. Pryderi should have been there to see me, it would have brought back some tender memories for him, I'm sure. Down the two of them went like one of those sacks of potatoes Stakis was always peeling. If I'd wanted to, now was the time to go through my whole repertoire of tai chi moves and reduce them to submission but, on a whim, I decided to do it the easy way. As I landed on top of them I pressed first the Welsh Dragon ring on my left hand, aiming at Crad, and then the map of Cymru ring on my right hand, aiming at Sharona. "Whoosh,' the rings sent a thin jet of cold liquid into both their faces. There, that ought to keep them quiet for a while, or a few minutes at least, while I decided what to do next. The liquid was harmless enough with no toxic after effects—my man in Aberbargoed had taken good care of that, but it meant that now *I* had the guns and now *I* was in charge.

Time to check Caratacus ap Cadwaladr's pockets while he was still out. Hmm, nothing very incriminating there, no signed confessions admitting to any unlawful killings in the last few weeks, no clues as to where to

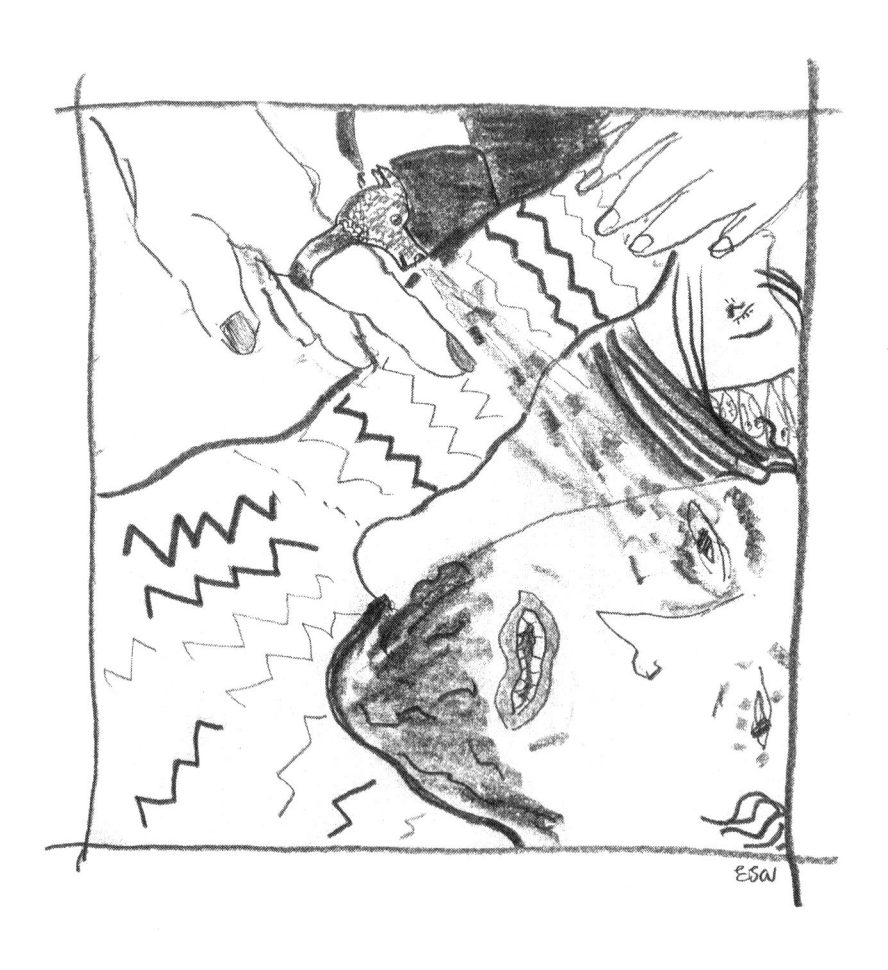

As I landed on top of them, I pressed first the Welsh Dragon ring on my left hand, aiming at Crad

find Madge Breese's record of our National Anthem. Ah, a bunch of keys including a car key, they might come in handy . . . I pocketed them just in case. It was the same with Sharona — no references to tangerine dresses, or dogs called Hector or Victor or Nestor, or whatever the mutt's name was, to be found anywhere on her person. I was no further forward in my quest for justice, truth and the Welsh Republican Way. Oh well, nothing to be done about that . . .

Then a thought occurred to me. Quickly, I checked the various rooms leading off the kitchen. There was a lounge, three bedrooms and what looked like a games room. There was nobody in any of them but they all seemed to be furnished in exquisite taste. I would have liked to have lingered a little longer, given all of these rooms a proper once over, but I had no time for a guided tour, of course, Crad and Shar might wake up at any minute. I just had time to notice all of the rooms had keyholes meaning they could be locked but before I could try any of the keys, I had taken from Caratacus ap Cadwaladr's pockets, I heard signs of movement coming from the kitchen. Uh, oh, the sleeping beauties were beginning to come round. I backed away from them, taking good care to keep what used to be their guns trained on the two of them.

Caratacus was the first to come to his senses. As if through a clearing haze, he saw me and took in the situation. "What the . . ." he said, "Price, how come . . ."

"How nice to have you back with us, Crad," I said, "now if you'll just answer a few questions, I'll be on my way..."

"Get knotted, Price," he said, giving me one of those if looks could kill, I'd have been thrown off a boat into the Cardiff channel, wearing cement boots by now and consigned to its depths for a long, long time looks.

"Get knotted," I said, "get knotted, hmm, I haven't heard that phrase in a while. Not very poetic, is it, Crad, especially coming from such a great performance poet as yourself and remember I've seen you in action. Now what was that question I wanted to ask you, oh yes, I remember..."

"I'm not telling you a thing, Price," he said, "what"s stopping me rushing you and taking our two guns back. A goody-two-shoes like you is hardly likely to kill me now, is she?"

"Maybe not," I said, "but I'm quite partial to shooting people in the leg, I used to do that quite often at one time. Apparently, it hurts quite a lot. Fancy your chances, Crad? Come on, rush me, there's a good boy..."

Before he could answer, Sharona Haf began to rejoin the land of the living, "what, where... where am I?" she stammered. Then, her eyes took in me, shooting me a look of pure hatred, and if looks could have killed etc, etc... "Hey, you've got my gun," she said, "give it back to me."

"Sharona," I said, "how nice to have you back with us. We've just been playing a game of Twenty Questions, but Crad's being a bit of a spoilsport and doesn't want to play anymore, so you can take his place. You'd like that, wouldn't you? Now about that dog of yours —what was his name again — and those tangerine dresses? I assume you must have had more than one of them, you being a dyed in the wool Blackpool supporter and all. Now I come to think it, they may have really suited your complexion and while I'm at it, who is Amber Bernstein and where is she? Is it you? And what about all those owls of yours—is there some deeper meaning behind all that? Maybe, you're really a Sheffield Wednesday fan, after all? Come on, you can tell Auntie Astrid."

Sharona Haf looked at me incredulously. "If you think I'm going to answer any of your stupid questions, Price, you've got another think coming." She spat out the words. "I'd rather be trapped in a very small broom cupboard listening to your precious President Hopkins's collected speeches for hours on end. Why I've a good mind to . . ."

"Do what, Sharona?" I said, "a good mind to do what? Pray, do tell. I'd really like to know. Rush me, perhaps? Try and get your gun back off me and just when I was getting attached to it? I've already had that conversation with Caratacus here, but he saw sense and thought better of it, didn't you, Crad . . ."

Caratacus ap Cadwaladr opened his mouth as if to say something, probably to congratulate me on my superior wit and wisdom, and attempt to persuade Sharona of the error of her ways, but I never got to hear what exactly he was going to say, as just then there came the distant sound of a car seemingly being driven very fast and heading towards us. It still sounded a long way off but at the speed it was being driven I could tell it wouldn't be very long before it reached us, the big question, as far as I was concerned, at least, was, would it be friend or foe driving it . . .

CHAPTER 34

Well, we all looked at each other. I'd like to think it was the start of a burgeoning, deep spiritual communion between the three of us but somehow I didn't think so. Just who was coming our way and was it friend or foe? One thing was certain —we would soon find out.

Caratacus found his voice. "Now you're in trouble, Price," he said. "That'll be Mrs Big and her men returning from a mission. Give us our guns back now, there's a good girl, and we'll make sure she goes easy on you, won't we, Shar?"

"Yeah," said Sharona, "Give us our guns back, you ginger headed slag. If you know what's good for you, that is."

What to do? What would Inspector Barnaby have done. Cymru alone knew but somehow I didn't think he'd be showing up to help me before it all went pear-shaped . . . No, as usual, I was on my own, but just who was in that car —was it Mrs Big & Co, as Crad and Shar seemed to think, or someone else, more friendly disposed towards me. I looked at the two of them. I could shoot them both dead on the spot . . . Not a good idea. True they would be out of my hair and I would be free to concentrate on other things, like getting out of here, but that would just bring me down to their level and I liked to think I was better than that. I made up my mind.

"Right," I said, "both of you into that bedroom —now", pointing in the direction I meant with my two guns.

"And if we don't," they both said, more or less simultaneously.

"Well, I will just have to persuade you then, won't I," I said, "I assume you are still both very much attached to the use of your legs . . ." and I did some threatening waving of the guns of my own.

Reluctantly, the two complied. Once inside the bedroom I stashed one of the guns in my pocket, taking good care to keep the other trained on the poet and his 'gangster's moll,' meanwhile fishing around in my other pocket for the keys I had taken from Caratacus earlier, hoping one of them would fit the lock to this bedroom door.

"Right you two, on the bed," I said, "and keep your hands above your heads, both of you. You can recite some poetry while I'm gone, Crad, keep you both occupied, I'm sure you've got a love poem or two hidden away in that brain of yours somewhere."

"Oh, go stick your head in a bowl of hot *cawl*, Price," said Caratacus, "what do you know about poetry, or love for that matter?"

It's people like you give poetry a bad name, I thought, but, to tell you the truth, I wasn't really listening, I had other things to do. I was already out of the door before you could say Penllergaer, or even Penperlleni, and inserting the first key I found into the lock. Well, maybe it was serendipity or maybe it was the luck of the Prices (which hadn't been very much in evidence lately, I can tell you). Whatever it was, the key locked the door first time. Hallelujah! I backed away from the door which looked solid enough and would probably hold them for a while, if they tried to break out, and returned to the kitchen casting a wary eye over Sharona's vicious looking knives. I was tempted to take one or two with me just in case I had to do some knife throwing of my own but decided against it —I wasn't sure I could be trusted around knives, Sharona's or any one else's.

And now what? Suddenly, I felt like a combined force of rooks and jackdaws, straight arrowing their way, almost blind, into a dense bank of thick fog in the soon to be darkening evening sky, but nowhere near as clever. Those birds knew where they were going, heading for their winter's roost, and would get there eventually. As for me . . . Where was I going?

All I knew was that someone was coming to Cwrt-y-bela Farm and would be here soon. But who? And would they be for me or against me? Aye, that was the 64,000 Glyndwr question. And what was I going to do? Stay here and wait for them or try to make my escape? I had Crad's car keys. I could use them to make my getaway . . . If I stayed where I was, how long would that bedroom door resist Crad and Sharona's combined efforts to escape? Was there anywhere to hide around here? And if it was Mrs Big and her henchmen walking through that door, was I really going to pick them off, one by one, great shot though I was, reader? That could be an awful lot of legs to aim at. Questions, questions, a whole bunch of nothing but questions. That was all this case had ever been, right from the very beginning and still I had no answers to any of them.

What would Morgan Price, my late lamented and much missed husband have done? Sadly, he was no longer around to show me, or offer me the benefit of his years of experience, having been gunned down by a crazed individual during the course of one of our joint investigations that had gone badly wrong. Believe me, there wasn't a day went by that I didn't think of him or grieve for him terribly, but lately, although I hated to admit it, and it felt like the greatest of betrayals, my thoughts had, more and more, begun to turn to other men, to other men's arms to sometimes hold me through those long nights . . .

Suddenly, I felt very weary and an intense almost overpowering longing came over me to fall to my knees and cry my eyes out, shed bitter tears for everything that had happened, to let Mrs Big and company do their worst —what did I care what became of me? Maybe, it would be sweet release . . . And I would have done it too but just before I succumbed to this overwhelming feeling of despair, and fell to the floor in pain and sorrow, another voice rang out inside of me, telling me to think of others and not just me, me, me, my own selfish self all the time.

What about Stakis? Languishing in a Welsh Republican Police prison through no fault of his own and relying on me to get him out? I was the one who had put him in that predicament through my own stupid course of action, after all. What about Pryderi? Did he have any feelings for me or was I just imagining things? Would there be a future for us? A new life in store for me? Did I want there to be one? There wouldn't be, so much was certain, not if I was on my knees, crying my heart out in this Godforsaken kitchen, in this Godforsaken place, just waiting for the bad guys to come along and finish me off, there surely wouldn't be.

With an effort I threw off whatever black mood I had fallen into, drew myself up to my full height and gripped the evil duo's guns tightly in both my hands. If I was going out, it would be with an almighty bang, not with a crybaby whimper and I would make damn sure to take a few wrongdoers with me.

Now, as I stood there, still trembling, in my fevered imagination which had been working overtime, I half expected, once outside, to find Mrs Big and a car load of her henchmen all out to get me and do me wrong.

In my more optimistic moments I somehow

hoped to find Pryderi waiting for me in the AWR's (Army of the Welsh Republic's) latest top secret jeep ready and willing to whisk me away from all this. Maybe my 'favourite' three police officers—Pritchard, Sergeant and 'Stilts' would be there to welcome me 'warmly'.

Or even, ridiculous as it may sound, Edward Henry Davies riding his *Hebog*. But what would he be doing there? Even more ridiculous, I somehow entertained the briefest of brief notions that my old friend, The Bird Man, Daniel Owen, would be there, carrying my other old friend, Gelert, the African Grey Parrot along with him in a cage! Gelert had been a pivotal witness in a case I had been involved in earlier — the mystery of the Golden Lovespoons — even if he was an African Grey Parrot, he was still my Good Boy.

Get a grip, Astrid, I thought to myself, hallucinating already and I hadn't even taken any mind altering substances, illegal or otherwise. Time now to follow Lady Macbeth's advice and screw my courage to the sticking place. "Boudicca," I shouted at the top of my lungs, more to give myself courage than anything else, just as those Ancient Britons must have done, I fancied, and quickly made my way to the front door to see what fate awaited me . . .

CHAPTER 35

Brandishing both guns in front of me I kicked open the front door, still yelling, "Boudicca" at the top of my voice (well, it made *me* feel better, if nothing else, and I hoped it would scare the liver and lights out of any potential villains waiting outside for me) and stepped out into what . . .

Well, nothing really. There was nobody there in the open space before the farmhouse, just Crad and Sharona's car in the exact same place they had left it. There was no sign of anybody else anywhere to be seen but what about that car we had all three of us heard approaching . . . Cymru knew what had happened to that, but, it was undeniable, there was nobody there, I was the only person standing in front of that farmhouse.

My first thought was to get into Crad and Sharona's car and get the merry hell out of that place and back to Casnewydd as fast as it would take me. So I fiddled around with Crad's keys and, after a bit of searching, found the one to unlock the car door. Then I sat behind the wheel ready to go. It wasn't the *Pwca* (what car was?) but it would get me where I wanted to go, back to *The Lying Cod* and the safety of my own home, where I would have time, time to think and work out what my next strategy was going to be. Strategy. That was a laugh, considering my less than brilliant performance so far.

    I started the car and looked around me. Still no sign of anybody. It was all quiet on the Cwrt-y-bela front and that bedroom door still seemed to be holding Caratacus and Sharona. Damn, I thought, should have hidden those knives while I had the chance just in case they did manage to escape. Too late now, I was on my way, but, wait just a wild wimberry picking minute, maybe I should check those intriguing looking outhouses before I left, just to see what I could find, as I didn't fancy paying a return visit any time soon, and after all, I had the guns now, not the poet and his 'little friend'. The force was with me.

    Abruptly, I got out of the car, leaving the engine running and taking the guns with me. Like my old mam used to tell me, you couldn't be too careful. Swiftly, I ran to the first of the outhouses and kicked the door open with my foot. Luckily, for my peace of mind, there was no-one inside and nothing very interesting for me to look at. So far, so good. Keep going, Astrid, I told myself, this is going to be a piece of Welsh cake, you just wait and see. I moved on to the second outhouse and opened it the same way as I had the first.

    Once again, I was lucky, no wrong uns stepped out from the shadows to fill me full of lead, no weighted cosh descended on my pretty little Titian coloured head to send me crashing to the floor. I looked around me. At first glance this second outhouse seemed to be pretty much like the first —full of junk and rubbish from the main house that had outlived its usefulness, but then I saw them — five or six Super Dragons standing tall and proud in front of me —but when I looked closer, I could see they weren't intact by any means. The floor around them was littered with gouged out Super Dragon parts.

Somebody had been trying to get inside them, looking for something, obviously, but what . . . Drugs? Money? Smuggled artefacts? Cymru alone knew, as I certainly didn't. Hercule Poirot might have been able to tell me, but as usual, he wasn't around to put in his two Gwynfors worth (a hundred Gwynfors to the Glyndwr, remember, reader) and I wasn't going to stand here much longer waiting for him. Quickly I took out my mobile phone, I'd had the foresight to remove from the place in the kitchen Crad and Shar had left it, and took photographs of the vandalised Super Dragons from all angles. Now, it really was time to go.

CHAPTER 36

I walked out into the early evening sunlight, guns held straight out in front of me, just to be on the safe side, you understand, and headed for the car and my ticket out of here, this was one place I was very glad to be leaving behind me. Everything looked to be okay, there was no sign of anyone, as far as I could tell, Crad and Shar were still locked in the bedroom —maybe they'd given up trying to get out and turned their attention to some other kind of business . . . as long as it didn't involve me, what did I care.

    I placed my hand on the car door ready to open it when, suddenly, a voice rang out behind me, a voice I had heard before. "Going somewhere, Mrs Price?" the voice said. "Yeah, leaving so soon? That's not very neighbourly, is it?" said another voice, one I did not recognise, but one which seemed to have a pronounced New York twang to it.

    I wheeled around, guns at the ready in time to see Mrs Big standing at the door of the farmhouse flanked by the two rogue cops, Jude and Joe. In front of them was the Columbian hood, Rodrigo Rodriguez, whom I had last seen when we had found Stakis in the house in Cwm Hyfryd, and some other guy I did not recognise. This one looked to be about five foot eight, five foot nine, and was wearing a woolly hat, despite the hot weather, a golden earring in his left ear, track suit bottoms and trainers. Like all the rest of them, he was holding a wicked looking gun and it was pointing straight at me. Like all the rest of them, he looked as if he knew how to use it.

My first thought was how, in the name of Cymru, had I not heard them? How had I, O Great Detective that I was supposed to be, allowed them to creep up on me unawares? It must have been whilst I was too absorbed in looking at the Super Dragons and, consequently, wasting precious time —that and a false sense of security I had foolishly allowed myself to be lulled into but how had I not heard their car approaching? Surely, I would have heard that?

My second thought was, yes, I was now the proud possessor of two guns but the opposition had five of their own, all cocked and ready to send me into the next world before my time had come. Five guns against two, Astrid, not good odds, not good odds at all.

Well, there was nothing for it but to try and brazen it out. "Mrs Big," I said, putting on my saccharin sweetest smile, "we meet again. How nice to see you or should I call you Amber Bernstein? That is your real name, isn't it?"

Keep 'em talking, Astrid, for as long as possible. While there was talking going on, the less chance there was of a shooting war breaking out. All the same, I began to inch very slowly, so as not to draw their attention, and very patiently to a position where I might be able to get behind the car which would afford me some protection at least once the bullets did start to fly, as they inevitably would, sooner or later.

Inch by inch, Astrid, inch by painstaking inch . . . keep those guns up and trained on the opposition. "Who's your new friend, Mrs B," I said, gesturing at the guy with the New York accent.

"Cocky Marciano at your service, Mrs Price," said the woolly hat, "I've heard a lot about you . . ."

"Oh, nothing bad, I hope," I said, flashing him my most beaming smile and tossing my hair back.

"Only that you're a dangerous woman, Mrs Price, and a man needs to be careful around you . . ."

My, my, what a compliment, back handed or not, but take them where you can get them, I always say, take them where you can get them.

"Oh, Mr Marciano," I said, "you do say the nicest things. Tell me more . . . "

Marciano opened his mouth as if he was indeed about to say more, but just then Mrs Big interrupted. "Just a minute," she said, "I thought Caratacus and Sharona were looking after you, Price. Where are they?"

"Oh, those two," I said, "well, yes, they were 'looking after' me, as you so delicately put it, but then they decided they wanted to spend some time alone. You know what young people are like nowadays, can't keep their hands off each other. They're probably reciting poetry to each other right now, I shouldn't wonder, that Caratacus ap Cadwaladr has got a way with words, I must admit . . ."

Mrs Big shot a glance at me which didn't bode well for my future well being, I got the distinct impression she didn't really like me, didn't like me at all, I couldn't think why.

"Hey, Joe, Jude," Mrs Big positively barked out the order. "Get in the house and find out where those two fools are and get them here. Now!"

"But Mrs B," said my old 'friend', Jude, the *faux* policeman, or was he just a bent copper, I still wasn't quite sure. "Let me have a go at her, I owe her one after what she did to me in that house in Cwm Hyfryd. She made me look a right *twp* (idiot)."

"You'll get your chance later, same as the rest of us," said Mrs Big, "now do as I say and find those two morons." And Joe and Jude hurried away to do their boss's bidding. Well, the odds were looking a bit better now, but they wouldn't stay that way for long. I would have to move fast. The two 'cops' would soon find Crad and Shar and then I would be even more outnumbered than I was now. Inch by inch, Astrid, slowly, slowly catchee master criminal and her nefarious gang.

"Well, if that's all then, Amber," I said, "I'll be on my way. Lovely to see you again. Give my love to Crad and Shar, won't you. I'll just borrow their car to get me back home, if you don't mind. I'll leave it in front of *The*

Lord Raglan in Casnewydd, shall I, so you can pick it up later?" And I made to move towards the car door.

"Stay where you are, Price," said Mrs Big "right where you are. You ain't going nowhere. Boys, if she so much as touches that car door, let her have it."

"Yes, Mrs Big," said Rodriguez and Cocky Marciano in unison, almost as if they were willing me to touch the door.

"Aw, Cocky," I said, "all you really want to do is plug me full of bullet holes and just as I was beginning to like you . . ."

"Take no notice of her tricks," said Mrs Big. "The woman never stops talking. She's just playing for time, that's all, trying to drive a wedge between us. She may be holding two guns she probably took from Crad and Shar but I think we outnumber her in the guns department, the superior fire power is with us. As soon as Joe and Jude return we'll make our move and disarm her. It shouldn't be too difficult. Then we'll find out what she knows, what she *really* knows and who she's spoken to, get the names of those she's confided her suspicions to, that'll be *my own* particular pleasure, of course, and then I don't think Mrs Astrid Price, The Great Welsh Detective, or so she likes to think, will be seeing Abergynolwyn again or anywhere else for that matter. From what I've heard, the Welsh Republican Police won't miss her very much. Nor will anyone else, I shouldn't wonder . . ."

What to do, dear reader? What would Clint Eastwood have done? Bruce Willis? Big John Wayne? No use relying on those guys. They were never around when you needed them. The cavalry was never going to come over the hill. Not now. Not ever. One last desperate chance, perhaps, I thought to myself, what would Annie Oakley have done? Probably shot the three guns out of the ne'er-do-wells' hands and then peppered the ground around them so that they were hopping about like jackdaws on a gravestone. Not a bad idea, really. Not a bad idea at all, but would my shooting skills be up to it? It had been a long time since those days on the firing range, practising together with Morgan. Still I had to do something . . . Mentally, I prepared to fling myself to the ground, start firing and, if the worst did come to the worst to go down with all guns blazing, when suddenly . . .

CHAPTER 37

. . . When, suddenly, I heard a voice behind me, a voice I knew, a voice I recognised, but I couldn't turn around to look as Mrs Big & Co still had their guns trained on me, and wouldn't hesitate to shoot, I knew.

"Three against one," the voice was saying, "now that's not fair odds, not by a long way, not where I come from, anyway."

Pryderi, I thought, what took you so long? And then, rather inconsequentially, where did he come from, anyway? As usual, I hadn't a clue. Really, I knew so little about him. What his likes and dislikes were. How he spent his days off. What kind of music he liked. He had no noticeable accent, or none that I could detect, and I'd never really got round to asking him about his early days during our short-lived acquaintance so far.

"Now then, soldier boy," Mrs Big or Amber Bernstein, or whatever the name was that she went under, was saying. "We've got no beef with you. Our quarrel is with Mrs Price here. You wouldn't believe what trouble she's caused us and you wouldn't want to get involved in it, I"m sure. Why don't you just put that gun away and trundle back to your regiment, like the good military man you obviously are, and leave us all here to sort it out amicably? What do you say?"

"Well, I'd like to do that, I really would," said the

voice, but first I'd like to see what Mrs Price thinks about it all," and he stepped up right alongside me. Now I could see he was holding a gun of his own, but why hadn't he brought the rest of the Army of the Welsh Republic with him, or at least some of them (I could be really ungrateful at times, reader). Well, the odds had evened up just a little, but not by that much.

"What are you doing here?" I whispered to him by way of a welcoming opening remark.

"Oh, only taking a spot of unpaid leave," he whispered back, "just let's say I fancied taking a look around Cwrt-y-bela—I've heard so much about it. Love that golden yellow daffodil motif brooch in your hair, by the way, it suits you, I must say, very fetching . . ."

"Oi, you two," said Mrs Big, "What's with all this whispering, speak out loud and clear like the good citizens of the Welsh Republic you're supposed to be, can't you, and you, soldier, what's it to be then? Are you leaving quietly, or going down with Price? She's not worth it, let me tell you. Hey, wait just a little leek eating moment, you two don't know each other, do you, you seem awfully pally together, don't they, boys?"

And the two stooges nodded their heads in unison but I wasn't really listening to what she was saying, I was thinking about what Pryderi had just said. . .

Daffodil? Daffodil! For Cymru's sake, Astrid, how could you be so stupid and forgetful. What a right *twp* (idiot) I was and then some. The *twp* of all *twps*. The head *twp*. The *Capo twp* of all . . . I could go on, but well, you get the picture. Of course. What was the matter with me?

"Take my one gun, Pryderi," I whispered, "and keep me covered, I need to do something, it'll all become clear in a moment, trust me, I'm a private detective."

Well, if he had any doubts on the matter, he kept them to himself and did as he was told, just like a good soldier should. Slowly, and very carefully, I removed the golden yellow daffodil motif brooch from my Titian coloured hair.

"Here, Amber," I said, "catch," and hurled the brooch as hard as I could straight at Amber Bernstein, alias Mrs Big, a forward pass any American Football Quarterback would have been proud of — eat your heart out, Tom Brady. As it sailed through the air at what, it seemed to me, to be a pace to match that of those long extinct, former glaciers in Snowdonia, everyone stared at its prowess, as if mesmerised by none other than Paul McKenna himself.

"Catch it, Amber, catch it," I shouted, but I knew she wouldn't, not in a month of Saturdays, she would never have made our old Welsh Women's Rugby Team in a million of our Earth years, well, she might just have sneaked under the radar as a water carrier, on a day when we had all collectively taken our eye off the

Slowly, and very carefully, I removed the golden yellow daffodil motif brooch from my Titian coloured hair

ball . . . but I digress. She certainly took *her* eye off the brooch, as I always knew she would, and it dropped to the ground in front of her with a faint, metallic ring which was unfortunate, of course.

Unfortunate, that is, for her and her two 'goons'. A second or so after the ring had hit the ground, the stun gas it contained rose up in a cloud around the three of them, enveloping them in a thin mist. It wouldn't do them any permanent harm, of course, my man from Aberbargoed had vouched for that, and they would soon recover, but for the moment at least, they had been effectively 'stunned', unable to move in any way.

The beauty of it all was, and I knew this, was that the stunning effect of the cloud would have been confined to the three of them, and would not affect anyone standing a little way away from it, as Pryderi and I had been. I also knew there wasn't a moment to lose.

"Come on, Pryderi," I shouted, "quick, get their guns, I'll take care of Amber," and I ran towards the three prone bodies, Pryderi following swiftly after.

CHAPTER 38

I pulled Amber/Mrs Big up into a sitting position, and then dragged her further away from the house, throwing her gun to Pryderi as I did so, to go with the others he had acquired from Marciano and Rodriguez. We were getting to accumulate quite a collection between the two of us. Meanwhile the 'stun' cloud had begun to dissipate and our three 'opponents' were slowly coming round.

"Got any handcuffs on you, Pryderi?" I said, "just so as we can make these babies a little more comfortable, and our lives a little easier, if you see what I mean . . ."

He shook his head. "I knew there was something I forgot when I set out this morning," he said. "For Cymru's sake, Price, I'm beginning to be almost as forgetful as you. That's spending too much time with you, I suppose. Nice trick with the brooch, by the way, where did you learn that one?"

I was about to answer when Amber Bernstein began to come round. "Wha, wha's happening? Price? Wha are you doing here?" she stammered, obviously still dazed from the effects of the 'stun' brooch.

"Don't you worry, Amber," I said, "everything's all right, Astrid's just got a few questions she'd like to ask you, that's all. Now what can you tell me about a certain friend of yours? What was he — Czech, Polish, Slovenian? Or am I getting my Slovene mixed up with my Slovak? Come on, Amber, help me out here. Was he Bulgarian? Or Russian, perhaps? Something like that, but somewhere along the line, you and he had a falling out, didn't you, Amber? What happened to him? What can you tell me about that? And why are the Super Dragons so important to you?"

But I could sense the moment had passed and Mrs Big was now back to her old self, a feeling confirmed by her next few words. "Just Cymru off out of it, Price," she said, "why don't you. I'm not telling *you* anything. Not if you were the last person left to talk to in this whole, wide world."

"Aw, Amber," I said, "and there I was thinking we were getting along so well," but just then, there came a noise from the doorway and I looked up to find those two rogue cops, Joe and Jude, standing there, along with Caratacus, and, wouldn't you just know it, the cops with guns drawn and, as usual, pointed in my direction.

Where's my best female friend, Sharona, I thought fleetingly but I said, "Drop the guns, guys, and kick them away from you, or I swear I'll blow Mrs Big's head off. Do it, do it now!"

"You won't do it, Price," said Joe, "you're too soft, too full of the sour milk of human kindness. How about *you* drop *your* guns, you and that new found friend of yours and we just might let you walk out of here in one piece."

"Oh, won't I," I said, "I'd be doing the Welsh Republic a service and the whole world, for that matter. She's no use to me, anyway, she never answers any of my questions, she's just no fun any more. Now call off your dogs, Amber, or prepare to enter that new world we know nothing about . . ."

For a brief moment, I thought she was going to call my bluff and we were in for an almighty shootout when, suddenly, she crumbled and, in a small voice, said, "do as she says, boys, throw your guns away."

Joe threw his to the ground but Jude hesitated for a minute. I could tell he was itching to shoot, but in the end he, too, complied. "Now, down on the ground, all of you, all except you, Amber," I said, "you, too, Marciano and Rodriguez. Pryderi, see if those two 'cops' have got any handcuffs on them and do the necessary."

So now we had Pryderi and me against six of them, only this time we had all the guns, quite a nice big pile by now. "Well, well," said Pryderi, "these two so-called 'cops' have each got two pairs of handcuffs on them."

"Good," I said, "handcuff both of them, hands behind their backs and then do the same to Marciano and Rodriguez. That would take four of them out of the equation, leaving only Amber and Crad to perhaps offer any possible opposition, although I didn't think Mrs Big had much fight left in her. But Sharona? Where was

Sharona? I didn't like the idea of her being still at large and, possibly, up to all kinds of mischief, but before I could give this problem any more thought, a car drove up. It was one of those new electric hybrids which made little or no sound at all, thus making it relatively silent and why I hadn't heard it —   In that and all the recent excitement that had been going on here. Who was this now? I didn't recognise the car. What was it doing here? Was it reinforcements for the Big gang? And why did it have tinted windows, for Cymru's sake, so that I couldn't look in to see who was inside?

"Right," I said, "down on the ground, Amber, you too, Crad," and trained my gun on the car door as it began to open . . .

CHAPTER 39

"Come out, come out, whoever you are," I said (rather superfluously really, as they were coming out anyway, but never mind, it sounded good) "and come out with your hands up, right up, slowly now, where I can see them, I warn you, I'll fire, if you don't do as I say . . ."

Slowly, very slowly, one hand came out, followed by the other one, even more slowly. And then the voice behind the hands was speaking, a voice I recognised, a voice I knew. "Astrid," the voice was saying, "it's me, Dan, The Bird Man, I've got Gelert in the car with me. Don't shoot, please, he doesn't like loud noises. He's a sensitive little soul, as you well know, and must be treated with respect."

Right on cue, the parrot chimed in from the back of the car, "Hello, sexy, what a *pishyn* (pretty girl), she is, what a *pishyn* is the Master Detective, Mrs Astrid Price, what a real *pishyn*."

Yes, Gelert, enough of the compliments, I thought, tell me what I really want to know – who is this mysterious Central/Eastern European no one will give me a name for? What is the significance of the Casnewydd Super Dragons? What is the real name of Sharona Haf's dog? And, most important of all —What am I going to have to eat tonight?

"Hello, love," said Gelert, "how's it going?"

"Gelert, *Cariad*," I said, "my darling boy, "I've missed you."

"Yes, but not enough to come and see me," said Gelert."

He had a way with words that parrot, it could not be denied. "Dan," I said, "why are you here and why have you brought Gelert with you? Don't you realise this could well have been a 'war zone' you were heading into. And why are you driving around in a hybrid car with tinted windows and an African Grey Parrot sitting in his cage on the back seat?"

"Well," said Dan, "when I phoned you and that rather rude woman answered and didn't seem to know her Flat Holm from her Steep Holm, I thought something was wrong and then I thought I'd come out to investigate. I thought I'd spin that old yarn about being lost or needing a drink of water in this extreme heat . . ."

Then he stopped and took a closer look around him, at me and my motley crew of companions. "What's with all the guns, Astrid, I thought you didn't like them? And what's he doing here?" (This last question rather a pointed one, I thought.)

"I don't," I said, "but sometimes needs must. Like right now, for instance. As for Lieutenant Pryderi of the Llewelyn the Last Brigade, he is, how shall I put it, 'helping me with my enquiries'. You were saying about the tinted windows and driving round with Gelert?"

"Well," Daniel Owen said, "I've been meaning to

get a new car now for quite a while, the old one was getting really 'clapped-out' and then I thought, why not get one of those new electric motors, you know, save the world and all that . . . as for the tinted windows, I was tired of people giving me funny looks every time I took Gelert for his daily ride. I did try to persuade him not to come along today, but you know, he insisted on accompanying me. And, Astrid, I hope you don't think I was being entirely stupid coming here. When that woman failed the Steep Holm/Flat Holm test, I hope you don't mind, I contacted the Welsh Republican Police. They . . ."

" . . . are here already," I said, as a Welsh Republican Police car screeched to a halt in front of me, disgorging its passenger load of Inspector Sergeant, PC Pritchard and WPC Gwenllian 'Stilts'/Tall Girl Sempringham. I'd been so busy trying to get to the bottom of Dan Owen's labyrinthine explanations, I hadn't heard them coming either. Was my hearing going? Was I getting past it? Who knew? Maybe Dr Watson would have, Dr Blake even, but they weren't there, were they, as per, expletive deleted, usual?

"My, my," said Inspector Sergeant, "you have been busy, haven't you, Price?" And then, looking around him, "I thought you didn't like guns."

"I don't," I said, 'but sometimes . . ."

"You know, Price," said Pritchard, "some might say these people you have, uh, 'gathered together', they might be able to bring a good case of unlawful imprisonment against you . . ."

"What are you talking about . . . ?" I said, but Pryderi broke in, "Don't be ridiculous, man, this woman has done the Welsh Republic a great service by helping to apprehend these felons. Do your duty, Inspector and arrest them all now."

Well, Sergeant looked somewhat taken aback at this but, nevertheless, he motioned his two colleagues forward, mumbling something about 'reading them their rights'. Meanwhile, I was thinking to myself, was I a Super Psychic or what? Had I not envisaged such a scenario with all these various people arriving at the farmhouse, one after the other, just before I exited the place?

All it needed now was for Edward Henry Davies to join us . . . And lo and behold, I DIDN'T believe it, here he was now, alighting from his *Hebog* just in front of us . . . What was happening to me? And where had these seemingly newly acquired future foretelling powers come from all of a sudden? Was I really descended from a long line of Welsh psychics as my old mam had never tired of telling me, like my psychic *nain* (grandmother) years ago back home in North Wales and I had never really taken it seriously before now? Or was I just seeing things that weren't there?

Edward Henry Davies was looking at me strangely. "What's all this, Mrs Price?" he said, breaking into my inner turmoil, "What's going on and what's with all the guns? I thought you didn't like them?"

"I don't, Mr Davies, it's just . . ." I started to say and was just about to ask him what exactly *he* was doing here when, suddenly, all hell broke loose . . .

I had been so distracted by these constant new arrivals and visions of new found psychic 'glory' that I scarcely noticed Sharona Haf creeping up behind me until she was almost upon me . . . where the hell had she come from all of a sudden?

Before I could make a move, she had, unusually for her, ignored me and pushed Edward H Davies out of the way with a vicious shoulder barge — that girl's manners were terrible, I couldn't imagine what sort of finishing school she had gone to — then, before you could say Mynyddislwyn, or even Mynydd-y-Garreg, she had leapt onto Davies's *Hebog*, fired it up, turned it around in the direction of Casnewydd and was heading out of there at a rate of knots before any of us could make a move to stop her.

"She's taken my bike, come back with my bike, but wait a playwriting minute, that's her, that's . . ." stammered Edward Henry Davies.

"That's right, Mr Davies," I said, "that's your girl in the tangerine dress, the one you've been looking for all this time, aka Sharona Haf, but believe me, you're better off without her, she's mad, bad and dangerous to know and those are just her good points. She's not the one for you, I'm telling you. Forget her and find some home loving girl instead."

All was confusion and consternation at the Cwrt-y-bela farmhouse after Sharona's abrupt departure. Caratacus ap Cadwaladr was cheering his head off, Amber Bernstein looking pretty smug, considering the predicament she was in, and 'Stilts' was on the car radio to headquarters telling them to apprehend the fugitive, ASAP, adding she might be armed and was certainly dangerous. As for myself, I was thinking Sharona seemed to be able to handle the *Hebog* pretty well. In fact, there was something about the shape of her on that bike, as she hurtled away, that vaguely rang a distant bell with me, but, as so often with me, I couldn't quite place my digit on it. Oh well, it might come back to me later, but I wasn't going to put my Private Investigator's Licence on it.

Anyway, things started to break up after that. The Bernstein gang, minus Sharona, were ferried away in a fleet of Welsh Republican police cars with Sergeant posting a few of his men and women on guard at the Cwrt-y-bela farmhouse just in case there happened to be more of the gang at liberty than we knew about. I bade a tearful farewell to my old friend Gelert and Daniel Owen waved me a cheery goodbye.

I nodded to Pryderi. "When will I see you again?" I said. (Will I see you again, I thought, and do I *want* to see you again?)

"As soon as I'm able to get in touch," he said, "I would let you have my private number, only it's strictly against Brigade rules but you can always leave a telephone message at the Barracks for me — they're pretty good at passing them on. Stay safe, won't you," and he touched me lightly on the elbow. Proprietorially? Affectionately? Longingly? Then he was gone like last night's dream I could never quite remember.

Which left just me and Edward Henry Davies. Davies had lost his *Hebog,* whether temporarily or not remained to be seen, but I still had the keys to Caratacus ap Cadwaladr's car. "Come on, Mr Davies," I said, "I'll give you a lift back to Casnewydd. We'll be there in no time. Let's just hope we don't run into 'the light of your life,' Sharona Haf, along the way, that woman is a regular little she-devil and the sooner she's caught and safely behind bars, the better I, for one, will sleep at nights."

The drive back to Casnewydd ran smoothly, thank Cymru, no one ran out at us with designs upon our wellbeing, no one attempted to block our path to the Big City, no sign of the Welsh Republic's Most Wanted, otherwise known as Sharona Haf, anywhere, thanks be to Cymru again. If she had any sense that girl would be half way to North Wales by now and a safe house in Bangor, but something deep inside my soul told me Sharona wasn't particularly renowned for her sense, common or otherwise. Best to be on my guard still until she was safely apprehended and out of harm's way.

On the way back I attempted to interrogate Edward H Davies as best as I could, as to the reasons why he had turned up at Cwrt-y-bela Farm, when he did, but he was rather vague in his answers and noncommittal, only mumbling something about doing research for a new play he had in mind, and how he had been intrigued to see so many people milling about in the forecourt of the farmhouse, and had decided to investigate.

Sometimes I wondered about Mr Edward Henry Davies. Was he really the penniless playwright he claimed to be, coming up with obscure plays that very few people were interested in? And just why had he appeared at Cwrt-y-bela Farm, when he did, and, incidentally, provided Sharona Haf with a convenient means of escape?

Still, I had no proof either way and decided to keep my suspicions to myself for the time being, they might be unfounded, I might be imagining things, it wouldn't be the first time and I dropped him off in front of *The Lord Raglan* where I parked Caratacus's and Sharona's car right in front of a huge poster declaring in great big letters:

Forget England. Forget the Independent Welsh Republic. Join up with Ireland. Cymru knows it makes sense. Casnewydd knows it makes sense and YOU know it too! Vote Celtic Confederation. Vote the Celtic Confederation

Party for a new and better future!

Well, it took all sorts, I supposed. I was tempted to throw the car keys into the boot and be done with it, Caratacus ap Cadwaldr wouldn't be needing them where he was going, but then I decided to hold on to them for the time being, you never knew when they might come in handy. I said goodbye to Edward Henry Davies and watched him as he went on his way, still mourning the loss of his *Hebog*, I suppose, or was it the loss of Sharona Haf once more, so soon after finding her again? He turned the corner and I started walking the few blocks to *The Lying Cod*. The walk would do me good. I needed to clear my head. I had a lot to think about . . .

CHAPTER 40

When I got back to *The Lying Cod,* Big Zorba was there getting everything ready for the expected evening onslaught of customers. However hard I tried, I still couldn't get used to seeing him there instead of Stakis. Never mind, one day and pretty soon, if I had anything to do with it, my old friend would be back there in his rightful position, frying tonight. Zorba looked up and gave me a cheerful wave of his potato peeler. "All right, Astrid, love?" he said. "How's it going? Everything okay? Any news on Stakis?"

"Not so bad," I said, "and yourself? Anything to report?"

"No," he said, "it's been very quiet, very quiet indeed."

"Good," I said, "that's what I like —quiet, perfect quiet. I'll be away to my palatial apartment then," and I turned to mount the stairs to the flat.

"Okay, then," he said, "I'll see you around, oh, before you go, I've just remembered, mind like a thousand sieves, that's me, there was something . . ."

"Oh," I said, stopping dead in my tracks. "What was that?"

"Some bloke came in earlier looking for you," he said. "I told him I didn't know whether you were in or out, but he should go upstairs anyway, and find out for himself. I hope I did the right thing?"

"What did this person look like?" I said.

"Well, I'm not as observant as you are, Astrid," he said, "you being the great detective and all, and to tell you the truth I wasn't taking that much notice, being up to my eyes with potatoes at the time, but if you put me up against that wall and threatened me with a sawn-off shotgun, and other unmentionables, I'd have to say he looked a little like a military man to me."

"Thanks Zorba," I said. "You've been a great help. You did the right thing showing him upstairs. And don't worry about Stakis, we'll get there, we *are* getting there."

Slowly I climbed the stairs to my 'palatial' pad, mulling over the day's events so far. When I reached my front door I saw that someone, the 'military man', perhaps, had left a little collection there for me to find. There was a single red rose and what looked suspiciously like a box of chocolates. Attached to the chocolates was a note. I picked it up gingerly and held it away from me, as far as my arm could reach. It didn't look like it was going to explode in my face, but you never knew in my game. I didn't recognise the handwriting which was bold and left sloping with many loops and flourishes and seemingly written in fountain pen (not many of them around, nowadays). It said:

And all because the Lady Loves Lovell's Delicious

Dark Mystery Chocolates!

I've booked a table for two at Die Sachertorte tonight. 8.30 pm. Will you be there? Wear what you like, no need to be formal. If you haven't showed by 9.00 pm sharp, I'll assume you'll have found something better to do and put it down to experience.
P.
PS. I would have put the box of chocolates on that same pillow you lay your head at night, together with this note, but I figured you wouldn't be too keen on me wandering round your flat alone, giving it the 'once over'. Besides, I didn't want to disturb that little card of yours you so prettily and discreetly placed in the right hand corner of your door. See you tonight, maybe?

Cheeky bastard, I thought. Too bloody right I wouldn't want you walking round my flat alone sizing up the joint. I had to admit though, a little part of me, just a tiny little part, was impressed by Pryderi's gesture, his, it has to be said, quite romantic gesture. But how did I know Pryderi had left the chocolates? I'd never seen his handwriting. For all I knew, anybody could have written that note and was this whole set up a trap? After all I only had the P. signature at the end of the note and Big Zorba's 'military man" description (and how reliable was that?) to go on. But how would the villains know about Pryderi? Maybe they had been keeping closer tabs on me than I thought. Maybe they had been tapping my phone? Reading my correspondence? Following my every, stumbling around, haltingly, in the dark, trying to put the piece of the jigsaw together, move? Maybe, just maybe, they had seen me and Pryderi together, had put six and nine together, and then come up with the Love Story of the century and acted accordingly.

Who knew? Certainly not Sam Spade, Philip Marlow and all the rest of them. Even if they did know, none of those guys would ever tell me anything. Maybe the Dark Mystery Chocolates were poisoned? Maybe they *would* explode when I opened them?

Or maybe, just maybe, I was getting a little bit too paranoid about the whole thing. Maybe. Maybe. They were going to have to put that word on my gravestone. Too many Maybes. There was only one real way to find out. Turn up at *Die Sachertorte* at 8.20 p.m., find a dark secluded doorway to hang out somewhere opposite the place and see just who went in the restaurant by the 'witching hour' of 8.30 pm. And, in the meantime, of course, DON'T TOUCH THOSE CHOCOLATES! And with that in mind, I lightly kicked the chocolates, oh so carefully away from me, retrieved my

ASTRID PRICE INVESTIGATIONS
NO CASE TOO SMALL FOR US TO SOLVE

card where I had, oh so carefully, placed it that morning before leaving home and opened my front door, curious to know whether anybody had actually been inside . . .

CHAPTER 41

Once inside the front door I took a quick look around me. The flat looked exactly the same as when I had left it earlier. It didn't seem as if anybody had been wandering the rooms, snooping inside, but then Pryderi, if indeed Pryderi had written the note, was a professional. He would have known how to check everything but still make it appear as if nothing had been touched, and I wouldn't have put it past him to have inserted my business card back in exactly the same place, he had first found it, after he had closed my door behind him.

Now I had a decision to make: to go to *Die Sachertorte* or not to go to *Die Sachertorte*? That was, indeed, the question but not really a very difficult one to answer. I *was* going, there was no doubt about that, if only to put my mind at rest about who exactly had written the note and whether or not it would be safe to eat those chocolates he had left for me.

No, the more important question was this: what clothes should I wear to this 'assignation'? (It didn't feel right to call it a date, somehow.) The writer of the note, the mysterious P., who may or may not have been Lieutenant Pryderi, had said to 'wear what you like, no need to be formal' and that was what he was going to get. I tried on a few of my most precious items in front of the mirror, but in the end decided on something smart but casual, like designer jeans and a fashionable t-shirt and also some sensible shoes, just in case I had to do a 'runner' or even chase somebody down myself, before the night was out. I checked myself in the mirror again — yes, that would do, smart but chic, the Astrid 'look'.

Then I looked out of my window at the street below. There didn't seem to be anyone about. That didn't mean to say there *wasn't* anybody there, of course. There *could* be someone, lurking in the shadows, just waiting to ambush me when I was least expecting it. Still, nothing ventured and all that . . . I drew myself up to my full height, ran my fingers lightly through my Titian coloured hair and breathed in deeply. Then, gently closing my front door behind me, taking good care to place my business card in the top right hand corner as I did so, I made my way to *Die Sachertorte* and whatever fate awaited me there.

CHAPTER 42

Outside *The Lying Cod*, none of my worst fears seemed, happily, to have been realised. No one leaped out at me from darkened doorways, brandishing yet another big gun in my direction, and insisting I accompanied them on a ride to some place I really, really did not want to go. No one accosted me in the street asking for a light, or anything else they could think of, as an excuse to bash me over the head with a seriously blunt instrument. All was calm. All was serenity which was just the way I wanted it.

Somewhat reassured, but still wary, I continued on my way to the *Pwca* which I had parked just around the corner. Just above me, I heard the wistful, melancholic sound of a Welsh *Fado* (this summer's surprise hit music —how long would it last, I wondered) singer, and the accompanying plangent guitars, issuing from some of the upper floor apartments on the opposite side of the street. And then, before you could say Llanfihangel Ystern Llewern backwards, or even Llwynypia, I was upon it, my pride and joy, the light of my life, my love and my delight, my *Pwca*.

I took a quick look around me, nobody seemed to be about, no was watching, ready to pounce. I took another quick look — still nothing. Then, very carefully and very gently, I got down on my knees and looked beneath the car very closely and very slowly until I was satisfied that there was nothing underneath that shouldn't be there. All these precautions may sound a bit over the top, but it didn't do to be too careful in this day and age, especially when a known head case like Sharona Haf was out there somewhere, on the loose and maybe out for revenge, not to mention all the local low lifes who might have it in for me. Gingerly, I opened the car door and then I took a good look inside, relieved to know there was no one in there, no unwelcome stowaway, or stowaways, just waiting to spoil my evening.

    I sat down behind the wheel and took a moment to compose my thoughts. Then I put the car into first and ramped up the gears as I left *The Lying Cod* behind me. After a while I turned on the radio for some background noise, just in time to hear the well known voice of Brigantia Lightfoot say:

    And now we have some breaking news just in from the Welsh Republican Police. Reliable sources suggest they have succeeded in apprehending members of a dangerous North Walian gang specialising in gun running, drug smuggling and other nefarious crimes. Recently, their activities appear to have extended to the south of the Welsh Republic. One of the gang is, however, believed to be still at large. Details to follow shortly. Our sources say The Welsh Republican Police are close to solving the mystery of the whereabouts of Madge Breese's original recording of Mae Hen Wlad Fy Nhadau, *the Welsh National Anthem, which was taken from its museum case in Caernarfon some time ago. The recording is of historic importance and it is hoped it will be recovered undamaged. An announcement on this matter is expected very soon and we will be sure to keep our listeners and viewers informed. This is Brigantia Lightfoot signing off. There now follows a discussion programme on the relevance and significance of the 'craze' that has recently been sweeping the nation —* Welsh Fado *music.*

Well, well, I thought, trust the Welsh Republican Police to claim all the credit and not give so much as a mention to little old me, or anyone else who had helped them out upon their, sometimes, not so merry way. Never mind, I'm not bitter, well, not much and the main thing was that the case appeared to have been brought to a successful conclusion and it looked as if Stakis would be out very soon, a free man once more. Pryderi and I *might* or might not have a thing going (that remained to be seen) the weather forecast looked set on good for the foreseeable future and the sun would continue to shine for a while yet . . .

In fact, the only potential 'nagging doubt' gnawing away at me was, where was Sharona Haf? There was no telling what that girl would do, especially now she was on her own without Caratacus ap Cadwaladr to restrain her (if he ever did, that is). Somehow I knew I wouldn't really be able to rest easy until I knew for sure she would be locked away behind bars in Portmeirion and for a good while to come. I would just have to be on my guard, that's all and warn all my associates to do the same.

I switched off the rather interesting radio discussion about the merits, or otherwise, of Welsh *Fado* and parked the *Pwca* a couple of streets away from *Die Sachertorte*. So far so good. Everything was going exactly as I had planned it. As I made my way towards the restaurant, I did my best to blend in and not stand out from the crowd, whilst at the same time keeping a wary eye out for anything unusual.

There, everything was going according to plan, I was in *Die Sachertorte's* street and on time (the time I had set myself that is) 8.20 pm. Now, for that darkened secluded doorway, not too near the restaurant for me to be noticed by anyone, but from where I could observe all *Die Sachertorte's* comings and goings at my leisure.

A few minutes passed and I was unable to resist looking at my watch. 8.25 pm. Nothing much had happened. Just a stray dog running past me, trying to find its home, any home, for the night. There was no sign of Pryderi, or any one else for that matter, and *Die Sachertorte* itself didn't appear to be overly busy.

I shuffled my feet. Maybe this hadn't been such a

great idea, after all, and I was already beginning to wonder about Pryderi's punctuality, or, perhaps, lack of it, he was cutting it very fine for 8.30, the appointed time. Not a good sign in my book. Then I saw him. It was Pryderi all right. He was not walking down the street towards the restaurant, as I would have Imagined, but standing in the doorway of *Die Sachertorte*, looking rather resplendent in his military uniform, I thought and making me feel distinctly underdressed. He looked up and down the street, but didn't see me hiding in my doorway. Then he looked at his watch, shook his head and went back inside *Die Sachertorte*.

Good, so he had been punctual, after all, I thought, but there was no reason for me to be. No reason at all for me to appear too eager . . . Nothing like keeping a good man waiting and so I did before making my grand entrance around five minutes later.

As I stepped inside, I noticed the same Anton Karas look-a-like, who had been there when I had last visited with Pryderi, (it seemed a long time ago now) was playing a selection of what I took to be Austrian folk songs on his zither. Obviously, *Die Sachertorte* was having no truck with Welsh *Fado,* no matter how popular it might currently be in the rest of the Welsh Republic.

Within seconds of my entering what was a crowded restaurant, full of diners all enjoying the delights *Die Sachertorte* had to offer, a waitress was at my shoulder, in her smartly pressed black and white uniform, an Austrian hussar's shako on her head, wanting to know where I would like to sit. I looked at her, resplendent in her own particular uniform, and felt even more underdressed, in fact, I briefly thought of asking her if I could borrow her uniform for the evening, but before I could explain a table had already been booked for me, Pryderi had seen us and was gesturing towards his table.

He rose from his seat as I approached. "Price," he said, "lovely to see you. You made it after all, then? I was beginning to wonder. You're looking very nice tonight, I must say. Allow me . . ." and he, very solicitously pulled out my chair for me to sit. A gentleman, then?

"Yes," I said, "as you see, I had a little trouble with the traffic on my way here."

The waitress now approached our table which, I briefly noticed, was set with the usual array of cutlery and expensive looking linen napkins, and asked if she could take our orders.

She was wearing that same smartly pressed, black and white uniform with the same Austrian hussar's shako on her head, and she had that cute little Austrian accent all of the staff seemed to have, but for some reason her voice sounded vaguely familiar to me, as if I'd heard it somewhere before.

There was also a faint, but unmistakable,

lingering smell of stale cigarette smoke about her, something I had smelled somewhere before, perhaps, but to tell you the truth, reader, I hadn't come all the way here to spend my time worrying about the waitress's nicotine addiction. I looked up at Pryderi and smiled my best unsalted Welsh butter sweet smile. This was going to be a good night, I knew it in my Brecon Carreg bottled water.

"I'll have the vegetarian *Zigeunerschnitzel* with fried potatoes and a green salad, with a glass of *Echt Wiener Lagerbier* to go with it," I said, "and, oh yes, a hazelnut chocolate *Palatschinken* to follow with coffee to round it all off."

"Good choice," he said, and to the waitress, "I'll have the same, thank you," and she took our menus away but soon returned with our drinks.

Once she had gone, I put my hand on his hand. Well, I was an emancipated woman, after all. He looked at me rather curiously but didn't take his hand away.

"Are you always this forward?" he said.

"Only when the mood takes me," I said, looking deep into his hazel brown eyes. "Thank you for inviting me," I said, "and for the chocolates too. I'll look forward to sampling them later."

Pryderi gave me a strange look. "But I didn't invite you," he said, "you invited me. You left a telephone message for me at the barracks. And I didn't give you any chocolates either . . . "

"But I didn't leave a message . . ." I said.

Uh, oh, alarm bells were beginning to ring ever so faintly inside my head but still I didn't twig and persisted in looking into his eyes, his hazel brown eyes. And that, dear reader, might very well have been my undoing. I was so absorbed in acting like a lovesick teenager, so intent on unlocking the secrets of Pryderi's soul as reflected in his hazel brown eyes, so caught up in what our future together might be, if we were ever to have one, that I failed to hear the footsteps approaching our table, failed to notice the person standing over me until I heard Pryderi cry out in horror, heard rather than saw the cosh thud into the side of his head and caught the flash of the great big handled knife as it plunged towards me . . .

I caught the flash of the great big handled knife as it plunged towards me

CHAPTER 43

Instinctively, I somehow managed to throw myself to my left, and out of harm's way, as the knife slammed, harmlessly, into the table. That brief moment when the attacker's attention had been divided between Pryderi and myself had saved me, temporarily at least, but there was still the threat of the cosh to worry about and the knife, of course, as soon as the assailant wrenched it from the table. My brain had gone into overdrive, I was unarmed, no faithful Excalibur, no gun, after all I had been expecting nothing more than an enjoyable dinner date. Now, more than ever I needed all my wits about me if I was to survive.

I swept up the glass of Franz Josef *Echt Wiener Lagerbier* and flung it straight into the face of my opponent who, luckily for me, seemed more preoccupied with extracting the knife than using the cosh on me. It was a waste of good lager beer, of course, but needs must at a time like this. It was my devout hope that there would be many more such beers to come, as things stood, I had little else to cling to, but first I had to survive. Now I saw the face beneath the Austrian Hussar shako, the face of the waitress who had been serving us, the face of the waitress I had resolutely ignored previously, the face of Sharona Haf . . .

What was the matter with me? What had I been

thinking? I had been blind, so blind. The warning signs had all been there for me to see, but I had wilfully ignored them and for what? For this growing obsession with Pryderi?

Pryderi? Was he still in the Land of the Living? Had Sharona killed him with that sickening cosh blow to the head? I wanted to run to him, to hold his head in my hands, cradle him in my arms, but I had other things to think about now, like how I was going to get out of this place in one piece myself with a determined Sharona Haf dead set on finishing me off once and for all. What had Stakis said she was —a devil woman? That sounded just about right in my book.

The good news was that the beer I had thrown at Sharona's face had temporarily stopped her in her tracks. The bad news was that she had succeeded in pulling out the knife and was coming for me again but luckily the beer had given me just enough time to pick up my chair and hold it out in front of me.

"Think that's going to stop me, Price," sneered Sharona, "I'll do for you and then I'll finish your little friend off. Crad and I had a good thing going until you showed up, poking your interfering nose into everything. Well, you got Amber and the rest of them, but you're not going to get me. You're going down, Price," and she lunged at me with that great big handled knife of hers.

Somehow, I managed to fend her off with my chair, dimly aware of the rising panic and pandemonium in the restaurant behind me. People were screaming and shouting and, probably running for the door. I hoped someone, anyone would have the good sense to alert 'Stilts' Sempringham and her colleagues before it was too late.

I tried a counter thrust of my own with the chair to get her to move back, but she merely yelled in frustration, slashing at the wooden legs with the knife and crashing into the chair with her cosh. Don't go backwards, Astrid, whatever you do, don't go backwards. If I go backwards, if I can't see where I'm going, if I stumble and fall, then Sharona will surely have me and there's an end to it. No, remember your rugby training, move from side to side, more or less on the same spot, sway, sidestep, try to confuse her, keep her talking, but don't go backwards, no, don't go backwards.

"Sharona," I said, breathing heavily, as by now we both were, and trying to think how I could separate her from the knife and cosh, "before you kill me, just put me out of my misery. How did you manage all this tonight? We thought you'd gone back to the North and Bangor."

"Oh, that," she said, "that was easy, that's what I thought you would think. I disguised myself and went to that hovel you call a home. How can you live there? The dozy big guy behind the counter was too busy peeling potatoes or something to take much notice of me. Then I put the note and the chocolates in front of your door. Don't worry, I didn't have time to poison them or anything. They're perfectly safe to eat, not that you'll be in any fit state to eat them after I've finished with you, of course. I would have gone in to see the state of your 'apartment' but I was running out of time and had to leave. Then I left a message for your soldier friend at the barracks. He fell for it, as did you, Price, The Great Detective," and she laughed, but there was no mirth in the sound.

Before she could make another pass at me with that deadly looking knife, I spoke again. "What about the dog, Sharona, what was the name of the dog? Please tell me before you kill me. I'd just like to know before I go."

Sharona laughed again, "why are you so concerned about that bloody dog, Price. All right I'll tell you, it'll be like granting the condemned woman's last wish" and she flashed at me again with the knife, but I was ready and fended her off with my chair.

"Touché, Price," said Sharona, "if you really want to know, the mutt's name was Hector and I used to borrow him from the local WSPCA (Welsh Society of Prevention of Cruelty to Animals) to take for a walk every day. Anything to relieve the boredom of being stuck in that house by the cemetery every day waiting for a fresh consignment of Super Dragons to come through and with only Herb the Serb for company. God, was he boring. Almost as boring as your mate, that *twp* (fool) Stakis, always going on about how great you were, and how you were going to get him out of that house in

Cwm Hyfryd . . . it made me sick, I can tell you. How can you stand being around that guy?"

Suddenly, as I made a thrust of my own with the chair to force her back, a light went on inside my head, illuminating something I should have known, should have seen long before . . .

"So it was *you* then," I said, trying again to push her back with the chair.

"It was me what?" she said, lunging at me in her turn and making me realise once again, never had I been so glad to hold onto a chair, but I had been watching her hands, not her face, and again fended her off.

"You who fired the bolt at the tree that day in Coed Melyn Park," I said, "you who rode the *Hebog* away from there when I came after you in the *Pwca*. That's why those two bent coppers, Joe and Jude, stopped me because they wanted you to get away."

It had taken me long enough to work all this out, but it was all falling into place now, not that it would do me much good, unless I could find some way of disarming Sharona. I wasn't as fit as I used to be and the strain was beginning to tell on me. "It was you who made that threatening phone call warning me off the case right at the beginning," I panted, "you were the 'Perm' woman in that house opposite the cemetery, the one with all the owls, you left those notes for me there after you and Herb the Serb abandoned those houses . . ."

"Well, well," said Sharona, "the Master Detective strikes again. And you worked all that out by yourself, you ginger-haired South Walian bitch. I really would applaud, only, as you can see, my hands are rather full at the moment. And now that I've answered all of your stupid questions, there's no real reason for you to stay in this world any longer, is there. Goodbye, Mrs Astrid Price, I'd like to say that it's been a pleasure knowing you but it hasn't, it really hasn't," and she made a determined lunge at me with both knife and cosh.

A cold rage came over me. If I was going down, then she was coming with me, or my name wasn't Astrid Bronwen Price. "Boudicca," I shouted at the top of my lungs, at the same time feinting to my left and pushing forward with the chair as hard as I could. Whether it was my blood curdling war cry that did it, or whether she was beginning to tire, I don't know, but she visibly fell back a little, giving me my half a chance. Out of the corner of my eye I saw Pryderi's still full glass of beer on our table along with our two sets of cutlery.

I whipped the glass off the table and flung its contents full into Sharona's face. Then, as she reeled ever so slightly, I followed it up, throwing the knives and forks straight at her. She was wobbling now, there was no doubt about it and I brought my chair down hard on her knife hand. The great big handled knife, no doubt another one from the town of Solingen, the German equivalent of Sheffield, clattered to the floor and, as it did so, I smashed the chair down on her other hand still holding the cosh.

Then, I was on her, raining blows down on her, all thoughts of using my Tai Chi banished temporarily from my mind, I was so angry, all my pent up rage and frustration pouring out of me. "That's for Pryderi," I said, driving the punch in as hard as it would go, "and that's for Stakis, and this is with love from Astrid, the *Titian*-haired South Walian bitch," following it up with two more hefty blows as Sharona Haf began to wilt visibly under the savage attack, trying to cover her face with her hands and offering little or no resistance.

I swear I would have done for her, I was so angry but I heard approaching footsteps and looked up to see WPC 'Stilts' Sempringham running towards me, gun at the ready, closely followed by Sergeant and Pritchard and I came to my senses, just in time. "You're too late," I said, blowing hard, "the party's over, take her away," and I rushed to Pryderi's side, Sharona's shouts of "I'll get you for this, Astrid Price, you'll see if I don't," ringing in my ears.

CHAPTER 44

As I got to him, he was just beginning to come round, although looking distinctly groggy. He opened his eyes wide and saw me. "Price," he struggled to say, "you're still alive," and then, "have I missed all the fun?"

"Yes, on both counts," I said, "we're not having much luck with *Die Sachertorte*, are we?" trying to smile and reassure him.

I turned to Inspector Sergeant who was standing next to me. "Is there an ambulance on the way?" I said, "or a doctor? Pryderi needs to be checked out by a doctor. That was a vicious blow to the head he took."

"Yes," said Sergeant, "they're on their way. What about you?" Are *you* all right? This must all have been a severe shock to you. Maybe the doctor should take a look at you too?"

"I'm all right," I said. "I feel fine." But was I? Now that the adrenalin of the fight with Sharona was beginning to wear off, I could feel my legs beginning to shake, and the fact that I had a very narrow escape was beginning to sink in slowly.

Sergeant looked at me, almost solicitously, I thought, that wasn't like him, what was going on and brought me a chair. "Here," he said, "sit down here till the medical people arrive and hold his hand. He's had a severe shock too." And then, turning to *Die Sachertorte's* staff who were standing some distance away, having their statements taken by his men and women, he shouted, "one of you bring us some tea over here, three cups, hot, strong and sweet and make it snappy."

"But I don't take . . ." I started to say, but Sergeant interrupted me. "Drink it, Astrid," he said, "Drink it, it'll do you good."

Well, to cut the proverbial long story short, the ambulance soon arrived and took me and Pryderi to Casnewydd's new, state of the art *Lady Rhondda Hospital*, 'Stilts' Sempringham 'riding shotgun', in order to take my statement later.

The doctors examined Pryderi thoroughly and decided that no real, lasting damage had been done by Sharona's vicious blow to the head, but that he needed to stay in overnight as a precaution. As for me, they diagnosed a slight shock to my system which was only to be expected under the circumstances but that the effects would begin to wear off after a few hours.

WPC Sempringham duly took my statement and drove me home to *The Lying Cod*. "Are you okay, Astrid?" she said, "would you like me to come in and sit with you for a while? Just till you feel better?"

"Thanks for the offer, Gwenllian," I said, "it's very kind of you, but I'm a big girl now and I think I'll be all right, thank you, after all, nobody died, not even Sharona."

"No," she said, laughing, "somehow I don't think

that girl likes you very much, Astrid. Well, I'll be on my way. Look after yourself," and she started the car and was gone, leaving me alone with my thoughts and thinking to myself, as I mounted the stairs to my flat, maybe I needed to pay Branwen Guest and the Casnewydd Super Dragons another visit tomorrow . . . . it was just a hunch I had, but first I needed some 'me time,' a herbal tea, perhaps, a light snack, and then a long, luxuriant soak in a warm bath to wash all traces of 'the devil woman,' Sharona Haf, away, together with some scented candles and aromatic bath salts and all the necessary trimmings. Maybe some soothing music. And then sleep. Beautiful sleep. Precious sleep. Perchance to dream, as the bard would have it, but of what precisely or of whom . . .

CHAPTER 45

The next day I was up bright and early and the first thing I did was to call *The Lady Rhondda Hospital* to check on Pryderi's health. The news was good, they said, he was well and in good spirits but they were keeping him in for another night just to err on the side of caution. I'd check in again later, I told them. Relieved that things seemed to be going so well, I showered, dressed and breakfasted and was soon on my way to see Branwen Guest and the Casnewydd Super Dragons. Call it a hunch, call it a woman private dick's intuition, call it my inherited 'psychic powers,' call it what you will, but I had a feeling about them. In fact I had had a feeling about them for quite some time now but lately it had been growing in intensity.

Reflecting my mood, the sun was (once again) shining and I sauntered along without a care in the world although, once or twice, I had the strangest feeling that I was not alone, someone was following me, but each time I turned my head, I saw no one and nothing. Eventually I decided that recent events had made me even more paranoid than I usually was, or perhaps I was suffering from an attack of Post Sharona Haf Stress Disorder (that girl had a lot to answer for) but she was safely locked up and out of harm's way, and under constant guard, so I thought no more about it and carried on walking to my destination.

When I reached it, Super Dragon Central (the empty shop which Casnewydd City Council had temporarily taken over) was just as I remembered it from my earlier visit. It was fairly early when I got there but nothing much appeared to have changed: the same local artists were still hard at work, applying the finishing touches to the same ten or twelve fibreglass dragon bodies, drinking instant coffee out of a variety of cups and mugs, or just standing back and admiring their handiwork. The Dragons themselves were just as I recalled, all of them about five feet high from head to hoof.

A quick glance around the room revealed the same pots of paint, palette knives and brushes scattered everywhere, the same old newspapers strewn over parts of the floor and the same battered old armchairs and sofas offering a welcome rest to visitor and artist alike. It was like stepping back in time.

Just like before, no two Dragons were exactly the same, some were painted in bright, bold attractive colours, others featured a *smorgasbord* of differing motifs, local and international whilst still others were covered in surreal flights of fancy where the artist had really let their imagination take flight and soar to the heavens. One of them was the one I was looking for, but which one?

As I stepped further into the room I made a

beeline for the woman whose hair was tucked under a sort of bluish red turban. Just like the last time, she was still wearing the same overall, which had once upon a time been white but was now covered with paint, old and new.

"Branwen," I said, and, at the sound of her name, Branwen Guest stopped minutely examining her own Super Dragon and looked up.

"Why, Augusta," she said, "how nice to see you again, it is Augusta, isn't it, I thought you'd gone back up North, back to Bangor . . ."

Somehow, I hadn't the heart to tell her my name wasn't Augusta, well, not yet, anyway. "I couldn't keep away," I said, "Casnewydd kept calling me back. Anyway, my editor wanted some more local colour, so here I am again. Tell me, Branwen, just how heavy are these Super Dragons? I mean how many people would it take to lift one and shake it all about?"

"Goodness, Augusta," said Branwen Guest, "you do ask the strangest questions, I must say. They're comparatively light, I suppose, I don't know, maybe three or four people . . ."

"Branwen," I said, "I know this is going to sound strange to you, but could you and your colleagues just help me out, humour me really, by lifting each Super Dragon in turn and shaking it? How many are there? Ten? Twelve? It shouldn't take that long and my readers would be really interested in knowing the results."

Branwen looked at me as if I had fallen off the top of Snowdon in a raging gale and lost all my faculties in the process.

"Is this really necessary, Augusta?" she said.

"It's just a theory I've got," I said. "You want to be in the paper, don't you?"

"Well . . ." she said, rather doubtfully, "I don't suppose it can do any harm. What do you say, guys?"

The rest of the artists, who had been listening intently to our conversation, whilst pretending to be hard at work, probably agreed with Branwen that I had no marbles left to speak of, if indeed, I had ever had any in the first place, but they nodded in agreement. What the heck, I suppose it broke the daily routine up a bit.

Three or four of them lifted up the first Dragon with comparative ease and shook it all about, rather sheepishly, it must be said, but no sound could be heard from within the fibre glass body, but by the fourth or fifth Dragon, they were getting into their stride and giving each 'beastie', a good old shake, even Branwen joining in enthusiastically, but still no sound came from within the Newport Super Dragons.

When the same thing happened with Dragons six to ten, namely, they were given a good old shake but we could hear nothing, I began to wonder whether my theory had been right after all. Dragon Number 11 went the same way which left only one remaining, coincidentally, Branwen Guest's own Super Dragon.

This then was the acid test. If this last one 'failed,' I would walk away feeling like a fool and with a lot of egg on my face. "One last try, guys," I said, as they hoisted Branwen's Dragon up and began to shake. There. It was there slight and rather faint but it was an unmistakeable rattling sound nevertheless. Something was inside Branwen Guest's Super Dragon but what? That was the question. I had half an idea but I couldn't be sure.

"Well done, people," I said, "now to open it up and see what's inside. Anyone got a grinder?"

"Oh, really, Augusta," said Branwen Guest, "I must protest, this is going too far . . ."

"But don't you want to see what's inside, Branwen?" I said, "if it's what I think it is, we could be on to something big. We just need to cut open the space between the wings so that I can put my hand in and pull whatever it is out. My paper will reimburse you, if that's what you're worried about and bring in someone to fix the Dragon so that it's as good as new. What do you say?"

Well, Branwen ummed and ahhed for quite a while but finally she gave her consent. A grinder was found from somewhere and one of the burly artists donned protective mask and gloves and set to work, whilst someone opened the door to let the air in, and everyone stood back at a respectful distance.

In no time at all, or so it seemed, the burly artist

had opened a gap wide enough for him to put his gloved hand inside the Super Dragon. Carefully, he pulled out what appeared to be a Tesco's Cymru plastic bag folded over. Even more carefully, he wiped away the fragments of fibre glass from the bag and handed it to me. (They seemed to have accepted me as their leader.)

Equally as carefully, I slowly opened the bag and pulled out what seemed to be a single-sided 7-inch disc. I turned it over. I had suspected it but was still shocked to hold it in my hands. "It's the missing Madge Breese recording," I said, "People, rejoice, we've found the recording of her singing *Mae Hen Wlad Fy Nhadau* which was stolen from the museum in Caernarfon. Well done, everybody."

A collective gasp went round the room interrupted only by a voice saying, "I'll take that disc off your hands now, Astrid, thanks for finding it for me," a voice I knew, a voice I recognised . . .

CHAPTER 46

" 'Stilts,' " I said, (old habits die hard) as I turned round and looked straight at WPC Gwenllian Sempringham. Where had she come from all of a sudden? Had she been the one that was following me earlier on, I thought, but I said, "I mean Gwenllian, you look so different out of uniform, but what are you doing here? And why are you pointing that Welsh Republican Police regulation issue revolver straight at me? This is some kind of joke, surely? I thought we were friends . . ."

"Don't kid yourself, Astrid," she said, "we were never friends, we've never been friends, you and I, even when we were in the Welsh Women's rugby team together, it was always *me*, *me*, *me* with you, the controlling outside half, the show-off number Ten, dictating tactics, only thinking of her own personal glory. None of the other girls liked you, you know that, don't you, always bossing people around, telling them what to do . . . Now hand over your find to me and I might just let you live."

"But why do you keep calling her Astrid all the time?" Branwen Guest broke in, "she's Augusta Hall, the newspaper reporter. She wrote *How Mean Was My Valley,* you know."

"My rear end, she did," said 'Stilts', "she's Astrid Price, a somewhat incompetent private investigator and former rugby playing poseur. She's been having you on, lady, she's good at that."

I could see Branwen looking somewhat crestfallen at this revelation and felt a twinge of conscience at my deception, but I had other things to worry about at the moment, such as how was I going to remove this latest obstacle to further progress in my life.

"Tell me, Gwenllian," I said, "just out of interest, are you a member of the Amber Bernstein gang? Is that what this is all about? You're here to achieve what the rest of the gang couldn't accomplish? Find the Madge Breese recording?"

"Huh!" said Gwenllian, "the Amber Bernstein gang. Those losers. D'you think I'd waste my time with them? Mrs Big? Don't make me laugh . . ."

"But what about Joe and Jude?" I said. "Those two rogue policemen? Didn't you feel any affinity with them?"

"Those two," said Gwenllian, "small fry both of them, the only similarity between them and me is that we were all using The Welsh Republican Police force for our own ends. Did you know we found out one of them, Joe, I think it was, telephoned you, trying to warn you not to go to Cwrt-y-bela Farmhouse? Must have a soft spot for you, I suppose, can't think why . . . Now, stop talking and hand over the recording, before I shoot you down here on the spot and take it anyway. What's it to be —with —or without your blessing?"

"But 'Stilts'," I said, "I mean Gwenllian, you swore an oath to uphold the values of the Welsh Republic when you signed up to enforce our laws. Surely that means something to you. This here is one of our greatest icons and belongs in the museum in Caernarfon. Now put down the gun, there's a good girl and let's talk this over and come to an amicable agreement."

"D'you know how much a WPC earns in a month in this ramshackle Welsh Republic of yours, Astrid, chickenfeed, that's what. That disc is going to be my passport to the life of luxury I've always craved. There are lots of private investors willing to pay good money for it and I'm about to make their dreams come true. Now hand it over and stop calling me 'Stilts', I hated that nickname and still do, I went along with it for the sake of the team but . . ."

"But what about PC Pritchard and Inspector Sergeant," I said, "won't you be letting them down, they believe in you."

"Those idiots," she said, "I'm head and shoulders above them, and not just as far as my height goes, I'll be glad to see the back of both of them. And don't think I don't know what you're doing, Astrid, trying to stall, trying to keep me talking while you come up with some plan to save your posing outside half skin. Well, it's not working with me. I see right through you. Now, for the last time, give me what I need, what I want, my meal ticket to a better life, there's *a good girl*, or . . ."

"Okay, Gwenllian," I said, "you win, I give up, you've seen through all my tricks, here's your recording, I hope you enjoy your new life," and I spun the single-sided 7-inch disc containing Madge Breese's historic version of *Hen Wlad Fy Nhadau* through the air like a frisbee on the beach, but not to WPC Gwenllian 'Stilts' Sempringham, oh, no, not to her.

"Catch it, Branwen," I shouted, "catch it, don't let it drop, for Cymru's sake!"

'Stilts' Sempringham stared, as if hypnotised, as she watched the disc flying through the air, oh, so slowly, or so it seemed to everyone there. "You crazy woman . . . " she started to say, but she never finished the sentence, as I slammed into her, low and hard, remembering my coaching sessions at The Casnewydd Young Maidens all those years ago, grabbing her around the knees in one of my finest tackles, before she could get a shot off.

Down she went like my bank balance at the end of the month and the gun clattered from her hand to the floor. The bigger they are, the harder they fall, indeed, I thought. "Get her gun," Branwen, "I shouted, "get her gun, quick!"

'Stilts' Sempringham was bigger than me and heavier than me. She managed to escape from my tackle and came gunning for me, as I backed away, but she was just a lumbering second row forward really, and I easily sidestepped her clumsy attempt at a haymaker. Then I

"Don't let it drop, for Cymru's sake!"

pivoted and Tai Chi hooked her in the side of her throat. Down she went again like *The Titanic* after its disastrous encounter with the iceberg, but, to give her her due, she got straight back up again, although a little more slowly this time, and tried to rush me like one of those raging bulls from Pamplona in the north of Spain. I let her go by and then, at the last moment, stuck out a leg for her to fall over. Down she went like one of those falling leaves in autumn they're always singing about, only harder, a lot harder. This time she didn't get up. Job done, I thought, and hoped there weren't any more bent coppers or unpleasant surprises, somewhere around the corner, just waiting to leap out on me and make my life a misery. There were only so many of those a girl could take.

To my complete surprise, the room burst into spontaneous applause and I found myself, almost unconsciously, taking a bow. Well, why not, I thought, enjoying my moment in the limelight, it wasn't every day I found myself able to rescue precious historic artefacts and thwart yet another dastardly villain at the same time. I basked in the approval of my peers for just a little attention seeking minute . . .

"Augusta, Astrid, whoever you are, whatever your name is, that was wonderful," gushed a beaming Branwen Guest, "but, please, please, don't ever do that to me again, will you, for one heart stopping moment, I really thought I was going to fumble the catch and drop that priceless Madge Breese recording . . . oh, it doesn't bear thinking about."

The thought had crossed my mind too, but I wasn't going to tell her that, I didn't want to hurt her feelings, so I said, "I knew you were going to catch it, Branwen, I had complete faith in you. You don't think I would have thrown it otherwise, do you? Now if you'll just call the Welsh Republican Police for me and ask for Inspector Sergeant, oh, and hand me that gun while you're at it, I'll sort out young 'Stilts' here . . ."

CHAPTER 47

So that was, more or less, that. The Amber Bernstein gang were all safely behind bars, awaiting trial and, very possibly, nothing to look forward to but long prison sentences in Portmeirion. They had been joined in jail by the disgraced WPC, Gwenllian 'Stilts' Sempringham, who had put her own greed above loyalty to the Welsh Republican Police uniform. (In fact, I was beginning to think that that particular force was in need of a latter-day Hercules to clean up its very own modern day version of the Augean stables, especially as Joe and Jude, of the Amber Bernstein gang, were two other officers who had betrayed the trust put in them by the public.)

Lawyer Frost had wasted no time in 'springing' Stakis from prison as soon as it became clear beyond all reasonable doubt that Sharona Haf was behind the knife murders of Red Iolo and Culloden Jimmie. My old friend walked free from jail without a stain on his character.

Meanwhile, it was becoming clearer by the day that Sharona Haf, the 'she devil,' the 'devil woman' was also responsible for the death of John Henry Sienkiewicz, or Polish John, the small time crook, well known in North Wales criminal circles, who had been stabbed in the back with what the local police described as 'a great big handled knife', when all this first broke upon my consciousness.

From the dribs and drabs emerging from Welsh Republican Police headquarters, it appeared that Sienkiewicz had been part of the Amber Bernstein gang, and had been with them when they had stolen the Madge Breese recording from the museum in Caernarfon. Sienkiewicz must have spotted an opportunity to double-cross the rest of the gang and keep the recording and its money-making potential for himself.

Somehow, he had seized the disc right in front of the others' noses, given them the slip and had made it as far as Bangor, when they caught up with him, amazingly, at the very place where the Casnewydd Super Dragons were being made. Seeking sanctuary, Sienkiewicz had broken in and just had time to secrete the Madge Breese recording inside one of the Super Dragons, thinking he could come back later to retrieve it at his leisure, but his plans never came to fruition, however, as Mrs Big and her people were waiting for him on his way out.

They eventually forced him to reveal what he had done and then, presumably, Sharona finished him off when he was no longer of any use to them. Then, they tried to retrieve the stolen 7-inch disc but they were too late. The Super Dragon in question had already passed along the conveyor belt, been completed and was already on its way south with the rest of the consignment to Casnewydd.

As for Pryderi . . . Ah, Pryderi . . . He was released from *The Lady Rhondda Hospital* with a clean bill of health, and no lasting after effects despite Sharona's best efforts, but before we could hook up together for an evening meal at a restaurant of our own choice, not, I hasten to add, *Die Sachertorte* — lovely as it was, that place held too many associations now for both of us, Pryderi's regiment had been called up for active service, probably somewhere near one of the Welsh Sea ports in the face of growing Irish hostility towards the Welsh Republic, or along the English border, where rumours were rife of impending trouble with our giant neighbour, despite the indefatigable diplomatic efforts of our Foreign Minister, Margaret Hanmer, in both Dublin and London, but it was all very hush-hush and I had no real idea where he was. There was a strict communications blackout in operation too, so there was no way of getting in touch with him. And where did all that leave us and our fledgling 'relationship,' if you could call it that . . .

Would we fly, faultlessly, like two rooks or jackdaws through the gathering dusk towards their evening roost and stay together or would we plummet to earth like that Greek boy in the legends, (what was his name again?) and perish separately, our overweening ambition having done for us? Well, we would find out eventually, one way or another . . .

And Edward Henry Davies? He turned out to be

kosher after all, despite my misgivings about him from time to time, with no criminal connections of any kind. He even stumped up for free tickets for me and a few friends to see his latest offering *Aneurin Bevan — What Might Have Been*. The programme notes even said *Inspired by my friend, Mrs Astrid Price*. I glowed inwardly. Well, why not? Take the compliments where you can get them, I always say.

Unfortunately, however, Edward Henry Davies's infatuation with Sharona Haf showed no signs of diminishing. Quite the contrary, in fact. In spite of the overwhelming body of evidence against her, and the almost racing certainty that she would be convicted of at least three murders at her forthcoming trial, not forgetting her attempts to murder both Pryderi and me, Edward Henry Davies insisted on standing by her, writing her letters, visiting her in the Welsh Republican Police cells, and even talking of visiting her once she was a prisoner in Portmeirion when, as seemed almost inevitable, she would be sentenced to spend, if not the rest of her days, a considerable part of her life there.

I had tried in vain, on more than one occasion, to get him to see sense and forget this dangerous obsession with Sharona Haf. In vain, did I try to convince him that she was using his infatuation for her own, no doubt nefarious, ends, but he would have none of it. I could see no good coming of all this, I could feel it in my Brecon Carreg bottled water, but Edward H Davies would not hear a word against her, claiming she had become a reformed character and 'had seen the light' since she had been arrested and after several intense conversations with him had finally seen the error of her ways. Well, he was over twenty-one and, supposedly old enough and able enough to make his own decisions . . .

As for the elections, well, election night finally came around and President Mary Hopkin's Those Were The Days party was voted in again, but this time with a much reduced majority, so that coalition talks between them and some of the other, smaller, parties would soon be taking place in order for them to form a viable government. Maybe Ivor Hale's Generous Party's time had finally come . . .

So I had lots to mull over as I walked with my companion across the old town bridge on a balmy evening in early summer. A full moon was shining, high up in a clear sky and the tide was rising on the Brown River, lapping against the bridge's supporting pillars.

Downstream and not very far away, another bridge — the Casnewydd Michael Sheen Pedestrian Footbridge —was illuminated by a myriad of shining lights. It was a scene only a romantic poet could fully have done justice to (but not, please Cymru, Caratacus ap Cadwaladr — for obvious reasons I'd gone right off his poems and was less than impressed about all the dark rumours circulating about his plans to put pen to paper, once his sentence had been passed, and

A full moon was shining, high up in a clear sky

eventually publishing a limited edition of *Poems from Prison*) and it made Casnewydd, even if only for a few fleeting moments, seem magical — not a word one normally associated with the city. Arm in arm with Stakis, my friend and confidant, now, thankfully restored to freedom, I surveyed the scene. For the moment, all seemed calm, just like the river below, but somewhere along the line, I knew it, a new case was waiting . . .

POETRY BY ALAN RODERICK

AFTER YOU'D GONE (amazon.co.uk) contains poems written by Alan Roderick after the death of his wife, Božena, on Christmas Eve, 2015. The overwhelming majority deal with the aftermath of this devastating event, the days immediately after the funeral and his attempts to come to terms with his loss, but the collection also describes the places he visited, at home and abroad, in the years that followed Božena's death and imagines political firebrand Rosa Luxemburg and soul singer Gladys Knight travelling to Newport, as well as revisiting the Orpheus legend and the impact on him of Hitchcock's film Vertigo.

JOHN FREEMAN: (Chose '***AFTER YOU'D GONE***,' as one of his Books of the Year 2020 for *THE LONELY CROWD* magazine.) *After You'd Gone* is a classic articulation of devotion and sorrow, which will find an echo in the mind and heart of any reader who has known bereavement.

JOHN FREEMAN: *Verlaine wrote about Tennyson's In Memoriam that 'when he should have been broken-hearted, he had many reminiscences'. There is reminiscence in this beautifully produced memorial by Alan Roderick to Božena, his wife of forty years, but there is also, as well as pictures, travel writing, and excursions into popular culture and classical mythology - Orpheus and Eurydice, particularly - what Keats called the true voice of feeling. The best of these poems, and there are plenty of them, speak with a courageous simplicity out of grief and to any experience of grief the reader may bring to them. It takes tact, artistic restraint and skill to let this truth come out so purely, without adornment, as in 'Everyone says': 'be strong, stay/strong, sei doch/stark, but how/ can I when you/are gone, lost/ to me forever.' As a survivor at the end of King Lear says, 'The weight of this sad time we must obey, Speak what we feel, not what we ought to say.' It is not as easy as it looks to 'speak what we feel' in verse but Alan Roderick has succeeded, and in so doing he has spread a balm upon the world.*

VIVIEN FREEMAN, (the author of The Escape of Rose Alleyn) chose **'AFTER YOU'D GONE**,' as one of her Books of the Year 2020 for THE LONELY CROWD magazine. Vivien said this about **AFTER YOU'D GONE**: Alan Roderick's **AFTER YOU'D GONE** is a record of his grief after the loss of his wife, Božena, in 2015. The honesty of these poems is beautiful, touching the heart and making of grief something transcendent. There are also moments of humour. It is a superb production, with photographs including reproductions of fine self-portraits by Božena. I came away feeling uplifted. This is a collection to which I shall return.

VIVIEN FREEMAN: *What a beautiful and moving book AFTER YOU'D GONE is. Both poems and illustrations, including Božena's lovely self-portraits, are candles in a dark world spreading their light."*

PATRICK JONES: *…engaging and beautifully written heartfelt truths...powerful collection and a wonderful tribute...It is a very brave book...very moving, very honest and truly human."*

ANNA LEWIS: *I bought 'AFTER YOU'D GONE' a little while ago, and have been reading through it a few poems at a time. It is really beautiful. I have always loved hearing (Alan) read (his) poems, but it is even better to see them written down."*

MIKE McNAMARA: A searingly unflinching evocation of devastation that evokes the loss and longing in a sincere and open hearted manner. Roderick laments the wife, soulmate and lifelong partner who has passed away attempting to turn back time, invoke the spirit or even encounter the doppelgänger of this one love. His contemplations veer between love and almost worship. The memory of the dead is transfigured in various roles, times and settings. In effect his is the written word that paints his own Desolation Angel. The haunting solitude and longing resonate for sometime after closing the book. Brave heart.

SELECTED POEMS (amazon.co.uk) Alan Roderick's collection of the poems he wrote between 1978 and 2015 reflects his interests and enthusiasms. Here you will find poems about Romans and Ancient Greeks; poems about Wales and its language; poems about Cardiff and Newport; Love Poems; poems about Cats, Flowers, Birds and Animals; Food and Drink; Slovenia; Gaelic speaking Islanders; Elvis Presley and Bruce Springsteen; mobile phones; painters and paintings plus the author's Haikus and some of his German language poems.

AMAZON REVIEWER: *A 400-page collection of entertaining poems with a Welsh flavour, occasionally serious. Instantly understandable and engaging. Think Liverpool poetry of the 1960s transferred to modern-day Newport, South Wales, and given a Welsh bardic twist. Everyday themes brought to life with a pleasantly wry sense of humour.*

JOHN FREEMAN: ***The Selected*** *is predominantly joyful, full of playful and hilarious wordplay, as well as manifesting a deep knowledge of and pride in Wales. A minority of the poems, and some of the best, are written in German and addressed to his late Slovenian wife.*

Twelve Days In Intensive Care

October 21st to November 1st, 2010, A Poetic Record

Alan Roderick

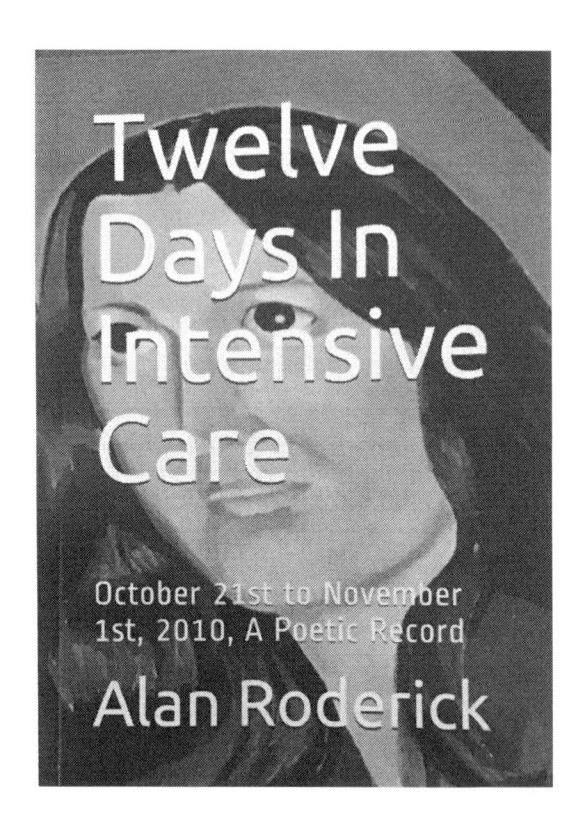

TWELVE DAYS IN INTENSIVE CARE: In October, 2010, Alan Roderick's wife, Božena, who had been ill for some time, was rushed to Newport's Royal Gwent Hospital. On arrival, the doctors were unable to pinpoint her illness and transferred her to the Intensive Care Department, where she was put into an induced coma, whilst they investigated further. Božena had previously spent two long periods at Cardiff's Velindre Cancer Centre battling Non-Hodgkin's Lymphoma.

Eventually, the Royal Gwent doctors discovered the Lymphoma had returned and took steps to combat it. Luckily, Božena successfully fought off this latest Lymphoma attack and lived for another five years. These poems are a record of my daily thoughts and feelings during the time Božena was in the Royal Gwent Hospital's Intensive Care Department, a poetic diary of those stressful days.

JOHN FREEMAN: *Twelve Days* has a simplicity and intensity which is admirable.

BOŽENA'S BOOK (lulu.com) Edited by Alan Roderick
Božena Marija Roš was born in Laško, Slovenia but brought up in Žalec where her burgeoning artistic talent led her to take lessons with the renowned Slovenian painter, Žuža Jelica. After studying at the University of Ljubljana she worked as a librarian at the Stadtbücherei in Remscheid, West Germany where she met her future husband, Alan Roderick. They eventually moved to Newport, South Wales where Božena studied Graphic Design at the prestigious Newport College of

Art. After graduating she then had a variety of jobs making use of her artistic skills and talents and also illustrated many of Alan's books as well as exhibiting her paintings at many local venues and playing an active part in the Newport and South Wales arts scene. BOŽENA'S BOOK pays tribute to her memory and her vibrant artistic and literary abilities.

Printed in Great Britain
by Amazon